THE MEMORIES OF MARLIE ROSE

What Reviewers Say About Morgan Lee Miller's Work

The Hues of Me and You

"*The Hues of Me and You* is an enjoyable second chance romance. Miller is known for them and those that like this type of trope will find that she easily nails their nuances. She understands the basics of a good second chance: She gets the main characters right." —*Women Using Words*

"This is a lovely easy to read romance. It's low on the anguish and high on the super cute sweet moments and it was just what I needed to kick off 2023! This book has a great storyline, a brilliant cast of characters, and enough of that sweet, lovely romance to keep you turning the page. I devoured it and loved it."—*Lesbian Review*

The Infinite Summer

"*The Infinite Summer* by Morgan Lee Miller brought back a lot of nostalgic memories of my own youth, especially that summer between high school and college…and that really fun summer after high school. I hope it does the same for you."—*Rainbow Reflections*

"There is something about Morgan Lee Miller's writing that gets me every time…but all in all, Miller delivered yet another enjoyable story that made nerd me happy."—*Hsinju Lit Log*

All the Paths to You

"This book made me, a self-proclaimed hater of sports, care about sports. Even sporting events that were purely fictional. That in and of itself is impressive. ...My god, Kennedy and Quinn are such a cute couple, I love them!! I ship them so much it isn't even funny. Their chemistry is through the roof to be honest."—*Day Dreaming and Book Reading*

"*All the Paths to You* is the kind of romance that makes your heart ache in all the right places."—*Hsinju's Lit Log*

"This book had a lot of feel-good moments and I still have a big smile on my face. ...This was the feel-good and even a little inspirational book that I needed right now."—*Lez Review Books*

"I can strongly say that this is one of my new favourite books (and series) and is definitely a contender for my favourite book of the year so far. ...I'm so happy I had the chance to read it and I don't think I could ever recommend it enough!"—*Althea is Reading*

All the Worlds Between Us

"This book is really sweet and wholesome and also heartbreaking and uplifting. ...I would recommend this book to anyone looking for a cute contemporary."—*Tomes of Our Lives*

"[*All the Worlds Between Us*] deals with friendship, family, sexuality, self-realization, accepting yourself, the harsh reality of high school and the difference between getting to tell your own story and having your own story exposed. Each character plays a vital role...and tells the story of this book perfectly."—*Little Shell's Bookshelf*

"If you're looking for an easy, quick cute f|f read, you should give this a try. ...This was a solid debut and I can't wait to see what else this author publishes in the future!"—*The Black Lit Queen*

"This book took me straight back to all of my gigantic teenage emotions and got right down to the heart of me. I'm not a swimmer and I wasn't out in high school, but I swear I was right there with Quinn as she navigated her life as a competitive athlete and a queer kid in high school. Experiencing love and betrayal and triumph through her story was bananas. Morgan Lee Miller, you ripped my heart right out with this brilliant book."—Melisa McCarthy, Librarian, Brooklyn Public Library

"I'm always up for fun books about cute girlfriends, and *All the Worlds Between Us* was certainly that: a super cute ex-friends to lovers book about a swimming champion and her ex-best-friend turned girlfriend. …*All the Worlds Between Us* is a great rom-com and definitely recommended for anyone who's a fan of romance." —*Crowing About Books*

"[*All the Worlds Between Us*] has all the typical drama and typical characters you'd find in high school. It's a tough, yet wonderful journey and transformation. The writing is divine. …It's a complicated tale involving so much pain, fear, betrayal and humiliation. *All The Worlds Between Us* is a terrific tale of taking what you want."—*Amy's MM Romance Reviews*

"Morgan's novel reiterates the important fact which should be repeated over and over again that coming out should always be done on one's own terms, and how this isn't a thing that any other people, straight or queer, should decide."—*Beyond the Words*

"Finally, a sporty, tropey YA lesbian romance—I've honestly been dreaming about reading something like this for a very long time!" —*Day Dreaming and Book Reading*

Hammers, Strings, and Beautiful Things

"There's more going on than first appears and I was impressed that Ms. Miller won me over with a well written book that deals with some more serious issues."—*C-Spot Reviews*

"*Hammers, Strings, and Beautiful Things* is an emotionally raw read with plenty of drama. The journey Reagan and Blair share is rough in places but there is a beauty that you won't want to miss out on."—*Lesbian Review*

Before. After. Always.

"Miller tackled the tough subject of grief in *Before. After. Always.* It didn't feel too painful reading, but all the emotions were there."
—*Hsinju's Lit Log*

Visit us at www.boldstrokesbooks.com

By the Author

All the Worlds Between Us

Hammers, Strings, and Beautiful Things

All the Paths to You

Before. After. Always.

The Infinite Summer

The Hues of Me and You

The Memories of Marlie Rose

THE MEMORIES OF MARLIE ROSE

by

Morgan Lee Miller

2023

THE MEMORIES OF MARLIE ROSE

ISBN 13: 978-1-63679-347-4

THIS TRADE PAPERBACK ORIGINAL IS PUBLISHED BY
BOLD STROKES BOOKS, INC.
P.O. BOX 249
VALLEY FALLS, NY 12185

FIRST EDITION: DECEMBER 2023

CREDITS
EDITOR: BARBARA ANN WRIGHT
PRODUCTION DESIGN: SUSAN RAMUNDO
COVER DESIGN BY INK SPIRAL DESIGN

Acknowledgments

Writing this story was a challenge that took me on quite the journey. The idea originally came to me when my maternal grandma, Marlene, was diagnosed with dementia, over a year after my maternal grandpa passed away from Alzheimer's. Both of my maternal grandparents lost their memories, and I couldn't help but wonder about my own, and if I'm destined to lose them just like they did. I imagined what it was like to lose your memories—the good and the bad. I wanted to explore the idea of someone who was so overcome with heartbreak, grief, and pain that they would go to the extreme and willingly erase parts of their life.

Then, right as I started writing this story, my mental health took a drastic turn, and just like my main character, Marlie Rose, I found myself at rock bottom, weighed down by past and current traumas that made it extremely difficult to get out of bed. Trying to write while at rock bottom feels like wading through cement, and there were times I truly believe I couldn't do it...or make it out. But eventually, the days became easier, and as I powered through the pain, Marlie Rose sprang to life. What became a challenging story to write for a myriad of reasons ended up turning into the healing journey I desperately needed.

For a while, I felt incredibly alone, but once I started healing, I realized I was anything but alone. I had an amazing support system at home and incredible friends in this writing community who stuck by my side (you know who you are), checked in with me daily, and were rays of light on my darkest days. All these people are even more special to me, believing in me when I didn't believe in myself, loving me when I didn't love myself, and supporting me when I felt like giving up. From the bottom of my heart, thank you so much for being there. You helped more than you probably know.

As always, a huge thank you to Rad, Sandy, my fabulous editor, Barbara Ann Wright, and everyone else at BSB for letting me live out this dream of writing stories. Endless gratitude to my amazing my beta readers for all of their time and the invaluable feedback they provided.

I named Marlie Rose after my grandma, Marlene, and great-grandma (Nana), Mary Rose, who helped inspire my main character. In July 2023, one of my favorite aunts, Gayle, passed away. Our last conversation was filled with laughter, reminiscing all of our shared memories, and she expressed how proud she was of me and my writing. I got to talk to her about this story, and I'm so glad I had the chance to tell her that this book was going to be dedicated to her. My nana, grandma, and Aunt Gayle are three of many amazing and inspiring women who helped me become the person I am today. I have so many wonderful memories with them, ones I'll hold extra tight now.

Last but not least, the biggest thank you and hugs/enthusiastic waves to my readers. Your support means the world to me.

Dedication

To Aunt Gayle,
I'll forever cherish all the memories with you.
Love you and miss you terribly.

CHAPTER ONE

Present day, September 2016

"Are you sure you want to do this?" I see the fear rounding Kristina's eyes as we sit in the waiting room of the Farrow Neurological Institute of Malibu. It's about the millionth time she has asked. I understand she's concerned, but I'm certain this is what I want to do, what I need to do in order to live again.

I'm tired of my days dragging on like I'm wading through cement. I'm tired of looking forward to going to sleep and dreading waking up in the morning. That's not living. That's rotting from the inside out, and for years, I tried everything to help my depression. Therapy. Anti-depressants. Yoga. Mediating in my backyard that overlooks the Pacific Ocean. They say, "This too shall pass," but I'm starting to wonder if all my pain, heartbreak, and grief has stacked and compounded into a boulder too heavy to move out of the way.

"I'm sure," I say. "I know you're worried about me, but I've thought about this for months, and ever since I got the results of the investigation, it's sealed the deal."

"Marlie, I know that was very hard to process. I can't even imagine what you must be going through, but are you really sure this is the right approach?"

Kristina is more than an assistant to me. She's been with me for five years, and even though she's thirty and young enough to be my daughter, she's one of my dear friends. We talk about everything.

I've been there for her when she went through a horrible breakup, she was there for me during the last horrendous year and a half, and she was there to catch my fall when I found out about the private investigation. She told me once that she considers me to be her California mom, and I know that her constantly asking if I'm sure about this is just her way of looking out for me as if we were family.

And honestly, right now, she's the closest family member that I have.

"I've tried everything," I say. "I'm so tired of feeling this way. I don't think I have much to lose at this point."

"Marlie, that's not true," she says, resting a comforting hand on my wrist. "What about your comeback? Helen keeps texting me about the *Hello, Dolly!* script. That could be so amazing for you. Don't you think being back on stage will help?"

"It didn't help before. Why would it be any different now?" Growing up with nothing made it easier to sacrifice everything. The illusion that money bought happiness was stitched into me, and I grew up chasing everything I never had. I kept running until I saw my name spelled out on the Times Square marquees, until scripts landed in my hands like snowflakes, until I had enough money to buy beautiful Upper West Side row houses and a Malibu house planted on top of a hill overlooking the ocean, and until I became one of the seven women to achieve EGOT status. I really thought that finally winning an Emmy and joining the likes of Helen Hayes, Rita Moreno, and Audrey Hepburn would fill in the missing piece I'd been searching years for to feel complete.

But I've learned the hard way that money and success didn't glue my broken pieces back together like I thought it would, and it didn't bring my loved ones back. It only provided an illusion of happiness to those looking from the outside, but it didn't heal my shattered heart rotting from the inside out.

"Ms. Rose? We're ready for you," a woman in baby blue scrubs says in the entryway.

I turn to Kristina. Her brown curls fall to her shoulder, her face sun-kissed after spending Labor Day weekend in Palm Springs. However, a frown still finds its way onto her lips. I offer her an encouraging smile and rest my hand on her shoulder. "I'm going to be okay, I promise."

She thins her lips and nods. Doubt still rounds her dark brown eyes. "Okay, I'll be here when you get out."

I follow the nurse into a small examination room. She hands me a thick packet of paper that I've seen before. In a big, bold font, the title reads, "The Guide to Neurological Reimaging." As someone who has spent the last forty-four years reading scripts, I'm highly skilled at memorizing packets of text. I've read it front to back multiple times and followed the steps outlined before starting the procedure. I know that there could be up to eight sessions over the course of four weeks. I know based on my research that neurological reimaging is an experimental procedure for those battling with severe depression, PTSD, trauma, grief, heartbreak, and certain addictions.

It works by erasing unwanted memories.

Dr. Pierson greets me with a firm handshake in the examination room and sits in the chair opposite me. "Well, today is the day, Ms. Rose. How are you feeling?" He gives me a friendly smile, encouraging.

"Nervous, anxious, but ready to get started," I release with bated breath.

He nods and pulls out his clipboard. "Have you followed the steps outlined in the packet? Have you removed anything that holds a strong emotional connection? Or at least, packed it away?"

"I have, and I gave it to my assistant so the boxes aren't even in the house."

"Good, good. And you know that during this four-week procedure, we strongly advise you not to travel, especially to any places that hold sentiment, grief, or trauma."

"I don't have any travel plans in the next four weeks. That won't be a problem."

He nods, glances at his clipboard, and then back up at me. "I assume you've read the entire packet, correct?"

"I have. Multiple times," I say with the smallest laugh. "I think I have an understanding of how it all works."

He smiles. "That's good to hear. Eighty-eight percent of our patients have maintained targeted memory loss for two years and counting."

"What about the other twelve percent?"

"The other twelve percent did have some memories come back, but we found that was because they came across an item or went to a place that held significance in their lives. Memories are represented by a collection of neurons spread throughout the brain, meaning certain details are located in different parts of your brain. The easiest way to explain is to think of each memory as a forest. There are a number of trees, each one holds a specific detail of a memory. Our technology is going to bulldoze the trees, but some have larger root systems than others. Some details will tangle into other memories. That's why it's extremely important to get as detailed as possible so we can see how deep these memories run in your brain, and why it's critical to avoid anything or place that holds significance. Exposure increases the chance of you stumbling on a root of a memory and spawning it again. The further into the sessions you get, the more the risk of getting them back decreases."

"I understand."

The thought of getting in-depth about the nitty-gritty details of my life to a group of five strangers causes discomfort to prick down my spine. Being open about all facets of my life is something I'm not used to, something I've been able to dodge during interviews for over forty years now. I have to trust a practical stranger with it, but his warm smile goes a long way toward putting me at ease. I know it's something I have to get over if I want to shed the awful memories.

"While you recall a specific memory, you might come across details that confuse you. We erased the memory, but there might be roots that travel into another one. Many times, this happens when someone recalls a conversation. And we've noticed that the stronger or more emotional the memory, the more painful the headache can get. That's why we schedule a few days between sessions, but it's nothing ibuprofen can't fix. I've seen patients struggle with headaches and confusion throughout the course of treatment, but just like art, we need to trust the process. It will all come to fruition after the final session."

"I think I can handle the confusion, and I'm sure the headaches are nowhere near as painful as everything else I feel."

"Now, I know recalling some details might feel like too much information, too personal, too embarrassing, but my team and I are not here to judge your life. We're here to help, to relieve you from the pain you're feeling."

He explains what happens during a session: I'll wear what's called a dTMD helmet, short for a deep transcranial magnetic device, made of electromagnets. Because neurons live all over the brain, the helmet will locate and trace the neurons that hold a specific memory. Dr. Pierson and his team will use computers to record the neural activity. Then, after about thirty to forty minutes, the computers and helmet will work together to create low frequency light pulses that will destroy the neurons, weakening their connections.

Who am I kidding? None of it really makes sense to me. I'm a Broadway performer, not a neuroscientist. But I pretend like I know everything Dr. Pierson is saying by nodding along. I shouldn't, but I trust people who have dedicated their lives to researching and implementing this procedure. I trust the hundreds of patients who are now living the lives they hoped to have.

"Do you have any questions before we begin?" Dr. Pierson asks.

"I don't."

"If at any moment, you want to stop, we can. Nothing will happen until you give me your consent."

"I understand. Thank you." Honestly, the more he speaks in scientific terms, the more nervous I'm becoming. I can feel adrenaline, anxiety, and nerves congeal in my veins. I have a feeling they'll go away once I get through the first session.

He gives me a professional smile. "If you don't have questions, you can follow me into the examination room."

I walk down a hallway that feels never-ending. "Somewhere Over the Rainbow" pops into my head. My pulse twitches in my neck, and pain yanks in my stomach. It's a song that once brought me comfort, a song my mother used to sing to me, a song I sang in my head to calm my nerves before performances or anytime I felt panic snake around me.

It becomes an ear worm while walking down the hallway. But after finally getting the answers about my mother that I've been asking for most of my life, I'm eager to erase the heartbreak that taints my once favorite song.

Inside the examination room, four other people in white coats sit at a long table with five computer screens and a few machines I don't recognize. Across from them is a padded examination chair reclined at an angle. Behind it is a machine with a helmet on the end. Dr. Pierson gestures for me to sit. Once I do, one of his team members with "Dr. Wilson" stitched in navy embroidery places the helmet over my head.

"There's a lever on the side of the chair so you can adjust it to your liking," she says with a smile. Like Dr. Pierson, her smile seems friendly and nurturing. "Make yourself as comfortable as you can. The more comfortable you are, the more you can focus on recall."

"Thank you, Dr. Wilson."

Her smile grows into a more bashful one. "I just want to say that I absolutely love 'Sincerely, Yours,'" she says, lowering her voice as if she knows she shouldn't bring up any topic other than erasing memories. "It's one of my favorite movies."

She looks like she's in her early forties, which means she was most likely a child when the movie came out in 1980. Movie critics and enthusiasts claim it's one of the most iconic movies of the eighties, so I assume that she watched it once she was old enough for a PG-13.

"Oh, I'm so glad to hear that. Thank you so much."

I see excitement glimmer in her eyes as she flashes one last smile before situating herself at the table.

"Are you comfortable, Ms. Rose?" Dr. Pierson asks from the table.

"I'm as comfortable as I can be."

I want a drink to calm the nerves aching in my stomach and to dilute the feelings bubbling to the surface, but I know there's a ninety-nine percent chance that Dr. Pierson doesn't have a secret bar in the building.

"Great. I'm going to dim the lights. As I'm sure Dr. Wilson explained, we want you to be as calm and comfortable as possible." The fluorescent lights turn off, and another doctor turns on soft lights next to the computers. It's much more relaxing than the bright and irritating fluorescents. I feel my body sinking into the surprisingly comfortable chair.

"What I'm going to have you do is start back from the earliest memory you can think of," Dr. Pierson continues. "Think all the way back to your childhood and try to search for that very first memory and then walk us through it. You'll recite your entire life story. We want every memory, every detail, and every feeling. The more details we get, the better we can target the neurons. I'll let you know when it's a good time to stop, and I'll ask if you would like to keep everything you just recalled, keep parts, or delete it all. We will also delete the memory of you recalling and asking to delete it. Just remember, once you delete, it will be erased. You'll hear clicking sounds through the earplugs we'll give you and feel a knocking, tapping, or tingling sensation on your head. There might be some scalp discomfort that lingers afterward, most likely with a mild to moderate headache, but again, it's nothing pain medication can't fix."

"And what will replace the memory?"

"Nothing. We don't remember everything. It will feel like you can't pinpoint the beginning of someone or something in your timeline. You might be a little confused at first when you come face-to-face with something that's part of an erased memory. For example, if we erase your childhood home and you revisit it—of course, after the procedure is fully completed—the home might seem familiar, but your brain will cover up that hole and process it as something dreamlike or déjà vu."

This is all starting to feel very weird. My stomach ache intensifies, as if I ate something it didn't agree with.

"Any last questions, Ms. Rose?"

I'm so eager and focused on getting started, I feel a bit detached from reality, even more so than I've been for the last year and a half.

I have to be in order to mentally prepare for the procedure. I need to let go of the memories I want gone before discarding them. "I don't have any. I'm ready."

"Close your eyes. Take as much time as you need to relax and sift through your memories. When you have found the very first one, start from there, and please try not to leave any details out."

I close my eyes and take in a deep breath until I feel the air reach the bottom of my lungs. I slowly exhale through my mouth, a technique I've been practicing with my therapist for the last several years. I sing "Somewhere Over the Rainbow" one last time as I almost see my life rewinding like an old VHS tape until the closest thing that feels like a childhood home to me fills my mind.

I'm around four years old, which means it's 1958. I can't help but smile because I might not have known all the things I didn't have back then, but I had my parents surrounding me. I didn't know how poor we were. I didn't know about my mother's alcoholism. I didn't know about my father's dangerous job as a longshoreman at the Brooklyn docks. I didn't know we lived in the projects until the private investigator's folder filled in all the blanks that my memories couldn't.

What I do know is that it was one of the happiest times of my life, though the memories are frayed and thin like a beloved and overused T-shirt. It was a simple time for me, one filled with the greatest amount of pure love I've ever encountered in my sixty-two years on Earth.

It's time to let go of the hurt that has polluted my favorite song.

CHAPTER TWO

My first memory is of my mother singing.

I watched her from the living room chair. She always looked out the west-facing window, especially when an amazing sunset colored the sky, though most of the view was obstructed by the identical apartment building next door, all part of the Red Hook Houses. Every day, she stared out the window and sang along to the radio or whatever song was in her head. It wasn't until years of ruminating on this same memory that I wondered if she always stared out that west-facing window because that was where Manhattan was.

She had an affinity for Manhattan that sparked my own. I don't have many memories of my father. I know I had the same dark brown hair as him, my mother's blue eyes, and I think I remember my mother telling me I had his smile too. I remember the three of us walking down Coffey Street until it pooled into New York Harbor. We walked to the end of the pier offering a beautiful view of the tip of Manhattan to the right and the Statue of Liberty to the left.

"I've always wanted to live there," my mother said while staring across the river. "Manhattan is the land of dreams."

My father wrapped an arm around her and kissed her cheek. "Red Hook is our start, but Manhattan will be our end."

She smiled at that promise. She didn't smile often, but she did when thinking about Manhattan…or singing.

Manhattan was the land of skyscrapers, theater, and colorful lights from Times Square. The movie and Broadway stars lived there while the rowdy sailors and gangs lived in Red Hook, adding to its horrible reputation. Sometimes, it felt like the skyscrapers taunted us. The land of dreams rose in visible, sturdy structures while Red Hook didn't have any skyscrapers at all. Our docks were run by the mob while Manhattan was run by show business. The "Waterfront Mob" fed off the working class while the longshoremen risked their lives every day hauling cargo from the ships, all while losing fingers and limbs. It was no surprise my parents' dream was to escape the continuous spiral of a decaying Red Hook, and because of them, their dreams became my own.

My mother found hope looking out that window, as if she could see her dream manifesting in the distance. I could tell because her frown curved upward just a fraction. When she decided to hum a song while looking out that window, the soft smile grew brighter. It was the only time she seemed in her element, and I saw the weight of the world vanish from her shoulders. Whenever my mother sang, she had this glow on her face, and even though I barely knew anything about the world, I knew that my mother became captivating when she sang. I stopped playing to watch her. Her voice was velvety soft, as if she held back from fully drenching our small apartment in her voice, but it was strong.

She sang to me when she brushed my knotted hair after a bath. She sang when she tucked me into bed, and I sang with her. The soft glow of the nightstand lamp contoured her facial features, highlighting that special smile she wore when she put me to bed. She sat on the edge, combed her fingers through my hair, and sang "Somewhere Over the Rainbow." Eventually, I learned how to sing it back to her.

"You have the most beautiful voice, my Marlie Rose," she said when I sang along. "I just love it when you sing." She had the biggest smile, and whenever I think about her, I remember the glow radiating from her.

It became our own language. I learned all the songs she sang, and while she cooked, I helped her bring bowls and plates to the table, and we sang together. Sometimes, the two of us squeezed onto one living room chair. I cuddled into her side, and we listened to the radio until she started cooking dinner, making sure it was ready by the time my father arrived.

One memory I do remember of my father: I must have been about six. He came home late. It was dark. He always worked long hours and came back with dirt all over his hands and face. We didn't eat dinner until after he bathed. I was already at the kitchen table and sang "Somewhere Over the Rainbow" to my mother sitting across from me. It was something to pass the time while my father washed, and my grumbling stomach had to wait.

"You should hear your daughter sing," my mother said, that vibrant smile on her face. "Doesn't she have a hell of a voice? Go on, Marlie Rose. Keep singing for your father."

So I sang "Somewhere Over the Rainbow" again, my first performance for my father. I watched his smile grow, and his sparkling dark eyes caught a peek at my mother, who didn't take her eyes off me. She rested her chin on her palm, staring as if I was something miraculous.

"I didn't know you could sing like that, Marlene," my father said and squeezed my shoulder. He always called me Marlene, while my mother called me Marlie Rose.

"She's been doing it often while you've been at work."

"Well, I love to come home to both my girls singing. I bet if you keep up with it, you'll be as good as your mother."

It's strange how most of the memories of my father are short and vague, almost translucent, but the entire day he died is in vivid detail. It must have been about half a year after that walk down Coffey Street; I was six, singing Elvis Presley's "Can't Help Falling in Love" with my mother as she made oatmeal and toast. She burned my toast that morning, caught up in singing with me. I happily ate it anyway because I've always preferred my toast on the darker side. My father had come out of the bedroom and asked my mother what was wrong because she became silent, and her eyes became glossy.

My father lifted her chin so she met his eyes. "Honey, what's wrong?"

"I burned the toast."

He looked over at me and smiled. "Marlene seems to be enjoying it."

"I am enjoying it," I said and took another bite.

But my mother didn't look over. She went back to the sink and started washing dishes. He gave her a kiss on the cheek. "It's okay, hon. I promise. I love you."

"I love you too."

He kissed her on the lips and then came to me. I jumped off my chair, and he scooped me up, twirled me around like he did every morning, and kissed my cheek. "Love you, Marlene," he said.

"I love you too, Daddy."

"You'll sing for me when I get home?"

"Yes, I promise."

"Good."

He snatched his paper bag lunch and walked out the door.

That was the last time I ever saw my father.

It was the most ordinary morning. My mother walked me to school; it was mid-December, and my teeth chattered the entire time. Even my mother's face was red when she dropped me off. A dusting of snow had clung to the sidewalk and trees as the smell of winter clung in the air. That day in music class, we sang carols, and it made me even more excited for Christmas. I don't remember Christmases being extravagant, but I remember the tiny tree in the corner of our living room and how my mother and I sang to my father, who sat in the chair, his eyes wide and expressive.

The ordinary morning turned into an ordinary afternoon, but everything changed when night fell, and my father still hadn't come home. Dinner waited on the stove. I complained because I was hungry. My mother made me a plate of food and sat at the table as I ate, her eyes fixed on the front door. She looked scared. I could sense something wasn't right. It was one of the very few evenings I remember my mother not singing.

I was fresh from the bath, wrapped up in my quilt when there was a knock on the door. My mother was quick to open it. I hopped out of bed and peered around the corner of the doorway and spotted a man I'd never seen before. His face was shiny, as if he'd spent the day sweating, and just like my father, his hands, arms, and face were covered in blotches of dirt and oil. He took off his flat cap and said something I couldn't hear, but whatever he said made my mother shriek and collapse on the ground. He glanced at me, and I'd never seen that look on anyone's face before. It was like he had looked death in the eye, and knowing what I know now, he had.

As I grew into adolescence, finding a sense of identity was crucial for me. I wanted to know where I came from and was desperate to find out any details about my family. If it wasn't for the birth certificate my mother had packed in my suitcase with the rest of my belongings, I wouldn't have known my father's name. For the next ten years, the only thing I had of him were the memories that had started fading and his name on my birth certificate. William George Hatcher.

One day when I was sixteen, I ventured to the Brooklyn Heights Library to find answers. I scoured all the newspapers from December 1960 to see if something could give me any kind of clue about my father's death. I ended up finding *The New York Times* article about the harrowing disaster on the *USS Constellation* at the Navy Yard that had killed fifty people. I stared at the image on the front page of a massive smoke cloud cloaking the aircraft carrier, and all I did was wonder what would have happened if it had never caught fire. Then, I found the obituaries and my father's name.

My mother's smile never came back, even when I tried singing to her. I don't know if she ever knew what had happened to my father. If she did know, she never told me, and it added to my growing curiosity as I grew. She explained that my father had died and that he wasn't coming home. That part I understood, but I never understood how. Now, I think I understand why my mother never told me. I was only six, barely able to grasp the concept of death. Seeing the image of the massive ship in flames when I was sixteen was enough to give me nightmares for a month.

During the two years after he died, I watched my mother fade slowly. Her singing hushed to hums, and her hums hushed to silence. I had to learn how to cook and take care of her as well as myself.

During my last months with her, the radio would play as she stared silently out that window with a glass of brown liquid in her hands. When she was drinking, she cried a lot. I've since realized it must have been whiskey to ease her pain.

I tried singing "Somewhere Over the Rainbow," and instead of the smile I always looked forward to, she yelled, "Stop singing that song. I don't want to hear that song!" She tossed the glass across the room. When it clanged against the wall and shattered, the whiskey dripped down the white walls. I fell to the floor and started sobbing. I'd never seen her so angry. She was always so quiet, reserved, and docile, and with that horrible angry tone and shattered glass between us, she was unrecognizable.

My father died and so did my mother's will to live. I lost both my parents in that accident.

That day, my mother gave up on everything: her life, our life, me. The several weeks between the night she threw the glass to the last day I ever saw her was like living in purgatory. I barely existed to her. She hardly ate. She hardly spoke. She didn't sing. All she did was drink her brown liquid and stare out that window.

I always thought she looked out as a way to escape to a dream where the three of us lived more comfortably in a neighborhood free from decay and the mob. But as I grew up, I began to wonder if after my father died, she looked out that window as a way to escape from the life she didn't want anymore.

The last day with her was a rainy day in January. Fog hung low in the morning and obstructed the view from the window, but she still stood there for what seemed like an hour. It's clear to me now that she wasn't staring to take in the view. She was lost in her own mind. By then, I was used to her zoning out for long periods of time. I knew how to entertain myself, how to get ready for bed by myself. I was eight.

I made some toast and brought her a plate. She held it and continued getting lost in her trance. I don't think she ever ate it. A ghost floating through the house had more life than her floating through that day. Her eyes were swollen and red, and the one time she looked me in the eye, I noticed how hollow her stare was.

My father's death had chipped away large parts of my mother until there was a hollow shell. The way she looked at me that day, I understood that the life we once had was never coming back.

I came home from school to find her packing all my belongings in a suitcase. "Mommy, what are we doing?" I asked.

She didn't say anything. She went to the dresser and rummaged through pairs of underpants and socks and shoved them into the suitcase.

"Are we going somewhere?"

She stopped and glanced over. "Yes," she replied, the tone as empty as her eyes. She handed me my teddy bear and grabbed my hand. She ushered us out of the apartment, and I had no idea that was the last time I would ever be home.

I watched her the entire bus ride as she clung to my suitcase in her lap, staring toward the front. Only the sounds of raindrops splattering against the windows filled the bus. It was scary how mechanical my mother seemed. I clutched my teddy bear, rested my chin on top of his head, and felt him become just as wet as my face as I willed my mother to look at me.

She pulled the bell cord, and a minute later, the bus pulled over and lowered. She grabbed my hand and tugged me with her. It wasn't a suggestion. It was a demand.

"Mommy, where are we going?" I said and wiped the rain from my face. It was pouring, falling sideways. We had only walked a couple of blocks, and my clothes were already soaked.

She clung to my hand almost protectively, the one semblance of my mother still living inside. "We're going somewhere safe."

I thought that protective and nurturing squeeze really meant something.

She stopped at a corner with a four-story brick building hidden behind a few trees. A couple of windows shone through the darkness. She set the suitcase next to me. My teeth chattered, and I could feel myself on the verge of crying from how miserably cold and soaked I was. What stopped me was my mother kneeling on the sidewalk, seemingly not caring at all about the rain seeping through her pants. I forgot about the cold and the wetness because finally, my mother was looking at me, her eyes filled with a modicum of the mother I had desperately missed for two years.

"Here's what you're gonna do, my love," she said and wiped the water off my cheek. "You're going to walk into that building, all right? They're going to have a nice big bed for you—a warm bed and hot tea—and they're going to take care of you."

It was the most motherly she had been in two years. It stunned me right in the middle of the storm. My heart burst open. I was hopeful that it meant we were going to restart our life together, that all we needed to do was walk into that building, drink some tea, fall asleep in the warm, comfortable bed, and my mother would be put together enough to sing and smile at me again.

"Are you coming with me?"

She thinned her lips, and sadness started to glisten in her stare. "I can't, love."

"Why not?"

Her thumb grazed my cheek. "Because you're going to have a much happier life there. You're always going to have a bed, you'll always have food, you'll always have someone to take care of you. You'll always be warm. You'll have so many friends. Doesn't that sound nice?"

"But I want to be with you," I said against chattering teeth. If it was nice, why did it make her sad?

"You will. I'll come back and get you. Mommy needs to figure a few things out, okay? But once I do, I'll come back for you, and we'll finally have that big apartment Daddy always talked about, the one where you can see the Statue of Liberty outside your window."

"In Manhattan?"

She nodded. "Yes, in Manhattan."

"The land of dreams?"

She sucked in her lips and tucked a wet tendril of hair behind my ear. "In the land of dreams."

"When you come back, can we sing together again?"

She dropped her head and swatted at her eyes. After collecting herself, she met my gaze again and said, "You always keep singing, my Marlie Rose."

I shrugged. "You told me not to."

"No, honey, no," she said, taking my face into her soaked palms. "I don't want you to stop singing. Your singing is the best sound in the entire world."

"Then why did you tell me to stop?"

"Because—" Her voice cracked. She blinked rapidly. "Because Mommy was sad. Mommy *is* sad, and sometimes, she doesn't want to hear or see the things that remind her of Daddy."

"Why not?"

"Because I miss him, love. I miss him terribly."

"I do too."

She wiped my face again only for more rain to stream down it. "Your voice will always be my favorite. Please promise me that you'll never stop singing, even if people tell you to. Never stop."

"I'll keep singing if it means you'll be happy again."

"Oh, honey. There are a lot of things that I need to be happy, but if you keep singing, I'll always be one step closer. Do you understand? Do you understand how important it is?"

I nodded as I watched her struggle to not break down in front of me. Seeing her fight so hard made me cry again. She scooped me up and held me the longest and tightest she had ever held me. Since my father died, our hugs had been sparse. On the good days, I got a loose hug and a kiss on the cheek, small reminders that my mother still loved me.

I'll always remember that hug. It was tight and reluctant to let go. The hug filled the void of the last two years because with just one embrace, she reminded me that she loved me. Her arms swaddled me, and I felt so protected for just a few seconds. It made me forget about the rain, my chattering teeth, and the goose bumps up and down my arms and legs. When she broke the hug, she kissed all over my face and palmed my cheeks, "I'll always love you, my sweet Marlie Rose. Remember that, okay? You'll remember how much I love you?" I nodded, but the emotion balled in my throat so tightly that I couldn't say anything back. "Now, go on. Go inside and get warm."

When I hesitated, she pushed my suitcase to me. "Go on, love. Go inside. Get warm. It will be okay."

I listened to her like I always did. And once I felt the warm air hit my face when I stepped inside the home, I turned to get one last look at her, but she was already gone.

❖

I'm still not sure if my first foster family was my one blessing in the foster system or a curse.

The woman who ran the Kindred Hearts Children's Home for Girls, Mrs. Lyons, told us we weren't supposed to get attached to our foster parents or foster siblings. It was best to not get attached to anyone, even at Kindred Hearts, because we weren't sure of how long we would stay. Whenever Mrs. Lyons told us that, I clung to hope that I would go back to Red Hook whenever my mother walked through the doors again.

Every morning, I reminded myself, "Do not get attached to anyone. This is temporary. You'll go home soon when Mom gets better." Every night, I curled up in my twin-sized bed while around me, nine other girls did the same. I held my teddy bear close; the smell of home still clung to its fur. I closed my eyes and willed my mother to come back before I drifted off to sleep.

It was February of 1963, about a month after my mother dropped me off, when it was finally my turn to get summoned into what we called the adoption room. A couple greeted me with wide smiles. Mrs. Lyons introduced them as Mr. and Mrs. McCoy from the Upper East Side.

They certainly didn't look like they belonged in Brooklyn. Mr. McCoy wore a nicely pressed suit, and Mrs. McCoy wore a teal dress and a pillbox hat. They looked like wealth, like a couple who came fresh from Manhattan. Women in Red Hook didn't dress like Mrs. McCoy, and I had never seen someone wearing pearls and matching earrings. They flashed me friendly smiles, as if they were genuinely excited to meet me. They even went upstairs to help me pack my clothes and teddy bear and carried my suitcase to the cab.

"62nd and Third, please," Mr. McCoy said to the driver. "Manhattan."

The tugging in my chest that had been persistent since my mother had left loosened. "We're going to Manhattan?"

Mrs. McCoy smiled. "We are," she said sweetly.

"I've never been to Manhattan before."

"You're going to love it. It's a nice little neighborhood just a few blocks from Central Park."

It was the first time in a month that I was excited about something.

The whole ride, I had my face practically pressed against the window. It was the first time I'd gone over the Brooklyn Bridge. The distant skyscrapers rose above me once we turned onto FDR Drive and headed uptown. I hadn't even stepped out of the car yet and was already in awe of how everything was larger than life. While my heart ached and longed for my parents, it still erratically sputtered at knowing I was in the land of dreams, that while I waited for my mother to get better, at least I could find a pocket of happiness somewhere.

Don't get attached, Mrs. Lyons's voice reminded me, and maybe I needed that reminder because just five minutes inside Manhattan, I wanted to stay forever.

The McCoys lived on 62nd Street, a quaint street lined with rowhomes. Inside was the most beautiful home I'd ever seen. Two floors, a large family room with a bay window, modern appliances, a large kitchen, but the best part of the first floor was the color TV. Throughout my whole time in foster care, no home was as extravagant as the McCoys'. The McCoys' house was exactly what I expected a house in the land of dreams to look like.

Do not get attached.

"Our daughter, Susie, has been really looking forward to having a sister," Mrs. McCoy said as Mr. McCoy paid the cab driver and hauled my suitcase out of the trunk. "She's eight too. The same age as you. You two will share a room, but you will have your own bed and your own closet. We might have bought you a few housewarming gifts."

Susie McCoy was anything but thrilled about my arrival. When her parents led me upstairs into our shared room, Susie sat on her bed, sandy-blond eyebrows furled so tightly, I thought they would never manage to untangle. She brushed her Chatty Cathy doll's blond hair and didn't look up.

"Susie, your foster sister is here," Mr. McCoy said gently, as if knowing if he said it any louder, Susie would explode in rage.

She continued to brush her doll's hair, this time with her bottom lip protruding.

"Susie," her mom said soothingly. "It's not nice to ignore someone."

"I don't want a sister," Susie screamed, tossed her Chatty Cathy on her bed, and ran out of the room.

Mrs. Lyons's voice rang through my head again. I told myself that it was easy not to get attached to Susie McCoy. So I had that working in my favor.

While Mr. McCoy attended to his fussy daughter, Mrs. McCoy showed me to my twin bed where a boxed Barbie doll waited for me, propped up against my pillow. She showed me my closet of brand-new clothes that she said I could keep, and Mrs. McCoy had knitted me my own purple blanket that was almost identical to the pink one Susie had on her bed. All the new clothes, toys, and blanket distracted me from Susie McCoy throwing her tantrum out in the hallway.

"Don't worry about Susie," Mrs. McCoy said and tucked a strand of hair behind my ear. "She's just having a bad day. She really wants a sister. It's all she's ever wanted. She'll come around, I promise."

Susie didn't attempt to come around until a week later when she extended the thinnest olive branch to me in the form of a Barbie doll. Well, she told me to bring over my Barbie. I wasn't allowed to play with hers. She had a Barbie Dream House that I was in awe of at first.

Right as I was about to sit my Barbie on the pink and blue plaid couch, Susie swatted my hand away. "*Don't* touch the Dream House."

I listened to whatever Susie wished and demanded. I considered myself lucky that she had finally come around and wanted to play with me. I was an eight-year-old desperate to fill the absence of my missing parents. I was willing to follow whatever rules there were if that meant she liked me enough to talk and play with me.

Susie and her friends at school made it even easier for me not to get attached. Even though Mr. and Mrs. McCoy told Susie to walk with me, she walked ahead with her friends, leaving me to trail behind. The first day at my new school, I overheard Susie and her friends snickering and looking back at me.

"Is she like Little Orphan Annie?" Susie's brunette friend, Debbie, said.

The nickname stuck after that.

Susie was smart enough not to say it at home, but once we stepped off the stoop and entered the public domain of the sidewalk, Little Orphan Annie was what they called me. On the two-block walk to school, in the hallways, at lunch, on the walk back home. One day, I decided that I had enough and started eating lunch in the bathroom. I ate my lunch, hummed "Somewhere Over the Rainbow," and reminded myself that staying with the McCoys was just temporary.

As my birthday approached the following month, Mr. and Mrs. McCoy asked over dinner what I wanted to do. "We can do whatever you want, Marlene. It's your day," Mrs. McCoy said.

I felt like she'd told me to go wild in a toy store. I didn't even know all the options. I sat on it for a few days, and while I did so, it gave Susie plenty of time to tell her friends that my day was coming up.

"What do you want for your birthday, Marlene?" her blond friend, Cynthia, asked.

I shrugged. "I'm still thinking."

"I suggest you get a Little Orphan Annie doll," Debbie said. "It's…kind of cute."

"Is it?" Susie said.

"Not at all."

The three of them laughed the rest of the way to school.

The first half of my ninth birthday was horrid. I had already been dreading it because it was the first birthday without my parents, and all I wanted was for my mother to knock on the McCoys' front door and take me back to Red Hook. But the icing on top of the cake was when our class sang "Happy Birthday" to me, but I heard Susie and her two friends sing "Annie" instead of "Marlene." It deflated any lingering happiness, like they'd snatched my birthday balloon and squeezed it slowly until it deflated. I didn't even eat lunch that day because I was too busy in the bathroom crying.

I remembered my sixth birthday and how my father had come home a little bit later than usual because he'd stopped to get me a birthday present. It was Teddy, the brown teddy bear that I cuddled to sleep every night. I squeezed Teddy extra hard at night during my first month at Kindred Hearts and all throughout my stay at the McCoys'.

But Mr. and Mrs. McCoy had other plans.

Because my parents couldn't afford many things to spoil me with, I had no idea about all the things I could have for my birthday. I told the McCoys I wanted a chocolate cake, and even if they had given me that chocolate cake, I didn't think it was going to be enough to take back the hurt that Susie and her friends had caused.

"Happy birthday, Marlene," Mr. and Mrs. McCoy both cheered when I came home from school.

There was a chocolate cake with nine candles, but I was right. Even though the chocolate cake looked delicious, and there was some comfort knowing that at least Mr. and Mrs. McCoy were nice to me, Susie and her friends' words were too powerful for a cake to remedy.

They sang happy birthday, much to Susie's dismay, but after what she'd pulled earlier, I enjoyed watching her bottom lip pout and her smirk finally fade away. When Mrs. McCoy gave me a slice of cake, the tightness in my throat loosened for the first time that day. At least I was safe with them around.

"We also have another surprise," Mr. McCoy said and slid four tickets my way.

They were tickets to a Broadway show. I lowered my fork and stared at the McCoys in awe. I never knew how much I wanted to go to a Broadway show until I saw the tickets in front of me.

"We figured since you love singing so much that you might enjoy seeing a show," Mrs. McCoy said. "It's supposed to be really good. It's called *The Sound of Music*."

With the tickets in hand, I became more understanding of how protective Susie was over her Barbie Dream House because I didn't want her grimy hands ruining my ticket the same way she'd ruined the first half of my birthday.

"Is this really real?" I asked.

Once I'd crossed the Brooklyn Bridge into Manhattan, it was like getting to the other side of the rainbow my mother had sung about. I'd left my black and white world of Brooklyn and woken up in the colorful land of Manhattan, as magical as Oz. Some parts seemed a little too good to be true, like going to the theater for my birthday. I was afraid of waking back up in Brooklyn before getting to see the show.

Susie rolled her eyes, but Mr. and Mrs. McCoy smiled. "Yes, they're real, and we're going tonight," Mrs. McCoy said. "So how about you two shower, change into your favorite dresses, and we'll have a nice dinner before the show. How does that sound?"

"It sounds wonderful," I said and ran upstairs to get ready.

Finishing the chocolate cake could wait.

I watched as Mrs. McCoy curled my shoulder-length, dark brown hair in her bathroom mirror. It was the first time I had ever done anything with my hair. As she did, I looked at myself in the mirror and how my bright blue eyes stood out against my dark curls and eyebrows. I recognized the joy and excitement adding color to my eyes. On some days, they looked light gray, but when I saw myself in the mirror that afternoon, I saw nothing but baby blue and the small dimples that punctuated my growing grin. I pushed aside the first half of my birthday to the back of my mind. It didn't matter at that point because I was going to the theater...in the land of dreams.

We took a cab to the theater district, and I couldn't take my eyes off the kaleidoscope of billboard lights and the marquees flashing names I'd never heard of before. It was the first time I'd seen the glowing lights of Times Square, and the energy surrounding me looked and felt like the excitement inflating my chest. Everyone walking around had the same smiles, eyes fixed skyward at the billboards and skyscrapers that seemed even larger than they had appeared when taunting Brooklyn from the distance. We were in the heart of New York City. Times Square pumped energy and life throughout the streets.

"Wow," I muttered under my breath. "Is this Times Square?"

Mrs. McCoy squeezed my hand. "It sure is. It's something, isn't it?"

I was in the heart of the land of dreams. I thought of my mother and wished so much that we could be in the cab together, taking in all the lights and sights. I wondered what she thought of Times Square the first time she'd seen it.

Mr. and Mrs. McCoy treated us to dinner at Sardi's on 44th Street before the show, and I realized ten years later it was a famous staple of the Broadway community, and that was the place spectators went before or after the show—if they had money. Sardi's was the spot for the Tony Awards' after-party and a favorite spot for Broadway performers. But back when I was nine, I didn't know anything about it except that it was the fanciest restaurant I had ever been in, with white tablecloths and menu items I didn't know how to pronounce.

It must have been a treat for Susie too because she joined me in admiring all the fancy plates dancing around us and pointing at the caricatures covering every inch of the dark red walls. It was the first and probably only time during my stay with the McCoys that Susie and I shared the experience instead of competing for it. For just that night, I felt like I had a semblance of a friendship with the girl whose room I slept in every night.

Just when I felt like Manhattan couldn't get more extravagant, I stepped inside the Mark Hellinger Theatre lobby and was greeted by the two-story rotunda ringed by eight gold columns. It was everything I'd imagined a theater to look like. I took it all in, twirling in circles and accidentally making myself dizzy as I stared at the murals that made up the domed rotunda.

We had orchestra seats, and Susie and I continued our thin, developing friendship by awing over how close we were to the stage and how extravagant the theater looked. "Doesn't it seem like we're in a castle?" Susie said.

It was even better than a castle. We were in a theater.

Once the lights dimmed and Maria belted out the first notes of "The Sound of Music," I gripped the arm rests, and my eyes never once left the stage. I was fully entranced with the actors, the music, and the theater. I wondered what it was like to sing in front of the packed audience. When the crowd cheered and clapped after every song, I imagined myself on that stage and how it must have felt to be rewarded and admired for such a performance. I imagined myself going to Sardi's for dinner, seeing my own caricature on the wall.

Susie and I went home singing "My Favorite Things," "Do-Re-Mi," and "Sixteen Going on Seventeen," and the musical hangover that bonded us lasted several days. I wasn't Little Orphan Annie after the show. It was the closest we ever came to being sisters. She invited me to play Barbies, and our Barbies went to the theater together. We took turns singing and dancing and even put on the dresses we wore that night and pretended like we were going back to Sardi's and the theater.

That only lasted about two weeks. While I clung to every part of the Mark Hellinger Theatre like it was the tallest monkey bar, Susie's friends, Debbie and Cynthia, started calling me Little Orphan Annie again, and it was like Susie pushed me off, and I landed on my face.

"It was because you got attached," I mumbled to myself on the walk home from school with Susie and her friends at least twenty paces ahead of me. "You weren't supposed to get attached."

It was like the night at the theater had never happened. It was gone in a blink of an eye. I tried singing to myself when it was bedtime, but Susie was quick to shoot a glare at me. "Stop singing, it's annoying," she said.

"You used to like singing with me."

"Well, I don't anymore."

The McCoys were quick to notice that I had stopped. They must have clung to my birthday night too because when Susie decided it was over, the dream ended for all of us.

"I miss your singing, Marlene," Mrs. McCoy said at dinner one night. "How about you sing us your favorite song from *The Sound of Music*."

I used my fork to play with my diced carrots and peas. "I don't want to."

"Why not?" Mr. McCoy said. "You and Susie sang it all the time."

I looked over at Susie, who eyed her plate rather than acknowledging me. I was so tired of her treating me like dirt when her parents weren't looking and then acting innocent whenever they were there to witness it. I must have been so tired of being at the McCoy's that I lost the will to keep trying with them. As lovely as Mr. and Mrs. McCoy were, Susie McCoy made living in their beautiful, extravagant house unbearable.

"Susie told me to stop," I said.

She quickly gave me a look, like I'd just spilled her biggest secret like cranberry juice on the living room carpet. And the thing was, I was glad I said it. I was glad she looked terrified. At that point, I'd spent five months allowing her to bully me and hadn't spoken up once.

"Susie, is that true?" Mr. McCoy asked sternly.

"No, it's not true," she said in a desperate panic.

"And she and her friends keep calling me Little Orphan Annie," I added for extra measure. It was a bit entertaining to watch her squirm in her seat. I tried to bite back the grin, but I'm not sure how well I did. I also didn't really care too much if the McCoys noticed at all.

Susie's mouth dropped. So did Mrs. McCoy's. "Susan," Mrs. McCoy snapped.

"That's not true, either!"

"You and your friends sang Annie instead of my name when the entire class sang me happy birthday."

"She's lying."

"I'm not. You've been calling me Little Orphan Annie since I came here."

At least Mr. and Mrs. McCoy didn't brush the newfound knowledge underneath a rug. An intense lecture ensued, and I excused myself to the top of the stairs where I eavesdropped. Susie cried and insisted I was lying. I swiped my eyes and told myself that whatever happened after this would be better for me. Susie McCoy had made living there so miserable that only a fraction of me was sad when Mr. and Mrs. McCoy brought me back to Kindred Hearts. Mrs. McCoy was the one crying the entire cab ride back to Brooklyn while I sat emotionless next to her.

"We're very sorry, Marlene," Mr. McCoy said, struggling to look at me as we stood outside Kindred Hearts in almost the same spot where my mother had dropped me off six months before. Their eyes were glossy. They both couldn't look at me, and Mr. McCoy never let go of Mrs. McCoy's hand.

"Susie doesn't like me," I said with a shrug. "She wants a sister she likes."

Mrs. McCoy cried harder.

"It's more than that," Mr. McCoy said. "You deserve a sister who treats you better. You're a wonderful girl, Marlene. There are so many little girls looking for someone as wonderful as you."

"Tell Susie I'm sorry that I touched her Barbie Dream House. I think that's why she doesn't like me. She told me I wasn't allowed to play with it, and I did anyway. Thank you for taking me to the musical. It was the best present I ever got, and thank you for the clothes, blanket, and the Barbie."

Mrs. McCoy swatted at her eyes. "Thank *you*, Marlene." She tucked a curl behind my ear. "You were so wonderful. We enjoyed our time with you very much. It's just that…" She stopped and looked at Mr. McCoy, who pressed his lips together and shook his head. Mrs. McCoy looked back at me with flaring nostrils. "You're going to make a family so happy, Marlene. I'm sure of it."

I'm not sure why the McCoys returning me like a dog didn't haunt me the way it should have. Maybe it was because they gave me such an extravagant life for those five months that seemed more like five years being around Susie. Part of me always knew that it was all too good to be true.

I guess I had always known that living in the colorful world of Oz was temporary, and it was just a matter of time before I woke up back in my world of black, white, and gray. I would have taken that world over the wonderful land of Oz any day if it meant I got to live on the other side of the rainbow, home with my mother.

CHAPTER THREE

The McCoys were just the start of my journey through what seemed like every single foster family in all of New York City.

I learned soon after that dealing with Susie McCoy was just a little bump compared to other families that made up the foster care system.

I spent four months with the Porters in Bushwick, who clearly looked at each foster child as a paycheck. Sometimes, I wondered if they even knew they were responsible for taking care of the four other kids inside their home.

Throughout 1964, I hopped between five different families, spent about a couple of weeks in between each one. I hoped that each family was going to be as accepting and warm as Mr. and Mrs. McCoy. That's why I don't want to erase them completely. They were the rare ones in the foster care system, even with their brat of a daughter. They were there to take care of me; they provided me with safety. But the families following the McCoys did the bare minimum. They were motivated by money, not their hearts. I can't even tell you the names of many of them because there was no relationship. They just existed, provided a home, accepted the money, and fed us average-at-best casseroles.

It wasn't until the start of 1965 that I landed at the Chapmans in Ridgewood, another memorable stay but not for the right reasons. It was in early January because Mr. Chapman announced he'd finished the last of the New Year's liquor before running to the store to get more and then drunkenly grumbled to himself about how President Kennedy was actually killed by the government. Usually, when the night turned into that, I hid in my room with the other girl they were fostering, Judy, who was a year younger than me.

Mrs. Chapman was a doormat and stayed in her room to read while Mr. Chapman drank booze and watched TV. He hated everything. He yelled when Mrs. Chapman didn't cook a perfect dinner, he yelled at me to shut up whenever I sang to Judy in our room, and he yelled at Judy for not talking at all. Mr. Chapman yelled for no particular reason. In his drunken grumblings, he said more than just JFK conspiracies, and I once overheard him recalling something from the war. I didn't quite understand it then, but Mr. Chapman must have been battling a lot of demons that he brought back from Korea.

One time at dinner, he had already broken into one of his whiskey bottles. Mrs. Chapman was quietly asking Judy and me about school, as if she was afraid that if she spoke too loudly, Mr. Chapman would snap at her. I answered all her questions as Judy kept to herself.

Mr. Chapman eyed Judy and I like we were filthy dogs from the streets that his wife had dragged in. He pointed to Judy and slurred, "Does this child even speak?"

Judy's shoulders hunched as if she was trying to make herself disappear.

"She's shy," I said.

He gestured to me. "Does this child ever stop singing?"

I wanted to say something back, but it wasn't until my stay with the Chapmans that my gut started speaking to me loudly. At that particular moment, it told me to stay silent and to just let Mr. Chapman say whatever he wanted. I was only eleven. I hadn't figured out the world yet. I hadn't figured out the importance of listening to your gut.

While I understood Mr. Chapman was a mean drunk, I hadn't endured anything except for his yelling and drinking. I thought by saying, "I'm not singing now," that I was defending myself and Judy against his wrath.

In return, he hit me.

Judy and Mrs. Chapman gasped and cried, and while the rising emotion tugged on my throat, I couldn't cry in front of them. I refused to give Mr. Chapman that satisfaction. Judy and I didn't finish dinner. I didn't cry until our bedroom door was shut, and even then, I cried into my pillow because I didn't want Judy to hear. She was so distraught, and I wanted to protect her as much as possible.

We stayed in our room as much as we possibly could for a good week, too scared to eat. After that, Judy and I knew better than to get in Mr. Chapman's way.

The very thing that saved Judy and me was *The Sound of Music* movie. When it came to theaters, I was so desperate to see my first Broadway play again, to hear the beautiful music, to see my favorite story play out on the big screen, I convinced Judy to sneak out of the house and see it with me. Even though my gut warned me to stay put and not steal three dollars from Mr. Chapman's wallet, I ignored the feeling. I figured going to the movies meant we would be out of Mr. Chapman's way, and he wouldn't notice or care since it was clear he didn't care about Judy and me at all.

Judy and I scampered a few blocks to the Ridgewood Theatre. My eyes stayed fixed to the screen. I watched in awe as Julie Andrews spun in an Austrian meadow, belting out "The Sound of Music." I whispered every lyric Maria and Liesl sang and was so mesmerized at how gorgeous Charmian Carr was. I was drawn to her, and I wasn't sure if it was because she was so beautiful or if I appreciated her as Liesl so much that I wanted to be her. Looking back, that night was the first inkling that I was attracted to women.

I walked back to the Chapmans that night with Judy, telling myself that one day, I would be a Broadway performer, and I was going to play Liesel.

When Judy and I attempted to sneak back into the Chapman's house, we walked in to find Mr. Chapman in his chair staring daggers at us. His dark brown eyebrows strung together, and a belt waited in his hand.

"Where in God's name were the two of you, and who went through my wallet?"

Judy's waterworks were instantaneous. She cried into her palms, and it only fueled Mr. Chapman's glare as he stood and hovered over us. He already smelled like whiskey.

Judy was horribly shy. We'd lived together for four months at the Chapman's, but I could count the number of times she spoke to me on two hands. Because she hardly spoke, I felt this overwhelming need to protect her from the wrath I could see taking over Mr. Chapman.

"I did it. It was my idea. I wanted to see a movie. Judy didn't do anything."

Luckily, he didn't touch her. She scampered to her room while Mr. Chapman belted my wrist. I bit my tongue to stop the yelp that hummed against my tightly closed lips and swallowed the continuous yanking in my throat. Although a welt instantly started forming on my wrist, Mr. Chapman didn't whack as much nonsense as he intended out of me because I still used that hand to call Kindred Hearts. I almost didn't because that would involve the enormously risky move of tiptoeing out of my room after-hours and using the phone. But my gut told me to risk getting hit again.

I peeked into the hallway to double-check that Mr. and Mrs. Chapman were long asleep. When I realized the coast was clear, I crept out of my room and walked to the kitchen on the balls of my feet, my heart thrumming so hard, it started to hurt. I picked up the phone and moved my finger along the dial, cringing each time the number made a click that seemed loud enough to wake up the house. Mrs. Lyons answered and listened to my cries about being hit by Mr. Chapman. She was quick to pound on the Chapmans' front door forty minutes later with two police officers behind her. While the police dealt with an angry and still drunk Mr. Chapman and a bawling Mrs. Chapman, Mrs. Lyons helped Judy and I pack up our belongings and whisked us back to Kindred Hearts.

If there was one thing I learned from the Chapmans, it was to always listen to my gut.

Once we settled into the safety of our twin beds, Judy shifted onto her side and said very softly, "Thank you, Marlene."

❖

The longest I ever lived with any family were the Schwartzs in Astoria from June 1965 to June 1966. In a sea of incompetent, negligent, and abusive foster parents, only two couples stuck out as suitable parents: the McCoys and the Schwartzs.

Mr. and Mrs. Schwartz were a young couple. They must have been in their early thirties. The best thing about them: they didn't have any children, and they loved music as much as I did. They had a Steinway piano and a record player in their living room.

On the first day, Mr. Schwartz asked me if I loved music, and after I nodded enthusiastically, he introduced me to his impressive record collection. From Ray Charles and blues to Johnny Cash and country to Jerry Lee Lewis and Elvis and rock 'n' roll. He played an album after dinner, and the three of us listened in the living room, bopped our heads, and sometimes Mr. and Mrs. Schwartz danced, and then we sang together.

The best part about the Schwartzs' home was their baby grand Steinway. I was drawn to it the moment I arrived. I stared at it with absolute wonder and once peered inside the open lid at the soundboard. The only thing more beautiful than that baby grand had been walking down Broadway and 7th Avenue that night of *The Sound of Music* when the billboards and marquees colored the city in a kaleidoscope of lights.

"Pretty neat inside there, huh?" Mr. Schwartz asked.

I jumped and backed away from the piano. I wasn't sure of him yet. After my time at the Chapmans' and floating between other incompetent families, I wasn't sure how Mr. Schwartz would have liked an eleven-year-old with her head sticking inside his piano.

He must have seen the fear detailing my face because he flashed me a warm smile and raised his hand as if to comfort me. Both he and Mrs. Schwartz had a friendly smile. That was how I knew that living with them reminded me of my time at the McCoys. I can tell an awful lot by how someone smiles at me. That and their house felt like the closest thing to home in a long time.

"You know how to play the piano?"

"I don't," I said. "Do you?"

He sat at the bench and tickled the keys in a way that proved he really knew how to play. Whatever the song was, it sounded like rock 'n' roll and convinced me to sit on the bench next to him.

"Can you teach me how to play a song?"

And he did. Every night until I grasped it, Mr. Schwartz sat with me on the piano bench after dinner and taught me the basics: how to read music and the notes of the piano. My first song was "Heart and Soul," and then I begged Mr. Schwartz to teach me "Somewhere Over the Rainbow." I told him it was my favorite song, and it reminded me of my mother.

A couple of weeks later, I knew how to play it, and every time I did, memories of my mother piled in my mind, and I could almost hear her sweet, soft voice singing out that window. I sat on the bench after dinner and played for Mr. and Mrs. Schwartz. Mr. Schwartz looked so proud of my progress, and Mrs. Schwartz looked amazed.

"You picked this up so quickly, Marlene," she said and squeezed my shoulders.

"It's impressive, isn't it?" Mr. Schwartz said. "You must have a hidden talent."

Sometimes it brought me comfort, and on bad days, it made me so incredibly sad, I had to stop playing it. "Can you teach me another song?" I asked. While I heard the desperation in my voice, it didn't seem Mr. Schwartz caught on to it.

He took a seat on the bench with that friendly smile of his. "Want to learn how to play Mrs. Schwartz's favorite song? It's a good one. It was our first dance at our wedding."

He glanced at her with a special kind of sparkle in his eyes, as if the memory of their wedding night played in his mind. I loved the way those two gazed at one another.

"I want to learn everything and anything," I said.

It took me another couple of weeks to learn how to play "Can't Help Falling in Love" by Elvis. While I played it, Mr. and Mrs. Schwartz danced behind me, completely caught up in their own world. I glanced over, and the persistent clenching that had been following me ever since I'd arrived at Kindred Hearts loosened.

I could see the love they had for each other every time they exchanged a sweet glance or when they smiled at me. Anytime I played that Elvis song, it always made them stop what they were doing to give each other a look, and I knew that their faraway gazes reminded them of their wedding night.

All I wanted to do was play the piano. I was fixated on it from the second I got home from school until it was bedtime. Once Mr. Schwartz gave me the sheet music book to *The Sound of Music*, my obsession for playing magnified. Mr. Schwartz welcomed it. Instead of Mr. Chapman sitting in the living room drowning himself in alcohol and conspiracy theories, Mr. Schwartz watched TV with the volume down low and cheered as I played the songs I had long perfected or when I tried teaching myself new ones.

"George, Marlene needs to do her schoolwork," Mrs. Schwartz said one night, but there was a laugh in her tone.

"Music is better than schoolwork," he said. "It exercises the mind more than algebra."

"I agree," I said, and Mr. Schwartz gave me a thumbs-up and followed it with a wink.

"I don't think Marlene's teacher would agree with that."

"Her music teacher sure would."

Mrs. Schwartz laughed. "Marlene, how about five more minutes, and then it's homework time, all right? When you're done, you can play the piano until bedtime."

"Okay," I said, hopped off the bench and scampered into the kitchen.

Mrs. Schwartz smiled, ran a hand through my hair, and joined me at the kitchen table to help me. It was an incentive to get my homework out of the way.

That became the only rule in the Schwartzs' house. In order to play the piano, I had to finish my homework. Every day after school,

I did my homework so I had the rest of the evening to play piano. Every night, Mr. Schwartz spent an hour with me on that bench, teaching me how to read music. I was quick to pick up on it, and in a couple of months, I could play by ear. Mr. Schwartz thought it was the most impressive thing. He threw on one of his records and asked me to play the song. So I did.

"You've only been playing for three months, and you can play almost anything by ear, *and* you have a hell of a voice," he said. "Lois, we have a musical prodigy in our house."

The Schwartzs surprised me with singing lessons the following week. Every Tuesday, I went to Mrs. Robertson's for voice lessons. Mr. Schwartz told me she had taught several people who later went on to Broadway.

Never stop singing, my Marlie Rose, my mother's voice repeated in my head. It always swept through my mind whenever I stepped inside Mrs. Robertson's home on Tuesdays.

The Schwartzs even gifted me *Sgt. Pepper's Lonely Hearts Club Band* and *Revolver* Beatles' albums for Christmas. The last thing anyone had given me was the Barbie when I'd moved in with the McCoys and then a few red patches from Mr. Chapman's slaps.

I had outgrown my Barbie. I ended up giving it to Judy, who seemed to love it more than I ever did. But my records I knew I would never outgrow. It was the first present I ever got that felt like home to me. Music was my sanctuary. While Susie McCoy and Mr. Chapman had told me to stop singing, Mr. and Mrs. Schwartz encouraged my love to grow. They allowed me to listen to my albums, play the piano, and sing for them whenever I wanted to. As long as my homework was finished. I had so much more freedom at their house than I did anywhere else. Being with the Schwartzs, I felt fully comfortable living in my own skin for the first time in my life.

I didn't have to worry about them yelling at me or smacking me around. They held my hand as I waded through the heartbreak of being abandoned by my mother. They gave me a taste of what a loving family felt like, one that didn't consist of spoiled siblings or drunk foster parents. They gave me the closest semblance of what I'd had before my father died. They made it easy for me to get attached, and I did. I fell in love with them. They were the first family I wanted to adopt me. I easily pictured myself with them, and it made me excited at the idea of them becoming my parents. I knew they would give me a wonderful life. I knew they would always make me feel loved.

I learned throughout my journey in foster care that when I felt like I was living in Oz, it meant that I was closer to waking up in the black, white, and gray world. It always came, and with a snap of a finger, I was back to where I started at Kindred Hearts, lying in a large room with about ten other twin beds for girls just like me, wondering what could possibly be wrong with them for a family to not want to keep them.

I still wonder if they would have adopted me if Mr. Schwartz hadn't lost his job in June of '66. I was absolutely devastated when I had to leave them because they were tight on money. I sobbed for days. I tried finding them again when I was eighteen, but they no longer lived in their Astoria home. I wondered if money had gotten so tight, they'd had to downsize. I thought about them often, and I hoped they had the children they so desperately wanted. Those two were the best couple I ever came across in foster care.

I must have hopped through at least twenty families by the time I was fifteen. The older we got, the less valuable we were. Couples wanted cute little kids, not teenagers with attitudes. After a three-month stint with my last family, I heard Mr. Wolfe mumble to his wife, "Why are they all so bratty?"

Because being an orphan, I missed out on a lot of things, things kids with families took for granted. I lost out on having my own toys, my own bed, a hug from my parents, holidays with family, pictures of my youth, and consistent love, support, stability, and comfort. I got tossed around from family to family and saw shit that those normal kids didn't see. I saw adults smacking kids as easily as a housefly, I saw them checking their mailbox daily for their undeserved check for "helping" me, and then when I "proved" to them that I wasn't what they expected, they returned me.

I spent my youth fighting to keep my head above the treacherous waters.

So there we were as adolescents, learning all about periods and wearing bras for the first time but having so much life experience that our souls were twice our age, and you know what? It hurts. It hurts every single day, but then I was told to wipe that gross frown off my face because that wouldn't help me get adopted and that I should be grateful for everything I'd been given, as if I was given anything remotely shiny.

At fifteen, I had met so many adults that shouldn't have had custody of children. I begged Mrs. Lyons to stop placing me. I was at my happiest at Kindred Hearts.

I was shocked when she actually listened to me.

❖

"Okay, I think we have reached a good stopping point, Ms. Rose," Dr. Pierson says.

I open my eyes and find myself back in the examination room with five doctors in white coats staring at me over their computers.

"The next step is to think about what you would like to erase, and after you decide, we'll do that. I'll also erase the memory of you recalling it. You can take some time if you need—"

"I don't need any time," I say.

"You don't?"

"Dr. Pierson, you know what made me decide to go through with this procedure?"

"No. Would you like to share?"

Just thinking about the very incident that pushed me into the Institute stings my eyes and burns my chest. It sits heavy on my entire body and clouds all my memories. Ever since my mother dropped me off at Kindred Hearts, I strongly believed that she would come back for me. She promised me right outside that building. My whole career, there was always this hope hanging in the back of my mind that maybe she would be in the balcony, in the very back row, watching me perform, singing like she'd told me to keep doing.

Nine months ago, I couldn't take the curiosity anymore. I hired a private investigator to find out what had happened to her. I wanted answers. I needed them, actually. I spent my whole life wondering why she never came back.

According to the report, my mother checked herself into a rehab facility in Queens and lived in a halfway house until 1965, when she remarried and had a daughter. She had been living in Queens the whole time while I was in and out of foster care. Some of my foster families were in Queens. At some points in my childhood, my mother and I were only within a few miles of each other.

She and her new husband, Donald Roach, moved out of Queens and into Westchester in 1969. I guess her dreams went from Manhattan to the suburbs. She and Don lived in Westchester until 1992, when they retired up in Vermont.

And the report gutted me completely. It ripped through me more than my mother dropping me off at Kindred Hearts because at least when that happened, her promise had filled me with hope that gave me enough air to breathe through her absence. The older I grew, the more I wondered if she'd died. That would be the only reason why she never came back for me...why I still hadn't reunited with her.

But it turns out, that wasn't the case at all. She restarted her life and lived in Westchester and Vermont with Don until she died from liver cancer in 2010 at the age of seventy-nine. Their daughter, Laura Roach, is still alive. The investigator offered to research her, but I declined. I'm sure Laura is a lovely human, but finding any more about her would just break my heart even more. I have no idea if she knows anything about me or not. I assume she doesn't. I assume she would have found me or maybe she knows and is either too nervous to contact me or is also afraid of getting to know me as much as I'm afraid of getting to know her. I have a story that could shatter her perception of her mother if my mother was perfect to her. I hope she was, genuinely.

If the USS Constellation disaster never happened, my life would have been so different. I would have had a family. I think I was destined to grow up poor, but at least I would have had my parents. I can't say I would have ended up on Broadway. I always loved singing, but my passion and willpower to find my mother drove me to being adamant and persistent about getting onto a Broadway stage. Hell, my stage name was solely to grab my mother's attention. When I signed with my first manager, Glenn Kerr, he said that Marlene Hatcher wasn't a Hollywood name, and that before we did anything together, I needed a name powerful enough to light up the marquees like Marilyn Monroe, Joan Crawford, and Judy Garland.

"Marlene Hatcher is the name of a spinster," he said very bluntly in his office. It only mildly offended me, as I was eighteen, just legally an adult, and already a grown, middle-aged man was concerned about me becoming a spinster.

I swallowed back the bite I wanted to give him. I was in the office of an agent with a list of successful Broadway stars attached to his resume. I knew that Glenn Kerr had the power to turn me from a poor Brooklynite to a star with a snap of a finger. He tossed around a bunch of names that made me cringe. They didn't sound like me, and as someone who barely had an identity growing up, this was my time to create one. It was important to me to have a name I resonated with.

"How about Marlie Rose?" I said.

It was good enough for him. I signed all the papers, dotted all my I's and crossed my T's and just like that, I became Marlie Rose. Glenn didn't ask why I wanted the name. That's because in show business, the majority of the people you meet wedge themselves into your life because of money and power. They don't actually care about you. Glenn didn't care about me, and quite frankly, I didn't care about him. We used each other for money, and it worked out for both of us.

The only person to ever ask why I chose the name Marlie Rose was my good friend, Peter Arlo, and that's when I knew he was the first one on Broadway to actually care about me as a person rather than an entertainer or moneymaker.

"Can you tell us why you chose the name Marlie Rose?" Dr. Pierson asks.

I pause and remember the way my mother held my shoulders outside Kindred Hearts.

"My mother told me to always keep singing, so I did," I say, feeling a croak bubble up my throat. I cough to clear it. "I sang every day. After I signed with Glenn, I started imagining myself on the Radio City Music Hall stage, singing for a sold-out crowd and staring up at the third mezzanine level, searching for her in the back row. I pictured my name on the marquee, and if she happened to pass by to see her Marlie Rose up there, she would know it was me. She wouldn't have known anything about me if I went with one of the horrible fake names Glenn spouted off to me."

I shake my head, feeling absolutely foolish that I spent the majority of my life wishing and hoping that my stage name would be the very thing to lasso her back into my life so we could continue the rest of our years making up for all the time we never had with one another. "I really thought Marlie Rose would have worked. I really thought it would have brought her back to me, and now that I know that she continued on with a brand-new family, it's been so hard to find happiness and purpose in my life. Maybe this procedure will take the weight off me, and I can live the rest of my days not trapped underneath the things too heavy to move on from."

"I'm very sorry, Ms. Rose. That must have been really painful."

I swipe at my leaking eyes and swallow back the lump rapidly forming. "It was, which is why I would very much like to erase my parents, Red Hook, the investigation results, all of it."

"And what about the McCoys, Chapmans, Schwartzs, and the other foster families?"

I should want to wipe my memory of almost every foster home I walked through, and there are so many I couldn't wait to clear from my mind. The McCoys are more complex than the others. They introduced me to parts of the city I had always wanted to see. They gave me things I longed to have, and for a while, I did feel loved by at least Mr. and Mrs. McCoy and the Schwartzs at a time I desperately needed the reminder.

"Actually," I say and let out a deep sigh. "I think I want to keep those."

Dr. Pierson falters. "You want to keep this memory?"

I learned a long time ago to always listen to my gut. My gut is never wrong, and it's warning me to hold on to the McCoys, even Susie calling me Little Orphan Annie. "The McCoys helped me fall in love with theater," I say. "They introduced me to Broadway. My dream to be on Broadway was born the night they took me to see *The Sound of Music*. I spent my whole adolescence holding on to that dream. If I erase the McCoys, I erase all of the good they showed me. I erase the start of my dream."

"And the Chapmans?"

"I want to keep the Chapmans and all the other foster families."

Dr. Pierson pauses. "You would?"

"I have to know where I've been and why I ended up at Kindred Hearts and why that place is ironically so special to me. It's the closest thing I can call a childhood home, and what it means to me will be diluted if I erase all the memories that prove exactly why I'll cherish that place. But I would like to erase everything with my parents and Red Hook."

Time eroded most of my memories of my mother and father, and what remains are the ones I held on to tightly after all those years, the same way I used to cling to my teddy bear. But I found recently that clinging to hollow hope has led me to this dead end I've been stuck in for quite some time. All those years of desperately wanting and wishing and hoping lodged a permanent pain in my chest; growing up without my parents and the devastating confirmation that my mother never returned for me pales those eight years' worth of memories of her. As much as I love and miss my parents, losing them left me with so much pain, it was like a boulder sitting in my stomach every day, and with the report, that boulder grew ten times heavier.

"Okay, Ms. Rose. We will go ahead and erase these memories, including the investigation results."

Dr. Wilson comes over and hands me earplugs. "These will help drown out the clicking. Are you ready, Ms. Rose?"

"Yes." I close my eyes and attempt to seal the tears. My chest aches knowing that those few wonderful memories of my parents and the short good life I had with them will evaporate with a few zaps.

The helmet starts to warm up, and a few moments later, I hear the clicking and feel warm taps all over my head.

While I don't know exactly how my mother spent the rest of her life, I still hold on to one last bit of hope. I hope that the new life she found made her see blue skies, bluebirds flying, and that she, at least once in her lifetime, saw what was on the other side of the rainbow, just like her favorite song.

I tell myself that she did find that, and maybe that was why she wasn't able to come back to me. Maybe I was a painful reminder of everything she'd lost, just like how she is to me. If I'm about to wipe her clean, I'm finally able to let go of the anger and heartbreak of her wiping me clean too.

CHAPTER FOUR

No matter how many times I read the neurological reimaging packet, I wasn't prepared for the side effects: confusion, tiredness, and piercing headaches.

I lie in bed, chugging water, taking ibuprofen, even trying to take a relaxing bath to get rid of the headache. It's the kind that reminds me of hangovers throughout my twenties. I can't tell if it is a normal side effect or if it's because I erased a very big memory. I guess Dr. Pierson's technology is working because no matter how hard I try, I can't remember anything about the first session. It's like I sat in the examination room, had the helmet placed over my head, and the next thing I knew, I was in Kristina's car as she drove us back to my house.

It feels weird. Running through all the events of my life, my earliest memory is at age nine in an orphanage. Did I ever remember anything before nine? I must have because what else would I have erased? What else could have caused this massive throbbing headache? Dr. Pierson said to trust the process and give it time, so I pop more ibuprofen, chug water, and curl back in bed.

Two days later, Kristina picks me up in her white Land Rover with my cappuccino in the cupholder. She's too good to me. "How are you feeling?" she asks as I step up into her car.

"Extra old today," I say and take my first sip of caffeine. I hope it kills the lingering pain in my head. She backs out of the driveway and drives through the development and toward Route 1. "How was that date?" I ask. "You never told me about it."

"Hey, you remember?" she says with a smile.

"Of course. You were so excited about it. Let me live vicariously through you. I haven't gone on a date in ages."

"It went really well," she says, and I can see the excitement coloring her cheeks. "It's my turn to take her out next, and I have no idea what to plan. What do you think?"

I may be sixty-two and notoriously bad at maintaining relationships, but it doesn't mean I hate love. I love love, and I loved watching how nervous Kristina was for her first date with Lucy. I'm so desperate for love that I'll take it in any form, and that includes hearing the highlights of someone's date. "I'm not sure if I'm the one you should be coming to for advice," I say. "I have never been married."

"You've had relationships. You've been on plenty of dates. I'm sure you have had some great ones. What was your most memorable? It might help me think of ideas."

I quickly run through the dates that sweep across my mind. "It was with Elle. 1976. I rented out one of the bars at the hottest restaurant in New York City."

"Which one?"

"Windows on the World. Top floor of the World Trade Center. It was hands down the most scenic and extravagant restaurant I've been to."

"Wow," Kristina says. "That must have been really cool."

"Hundred and sixth and seventh floors. There wasn't anything like it. Still isn't. Anyway," I say and let out a heavy exhale. It's hard to talk about the Twin Towers without feeling pressure accumulating inside me. "I'm a little biased, but a date with delicious food and views goes a long way."

"Do we have anything like that here?"

"Axis LA by Serena DeLuca. I had my sixtieth birthday there. Fifty-third floor."

"That sounds wonderful, but I don't know how to even get a table."

I wave her off. "Don't worry about it. I'll arrange something for you."

She looks over like I just suggested something outrageous. "What? No, you don't have to do that—"

"I know I don't, but I want to. You seem to really like Lucy, don't you?"

She focuses back on the road, but a smile still lands. "I do. I don't know. I just feel different with her."

I smile because I know exactly what she's talking about. I felt it too once. I was in her shoes: daydreaming, giddy at the thought of the other person, equal parts nervous and thrilled. I see something familiar in Kristina that I can't turn away from. She's more than an assistant. She's a friend, a confidant, a daughter I never had. Having someone fill you up with that kind of rush is rare, and much to my own surprise, despite all the heartbreak, I still believe in love and romance. I know it exists because I experienced it once. It's something everyone deserves, especially someone like Kristina, who goes above and beyond her job to help me, not because I ask for it, but because she cares. I don't take that lightly at all.

"So she's someone special," I say. "And you should treat her that way. Let me help you."

"Marlie—"

I raise a hand. "No, I insist. Remind me after this session, and I'll see what I can do. It helps to be friendly with the owner."

"You're asking me to set a reminder in my phone to remind you to help me plan a date at a place out of my price range, and that's always booked?"

"Correct."

"I don't think I can accept that."

"Why not? You're always there for me. You make yourself available during hours you probably shouldn't—"

"Because I'm a single thirty-year-old. What else do I have to do?"

"Date. Hang out with friends. Watch Netflix. And maybe you do, but the fact that you're always there for me during my roughest moments? I appreciate it more than you know. So let me show you my appreciation, if you're truly okay with that…and trust me."

She looks over. "I trust you. I'm just…I'm not used to very nice gestures."

"You'll get used to it. Now, I have two conditions. One, you get a really nice bottle of wine. Two, you tell me all about it. I like details."

She laughed as she pulled into the parking lot of the Farrow Institute. "If you really insist, I agree."

"Perfect. I'll get in touch with Serena."

Kristina sits in the waiting room while I follow Dr. Pierson back. Dr. Wilson greets me with that same kind smile as I sit in the chair, and she situates the helmet on me. She turns off the overhead fluorescent lights, and the soft, warm lights flicker in, bringing instant calmness to the room.

"How are you doing, Ms. Rose?" Dr. Pierson asks. "How have the side effects been?"

"The headache was pretty bad, but sleep, water, and medicine did the trick."

"Good. Are you ready to start this next session?"

"I am."

"Good, good. How about you start after you told Mrs. Lyons you no longer wanted to be placed."

Pain swells in my chest. The first thing that fills my mind like a movie screen is Elle. I was fifteen when she walked into my life, and my entire world flipped. In some ways for the better because that was when I started to learn the importance of chosen family. My chosen family taught me how to love and to be loved.

Eleanor Olson's beautiful face takes up residence in my mind, and I watch as her face changes throughout the years. And while each version of Elle sweeps across my memory, the aching intensifies into a stomach cramp because while Elle taught me all about love, she also taught me all about heartbreak.

❖

There are people you meet and instantly know they're going to change your life forever. You don't understand why you feel drawn to them without knowing a single thing about them, yet, they're the only thing that holds your attention.

That's how I felt when I first saw Eleanor Olson.

I was fifteen, a seasoned veteran bouncing her way through the foster system. By then, I had become numb to it. I didn't have to repeat Mrs. Lyons's words any longer. The majority of the families I stayed with made it really easy to not get attached. If anything, I was more attached to Kindred Hearts, where I felt more love and acceptance with girls just like me than any of those families. I didn't need to impress anyone. I didn't have to worry about stepping on toes. I could just be myself, sing along to the radio, and watch TV with girls my age who knew exactly how difficult, confusing, and lonely our lives were.

But when I met Eleanor Olson, my world of gray finally saw color again.

I plopped my suitcase on an empty bed next to the girl with long, straight, blond hair, reading *The Wonderful Wizard of Oz*. Every twin bed had a nightstand to the right of it, and on Eleanor's were a stack of books. *A Wrinkle in Time*. *Harriet the Spy*. *The Outsiders*. *To Kill a Mockingbird*. A journal with orange and pink flowers and green leaves punctuated the top of the stack.

She was the most beautiful girl I'd seen since Charmian Carr in *The Sound of Music*, sitting alone on a twin-sized bed with a worn copy of a book in her hands.

She looked at me, her hazel eyes locking with mine for the first time, and my stomach flipped upside down. She was quick to look back at her book as if the rest of the room no longer existed. I knew she must have loved reading as much as I loved playing the piano and singing. She was so focused that I didn't want to interrupt her, so after unpacking my belongings for what seemed like the hundredth time, I went downstairs to the TV room where a few of my friends watched until dinner was ready.

Dinner at Kindred Hearts always had a bunch of things happening at once. Girls of all ages squeezed onto two long dining tables and spoke over one another. Eleanor ate in what seemed to be her own world. Occasionally, I stole glances, trying to get inside that world. Most of the girls I recognized, especially the teenagers I had grown up with. But I had never seen Eleanor before, and I knew there must have been a story as to why a fifteen-year-old had just landed at Kindred Hearts.

After dinner, the girls usually crowded around the TV but only if they were done with their schoolwork. The Schwartzs had instilled a wise schedule into me because even four years later, I always got my homework out of the way so I could listen to the radio or play the used Steinway upright in the library. It was the newest addition to Kindred Hearts, a donation from a couple who'd adopted a girl a few months prior to Christmas of '68. I could feel the piano crying out my name. I'd been away from it for three months and was itching to play.

Except this time, when I walked into what I expected to be an abandoned library filled with two bookshelves of donated books and the piano, I found the new girl sitting on the chair with her feet tucked underneath her, still enthralled in *The Wonderful Wizard of Oz*. Part of me almost walked out so my playing didn't disturb her. Unlike in the afternoon and at dinner, she finally looked like she had found some peace, and finding that at Kindred Hearts or in the foster system was a rarity that shouldn't ever have been tarnished.

So I began to walk away, figuring I would play another time or night. But right as I took a step toward the entryway, she glanced up, and those beautiful hazel eyes met mine again.

"Hi," I said with an awkward wave. She was so enthralled in the story, I wasn't expecting her to notice that I was even there.

"Hi," she said quietly, but there was the smallest curve to her smile.

I faltered for a moment. "I'm sorry. I'll leave—"

"You don't have to. You can stay."

"No, it's okay. I was going to play the piano but I can—"

She raised an eyebrow. "You play the piano?"

"Well…sort of. I've been out of practice for a few months."

"I've been here for three months and haven't seen anyone play."

"You've been here for three months?" She must have just arrived while I was with my last family.

"Yeah," she said and cleared her throat. "I really don't mind if you want to play. I enjoy music."

I sat on the bench, facing her. "I do too. I love singing a little more, though."

Her eyes widened. "You can sing too?"

"Just a little. Not as often as I used to."

"Why's that?"

"It seems to annoy a lot of people."

Her eyebrows pulled together. "How can singing annoy people?"

I laughed. "Maybe I'm not that good?"

"You should sing something, and I can be the judge of that." She closed her book like it was an exclamation point.

My cheeks absorbed heat as I swiveled and placed my hands on the keys. I hadn't touched the piano in three months, and I kept the singing to myself. Apparently, I did it too much, according to some foster siblings and foster families. So I'd kept it to myself, quietly singing in the shower or anytime I found myself alone.

I wasn't used to someone asking me to sing, not since the Schwartzs three years before. Not only did I want to take advantage of this moment, I wanted to impress this girl. Something about her was already captivating, and I couldn't quite pinpoint what or why. I just knew that I wanted her to enjoy the music I created.

I stared at the keys as I tried thinking of a song that would make the best first impression. The piano had seen better days. It was slightly out of tune but not so horribly that the new girl would sneak off into the kitchen to find a tomato to throw at me. As I straightened my back, the bench creaked, and because of my lack of practice, I worried that my fingers would fumble over each other.

I sucked in a breath and decided to go with "Somewhere Over the Rainbow" to complement the book sitting on her lap. I was surprised how well I had remembered it. My fingers danced along the keys almost perfectly, and while my voice was a little shaky, when I finished, I heard applause coming from more than one person. I quickly turned with a pounding heart to find Eleanor and the girls who had been in the TV room all gathered in the library with their eyes on me. Even Mrs. Hansen and the other houseparents stood watching me, smiling.

"Well, I think it's safe to say you know how to sing," Eleanor said with a small laugh, the first time I'd seen a full smile tugging her lips all day.

I had learned a lot about smiles while in foster care. The people who smiled the biggest and most frequently were the ones who were the most caring, like the McCoys and the Schwartzs. Susie and her friends had only smiled when they were with each other, and instead of soft edges and warmth, their smiles were prickly and sneery. Judy didn't smile much, but when she did, it was only with me, and there was warmth to it. I knew I could trust her, even if I only lived with her for a short period of time.

Eleanor's smile was bright, full, and captivating. It pinned me to the bench and washed me in an intoxicating warmth. "Really?" I said, still completely entranced with the heat spreading across my cheeks.

"Really. That was beautiful. I love that song."

"I love it too. It's one of my favorites."

"That's a very powerful voice for a fifteen-year-old," Mrs. Hansen chimed in, pulling my gaze off Eleanor.

Mrs. Lyons ran Kindred Hearts and facilitated adoptions and foster family placements, while Mrs. Hansen was the houseparent in charge of us. She started working at Kindred Hearts when I was fourteen, but she quickly became my favorite. Some women came and went during my time at the home, some were very strict, some were no better than the adults we had to live with in foster care, but not Mrs. Hansen. Her voice was sweet, she had one of those smiles that let me know her heart was made of gold. It reminded me of the Schwartzs' smiles.

"Can you play another song?" one of the younger girls asked, and a bunch of the girls nodded as if she'd had the most genius idea.

"Sure. Do you have any requests?"

The little girl shook her head. I faced the keys again and went through all the songs I'd memorized at the Schwartzs' house. I played and sang "Sixteen Going on Seventeen." More girls came inside and sat crossed legged around the piano, and a few even joined me in singing. I moved on to "Do-Re-Mi" and "The Sound of Music."

The library was the fullest I'd ever seen it in seven years of coming in and out. The girls started requesting songs, many of which I didn't know, but I kept a list in my head. I sang a cappella instead. All of us sang together, filling the library and the first floor of Kindred Hearts with something the walls didn't see too much of: joy, laughter, and music. All of us kids, and even the houseparents, sharing the night together. Music sewed our broken pieces together for just a moment, and for a bunch of kids who didn't have anything, we realized that we weren't as alone as we thought.

That was one of my favorite nights out of the ten years I was at Kindred Hearts.

When it was time for bed, Eleanor caught up with me as we headed up the stairs. "I'm Elle, by the way," she said, rewarding me with another kind smile. "Well, my full name is Eleanor. Eleanor Olson. But I go by Elle."

"I'm Marlene Hatcher, but you can call me Marlie."

"You have really striking eyes, Marlie."

The compliment forced me to stop on the landing. I'd been called a lot of things. Little Orphan Annie. Annoying. Little shit. Or just the sound of Mr. Chapman's hand colliding with my face.

It had been a really long time since someone had said something nice to me. I wasn't expecting it. I'd been told I had a good voice, but it had been a while since I'd even heard that. No one had ever told me I had "striking eyes" or that anything about me was beautiful until Eleanor Olson.

"Really?" I said, feeling as the compliment warmed my entire body up like a flannel blanket in the dead of winter.

"Really. Are they blue? Gray?"

"It depends on the day."

She smiled. "Whatever they are, they're very striking. It's groovy."

She led us to our bedroom. We grabbed our toothbrushes and walked together to the bathroom.

"You really learned to play the piano from a foster family?"

I squirted toothpaste on my brush and smiled at her in the mirror. "They were one of the good ones. I learned a lot from foster families, but most of them aren't good." I spat into the sink. "I've been here since I was eight, and I haven't seen you before."

Her smile faded, and I hated the sight of it dimming. "My grandma died three months ago." She looked away, spat into the sink, then cleaned her mouth with a towel.

I took that as a sign that she didn't want to talk about it. Something hung heavy between us, and I was desperate to push it away. "The foster family who taught me how to play piano gave me two Beatles' albums. Do you like The Beatles?"

"I love The Beatles."

"Maybe we can listen to them tomorrow after dinner?"

"That sounds groovy."

"Deal," I said and stuck out my hand.

When she shook it, I knew that Elle was going to be in my life for a long time. Something about her handshake felt like a promise that extended far beyond just the next evening.

The next night, I brought down *Sgt. Pepper's Lonely Hearts Club Band* and *Revolver*, and we listened to the albums on repeat until the younger girls tiptoed in and asked if they could listen with us. We crowded around the record player, and girls started filtering into the library like an accumulating puddle. We all sang, bopped our heads to the beat, and replayed songs that we loved.

Music really has the power to bring people with all sorts of backgrounds and broken parts together. During those nights in the library, it was hard to feel like an orphan when I had so many girls—and even Mrs. Hansen and Mrs. Lyons—around me singing, taking turns playing their favorite songs and records. Those evenings were something we all looked forward to. The TV sat alone while the library saw the most life it had ever seen in all my time at the home. My love for music deepened at Kindred Hearts. I realized how much I needed to have it in my life. It added light to my days, brought me closer with my foster sisters those last few years at Kindred Hearts, and stitched our broken parts into the closest thing we had ever felt to having a family.

My dream of being a singer was revived. It gave me a purpose. It gave me a hopeful future.

One day, early in the summer of 1969, Mrs. Hansen took the older girls to Morsey Records, a store a few blocks from Kindred Hearts. We had all grown to love our evenings in the library so much that Mrs. Hansen probably figured we would enjoy this specific outing.

"We should go to the listening booths," I said to Elle as we walked in and took in the rows of records. What was great about Morsey was that it still had booths where you could listen to the 45s without headphones. "That way, we can hear as many songs as possible and determine which one we want to buy."

We crammed into one of the booths. She pressed against me as she showed me all the albums in her hands. I smelled the shampoo wafting off her hair, and even though the scent was generic, and all the girls at the home used it, it smelled different coming off her. It smelled better, fruitier, and it made my stomach flutter.

When she looked at me with those hazel eyes, I noticed how the flecks of honey-brown swirled with amber and green. "What do you want to listen to first?"

I was too distracted by the butterflies in my stomach to know which 45s she read off to me. I scrambled to find an answer and went with the first album on top of the stack in her arms, *Pet Sounds* by The Beach Boys. "Let's go with The Beach Boys."

Her smile grew. She slid the record out of the sleeve and placed it on the turntable. "That's exactly what I was thinking."

After The Beach Boys, we listened to Bob Dylan, Jimi Hendrix, Aretha Franklin, and Elvis. "You should learn how to play this song," Elle said as we listened to "Can't Help Falling in Love."

I smiled proudly. "Already know it."

"And you haven't played it?"

"All the girls want me to play *The Sound of Music* or The Beatles."

"Maybe sometime, you could play this one," she said. "My grandma loved this song. It reminds me of her."

She moved her gaze off me and looked at the ground. She started nodding slowly, as if she wanted to immerse herself in the song.

Mrs. Hansen bought us each an album to take home. No other houseparent would have done that, but Mrs. Hansen treated us like her own daughters, and for many of us, it was the first—or one of the very few times—we had a nurturing mother figure. None of us had much. We could fit everything we owned in one suitcase, and most of the things we had were overly worn clothes that were hard to replace with our lack of money and growing bodies. So having our favorite album was like acquiring a bar of gold. We had something that was specifically ours.

Mrs. Hansen didn't have to chaperone a handful of teenagers to the record store that day. But she did, and it was one of the reasons we all loved her.

Don't get attached.

Elle bought *Pet Sounds* by The Beach Boys, and I bought *I Never Loved a Man the Way I Love You* by Aretha Franklin. I loved her voice, how rich it was, how it came from the pits of her stomach and filled a room. I wanted to sound like that, or at least, get my voice to fill a room.

With our new albums, the evenings became richer with music, singing, and camaraderie. Sometimes, Elle sat in a chair and read or wrote in her orange and pink flower journal, but even with a book in her lap, she still bopped her head and occasionally looked up to take in the scene. I hated how many times she caught me staring at her. I couldn't help it. She was just so beautiful sitting there completely content.

One of those nights, I mustered the courage to sit on the piano bench and play "Can't Help Falling in Love." Ever since Elle had requested it, I'd practiced in bed, playing an invisible piano underneath the covers to see if muscle memory still lived in my fingers. It was safer to practice there than on the piano for everyone to hear me fumble. I didn't want Elle to hear a butchered version of the song that reminded her of her grandma. When I was ready, I barely brushed my fingers along the keys, putting the muscle memory to one last test. Then, I played the first chord, cleared my throat, and pretended I was just singing for the Schwartzs, a two-person audience much less intimidating than my audience of Elle and only Elle. Somehow, I managed to sing and play with only a few fumbles.

"Wow, that was beautiful," Elle said, causing me to turn.

When I met her gaze, a rush of heat drenched me, stronger than when I nervously performed for her. "It was?"

She let out a chuckle. "Of course it was. You should play it again and hear yourself."

"Do you want to hear it again?"

"Absolutely. It's one of my favorites." She glanced at her journal on her lap. "It reminds me of my grandma. I miss her. A lot."

"What do you miss the most?"

She thought for a moment. And I learned that whenever she really thought about something, she pressed her lips together and sometimes chewed on the inside. "Her warmth," she said, eyes still on her lap. "She had so much warmth. It made up for my parents."

"What happened with them?"

She shrugged and started picking the corner of her journal. "My mom had me when she was young and loved drinking and drugs more than me. I've always lived with my grandma while my mom came and went. Sometimes, she stayed with us for a few months—a few good months—and then, she was gone. She and my grandma fought a lot."

"About what?"

"Her. I heard my grandma saying she was raising two children, and one of them was too old to be a child. They didn't get along, but my grandma and I did. She was the mother I never really had."

"What about your father?"

"He was never in the picture." She paused and finally looked back up. "What about your parents?"

I don't remember my parents, but I feel like I must have told Elle something because we had a conversation, though I don't remember what I told her.

"It's nice to hear the song though," Elle said. "It's like all these memories of her come back to life, and it makes me feel...I don't know."

"At home?"

The smallest smile appeared. "Yeah. Exactly that."

"I'll play it whenever you want, you know. Just say it, and I'll do it."

"You would?"

I nodded.

"Can you play it again?"

I swiveled and performed the song two more times. I didn't know why I was so drawn to her then, but I know now that my feelings for her started at fifteen, a seed of a crush buried so deep inside me that by the time I was able to recognize my feelings, she had already claimed my heart entirely.

❖

After our trip to Morsey Records, Elle and I made it a weekly adventure that summer. We squeezed into those booths and listened to all the greats: Led Zeppelin, The Who, The Rolling Stones, The Velvet Underground, and David Bowie. How couldn't we? We were teenagers during the year that defined the music of our generation. I couldn't stay away, which is why Mr. Morsey, the store owner, gave me my first job. I made minimum wage, a dollar thirty, and collected my earnings in an old Smucker's jelly jar and hid it in my suitcase, wrapped up in a pair of flood pants.

It was a good thing that it was the best year for music because we needed an escape that summer. The whole world did. I cried when I found out Judy Garland died that June in London. I played and sang "Somewhere Over the Rainbow" on the piano for weeks, and Elle even read the younger girls chapters of *The Wonderful Wizard of Oz*.

Later that month, I found Mr. Morsey behind the counter reading the *New York Daily News* with the front-page headline that read, "Homo Nest Raided, Queen Bees Are Stinging Mad."

On my lunch break, I went to the nearest newsstand and read all the articles about what had happened at the Stonewall Inn in Greenwich Village, including the horrible words I read in *The Village Voice*. I was only fifteen. I hardly knew anything about myself or understood what it meant to be a "homosexual" and what "cross-dressing" was. But I was old enough to feel empathy for those Stonewall Inn patrons, and even if they were "homosexuals" or wore the other gender's clothes, it didn't mean they deserved to be attacked by police batons and arrested.

I was so bothered by what I read, I tossed the paper in the trash the second I was done with it. I went back to Kindred Hearts and asked Mrs. Hansen what those words meant. She was in the TV room, watching the news while knitting.

"Where did you see that, Marlene?" she said, lowering her needles onto her lap.

"It was all over the newspapers. I wanted to know what happened, so I bought a paper."

She told me to never repeat those words again. I felt a huge wave of heat wash over me for saying something horrible that I didn't know was so bad.

"If those words are bad, then why are the papers saying them?"

"Because people are cruel, including some journalists."

"Why did the police beat up all those people? What did they do wrong?"

Mrs. Hansen pressed her lips together and then looked at the ceiling as if filtering her thoughts. I could tell she was struggling to find the right words, piquing my curiosity even more. "You know how men and women meet and sometimes fall in love?" I nodded. I understood that. I saw it in the movies and TV shows. "Sometimes, men fall in love with men, and women fall in love with women."

"Oh," I said, paused, and realized I didn't understand the controversy. "What is cross-dressing?"

She took another moment to think about her words. "Sometimes, men dress up as women, and sometimes, women dress up as men."

I thought, that was it? That was why the police whipped out their batons, that was why the newspapers said horrible things? Because people loved one another? It wasn't like I had too much experience with love or perfect families. I could only compare it to the foster families I'd stayed with, and while I strongly believed some of those adults had no capacity in them to love another human—or themselves—I saw how the Schwartzs had looked at each other and danced every night. They weren't like the other foster families.

I'd never seen a man fall in love with a man or a woman fall in love with a woman, but even then, I couldn't grasp why that was so problematic. Maybe it was a part of my subconscious already warning me that I'd fall madly in love with a woman, or maybe it was because I was so desperate for any ounce of love at fifteen that I couldn't fathom why anyone opposed any form of it.

Maybe it was a little bit of both.

"What's bad about that? I don't get it."

Mrs. Hansen rested her hand on my shoulder. "Depends who you ask. Some people think it's bad. They say it goes against the Bible. Some people don't think it's wrong at all. But either way you believe, it's illegal."

"It's illegal? Why?"

"It just is, sweetheart. Sometimes, laws aren't just."

"Do you think it's bad?"

Her eyes rounded with sympathy. "I think the police going there and hurting innocent people is bad. I don't think expressing love or living authentically is bad at all. I think love in any form is the best thing that can happen on this earth."

More than fifty years later, what she said hadn't aged one bit, and though we never spoke about Stonewall or the LGBT community ever again, whenever I think of Mrs. Hansen, I smile. She was in her fifties. She grew up in a time where the majority looked down on the minority.

But she never did. Why? Because some laws—especially during that time—were not just.

A month after Stonewall, we sent men to the moon. All of us crowded around the TV and stared in awe when Neil Armstrong and Buzz Aldrin took their first steps. We all clapped, cheered, and fixed our gazes on the black-and-white TV as the two of them planted the American flag on the moon.

The next day, Elle and I walked down the Brooklyn Heights Promenade with ice cream cones. The entire summer, we took advantage of the fact that we were old enough to wander outside of Kindred Hearts without a chaperone. Walking along the promenade with ice cream had become a frequent occurrence. Working at Morsey Records afforded me the luxury of having every album at my fingertips and money to buy Elle and I the occasional treat.

It bought me more time to be with her.

We found a seat on the bench and admired the Manhattan skyline on the other side of the East River. I was in a bit of a daze, still processing what had happened the night before. Humans had landed on the moon. It was hard to comprehend at first. That little rock that glowed in the night sky had human footprints on it now.

"If we can send humans to the moon, we sure as hell can get out of here," I said and licked my chocolate ice cream cone and stared at the Empire State Building in the distance.

The moon was something we saw almost every night, glowing and twinkling from a distance, reminding us there was more out there than our little world. I couldn't help but view Manhattan the same way. The skyscrapers we saw almost every day, twinkling from a distance, reminding us there was more out there than Kindred Hearts and Brooklyn.

"You want to leave Brooklyn?" Elle asked with raised, curious eyebrows.

"I've always wanted to leave Brooklyn. What's for us here?"

She pulled her gaze off me and back at the skyline. The skyscrapers started flickering against the dusk as streams of orange and yellow streaked across the sky. "Yeah, you're right." She paused, licked her mint chocolate chip cone, and then said, "I worry about leaving because my mom is here somewhere. Don't you feel that too?"

I'm not really sure why she asked, and I forgot what I said, but there wasn't anything tying me to Brooklyn. I wanted out. I wanted to live between the skyscrapers and have the Manhattan lights flicker against my bedroom walls. "I can't wait until I turn eighteen. Once we're done with high school, I'm booking it. You want to come with me?"

"Where would we go?"

"Where would you wanna go?"

Elle licked her ice cream. "Hmm, California sounds groovy. Maybe San Francisco. All the songs about San Francisco make it sound like a lot of fun."

"It sounds pretty far-out, doesn't it?"

"It does. Oh! Maybe London or Paris. I've wanted to go to Paris since I was little. I loved the book *Madeline*."

"Then let's go."

Elle's dreamy smile faded. "What?"

"Let's go to San Francisco or London or Paris. We can go once we turn eighteen. There's a whole world out there, Elle. We deserve to see more than just Brooklyn."

"There's a small problem in your plan, Mar," she said, and it was the first time she'd used that nickname. I loved it. We had only known each other for five months, but I felt like I'd known her so much longer. It made me wonder if she felt like she'd known me longer too since she was the first person to give my nickname a nickname. "We need money."

"I got the job at Morsey Records because I want to have enough money to get out of here. I'm saving up, and if I keep working there until I'm eighteen, I'm sure I can afford both of us moving out of Brooklyn. If you want to, that is."

She thought about it while taking another lick. "It's a bit silly to feel tied to Brooklyn, isn't it? Especially when my mom was hardly ever a mother."

"No, I don't think that's silly."

She looked at me as vulnerability slashed across her features. "Really?"

"Why is that silly?"

She shrugged and faced Manhattan. "Because she was never really in my life as a mother figure. If anything, she's always been, I don't know, a problem."

"She's still your mother, even if she's caused you a lot of pain."

She blew out a heavy breath. "I shouldn't wait around for her to want me, you know? I've waited fifteen years. If she doesn't come get me by the time I'm eighteen, maybe I should stop waiting. I gave up my childhood waiting for her. I'm not going to give up adulthood." She met my gaze. "I'm interested. I should get a job too. Maybe I can get one at the library?"

"Maybe. I'd bet you would get it easily. Just show them your book collection or those journals you write in every night."

"I'm not sure that's how it works," she said with a laugh.

"What do you write, anyway? Anything good?"

"I just write about my day, observations, my thoughts."

"Can I read one?"

She pushed my arm. "No, you can't. That's the whole point of a diary. It's for the writer's eyes only."

"What if I buy all the ice cream cones for the next year just for one page?"

"Do you even have enough money to make such a big promise?"

I thought about it, noticing how the whips of orange and golds started mixing with the crawling of the night sky. "Not yet, but I'm going to keep working with Mr. Morsey, and in three years, we'll have enough money to go anywhere, and that means I'll have enough."

"If you can get us out of Brooklyn, I'll let you read one entry of my journal." Elle stuck out her hand, and excitement inflated my chest.

"Deal," I said, shaking her hand and sealing our promise.

CHAPTER FIVE

Working twelve hours every weekend for three years added up. Because women couldn't open their own bank account without a husband cosigning, I accumulated so many Smucker's jars that I needed to buy a larger suitcase to hold them.

But it meant I had my own money, and Manhattan was no longer as far away as the moon seemed to be. Elle and I often took the subway into Manhattan and walked around Times Square and Central Park on the weekends. We pretended that we had enough money to afford an apartment that overlooked the park. I'd be on Broadway, and Elle would be going to college to study education, communications, or literature. She had been working at the Brooklyn Heights Library for almost as long as I had been working with Mr. Morsey.

"You really think we'll live here one day?" she asked as we walked up 5th Avenue, admiring the apartment buildings to the right of us.

I couldn't help but think of the McCoy's when we reached the intersections of 5th and 62nd. An intersection I had crossed numerous times nine years prior. It brought back a flood of memories, being left out and bullied by Susie and her friends. While I dreaded that walk to school every day, Elle standing beside me lifted that heavy weight I once carried on my shoulders on that walk up 5th Avenue to school.

"I used to live down there," I said, hooking a thumb down 62nd Street. "It was my first foster care placement."

Elle's eyes widened as if I'd told her I lived in a castle and was a princess. "Are you serious? You lived here by Central Park?"

"For five months. It was a beautiful home. They were really rich, but their daughter was a spoiled brat," I said. "At least they took me to my first Broadway play for my ninth birthday. We saw *The Sound of Music*, and that's when I wanted to be on Broadway."

"You should sing more," she said. "Get your voice outside of Kindred Hearts. People sing on the streets all the time. Maybe if you do it on Broadway, someone will notice you."

It hadn't crossed my mind before. It was fall of 1971. While I worked so hard to save up money to leave, I hadn't worked hard to get my voice out there except for all the girls staying at Kindred Hearts, and they weren't the ones getting people onto Broadway stages.

"You're a genius, Eleanor Olson," I said.

She shrugged, but a smile landed. "I read sometimes."

"You think it'll work?"

"I have no idea how it works, but it doesn't hurt, right? You could make some extra money doing it like all the other street performers, at the very least. But your voice is so good, Mar, I bet it will stop a powerful Broadway person. I'm almost sure of it."

I loved whenever she said my nickname. She was the only person who called me that, and every time she said it, it made my stomach flutter. I was sold just from that.

The next week, I went back into Manhattan and stood outside the Mark Hellinger Theatre, eyeing the *Jesus Christ Superstar* banner hanging in front of the marquee. I had a large Smucker's jar at my feet with "Tips" in permanent marker. I sang right outside the theater for three months until one December night, everything changed.

It was as if the seventeen Christmases of barely getting any gifts to unwrap morphed into one life-changing gift. It might not have been an actual gift wrapped in beautiful paper and a bow under a sparkling Christmas tree, but it was in the form of a middle-aged man wrapped in a tweed double-breasted coat, with a brown horseshoe mustache and short, wavy brown hair. I would have missed him completely if it weren't for the fact that he stopped walking and watched me sing from a couple of feet away as he smoked. He was on the shorter side, might have only had a few inches on me, and I'm five-seven.

I was in the middle of singing "Ave Maria" with a handful of people standing around me. I shivered in my worn coat donated the Christmas before, but I couldn't let the people on the street know how miserable I was. Misery didn't make much money. Talent did. The people watching had impressed grins that met with the redness of their cheeks. I knew they were about to go into the theater based on the suits and dresses under their coats. That was when I noticed the man off to the side, puffing on his cigarette and studying me in a different way than the others.

He watched me intently, not in a creepy way, but as if he was trying to find something in me. It wasn't until I finished the song that he flicked his cigarette on the ground, stomped on it, and took a step forward. "That's a great voice you have," he said.

"Thank you," I said as my teeth chattered.

"Where did you learn to sing like that?"

I shrugged. "I've been singing my whole life. Took a few classes a few years ago."

He gave an impressed nod. "I can hear the lessons."

"You can?"

He laughed. "Kid, I've been listening to singing voices for longer than you've been alive. I have to say, though, I wasn't expecting that voice to come out of you."

"Well…it did."

"What do you plan on doing with that voice?"

"Right now, I'm just trying to make some extra money so I can move out of Brooklyn."

He chuckled. "I don't blame you for that."

"And then maybe one day, I can sing in there." I pointed behind me at the Mark Hellinger Theatre.

"Do you know any showtunes?"

"I do."

"How about you sing one?"

I looked around at the festive lights, but I didn't question the request. If a decent tip was coming my way, I'd sing a showtune in the midst of Christmas spirit and festive decorations. So I sang "Sixteen Going on Seventeen."

By the time I finished, the man's dark eyebrows scrunched together, but he wore the smallest grin. "What's your name?"

"Marlie Hatcher. Well…Marlene Hatcher."

"How old are you?"

"I am seventeen going on eighteen," I sang it in the tune of the song.

He chuckled. "Clever."

I grinned, proud I could get someone to laugh at my horrible attempt at a joke.

The man plucked a business card out of his wallet and handed it to me. "I'll tell you what, the moment you graduate high school, you give me a call. You've got a hell of a voice, and it'd be a shame to let that voice go to waste." The card said, "Glenn Kerr, Talent Manager," with a phone number and address on Broadway. "If you want to sing inside one of these theaters, keep singing. Every day. Oh, and take an acting class. Do those two things, and I can make you a star."

After Glenn Kerr said that, I stared at the business card as if it was the golden ticket to Willy Wonka's chocolate factory, and the average looking, middle-aged man with the horseshoe mustache was Willy Wonka himself. "You can?"

He nodded. "Don't lose that card, and don't forget to call me in June."

I kept his card hidden in one of my Smucker's jars until the last day of high school in June of 1972. By then, I'd forgotten which jar it was in. I dumped at least five jars onto my bed, searching for this card.

Elle walked into the bedroom and gasped. "Marlie, is that…all your money?"

On the sixth jar, I found the card, and held it up in the air. "Found it!" I looked at all the money sprawled across the bed. "Oh yes, this is my money. Do you think we have enough to get out of Brooklyn?"

She laughed. "How about you go call the agent while I start counting all this."

"Okay, thank you. Also, don't let anyone touch it. I'll be right back."

Fifteen minutes later, I had an appointment with him in two days at his office on Broadway. I ran back into my room, and Elle had most of the money shoved back into my jars.

"Leave five bucks out. We're getting ice cream, my treat," I said and snatched a five off the bed. "I have an appointment with a Broadway talent agent on Friday, and we're going to celebrate."

We shrieked, jumped up and down, and Elle had a few tears in her eyes. I swatted them away and palmed her face. Something took hold of me in that moment. Having her beautiful eyes stare up at me like that with absolute wonder caused my stomach to shift. The feelings collected like a puddle in me. I wanted to kiss her, a desire that had accumulated from a raindrop to a lake over the last three years.

I knew I couldn't, though. We were best friends, and she had spent the last several months talking about her crush on a boy at the library. Sam. Anytime she mentioned his name, I had to suppress an eye roll. Her crush forced me to attempt to drain that lake of desire until it was back to a little raindrop.

So I dropped my hands and felt the immediate loss of her skin against mine. I was doing a terrible job of taming my feelings. While my crush gnawed on my chest, I tacked on a smile that I hoped masked those feelings from making themselves known.

"Let's go," I said. "We have a lot to celebrate."

We went to our favorite shop and walked along the promenade. As always, we found a bench and stared at Manhattan. I studied the new construction in lower Manhattan poking through the skyline, the scaffolding around the half-built Twin Towers. For the first time, Manhattan didn't feel like worlds away. It felt within my reach, and I wondered, sitting on that bench and eating my strawberry ice cream cone, if that meant something. Maybe it was my gut's way of telling me this was my ticket out of Brooklyn.

"What happens if I get signed with this agent?"

Elle furrowed her eyebrows. "What do you mean? You become a Broadway star. That's what happens."

"No. I mean what happens to us. Are we still getting out of here together?"

"The real question is, do you want to still get out of here together when you're all rich and famous?"

I rolled my eyes and nudged her elbow. She laughed. "Of course. I just wasn't sure about how you felt now that the time has come."

"Well, still no signs of my mom," she said, but while I noticed the sadness in her eyes, there was defeat and anger in her tone. I couldn't blame her. I understood her anger and her hurt. "I shouldn't have to wait for someone to want me. I want to see what else is out there. I want to get out of here and restart."

It was the biggest incentive to sing my heart out for Glenn Kerr. Not only for me to have a chance on Broadway but to have the ticket out of Brooklyn for a chance to start fresh as legal adults.

Two days later, Elle and I followed the address on Glenn Kerr's business card and stared up at the Paramount Building. The lights from the Times Square marquees danced along the limestone piers. This was Broadway. Art Deco architecture, Times Square lights, musical billboards. I sucked in a breath of the warm June air, and Elle and I walked into the building and ascended to Glenn Kerr's thirtieth floor office. The sign on the door read, "Kerr Talent Agency," and when we walked inside, we were greeted by the scent of tobacco smoke.

There was only a blond secretary with red glasses behind the desk. She didn't even look up to acknowledge us, and it made me wonder if we'd crept in so silently that she didn't hear us.

"Excuse me?" I said softly and insecurely.

That was probably why she didn't bother looking up from her typewriter. She kept clanking away. She smacked the lever of the carriage return and continued typing.

I cleared my throat, prepared to be louder the second time around. "Excuse me? I'm here to talk to Mr. Kerr."

"Do you have an appointment?" she asked, not giving me the decency of eye contact.

"I do. One p.m."

She finally scanned me head to toe. Her dark blond eyebrows folded behind her glasses. Then, she turned to Elle and did the same thing.

Elle and I exchanged an uncomfortable glance. I wasn't sure why the secretary was so rude. Maybe she hadn't taken her lunch break yet.

"She doesn't," I said. "She's just here to accompany me."

"Well, she'll need to stay out here." She picked up her phone, moved her fingers along the dial, and waited a few seconds until she said, "Mr. Kerr? You have a child waiting outside for you."

I cleared my throat when she slammed the phone back down. "I'm not a child, ma'am. I'm eighteen. I'm a legal adult."

She belted out a cackle and sipped her red-and-white can of Sego through a straw. "You can wait there." She pointed to the chairs behind us.

Elle and I took a seat as my blood started to boil along with anger and nerves.

"She's a real skuzz bucket," Elle muttered.

I roared with laughter, never expecting that to come from Elle. The secretary shot us a glare. I couldn't tell if she had overheard or if she was annoyed that I'd brought some laughter into the waiting room, but I couldn't have cared less at that moment. That one comment made me forget about my nerves until Glenn Kerr and his mustache opened the door.

"I remember you," he said with a point. "Marlie Hatcher, the young lady with singing pipes that you don't quite expect to come out of that body."

I suppressed the wince threatening to contort my face. I wasn't sure if that was a compliment or not. But I knew better than to fight him on it. This was a man who could start my career and make me Liesl the next time *The Sound of Music* came back to Broadway.

I stood and smoothed my dress, as if any wrinkles would ruin my chances at my audition. "Yes, that's me."

"Come on back, doll."

I took a step forward before glancing back at Elle.

"You got this, Mar," she said and gave me a thumbs-up and that beautiful smile.

My chest fluttered as I followed him through the doorway and into his office.

"So you wanna be on Broadway?" Glenn said, taking a seat at his desk and lighting a cigarette. He offered me the opened Marlboro pack. "Smoke?"

"No, thank you."

"Suit yourself."

I went from being called a child in the waiting room to being offered a cigarette by a middle-aged man. I was quick to find out right then and there how interesting being eighteen was. No one was really sure what you were. A kid? A young adult? Standing in front of Glenn Kerr, I knew that it didn't matter how old he saw me as. What mattered was if he saw potential in me.

"Now tell me, Marlie Hatcher, what's your dream?"

I watched the smoke from the tip billow up to the ceiling as I thought about it. "I want to sing for people. I want to be on stage. I want to play Liesl."

He laughed. "Doll, a million girls want to be Liesl. A million other girls with singing, acting, *and* dancing experience."

"I took acting classes like you said, and I haven't stopped singing. I've been practicing every day."

"Good. Now you're at the bare basics of show business." I had no idea if I should have been thankful or if I should have been offended yet again. He flicked his cigarette into the glass ashtray. "Let's listen to your singing chops again. Sing something."

"What do you want to hear? A Liesl song?"

He chuckled again, and it got under my skin how he laughed at me like I was a child, just like the secretary. Just like that, I went from being old enough to be offered a cigarette to being a naive child. My annoyance made me more determined to prove myself. He was right. A million other girls with more experience, who were prettier and probably had bigger boobs, wanted to be Liesl. What made me stand out? It sure as hell wasn't my C cups.

No, if I wanted to play Liesl, I needed to aim higher. This wasn't me busking on 47th Street for a few bucks like I had been doing since the fall. This was Broadway. I was standing in front of a Broadway agent. Behind him was a bookshelf with photos of him and dolled up men and women who looked successful, holding Tony awards next to Glenn Kerr clad in a tux. If I played my cards right and nailed this audition, I could be one of those people on his bookshelf with a Tony in my hand.

If I wanted that Tony, I needed to make Glenn Kerr believe I was a star. Liesl wasn't the star of *The Sound of Music*. Maria was. If I wanted to be Liesl on a Broadway stage, I needed to audition as Maria, and maybe then, I'd wipe the smirk off Glenn Kerr's face.

So I straightened my back, pushed through all the nerves coiling in my stomach, and belted out "The Sound of Music" as if I was in that Austrian field like Julie Andrews. I turned myself into Maria. I envisioned myself onstage of the Mark Hellinger Theatre, the first theater to spark my dream and the very theater where Glenn had discovered me. Ever since I'd bought the soundtrack from Morsey Records when I was fifteen, I had studied every note, sound, breath, and vibrato from Julie Andrews on the record. In the last six months, I had taken Glenn Kerr's advice like it was a Bible verse to empower me through the last several months of my adolescence. I had enough money to take those acting classes, and my teacher loved me so much, she gave me a few under-the-table singing lessons.

I'd worked hard for this exact moment in that nicotine-infused office.

Despite a whirlpool of nerves, there was still an undertow of confidence in all the work I'd done to get to this moment.

My notes filled Glenn Kerr's small office and probably outside into the hallways to hopefully Elle in the waiting room and Glenn's wet towel of a secretary. My vibrato and high notes wiped away his smirk like a chalk eraser in one swipe. He leaned into his desk, sucked in longer drags of the cigarette, holding in the smoke for a few moments longer. I know now that the last note I sang must have been powerful because there's always a certain kind of loud silence that follows something musically powerful. I call it the loudest rest. It was the first time I'd heard it.

A loud silence drew out for a few seconds too long, until Glenn hacked up a large cloud of smoke. After he sipped his coffee, he straightened and stared at me with dollar signs flashing in his dark brown eyes.

To fill the elongating silence, I said, "Do the other girls sound like that?"

I knew that there were, indeed, plenty of girls who sang like that somewhere in the world, but I sensed that I had to play the part twenty years beyond my experience in order for a Broadway agent to take an orphaned eighteen-year-old from Brooklyn seriously. Because before the song, he'd had a mocking grin. But afterward, I must have transformed into something miraculous. I didn't feel anything like Maria, but Glenn's stare made me wonder if he saw something I couldn't feel or see yet.

"Uh…no, no, they don't," he said and smashed the cigarette into the ashtray. He raised a skeptical brow. "You sure you're only eighteen?"

"Positive. March twenty-six, nineteen fifty-four."

"Fucking damn," he muttered. "Can you sing me the lowest note you can and then climb up to the highest?"

I nodded, sucked in an inhale, and did exactly what he asked. With each climbing note, Glenn's eyes widened.

"Fucking damn," he said again, this time with an impish grin as he stared up at the ceiling.

"Is that a good fucking damn or a…"

He cackled again and leaned into the desk. "You know what your range is?" I shook my head. "Three. Three octaves. You can sing *three* octaves."

"Is that good?"

"Is that good?" He laughed again, but this time, it wasn't a mocking laugh. It was the kind of laugh that told me he saw some greatness in me that I had yet to see in myself. "No, it's not good. You're not a Liesl." Right as I deflated and my eyes started to sting,

Glenn's smile grew, stopping me from crying. "Your voice is too powerful for Liesl, doll. That's the voice of a future Maria right there. You're one in a million. The teenage Julie Andrews. That's what you are."

I'd spent my whole life up until that moment thinking people couldn't distinguish me from a rat on the street. The only things that had kept me just the littlest sane were playing the piano, singing, and Elle. But then, I met a stranger who marveled at me more in those fifteen minutes than someone ever had in my life.

Glenn agreed to sign me right then and there after I promised to continue acting classes, musical theater singing classes, and speech classes.

"Speech classes?" I said, not expecting that to be thrown into the mix.

"Well...yeah," Glenn said very matter-of-factly. "We gotta neutralize your accent." He acted like he didn't have a thick New York accent too. "You've got the singing voice. Anyone with ears can hear that, and after you take more classes, you'll know the techniques that the Broadway directors are looking for. But you don't have the speaking voice. Anyone with ears can hear that too. You won't get those leading lady roles with that New York accent, doll. Broadway is the Hollywood of New York City, and Hollywood is elite. In order to fit in with the elite, you have to look, talk, and dress like them, and there's nothing elite about Brooklyn. Don't worry, though, we'll get you in top shape."

"But I can't afford all these classes."

He waved off my comment. "I can. That's part of the contract, doll. You're an investment, and once we get you into top shape, you're going to shine on that stage. Also, we're gonna need to do something about your name. Marlene Hatcher is the name of a spinster."

Show business was run by men. Still is. Men defined the beauty standards of women. We had to look, sound, and act like whatever those standards were that year. But I was eighteen, and an agent saw enough potential in me to help me clasp on to my dream. If shedding my accent and changing my name was going to get me out of Brooklyn and onto a stage in the land of dreams, I was willing to do whatever it took.

Once we agreed on my stage name and all the classes that would get me ready for auditions, I signed every paper I needed to that locked me into the Kerr Talent Group. By the end of June, Elle and I had escaped Brooklyn Heights and started the first days of our new lives in the heart of Manhattan.

Though, in 1972, the magic of Manhattan had started fading. Times Square's boisterous light display of Broadway shows and movies were getting replaced by adult theater advertisements. The sparkle of Times Square when I first saw it with the McCoys had lost its shine, and a different kind of darkness fell with the night. But I had experience with that already living throughout Brooklyn and Queens. I wasn't scared of a little grit.

I started out on the last row of the theater. That meant there was nowhere for me to go except closer to the stage, and I'd keep going until I was on that stage. Those "normal" kids who I used to be jealous of, like Susie McCoy and her friends, who grew up with parents and lived the dream in a New York brownstone, might have viewed Manhattan as a star falling from grace, but orphaned kids like Elle and me, who grew up admiring the skyscrapers on the other side of the East River, still saw it as the star we'd spent our whole lives wishing on.

Our first apartment in Manhattan was at The Whitby on 45th. Glenn recommended it because that was where many of the actors, performers, and writers trying to make it stayed. Elle was in the minority of tenants who had no interest in trying to get on Broadway. We crammed into a one bedroom on the sixth floor, shared a bed and a room, though we had already gotten used to that at the home. The kitchen could barely fit both of us, and our living room was big enough for a love seat, a two-person table, and my very first record player that I treated us both to. The apartment was small, but it was ours and more than anything we ever had in our lives.

As a move-in present, Glenn gave me a wicker basket of grapefruit and two packages of Sego, the same drink his secretary had been drinking the day of my audition. I gave him a confused look. "What's this?"

"Consider this a 'show business starter pack,'" he said through his cackle.

I took a closer look at Sego and saw "Liquid Diet Food" on the can.

"Eat a grapefruit with the Sego," he said. "At every meal. It keeps the weight off."

I looked at myself, trying to see if I could find the weight he'd alluded to. I was five-seven and around a hundred and forty-five pounds. "What are you trying to imply?"

"You want to be on Broadway, Marlie? You're taking acting, singing, and speech classes to sound like a leading lady, and if you stick to this diet right here, you'll *look* like a leading lady come audition time. Trust me."

And I did. I was a seed, and he told me that in order to grow, I needed to eat a grapefruit at every meal, drink a Sego, and ditch all the diner food that I'd been consuming ever since Elle had got a waitressing job at a Howard Johnson's Restaurant a few days after we moved. I was eighteen years old and desperate to be accepted… by anyone.

"You're sticking with a salad?" Elle said, raising a skeptical eyebrow behind the counter at Howard Johnson's, a Times Square staple at the time. Glenn said it was a quintessential part of the Broadway scene, and that sometimes, patrons spotted Broadway stars after a show.

I'd just finished a long day of acting, singing, and speech classes, and I craved something delicious and fattening to fill my empty stomach, like a cheeseburger and a chocolate milkshake. But I wanted a role on a Broadway stage more. "Glenn says I need to look like a leading lady, and grapefruit, Sego, and salads will help me get there."

Elle's gaze raked down my body, and while I know she was probably looking for what little pounds I needed to lose to meet whatever the male standard was for that year, but my body reacted to her taking in every inch of me, pinpricks of pleasure.

There was nothing I wanted more than that chocolate milkshake to cool me down.

"Does he not have eyes? You have the most beautiful eyes. You are gorgeous and so is your voice."

My heart filled and sped up the same way it did when she first complimented my eyes the day I met her. It made my mind glitch right there at the diner bar, with no cheeseburger or milkshake to hide the heat slamming my face. "Wait, really?"

"Am I the only one who can see properly? Yes, you're gorgeous, Mar. Anyone with eyes should be able to see that. And I'm not sure you should be taking appearance advice from a middle-aged man with a horseshoe mustache."

I was so embarrassed by how quickly my body reacted to the compliment, I said the first words that came out of my mouth, hoping to wash away what I assumed to be beet-red blush on my face. "That middle-aged man with a horseshoe mustache has clients who have gone on to win Tonys, Grammys, and Oscars. I'll listen to whatever he says until I get one of those in my hands."

She gave me a side-eye and shifted her weight onto one leg. "Marlie…"

"What? This is my dream, Elle. I've been wanting this for the last nine years, and somehow, a successful Broadway agent signed a nobody orphan from Brooklyn."

"You're not a nobody. Far from it. You're right on the cusp of being something."

"Yes, a New Yorker without a New York accent," I said, trying to perfect my neutral speech like I had been doing for the last several months in my classes.

I meant it as a self-deprecating joke, but Elle's side-eye turned into a glare. "Just wait until you get your first role, and then I'm going to say I told you so. I'm also going to force-feed you a cheeseburger."

"Whenever I get my first role, then yes, I'll accept anything you want to give me…for one night only."

"I look forward to this feast," she said with a wink, and my whole body caught on fire.

I'm not sure if it was the grapefruit and Sego or if it was all the singing, acting, and speech classes I took throughout that summer that helped me land my first role in a Broadway musical. Maybe it was a little bit of both, though Elle was adamant that it was because of my talent. Whatever the reason, right before the new year, I got the call from Glenn that I got my first role. I yelled in my apartment, fell on the couch, and cried. Glenn quickly ended the call after that, but I didn't care.

I ran to Howard Johnson's and found Elle in her cute diner uniform behind the counter. "I got the part!" I said with my hands in the air.

A few customers glanced over as Elle set down the plates of food she carried in each hand. "You what?"

"I got the part. I'm going to be in a Broadway musical, *and* I have my own song. Can you believe that? My debut and I have my own song."

She ran around the counter and brought me in for a tight hug. I sank into her embrace, smelling her shampoo mixed with french fries. "You know what this calls for?" she said, her words landing on my earlobe and sending a shiver down my spine.

I broke the hug. I couldn't get too lost in her. "I made a promise, didn't I?"

"I expect you to be here at six p.m. sharp. No grapefruit or Sego. You're going to celebrate properly."

I followed through on my promise. I came back at six, and we sat at a booth and ate an entire basket of cheese fries while I feasted on the cheeseburger and chocolate shake I'd been craving since we'd moved into Manhattan six months prior.

I caught her staring at me with the softest smile. Somehow, on the most exciting day of my life, Elle had the power to make the whole world still. I lowered the fries. "What?"

She shook her head and glanced at her lap as her smile grew. "I'm really proud of you."

"You are?"

She met my gaze, and my stomach somersaulted. "Of course I am, Mar. You sound surprised. My best friend is going to be on a Broadway stage." She leaned into the table. "Please tell me you can get me a ticket on opening night."

"I'm not sure if I know anyone who can get a free ticket," I said. She tossed a fry at me. I picked it up and ate it. "Of course I can do that. There's no one I'd rather have in the audience the first night than you."

"Good. It's a date."

I thought about how I wished it could have been a date. Something fancier than Howard Johnson's. A place like Sardi's or anywhere with a white tablecloth, a candle in between us, and a menu where I couldn't pronounce half the items.

But I told myself that no matter how much I wanted that to be true, the chances were that it probably wouldn't happen. Elle used to like Sam from the library, and while he was out of the picture, I didn't look too similar to him.

Let go of your crush. It's not going to happen. She's your best friend.

❖

Rehearsals for *A Little Night Music* started the day after New Year's Day in 1973. Eight weeks before it premiered at the Shubert Theatre. Before rehearsals started at ten a.m., Elle insisted that I stop by the diner for a meal.

"But I have to eat a grapefruit," I said.

She playfully slapped my wrist. "Stop that nonsense. You deserve more than that chalky diet milkshake and grapefruit. I know a few people. I can get you a breakfast you deserve on your very first day."

"But Glenn's gonna—"

"He's not going to know anything, will he? Because he won't be at the diner. You know your grapefruit diet is outrageous, right?"

"Is it?"

"Have you looked at yourself in the mirror? You don't need grapefruit…or Sego. What you need is a hearty breakfast. You don't want your stomach singing with you because you didn't eat anything of substance."

I only had to sit on it for about five seconds before caving. I was so desperate for anything other than grapefruit—which I've never enjoyed—and chocolate chalk. Elle was right. Glenn wasn't ever going to know.

So I followed her into the diner, took a seat at an empty spot at the bar, and watched Elle in work mode. She looked adorable as a Johnson Girl, wearing an aqua and white A-line dress with a white apron around her waist. Her hair was up, and an orange and pink floral scarf wrapped around her head. She'd started wearing scarves in her hair when we moved to Manhattan. I already thought that she was the most beautiful woman I'd seen, but there was something about her accumulating collection of silky scarfs that really did me in, especially when her hair was down, and she added the scarf to her look. I didn't need a cup of coffee with extra cream and sugar when I had Elle handing me a plate of bacon strips, a toasted English muffin, two eggs, and a glass of grapefruit juice while looking that absolutely breathtaking in the most nonchalant way.

I was starving, yet my stomach was so full of knots that I struggled to finish my plate. I picked at my food, stared into space, and hoped that my imposter syndrome subsided. Before rehearsals even started, I was worried about not belonging in a cast of seasoned actors.

A gentle hand rested on my wrist, pulling me back to the present moment. Elle leaned on the counter, smiling at me, and it filled me with enough contentment to untangle a few of those knots. "You look like you're ready to hurl onto your plate," Elle said softly.

"I feel like that might happen."

Her grip tightened. "You're going to be okay. I promise. You earned that role. You deserve to be there. Walk in there believing that."

"I'll try my best."

Walking into my first rehearsal with zero experience in a room filled with Broadway veterans made me feel like I'd won a backstage ticket instead of earning a role in the musical: the eighteen-year-old with no experience except for singing to her orphanage and people on the streets in a room of actors with impressive resumes. The first half of rehearsal, I didn't say much. I took my script and immersed myself in it, highlighting my parts while the rest of the cast filtered into the room. When it was lunch, I stayed in my chair and quietly scooped spoonfuls of grapefruit, forkfuls of salad, and drank my Sego.

I heard whistling coming from behind me growing louder until I found the actor who was playing my older brother, Henrik. He was four years older than me, very tall at six-three, and had dark shaggy hair with natural loose waves that covered his forehead. Out of all the chairs along the entire long table, he sat in the empty one next to me and dumped out the contents of his lunch: a Tupperware of Hawaiian meatballs and an apple. He continued to whistle while he stabbed his fork into a meatball.

"'Vincent' by Don McLean," I said, finally recognizing the song.

He swallowed and smiled. "It's a good one, isn't it? It's been in my head all day." He stuck out his hand. "I'm Peter. Peter Marotto, but everyone here knows me as Peter Arlo." He had a big smile, one that radiated warmth just like his soft, light brown eyes.

I shook it. "Marlene Hatcher, but I've been told that's the name of a spinster, so now I'm Marlie Rose." He let out a full-bodied laugh, his bright white smile taking up more of his face. I smiled at my accomplishment. "I actually know who you are."

"Oh, you do?"

"You're Jesus."

He let out another laugh. "Yes, I guess I was."

"I remember your face on the *Jesus Christ Superstar* billboards. I used to sing right outside the theater. That's when Glenn Kerr discovered me."

"You're the singing girl outside the theater?" He directed a point at me. "We used to talk about you."

I lowered my Sego can. "You did?"

"Yes. The cast talked about that girl with the voice who was singing outside. One of their wives walked past you. Huh, small world." He popped a meatball in his mouth. "Glenn Kerr is also my agent. He told me to look out for you. Also said you live in the Whitby. So do I. Ninth floor."

"I'm on the sixth."

"Well, look at that. Same agent. Same building. Same musical. Sounds like you're following me, Marlie Rose."

"It got me in this musical, so I don't regret a thing."

There was something about Peter Arlo that drew me to him. He was so full of life. He was kind, excited, and had such a strong presence. Every day, we had lunch together. We got to know each other quite a bit during the break. He was the oldest brother of five kids from a very Italian Catholic family from Worcester, Massachusetts. He said his family was so Catholic that they all had biblical names, and the three boys were named after the Apostles. "I'm Peter James, then there's Matthew Thomas, Mary Elizabeth, Ruth Eve, and Andrew Phillip." All five spent twelve years in Catholic school and had to go to Catholic colleges. He was four years older than me, a recent graduate from Boston College and had immediately "bugged out" of Massachusetts. I told him about my childhood growing up in an orphanage in Brooklyn, and that I too was desperate to "bug out" of where I came from.

Just like the lead, Nancy Osbourne, who played Anne Egerman, he was extremely attractive, and his vibrant and contagious smile was mesmerizing. He didn't make me nervous like Nancy Osbourne did. She was star-worthy beautiful. She had at least five inches on me. Long, straight, dark brown hair that she often wore in a high ponytail during rehearsal. Occasionally, she wore these black, hexagon-framed glasses. She was the kind of beautiful who commanded a room. I stole too many glances during the first week. Every time she caught me, I flitted my gaze away.

She was also very intimidating. Unlike Peter, Nancy wasn't approachable or warm. She didn't talk to me for the first week. The second week, she started flashing me the smallest trace of a smile, as if half her mouth wanted to remain the unapproachable starlet while the other half wanted to rebel against the other and curve into a grin.

"I don't think Nancy likes me," I said while eating lunch with Peter.

He laughed. "Why do you say that?"

"She hasn't spoken to me yet, and it's the second week. Do you think she hates me for some reason?"

"Okay, I'm going to tell you something that a good friend of mine told me that's stuck with me for years."

"What's that?"

"You could stand silently in the corner of a room, and someone would still find a way to hate you because you chose the wrong corner."

I carried that line with me. It was one I needed to hear long before, when I kept questioning why no one wanted me, why I spent my entire childhood being tossed between families. It bothered me that, for the first two weeks, the star of the show spoke to everyone except for me during my very first rehearsal for a Broadway musical. It made me wonder if there was something about me that repelled everyone except Elle and Peter.

But I still didn't quite understand. I hadn't done anything wrong. "Okay…but that doesn't help solve the problem of why she doesn't talk to me. She's the only one who hasn't said anything."

"What I'm saying is, don't worry about whether Nancy likes you or not. You came here to act and be amazing on stage. Not everyone is going to like you, even if you're perfect."

"So she doesn't like me?"

"Two things could be happening here. One, she's let the lead role go to her head. I mean, she just played Sandy in *Grease*. She might be riding those coattails into this musical."

"What's the second option?" I said, hoping it was better than having a hothead on our hands.

A silly grin took hold of his face. He leaned in and nudged my arm. "She likes you."

"What? If she liked me, she would have talked to me—"

"No, Marlie, I don't mean like as a person. I mean that she probably thinks you're a stone-cold fox."

The embarrassment that settled all over my body felt like wearing a scratchy Christmas sweater. It was the first time I'd ever heard someone mention same-sex attraction so casually. I didn't know how to respond or react. Instead, I sipped my Sego, wishing it was a few degrees colder to put out the fire that claimed my face.

"You're almost as red as the inside of that grapefruit," he said.

I glanced around the room to make sure no one was around. As embarrassed as I was, there was still an undertow of excitement and arousal. Nancy Osbourne, the lead who'd just finished playing Sandy, thought I was attractive?

I became eager to find out.

With the possibility of Nancy thinking I was a "stone-cold fox," I was hyper-focused on Nancy the next few rehearsals. I foolishly stole too many glances, hoping to figure out a hidden clue to how she felt about me. She caught almost all of them, leaving me feeling flushed and distracted. For a bashful eighteen-year-old who hadn't even kissed anyone, it was mortifying.

Once lunch was called, Nancy stopped me on my way. It caught me off guard when her dark brown eyes bore into mine for the longest they had since rehearsals started. "You smoke?" She wiggled a pack of Virginia Slims.

I hadn't smoked in my life, but at the moment, I was willing to pick it up for a single lunch break if that meant an older, beautiful woman—and the girl I couldn't stop looking at for the last two weeks—gave me the time of day. I would have probably smoked the whole pack if that was what was needed.

"I do."

"Follow me," she said with a nod toward the end of the hallway.

I followed her to the back alley and watched her lips wrap around the cigarette. That was the first and only time I'd been jealous of a cigarette. After she took her first inhale, she offered me the pack, and I followed her lead. I placed it delicately between my lips and watched as her stare fell to my mouth. She took a step forward, flicked the lighter, and cupped her hand over the end of my cigarette as she lit the tip. I inhaled too much and almost hacked up a lung. She laughed, rested her back and one foot against the building, and continued watching me struggle, a smirk firm on her face, as if she was getting pure entertainment from my smoking. Her grin caused heat to spiral down my spine.

"So this is your debut, right?"

I cleared the cough tickling my throat as I puffed out a cloud of smoke. "It is."

"And your first cigarette, right?"

Despite the cold January air nipping at my face and fingers, a blush still found a way to slam my cheeks. I hurried up to try to think of something to say, but Nancy exhaled before I found the words.

"I was your age when I first started. It's okay if it's your first. Try to take smaller inhales, and you won't cough as much."

I nodded and listened. Just like that, I was able to inhale without a coughing fit.

"You have a really nice voice, you know. I'm sure it's going to sound even better with the orchestra."

"You think so?" I said, feeling my heart speed up. I went from getting the silent treatment to smoking a cigarette with the lead while she showered me with compliments. It was quite the drastic turn.

"I know so. It's pretty impressive that this is your debut, and you have a singing part. Must mean you have something. You have the beauty, that's for sure." She pulled a drag of her cigarette, and her brown eyes raked down my body and back up to my lips.

I didn't know what it all meant. I was eighteen and had never had a woman come on to me before. So I took another drag and said, "You've got it too. The acting, the singing, and definitely the beauty." I couldn't look her in the eyes, but I could tell from my peripheral that she smiled.

"Glad you think so," she said. "Peter and I were going to catch a movie this weekend. One of the theaters is replaying *Cabaret*. You should come."

"Oh no, it's okay. I don't want to interrupt your date."

She belted out a laugh. "Trust me, it's not a date. We're…well, we're not really each other's type. And if it was a date, a third person wouldn't get the invite. You should come. Have you seen *Cabaret*?" I shook my head. "Come. Consider it homework for *Little Night*."

Nancy Osbourne didn't have to ask me thrice.

I'm not sure what was more of an experience, watching *Cabaret* or sitting next to Nancy in the dark theater. I watched all the sensual dancing, all the cleavage, and the sexuality oozed into the theater. Nancy and I shared a tub of popcorn, and whenever our fingertips touched, feeling her fingers graze mine sent a zap through me that flickered low in my stomach.

When our fingers touched for what seemed like the zillionth time, she caught my stare, and as I looked back on the screen to focus on Liza Minnelli, Nancy leaned in, and her perfume enveloped me.

"You look really nice tonight."

Her breath tickled my earlobe, and the flicking in my stomach traveled lower right as she placed her hand on my knee and slowly glided up my leg until she reached my inner thigh. It was the first time I had felt the desire for Nancy's hands to run all over my body. I glanced over, Nancy smiled, and I wished so much that we had the theater to ourselves so those beautiful lips I'd spent weeks admiring could kiss me the same way the actors in *Cabaret* kissed each other.

As my heart thudded, I placed my hand on top of hers that was still lightly gripping my inner thigh, hoping that sent her a message of exactly what I wanted. We turned back to the screen, and honestly, I can't tell you what happened for the rest of the movie. I was too focused on my heart stuttering and my stomach swirling with excitement, anticipation, and arousal. Our hands stayed like that until Peter nudged her for a sip of Coke, and she removed her hand to pass him the cup.

When the credits started playing, everyone stood, and Nancy caught my wrist and whispered, "Want to come back to my place? Without Peter?"

I obviously agreed.

The second she led me into her Greenwich Village apartment, she palmed my face and kissed me. I couldn't believe that Nancy Osbourne—the lead of *Little Night* and *Grease*—was kissing me. Deeply and ravenously. I unraveled in her grip and sank right into it. I had no idea what I was doing, but I followed her lead. We toppled onto her couch, and she crawled on top of me, slipped me her tongue, and lit up my body in a fuzzy warmth that I'd never felt before. She raked her hands down my body just like her eyes hours before, and my skin felt like it was on fire, like Nancy Osbourne woke me from a deep sleep and made me feel like a bolt of lightning shooting against the night sky.

What started out as kissing for an hour straight led her to pulling off my top, and that prompted me to do the same to her dress. Soon, her mouth latched on to my center, her fingers slipped inside me, and her free hand grasped my breasts, twisting and caressing my nipples until I belted out a cry. My pulse twitched in my neck, and my entire body hummed with arousal and pleasure. It was the first time someone had made me feel hot, sexy, and desirable, and I couldn't wait to explore the female body that had made me feel like I could be on the cover of a magazine.

When it was my turn to put my mouth on her, I remembered all the movements and techniques she'd done to me, and given how vocal and reactive she was, I figured I didn't do too bad for my first time.

As I cabbed home, every spot Nancy had kissed and touched tingled on my skin. I wondered if the driver could see her kisses twinkling in the darkness like the neon lights in Times Square. As light as I felt, my body still sparking from Nancy, I couldn't help but feel utterly confused too. My first kiss and first time was with a woman, just three years after Stonewall; hell, her apartment was only several blocks from Stonewall.

It scared me how much I'd enjoyed it, how I hoped it would happen again, and how much I desperately wished it had been with Elle.

CHAPTER SIX

S o…I have to tell you something," Elle said, pouring herself a cup of coffee in our kitchen while I scooped a spoonful of grapefruit.

It was two weeks before *Little Night Music* premiered, and Glenn was adamant about sticking to my grapefruit and Sego diet in the days leading up to it so I could make a "good first impression" on the Broadway world.

"What's that?" I said and suppressed a gag from an extra bitter taste. I already had plans about eating a stack of pancakes at Howard Johnson's after the first week of shows.

"I have a date Friday night."

I lowered my spoon as Elle waggled her eyebrows. She had a little dreamy smile that hinted she was actually into this guy, and it threw me off guard. I didn't recognize this Elle, the one who had a bashful grin, as if David Cassidy had asked her out.

My stomach dropped. "What? You have a date? On Valentine's Day?"

"Yes, why do you sound so shocked?"

"I don't know. I just…I didn't know you were talking to anyone."

"Well, this guy has been coming to the diner every morning for breakfast, and I don't know, we just kind of hit it off. He's really sweet. His name is Robert." She had a faraway glance and a coquettish grin that made me want to regurgitate my Sego and grapefruit.

I gnawed on the inside of my cheek, trying to ease the jealousy tightening my jaw. "Robert? Not Rob. Robbie. Bob. Or Bobby? Just *Robert?*"

She let out a small laugh. "You sound irritated."

"I'm not irritated. Why would I be irritated?"

"I don't know. Why would you?" She waited for a response, but like the jealous, immature eighteen-year-old that I was, I sipped my Sego and avoided looking her in the eyes.

"Aren't you getting on with Peter?"

I looked back up, feeling my eyebrows pull together. "What? Peter?"

"Yeah. He's all you talk about." Her mouth stayed almost neutral, with the smallest curve in her lips.

"Wait, you think I have something with Peter?" A laugh slipped right out of me. When Elle frowned, I realized then that she had no idea.

"So you two aren't dating?"

"Absolutely not. He's like an older brother. I'm not into Peter, and Peter isn't into me. I'm not his type."

"What do you mean?" I directed a firmer stare at her, and her mouth parted once it finally hit her. "Oh," she said, drawn out, as if she finally got it. "I figured he's the one you've been with when you've come home late."

"He's not."

"Then, what have you been doing?"

An embarrassed heat draped over my body like a winter coat. "I've been out and about."

Her mouth dropped with intrigue curving the corners. "Out and about? With who?"

I scratched the back of my head. I felt like I was being interrogated at a police station. "Um, someone from the musical."

"What's his name?"

I looked at my grapefruit and scooped another bite. It bought me time to stall and think of a name.

"What's *her* name?"

I glanced up at the same time my stomach tied into large knots. "How do you know it's a she?"

"Because you ate your grapefruit instead of answering the question, and I know for a fact you would have just answered if it was a guy."

I lowered my spoon. "If it was a woman, how would you feel?"

Elle shrugged. "I wouldn't feel anything. Peace and love," she said lightly and held up a peace sign for comedic effect. It worked because she got a small laugh from me. "Who is she?"

She gave me a look of curiosity, not judgment. It was what made me feel safe enough to softly confess. "Nancy Osbourne."

"The lead?"

It was my turn to shrug. "She's beautiful...and sexy."

Elle nodded and drank her coffee as silence filled the kitchen. It was like that for a couple moments until she asked, "Do you like her?"

"I like fucking her."

She choked on her coffee. It splattered onto her face and shirt. "You're fucking her?" She glanced at the coffee dotting her shirt. She swore under her breath and turned to the kitchen to blot out the spots with a wet towel.

"What else do you think I'm doing at one a.m.? I'm not braiding her hair."

"I know that, Marlie. I was just...I don't know. I guess I wasn't thinking you were fucking someone."

"Maybe you'll get lucky on that date."

She shot me a glare. "Why are you acting so..."

"So what?"

"Jealous?"

I laughed. "I'm not jealous, Elle."

The lie felt like a wad of hair on my tongue. Of course I was jealous. I was jealous of the mysterious guy who could walk into the diner, order something bland like a vanilla milkshake, give her one compliment about how beautiful her eyes were, and that was enough to take her out on a date.

Meanwhile, I'd known how beautiful her eyes were. I'd had the placement and color of each fleck of brown, green, and gold memorized by the end of our first summer. The guy probably thought her eyes were light brown and focused more on how her legs looked in her uniform than all the subtle and obvious beauty that made up her, inside and out. He probably had no idea what her favorite Bob Dylan song was or that she couldn't stand John Lennon, though she kept that a secret from almost everyone. I was certain that a diner patron hadn't earned that little part of her yet.

I thought about it throughout all of rehearsal, and it must have translated to my face because Peter nudged my elbow during lunch, causing the scoop of grapefruit to fall back into the hole.

"What's the skinny, Marlie Rose?"

I knew I needed to get over it. Elle had every right to go on a date. It was just that I wanted to go on a date. I wanted to meet someone who made me smile the way the mysterious guy made her smile, and I knew that person wasn't going to be Nancy Osbourne, who I could tell was starting to lose interest in me the more we slept together.

"It's nothing," I said and put the fallen scoop of grapefruit back on my spoon, ate it, and winced.

"Well, that's a lie. Come on. You can tell me. What's going on?" I buzzed my lips and stabbed the grapefruit with my spoon. "Whoa, there. Apparently something."

"The person I like is going on a date."

"Who? Nancy?"

"No, not Nancy."

"There's someone else? Is she a cast member?"

"No."

He took a couple bites of his salad while thinking. Then, he gasped and squeezed my wrist. "Is it Elle?"

"Peter…"

"Oh my God, it is!"

My face caught on fire as if Elle could overhear our conversation. "Stop."

"If you like her, ask her out."

"You know it's not that simple." I didn't know how to ask for a date. I'd never even been on a date.

"You live in New York City," Peter said. "You're in the epicenter of the gay liberation. It's a little simpler here than other parts of the world, trust me. I can introduce you to some women, you know. I know a few people you might like who frequent some of the gay bars in the Village."

He could have taken me to every gay bar in the Village, made me meet every lesbian in the city, and I already knew that none of them would have made me feel the way Elle had made me feel for the last four years, like a light constantly flickering against the darkness.

❖

On February 25, 1973, I made my Broadway debut at the Shubert Theatre.

My sleep the night before was sparse. I kept waking up every hour, and when I went back to sleep, I kept dreaming about being onstage, the same dreams that had been recurring since about a month out from the premiere. Half my dreams involved a standing ovation, and Elle running onto the stage and kissing me. The other half were me missing my lines, Glenn storming down the aisle saying my accent was too strong, or Nancy and I were caught in the middle of necking and feeling each other up onstage, and the police barged down the aisle with their batons.

When I woke up, I was in my bed, the morning sun shining through the window and the smell of sugar wafting from the kitchen. I rubbed my eyes, stretched out the last bad dream, and shuffled into the kitchen where I spotted a bouquet of roses in a glass vase in the center of the table adorned with two empty plates, a plate of over-hard eggs, maple syrup, and two glasses of grapefruit juice. Elle was attending to something on the stove, her hair was up, and one of her cute scarves wrapped around her head matched the lavender robe she was wearing.

"What's all of this?

She glanced over her shoulder with a spatula in hand, and her smile widened. "Happy premiere day!"

That was when I spotted the chocolate pancakes cooking on the pan. My eyes widened. Ever since moving into Manhattan and having our own kitchen, Elle had picked up cooking. She had a hidden talent, especially with breakfast. She always knew how to crisp the bacon, how to make my favorite eggs to perfection, and her pancakes were always rich and fluffy. It was such a shame I couldn't fully indulge.

She brought over a stack of pancakes as I took a seat at the table. "These are for you," she said. "And so are the roses. A rose for Marlie Rose."

I smelled them. I'd never received flowers before, and the fact that they came from Elle and that sweet smile of hers made me melt in my seat, as if I was standing on the Shubert Theatre stage all by myself with the hot spotlights shining right on me. She placed her hands on my shoulders and tucked a loose strand of hair behind my ear.

God, did I want her to caress my cheek the same way Nancy did. If Elle did it the exact way I'd been imagining her doing for the last several months, it wouldn't be as empty as Nancy's touch. While Nancy had the power to make me feel like the end of a sparkling firework, she never made me launch off the ground. I stayed rooted in place, sparking, and that was it.

But when I imagined Elle palming my face, caressing my cheek, my arms, my body, kissing and moving against me the way Nancy did, I saw myself flying to the moon.

"I'm so proud of you," Elle said, and the smile tugged at my stomach. "I can't believe this day is finally here. You're about to sing on a Broadway stage. I'm so excited for tonight."

My God, she was so beautiful. Always had been, but it wasn't until that moment, when she stood in her scarf and robe, looking at me as if I'd done something truly miraculous when I hadn't even performed in front of an audience yet, that I finally found the words I'd been searching for to describe her since the day we met. The word that perfectly described Elle was something that sounded so simple at first look but so complex when my mind held it delicately like glass.

Eleanor Olson was the most stunning woman I'd ever seen. That was why she was able to make my heart quicken for the last several months whenever she looked or smiled at me. Now that I think about it, that was probably the first moment I knew that my feelings for Elle ran deep, and if I'd ever had the chance to kiss her, one kiss, those feelings would reach my core.

"Thank you," I said and rubbed the sides of her arms, wanting desperately to run my fingertips up and down as her proud grin and expressive eyes held me captive. "This is really sweet of you."

"You deserve all of it. You need to be well-fed for your debut, and don't worry, that's freshly squeezed grapefruit juice, so you can kind of still keep up the Glenn diet."

Once I got to the Shubert Theatre, adrenaline and nervousness took over my body. I sat in the makeup chair, zoned out while running through my lines and singing my solo, an entire song called, "The Glamorous Life."

"How you feeling?" Peter said, shaking my shoulders. He was in his costume, a black, three-piece suit, and his face was covered in makeup.

"A ball of nerves." I held out my hand and watched it shake. "See?"

He clasped them and gave them a reassuring squeeze. "You're so ready for this, Marlie. Broadway is ready for you."

"Elle's here. I got her a seat in the orchestra." I blew out a shaky breath. "It's a bit nerve-racking, don't you think? The idea of a loved one in the audience is just as scary as a sold-out theater?"

"I don't know."

"What do you mean you don't know?"

"My family doesn't come to my shows."

I frowned. "What? Why not?"

He laughed and gestured to himself. "You think a super Italian Catholic family likes that I'm a flaming homosexual? Absolutely not. Haven't spoken to any of them since I moved out when I was eighteen, five years ago."

"Peter, I'm so sorry. I…I didn't know—"

He forced a smile. "Don't be. They don't like me for who I love, then to hell with them. I'm not responsible for making my parents like me."

For some reason, this resonated with me. I zoned out thinking on his words for a few moments before he patted my shoulder. "You're going to be great, Marlie. I just know it. So does everyone else. And when you kill this performance, I'm buying you a drink. Bring Elle. Drinks on me. Now, come on. Let's do this."

When I stepped in front of an audience for the first time, I felt like I'd woken up in a completely different world. The weights on my shoulders and chest from childhood broke free. The lights warmed me up, the music flowed through my veins, and all those eyes on me made me feel seen for one of the first times in my life. It was the exact moment I'd been waiting for ever since the McCoys had taken me to see *The Sound of Music*. Though I couldn't see Elle, I could feel her staring at me and that giant grin that she'd worn when she'd presented my stack of pancakes that morning.

During "The Glamorous Life" solo, I stared at the balcony, wishing there was someone else in the audience. God, I really wish I remembered who this person was because I thought of them and how important it was for me to take control of the stage that was mine entirely so they knew that I'd made it.

I sang my heart out the same way I'd first sung at Kindred Hearts when I'd tried giving the girls a sweet distraction from the lack of everything else in our lives. The audience in the Shubert Theatre came to see the show for a reason, and while their attention was on me, I wanted them to focus on my singing, the music, and the energy pouring from the stage to help make them forget the things that haunted them outside.

After my solo, the crowd applauded, and hearing their reaction made me want to be glued to the stage for the rest of my life. Singing and performing for a crowd was a rush I'd never experienced before. It was addictive.

I'd finally found a purpose.

After the show, the cast filtered through the lobby after getting changed. Peter came up behind me and yelled, "Marlie Rose," before picking me up and twirling me around under the lobby's beautiful rotunda. "Marlie Rose, you killed it out there," he said and placed me back on the ground.

"Did I really?"

"Do you have ears? The crowd loved it."

I caught a glimpse of Elle waiting near the entrance, bundled up in her red wool coat. When our gazes locked, she smiled at me, warming me up more than my winter coat could.

"Bring your girl to celebrate," Peter said with a nudge.

"She's not my girl."

I could hear the disappointment in my tone. There was nothing more I wanted than to make her my girl, but she was still seeing Robert from the diner.

"You sure? Because she's looking at you like you are."

"I think she's just really proud of me."

"Probably. You did amazing out there. But also, I'd kill for a guy to look at me like that. Now, go invite her out with us. Tell her drinks are on me." He patted my back and pushed me forward.

I stumbled, feeling the embarrassment heat my face.

Elle laughed and started walking toward me. "You go from giving an amazing debut performance to tripping in the theater lobby," she said as she placed her hands on my arms, gently squeezing.

"Peter tripped me."

She laughed. "Marlie, you were so wonderful. My God, your voice. It sounds even more miraculous on a Broadway stage with an audience."

Before the show, when Glenn had wished me luck, he'd warned me about the reviews that were to come in the papers in the days following, and if I kept up with them, I needed thick skin. I'd told him that being an orphan in foster care had awarded me one good thing, and that was thick skin. The reviews and the critics didn't mean anything to me. They were strangers, and I'd learned the hard way not to give any weight to a stranger's opinion.

You could stand silently in the corner of a room, and someone would still find a way to hate you because you chose the wrong corner.

But I cared what Elle thought. She was the one person who knew everything about me. Well, almost, minus my feelings for her. "Really? You think?" I said as my heart raced.

"I don't think. I *know*. Your voice filled up the whole theater. The woman next to me whispered to her husband, 'Now that's a voice.'"

"Really?"

She laughed. "You sound so surprised."

"I just wanted to make sure I had a good debut."

"You had more than just a good debut, I promise you that. You gave me goose bumps."

"That's a statement."

"You're really meant for the stage. I always thought so. That voice of yours is bigger than anything I've ever seen or heard."

"I think you're being a little biased," I said, nudging her arm. I had to insert some comedic, self-deprecating humor to loosen how tightly her kind words swaddled me. The more she spoke, the more my heart thrummed, the more my body craved hers, the more I noticed how enticing her lips were coated in ruby lipstick.

"I might not know anything about Broadway, but I know what sounds pleasing to the ear, and your voice was very pleasing. I don't think you can fake goose bumps down your arms. I'm so proud of you, Marlie. You should be proud of yourself too."

It was the first time in my whole life that someone had looked at me and told me how proud they were, and that opening night was the first time that I felt like I was doing something right.

❖

A Little Night Music was nominated for twelve Tonys, leading the nominations for 1973 a month after it premiered.

My first Broadway show and my play was nominated for Best Musical, *and* I got an invitation with a plus one. There was no one else I wanted by my side but Elle.

I took us both out shopping for dresses. Elle put up a fight about me paying. She said she had some money saved up, but I insisted.

She had just started her first semester at CUNY studying education. I asked her to be my date, and I wanted to celebrate her starting college, something she had always wanted but had always worried about having enough money for.

We didn't see each other in the dresses until the day of the awards. It was Elle's suggestion to make it even more fun. We got our first manicures and pedicures and then went to the salon to have our hair styled. Peter stopped by with a bottle of champagne, already in his black tux. He poured us each a flute and listened to our albums on the record player as I got ready in the bathroom, and Elle got ready in the bedroom.

I was the first to emerge, finding Peter dancing by himself to "Crocodile Rock" by Elton John. When he saw me, he stopped and let out a whistle. "Damn, Marlie Rose. You look gorgeous."

I spun around in my gold, floor-length dress and caught another glimpse of myself in the mirror hanging opposite the closed bedroom door. My feathered, dark brown hair fell to my shoulders, my makeup and my dark eyebrows brought out the light blue of my irises and made me look a little older than nineteen. Even I was impressed. For the first time in my life, I felt like more than just an orphan. "Are you sure? I don't look like a Broadway rookie, do I?"

He laughed. "Marlie, for a split second, I wondered if I have the hots for you. I don't, for the record. I'm still one hundred and ten percent gay with a giant crush on Robert Redford. But you, my gorgeous friend, are going to be turning some heads."

I put a hand over my heart. "Aw, Peter. You're looking so handsome in that tux that if I were into men, I'd be approaching you at the after-party. Now top me off, will ya?"

He poured more champagne, and I joined in with him dancing as we obnoxiously sang the la-las while sipping champagne.

"Okay, how about this," he said as he twirled me around during the chorus. "Instead of approaching me, your most handsome guy friend, how about you approach Nancy Osbourne? Rekindle your lost affair?"

I let out a grunt and washed it down with another sip. "I think that ship has long sailed. Just a quick fling until she got bored."

He pursed his lips for a second and glanced over my shoulder. "Any progress with Elle?"

"You're just a jokester tonight, aren't you?"

"What? It's a legitimate question."

"Elle is dating *Robert*."

"Who's he?"

"A breakfast regular at Howard Johnson's."

"And she's going to keep dating him if you don't tell her how you feel."

"And make things weird? No, absolutely not. She's my best friend. She's the only person who has stayed in my life for this long. I don't want to ruin that. Plus, she's clearly into Robert. I have no idea if she's like us."

Just as Peter opened his mouth to say something, the bedroom door opened, and Elle stepped out clad in her metallic-olive halter dress.

My heart plummeted.

She stood there with her newly cut, French-girl fringe hair that fell to her shoulders, her bangs right above her eyebrows, and her dress revealing her shoulders and teasing her cleavage, showcasing just how gorgeous, sexy, and classy she truly was. Elle's beauty was a different kind of beauty than the Hollywood bombshells like Farrah Fawcett and Christie Brinkley. Just like Elle, her beauty wasn't loud. It was subtle, but God, that was what made it so hard for me to look away. To me, she couldn't get any more perfect. I would have never been able to tell that she came from a children's home; she looked like she grew up next door to the McCoys in their Upper East Side row house, and my God, did she take my breath away.

I must have stared a little too long while finding my breath because she started laughing and said, "What? Do I look okay?"

Her gaze met mine as if asking only for my opinion. Elton John's singing filled in the silence as I tried to conjure words to express how truly captivating she was. Luckily, as my mind sputtered, Peter stepped in.

"Are you kidding?" he said. "Both of you are foxy. That's a great color on you, Elle."

It was the first time I'd seen her dolled up, with makeup that punctuated the most beautiful features of her face. We hadn't gone to our senior prom because neither of us had wanted to spend money on dresses. But this felt like the prom we'd never had, another reason why Elle had wanted us to wait to see each other. Part of me wished I'd seen her in the dressing room with it on to prevent the heat snaking up my spine and spreading all over my face and neck when I saw just how beautifully breathtaking she looked. I could feel Peter staring at me, and the fact that I couldn't hide what I assumed to be a very noticeable blush was a sign that he'd bring this moment up later.

"What do you think, Mar?"

My chest clenched around the soft edges of my nickname, dulled by the vulnerability in her tone.

Peter poked my back as if nudging words out of me.

"You look…"

"Okay?" She scanned my body, and the temperature in the room rose a few degrees. I sipped champagne to offer my body some relief.

"You look…well…you look absolutely breathtaking, Elle. Wow," I said, releasing a warm exhale.

Her eyes softened, almost as if she couldn't believe what I said. "You really think so?"

It stunned me that she had no idea how beautiful she looked. "I know so."

She glanced at her dress before walking to the bathroom mirror. She studied her face and then twirled to get a full look at herself. When she faced me and Peter again, the smallest grin appeared, as if she could see a blip of all her beauty shining on me like a warm June sun.

"We're going to be in a whole theater of stars," she said. "I just want to make sure I look good enough to be two stars' dates."

I took a step forward and willed my heart rate to slow, but instead, it betrayed me and quickened. "First off," I said, grazing her arm until I reached her hand and gave her a reassuring squeeze. "I'm not a star. I've done one play, and the second I see Maya Angelou, I might faint in front of everyone."

She laughed, and it filled my chest. "I promise to make sure you don't faint in front of Maya Angelou."

"Please. That would be mortifying. This could very much be the only Tony Awards we go to because I'm not showing my face if I faint," I said with a laugh. "And second, most of the people going aren't stars. They're just like us, with their hair all done up and wearing fancy clothing."

"This is just the start for you. I can feel it."

"Could be, but we don't know. Plus, we'll be sitting next to the real superstar, Jesus Christ himself. We'll be in good hands." I gestured to Peter and winked.

He waved and stepped forward to top off Elle's flute. "Let's kill the bottle, dance some more, then take to the red carpet."

It didn't hit me until we arrived that I'd successfully escaped Brooklyn and my tumultuous childhood. With Elle beside me, I walked toward the entrance of the Imperial Theatre as if the red carpet was the Yellow Brick Road leading to Oz. Flashes and clicks from paparazzi cameras; a sea of long gowns and tuxedos so beautiful and elegant, I had only seen them in fashion magazines; and fans squeezed behind the red ropes lining the red carpet, begging for their favorite star's attention.

"I don't think we're in Kansas anymore," I whispered in Elle's ear.

Her eyes sparkled against the flashes of cameras. "We're on the other side of the world from Kansas, Mar."

I felt like a brand-new person walking down the red carpet in my dress. It was the most expensive thing I'd ever worn, and I felt fully immersed in the glitz and glam. I stole glimpses at Elle, who looked just as enthralled as I was.

We had just sat in our seats, surrounded by the rest of the cast, when she caught one of my stares. She smiled and leaned in. "What?"

My heart lunged against my ribs. I could smell the soft perfume wafting from her neck, and I so desperately wanted to bury my face in that column and smell her, kiss her, touch her. She was so beautiful, I spent the whole ceremony hyperaware of everything she was doing.

I had one eye on the stage while the other was on her, taking in every time she glanced around the Imperial Theatre, clapping whenever someone won an award, nudging me when they announced Maya Angelou's name as a nominee for Best Performance by a Featured Actress in a Play.

As much as I enjoyed watching and being part of the awards, a huge part of me wanted it to end so I could enjoy the night with Elle, talking, laughing, and taking in every inch of her in that stunning dress.

A Little Night Music won seven Tonys. Not only did we win Best Musical, but we also brought home the most awards. My heart soared anytime they announced us, and when we won Best Musical, Elle clasped my hands while our producer went onstage to accept the award and give his speech.

"Your first Broadway musical just won a Tony," she whispered in my ear, and her breath tickled my earlobe.

I swallowed the flutter. I wanted to freeze time. It had nothing to do with the Tonys and everything to do with Elle's arm hooked around mine, her breath caressing the sensitive part of my ear, and her scarlet lips an inch from my skin, the closest they had ever been. She had no idea that every little movement caused a chain reaction within me. When she pulled away, I started figuring out ways I could get her wrapped around me, close enough to the point where I didn't know where my breath stopped and hers began.

Luckily for me, the night was far from over.

The after-party was at Sardi's, of course. I took it all in for the second time: the dark red walls covered in celebrity caricatures, white tablecloths, and Broadway actors packed inside. Elle and I took several moments soaking up the scene before Peter squeezed in the middle of us and hooked an arm around our shoulders.

"The celebration continues, ladies," he said and escorted us to the bar. "Welcome to your first after-party. What are we drinking?"

Elle glanced at me and smiled. "Champagne?"

The bartender passed all three of us a flute. As I took my flute, I turned, rested my back against the bar, and took in the scene unfolding around me. It was a full circle moment. Ten years prior,

I'd walked into Sardi's as a guest, ready to burst with excitement that I was about to see my first Broadway play. It was the night that had forever changed my life. In a way, the second time I went changed my life completely too.

Before I was able to take my first sip of celebratory champagne, Glenn threaded his way through the crowd. "Marlie, come with me," he said. "I have people who want to meet you." He leaned in closer. "Important people who want to help you with your next gig."

I looked at Peter and Elle, and before I could get a word out, Glenn tugged me with him. Peter gave me a thumbs-up, as if letting me know Elle was in good hands while I was gone.

I met a lot of directors, all middle-aged men who scanned me head to toe when Glenn introduced me. Most of them had no idea who I was. A handful had seen my *Little Night* performance and expressed how they wanted me to audition for their musicals. I had to force my eyes to stay on the directors and producers, paste a smile on my face, and while I was ecstatic to be talking to them, my body ached to be next to Elle, have her so close to me that her words tickled my earlobe again, and I was wrapped up in her perfume.

After Glenn released me, I let out a sigh of anxious relief, pounded back the remaining champagne, and scanned the crowd for Peter and Elle. I couldn't find Elle's blond hair, but I found Peter ordering another drink. The only thing that could calm my nerves was a strong drink too. Ever since Elle had stepped out of the bedroom in that dress, I'd stiffen anytime she looked at or touched me. The more I dwelled on my feelings, the more Elle morphed into a different person. I couldn't take my eyes off her. I needed something to loosen the anxiety before she suspected anything.

Peter ordered me some more champagne and flashed me that impish grin. "I have some things to say," he said and squeezed my shoulder.

I pulled a long drink. "Oh, I'm sure you do, given that grin."

"We need to talk about Elle."

"What? Why? Is she okay?" I looked around to try to find her.

He laughed. "She's doing great. Don't worry. I took care of her while you and Glenn were schmoozing. She's in the bathroom."

"Oh, okay," I let out a sigh of relief. "Do I even want to know what you have to say?"

"I don't think you have anything to worry about."

"What are you talking about?"

"Marlie," he said and gave me this side-eye, like I should have known something obvious. He leaned in. "You know that girl is in love with you, right?"

I pulled away and felt the heat consume my face. His smile widened. "You're going to make it to Hollywood one day, Peter Arlo. Your acting skills are impeccable."

"I'm serious. You should have heard her talk about how proud she is of you and the way her eyes got all soft when she was talking about you. Don't worry. I asked her about her love life so I could compare how she reacts to you and the guy she's seeing and—"

I slapped his arm. "Peter!"

"What? I did research to support my hypothesis. You should be thanking me. Aren't you curious to know the findings?"

"Well, obviously."

He smiled. "She totally digs you. To the max. Much more than Robert."

My heart dropped as if his thoughts had shifted the ground, and I had to adjust to the new terrain. "You think?"

"I have four years on you, remember that. I know when people are interested, and you are interested in each other. Next time she talks about you and how proud she is, you really need to listen. Really watch her speak. Your youth is showing, Marlie."

That offended me. He knew it too. That was why he waggled his eyebrows when I made a face at him. The last thing I wanted people to see me as was an inexperienced, naive, nineteen-year-old. "Excuse me?"

"Once you trust what I'm saying, you'll thank me." He glanced over my shoulder. "She's coming back. Go chat with her while I do a lap."

As my stare drifted across the restaurant, I found Elle stepping out of the bathroom. Our eyes locked, and the heat on my face overtook my whole body. Even though I tried acting coy with Peter, the truth was, his observations about Elle bloomed hope in me.

Before that, I'd never considered acting on my secret feelings. In an entire restaurant packed with beautiful, famous, rich, and extremely talented men and women clad in tuxedos and ball gowns, my eyes still gravitated toward her, never flinching once.

"You're finally free," Elle said with a smile. The way her smile reached her sparkling eyes told me she was thankful. Elle was always the quiet one. She liked to listen and observe her surroundings rather than be the talker or the center of the room.

"I am. Did you do okay?"

"Of course. I finally got to talk to *the* Jesus Christ Superstar. He's very sweet."

"He is. I knew you would be in good hands."

I drained the rest of the champagne, feeling the bubbles cool my cheeks just a few degrees. Peter's words were still processing in my mind like clothes in the washer, soaked with absolute confusion. I asked myself the questions that scared me the most: Did I play it safe and always wonder what would have happened, or did I risk the only person who felt like home to me?

"Did you know that I've been to this restaurant before?" I said, trying to kick-start a conversation while Peter's words were still on the spin cycle.

She raised an eyebrow. "You have?"

I nodded and stared at the caricatures. "My foster family took me here for dinner when we saw *The Sound of Music*. I was so excited that I couldn't sit still or even finish my meal. I kept staring at this wall, thinking about all these faces, and after the show, it was all I could think about: singing, performing, being onstage and having people look at me the same way I'd looked at them that night. I know I've only been in one musical, but looking back ten years ago to now, my life has entirely changed in a way I truly believed wasn't possible." I glanced over and saw how intently she listened, like she took in every word and allowed it to envelope her. It was in that moment that I started to believe Peter's words because no one had ever looked at me that deeply before.

Elle placed a hand on my wrist, rubbing my skin with her thumb. I almost pulled away because the gesture seemed way too intimate for such a crowd. But the longer I had a front row view of how Elle's eyes softened on me, the slower Peter's words spun and started to settle into place. So I left my wrist in her grip, and my entire arm burned at her touch.

"Did you honestly think you wouldn't make it here?" Elle said. "Because even though we dreamed big and had our jobs at the record store and library, I still couldn't see myself getting out of Brooklyn. It was like a pipe dream."

"I don't know what I thought. I was so desperate to get out, I feel like I didn't have a choice but to make it happen. Yet somehow, we are here, an entire world away, living in the heart of the city and wearing the fanciest clothes we've ever worn."

"We must have done something right, don't you think?"

It was my turn to rest a hand on her wrist and caress it. She looked at the contact for a moment, and something about that zapped an electric current through me. "We must have," I said.

We ended up slipping out of the party early, both a bit over-whelmed by everything we had consumed. From red carpets to seeing the actual Tony Awards to famous Broadway stars, white tablecloths, and endless champagne. It was a little past midnight when we got back to our apartment. After swimming in Peter's conclusions about Elle's feelings for me, I'd become hyperaware of everything she said and did; the tiniest movements she made throughout the night held extra meaning. I caught her looking at me too long. I caught her catching the dip in my dress. I felt so much in that wrist touch and caress that I knew it was more than just a sympathetic moment between two best friends. At first, I told myself it was just me trying to fit the narrative to Peter's thoughts, like trying to fit a square peg in a round hole. By the time it reached midnight, something felt different between Elle and me. Every touch, eye contact, or unspoken word mattered. With the champagne encouragement flowing through my veins, I was no longer terrified about the intimate moments we had shared all night.

After stepping into our dark apartment, our gazes seemed to have been magnetized. I caught hers as often as she caught mine, and with every catch, there was sizzling contact that made the nerves in my stomach waltz.

I finally saw what Peter was talking about. There was vulnerability in her stare. I studied how her eyes softened when they landed on me. The way she looked at me was much different than how Nancy Osbourne had. Nancy had looked at me ravenously with the quest to get me naked. Elle's eyes cradled me as if I was everything to her, so much more than a naked body.

After I went to the bathroom, I stepped in our bedroom and watched her struggling to unzip the back of her dress.

"Let me help you," I said and closed the space between us.

She lowered her hands. I glided the stubborn zipper down to the small of her back and swallowed the tugging in my throat when I observed how smooth her skin was. The back of her dress opened, and as I took in the expanse, my heart thrummed as my confession danced on the tip of my tongue, the champagne, the early hours of the morning, and her exposed back lassoing my words and encouraging them to be free.

She turned, and her eyes met mine, and the way she stared at me was enough to undo all the feelings I'd been bottling up for the last four years. Now that I'd seen what Peter had, all my feelings pooled out the same way her dress relaxed against her body.

"Elle?" I said, though my throat was so dry, it sounded more like a croak.

"Marlie."

My stomach bottomed out. There was no question in her inflection. It was a statement, soft but with demanding undertones.

I stopped myself from thinking too much. I palmed her face. I paused, giving her a chance to stop it if she wanted. But when her cheek relaxed, and the vulnerability in her eyes sharpened to desire, I kissed her. Once her lips gripped mine, a fire ignited through my body, and I wondered if she'd thought about kissing me as much as I had because she kissed like she had been practicing it over and over in her head. As I glided my tongue along her bottom lip, a murmur seeped out of her and hummed against my mouth. A hot curl of desire rolled low in my stomach. I dropped my hands from her face and let them skim down her neck, her shoulders, where I slowly peeled the dress away until it hung around her waist. I wrenched my mouth from hers to take in the glorious sight of her bra. She fixed her hooded stare on me as she reached behind her back to unhook it. I lost my breath when she slipped out of it and tossed it on the ground.

"Elle." I stared at her beautiful, naked breasts.

She stepped forward until she was a whisper from my mouth. She planted a soft yet searing kiss before pulling away. "Take me to bed, Marlie."

I didn't wait another second. I pulled the dress down her legs, discarded it to the side, and lowered her to the bed. I wanted her body pressed against mine. Her fingers, lips, and tongue traced delicious invisible patterns all over my skin. I lowered myself on top of her and let her explore my body, first over my dress until she freed me from it.

Her naked body against mine flickered nerve endings that Nancy had never come close to finding. The way Elle kissed me, touched me, and loved me turned me inside out and sewed up all the worn and frayed parts that I was trying so hard to grow out of at nineteen. I wasn't a sex expert, but I knew that it was the first time I had been truly intimate with someone. I finally knew what it was like to be passionate and tender and encompassed in arousal by how Elle rocked her hips below me and moaned her pleasure into my ear. I knew how much it meant to her by the way we held each other afterward, not saying a word or shifting in our spots. We just lay there, our bodies entangled, not knowing where the other person started or ended. The silence and the heavy, ragged breaths said more than any words.

At the time, it felt like that night had shifted our worlds into place. Sleeping with Elle didn't feel wrong like the world painted it to be. It was the most wanted and loved I had ever felt.

❖

"This is a good stopping point, Ms. Rose," Dr. Pierson says.

I open my eyes and center myself in the present, loosening the grip the memory wrapped around me. One of the male doctors stands and flicks on the light. I wince at the brightness.

"We covered a lot," Dr. Pierson says. "Now, it's time to decide which ones you would like to keep and which you'd like to erase. From meeting Elle to your first night together."

The embarrassment crawls across my cheeks as Dr. Pierson refers to the memory I just recalled. I can't believe I spoke about it to him and his team, but their white coats remind me that they're professionals and that they don't necessarily care about my love life. They care about relieving their patients from grief, trauma, pain, and depression.

Even though I just recalled the memories, they quickly play again as if I press fast-forward and watch the snippets speed through. My lips tingle the way they always do when Elle used to kiss me. I'm amazed that even though it's been twelve years since I last kissed her, I still remember the patterns dancing across my lips and tongue.

I never thought I would lose her. I thought she was the one thing I would hold on to forever, despite all the ingraining Kindred Hearts had carved into us about how we should never get attached.

I did get attached to Elle, though. It was impossible not to.

I quickly ruminate on all the memories I have of her and how she's given me some of the best moments of my life as well as some of the worst. This is what happens when she sneaks into my mind, and our shared memories remind me of how I lost the only woman I've ever truly loved. It's not always the bad memories that haunt a person. It's the good ones too. Regret grows from the good ones. If nothing was ever good, there wouldn't be anything to regret. I've lived in regret for years while tossing and turning throughout the night about the what-ifs and what-could-have-beens.

My heart constantly aches without her. How could something that was once so wonderful and so beautiful end? It's something I've asked myself for years. I got too attached. Elle made it clear years ago that she was done with me, and it's taken me so long to accept that the Elle in my memory grew up. We both did. We grew up and drifted apart, no matter how hard we tried keeping a tight grip on what we once had.

A lump buds in my throat, and no matter how many times I try to swallow it, it becomes heavier. "I would like to keep everything before the Tony Awards, but please erase that night." The entire team directs their eyes on me, rounding their stares as if they are all taken aback. "I know what you're thinking: it's a fabulous memory. That's what makes it hurt so bad. I keep comparing where I am right now to those good memories, and sometimes, that is as painful as the horrible ones. How can I move forward if my mind still defaults to the best time of my life, the best years when Elle and I were together? It reminds me of everything I've lost, and I carry that weight with me every day. Have done so for years, and every time I think about those days with Elle, I feel like I lose more of myself in those memories. I want to live the rest of my days without feeling like my heart is this hundred-pound weight thrumming against my chest."

My first six years in Manhattan were the happiest years of my life, the years I constantly wished I could relive again when I was feeling extra nostalgic. I held on to the memories of Peter and me like a security blanket that he draped over me. We shared those, and because they were shared, I don't feel the need to erase them. However, my memories with Elle are split up and divided like assets in a divorce, and now our memories weigh like a batch of bricks on my sternum that I'm desperate to pluck off with Dr. Pierson's help.

"Okay, I understand. Then we'll move forward with erasing that memory of the Tony Awards, the kiss, and the bedroom."

I'm so sorry, my love, I say to Elle in my head as the tears brim.

The helmet warms up, and once the clicking taps against my brain, I close my eyes as my chest tightens with each noise.

I don't want to erase that night. It was special for so many reasons, but the immense pain of losing Elle has been sitting heavily on me for years. I have no other choice but to take the weight off.

CHAPTER SEVEN

After my second session, my headaches are mild, but more confusion starts to blanket my mind. It's a weird feeling to know that I'm getting my memories erased and not remembering much of anything I spoke about at the last session. I know that's the whole point of it, but it's like my mind can't keep up with the sudden disappearance of space. One part of my brain is searching for the missing piece while the other is telling me there's nothing there.

I remember that Dr. Pierson told me not to think about what memories could be missing. The reminder stops my head from searching, and instead, I try to distract myself with a shower. But as I step out of the shower, I'm ready for my next session. I'm eager to untangle the parts of my life that I've been struggling to free myself from.

"You have a date this Friday at Axis LA," I say to Kristina on our drive to my third session. "You're at a table right against the windows."

She slams her brakes when we reach a red light. "What?"

"Careful on the brakes."

"I'm sorry. But what?"

"You have a date on Friday."

"You got a table that easily?"

I laugh and squeeze her arm. "Hon, I know how to pull a few strings. I talked to Serena DeLuca personally, and she spoke with the general manager, and we got you a table. Serena says it's a great view. She said she'll even save a Brunello for you."

"I don't even know what Brunello is."

"Great," I say and pat her shoulder. "It will be an experience for both of you. It's delicious, by the way."

Kristina continues through the green light for a couple of silent moments. "All right, I'll accept this except now it's my turn to have conditions."

"Oh wow, demanding."

"You need to look over the script Helen sent you two weeks ago. The *Hello, Dolly!* revival. If you want to get back onstage, this could be a great opportunity."

"I'll look at it when I get home."

"You promise?"

"I promise."

For the rest of the ride to the institute, I wonder if getting back on a Broadway stage is something that I really want to do, something that would bring color back into my black, white, and gray life. It's been seven years since I was last on Broadway, playing Carmen Bernstein in *Curtains*. But between taking a much-needed break and movie roles since then, there's a part of me listening to the stage calling me back. I miss it. I miss singing and performing for people. I miss having a purpose. I miss feeling the warmth of the lights all over my body. I miss hearing the audience clapping, and I miss how the pit orchestra fills up the entire theater with beautiful music.

I miss all of it. Maybe the *Hello, Dolly!* script is my ticket back home.

"How was your weekend, Ms. Rose?" Dr. Pierson asks as he takes a seat at the middle of the table with the rest of the team. "How were the headaches?"

"In existence but manageable," I say as Dr. Wilson secures the helmet around my head.

"Good. That's good." Dr. Wilson turns off the light. "How about we start after *Little Night Music*."

I close my eyes and think back to the first memory, and all I can see is myself wrapped up in Elle on our couch.

❖

It was late March of 1973. It was after a *Little Night* show, and I had come home to find Elle reading *One Hundred Years of Solitude* on the couch, all tucked into a blanket while Joni Mitchell's "For the Roses" played softly. She looked so soft and comfy, and when she pulled her eyes off the pages and onto me, my stomach flipped. She sat up, patted for me to sit, and when I did, her beautiful eyes filled with this pure look of adoration, flitting all over her face before landing on my lips.

My heart quickened as she leaned in and kissed me softly. I have no idea what prompted her to kiss me then and there on the couch. But of course, I didn't question any of it because she made me feel like I could float away like a balloon. The lips I had imagined on me countless times before were finally kissing me. I was so desperate for her that I palmed her face to hold her there, not wanting her to pull away.

This is the first kiss that I remember, but it doesn't feel like that now that I think about it. I know I'm not supposed to poke at what feels like holes in my memory, but when I'd dreamed about our first kiss, it was grand, where I pushed her against the wall. But this was soft and tender...and subtle. Elle had this amazing ability to untangle my stress, anxiety, and exhaustion with her lips. Each movement unwound me and made me melt into her. I know we had sex many times, but I don't quite remember the first time, which is odd because I can recall every other time with perfect detail. I think our first time was on the couch that night in March of 1973, but even then, how we made love to each other was so seamless and perfect, like we already had each other's bodies mapped out.

Whatever the case is, I loved coming home to her reading or journaling while listening to music, and every time I did, she made room for me on the couch, wrapped an arm around me, and held me. If I could think about the most perfect years of my life, it was those four years Elle and I spent together.

During the summer of 1973, Elle worked every day at the diner while I started piano lessons and more advanced acting lessons. We came home and tried out new recipes in our small kitchen, trying to teach herself how to cook. I attempted to learn with her, but I somehow managed to mess up everything I tried. Eventually, I gave up, and Elle banned me from helping. My purpose in that kitchen became to steal kisses from her in between tasks.

On weekend nights, we met up with Peter, who introduced us to the underground gay scene, and Elle and I felt like we'd landed on the moon and had all the time to explore territory we didn't think we would ever see with our own eyes. Men dancing with men. Women dancing with women. Soft touches and kisses out in the open, right at the bar or on the dance floor. A place people were free to be themselves and love openly.

As we bounced around the gay bars on Christopher Street, my mind always defaulted to those articles about Stonewall and the horrible language that was just a small window into the giant world of homophobia running rampant. But we were lucky in one way: being in New York City.

Greenwich Village was the heart of the Gay Liberation Movement. Peter told me that before Stonewall, gay bars were owned by the mafia, and the West Village was run by the Genovese family, including Stonewall. There were rules the patrons had to follow. Men were only allowed to dance with each other if there was a woman in the center, and the men didn't touch. If they did, a mafioso sitting on a stool shone a flashlight on them. After three flickers, the mafioso called the cops. They had a deal with each other, and the mafia helped the cops meet their quota of gay men arrested each week.

"It's how Stonewall happened," Peter said.

But we were going out in a post-Stonewall New York City, and now men were allowed to dance with each other, which drew in tons of crowds. In some ways, Stonewall freed us. It was the aftermath that put gay rights on the front lines of political change and meant Elle and I could dance with each other in those sacred places. We took advantage of the new rules, and with the drinking age set at eighteen back then, at nineteen and twenty, Elle and I found ourselves immersed in the gay liberation movement and the sexual revolution.

One night out in the Village, I had finally grown comfortable touching and kissing Elle in the dingy basement bars. While it might not have been the most romantic spot in the midst of low-hanging tobacco and marijuana smoke and the smell of cheap beer, it made us feel the safest. I finally had the chance to kiss a beautiful woman in public without being ostracized or worse, arrested. I rested my hands on her hips, pulled her in, and savored the Rheingold Beer on her lips. "I like kissing you in public," I said and nibbled her earlobe, loving the way her body went limp in my grip.

She laughed and pulled back enough to look at me. "I like how handsy you get in public."

"It's hard not to. Look at everyone else."

Men making out with men, women making out with women. Everyone dancing, some couples slow dancing intimately, as if the songs made everyone in the mood to kiss in the middle of the dance floor. I loved every moment of it.

"You know, we can dip out of here and get a little more physical if you want," I said, leaning into her neck to plant kisses on the spots that drove her crazy. When I sucked on one of them, I heard the softest moan fill my ears.

"Marlie," she said through an impish grin.

I knew that look. If we were home, that smile would have dragged me straight to bed. "What? I want you."

"Stop making out you two. 'Crocodile Rock' is on. This is our song that will forever remind me of you two," Peter said, inserting himself into our little huddle and tugging on our wrists.

Now, I don't know why the song reminded Peter of us, but I put off kissing Elle to dance with him and everyone else on the dance floor. A few men had recognized Peter, called him "Jesus Christ Superstar," and formed a circle around him. He seized the moment, ran his hand through his sweaty brown hair, and conducted the entire bar to sing. He was a natural performer. Hopping around the circle, coaxing each individual person to join in.

I relied on those nights, dancing our problems away when *Flight* was pulled from Broadway after two weeks in March 1974. The power of Elle and Peter helped me through struggling with landing another role. Going to auditions only to not get the part started picking away at the excitement that moving to the city and landing a role in *Little Night Music* had created. Worrying about money became an issue again, the exact opposite of what I expected once I made it into the Broadway world.

Peter always knew how to pick us up. Between my struggle with getting a new role and Elle's stress over classes, Peter knew the exact time we needed a good distraction. He'd venture down the few floors that separated us and make us his nonna's gnocchi in pomodoro sauce. We listened to records from Simon and Garfunkel, Billy Joel, Elton John, and Led Zeppelin while making the gnocchi and sipping wine. It was such a process, I had no other choice but to focus on the task at hand.

"There's nothing little fluffy carb pillows can't fix, right?" he said and stuck out the wooden spoon slathered with pomodoro sauce simmering on the stove.

"You promise not to tell Glenn about the fluffy carb pillows?" I said, hesitating before taking my first bite.

He zipped his lips. "Your secret is safe with me, Marlie Rose. And forget Glenn. Nonna's gnocchi fixes everything. At least, that's what she used to tell me, and she was never wrong. When I was about ten, I got beat up at school, so we spent a Saturday making what seemed to be a million little gnocchi. I completely forgot about the shiner under my eye."

"Peter," I said, resting a hand on his arm.

"What? Oh, please. I just bought myself this far-out 1970 Alfa Romeo Spider. I'm doing just fine. I hardly think about Mark Weaver beating me up after Red Rover, but I do remember making gnocchi with my nonna. So good thing I'm putting you two to work. You're going to make so many that you're going to forget about those auditions, and Elle is going to forget about those tests she needs to study for. In forty years, you'll be thinking about that time you made gnocchi with me, drinking red wine and listening to 'The Only Living Boy in New York.'"

"Forget about the auditions," Elle said and planted a sweet kiss on my cheek. "Peter's right. One of the best memories I have with my grandma is making raspberry thumbprints on Christmas Eve."

"Why haven't we ever made those cookies?" I asked.

Elle shrugged. "I didn't want to stress you out with your diet."

"Cookies are quite the opposite of stressful. Plus, calories don't count during the holidays."

"You know, I think I read that in *Vogue*," Peter said.

"Okay, if you really want some cookies, we should make them this Christmas Eve," Elle said. "All three of us."

"I'm a horrible cook," I said. "I'm lucky I can sing a little bit."

"You can be in charge of the music and pour the wine," Peter said. "Let the real chefs take over the kitchen." He winked at me and then slung an arm over Elle.

"What I'm trying to say is," Elle chimed in after I tossed a gnocchi at Peter's chest, leaving a floury patch on his navy shirt. "I don't remember every single little bump in the road, though there were a lot of bumps with my mom. I just always associate raspberry thumbprints with my grandma, and my grandma always made everything a little easier."

"That's why we have each other, right?" Peter said, tossing an arm over my shoulders too. "Three misfits who found each other in the biggest city in the world, making life a little easier for one another."

"Exactly," Elle said.

"Let's make Nonna proud and give Glenn a big 'fuck you' with these gnocchi," I said. "And then we'll do it again at Christmas."

❖

My audition struggle finally ended when I got a supporting role in *Shenandoah* as Jenny in January of 1975. However, Glenn landed me another big audition that March, claiming this musical was going to blow up on Broadway.

"That's what you said about *Flight*," I said with a scoff as he puffed away on a Marlboro in his office.

"If we play our cards right, if you get this costarring role, it could get your name on the most wanted list."

I learned a few months later that Glenn knew what he was talking about because that big March audition gave me my first starring role: *Chicago*.

Glenn was right. *Chicago* spread my name around Broadway like wildfire. At least, that was how Glenn first described it to me before the magazine features did. To think I was this close to not getting it. The director, Rick Higgins, had his eyes on Judith Preston, a Broadway veteran with more than six years of age and experience on me. Rick Higgins wasn't sure if he wanted a twenty-one-year-old playing the part of Roxie Hart, but Glenn knew what he was doing and how to work the director.

Not only was my grapefruit diet strictly enforced leading up to the audition, but Glenn had apparently mastered the art of persuasion. I was impressed with how adamant he was about me getting this role that I instantly forgave him for his persistence on *Flight* right then and there. I wanted the role of Roxie Hart so badly, I made a deal with whatever higher power there was that I would eat an entire grapefruit without wincing for a whole year if I got it.

After I sang the song "Roxie," Glenn turned to Rick Higgins and said, "Can Judith Preston do that? Can she fill up this whole theater like that?"

"I'm not arguing about Marlie's voice, Glenn. I have ears," Rick said. "She can sing. Hell, she can sing better than the majority of the women on Broadway right now, and that's saying something."

"Can she sing better than Judith Preston? That's the real question."

"Judith Preston is twenty-seven and has had three lead parts under her belt."

"But you have the chance to launch someone's career. You have the chance for people to look back on this performance and say, 'I remember Marlie Rose when she played Roxie Hart. She created that role. She *is* Roxie Hart. And it's all because of Rick Higgins.' Sometimes, a fresh face is just as good as a seasoned veteran. If you don't snag her, *A Chorus Line* has their eyes on her."

A week later, Rick Higgins offered me my first leading role.

As the musical's success started to rise, so did my first Times Square billboards. The first one I spotted was in black and white. I was dressed as Roxie Hart, and it looked like I sat on the middle "*C*" in *Chicago*. What made it even more perfect was that it hung right above Howard Johnson's. I didn't believe it when Elle came barging through the front door after a late shift and told me. We ran the block over to the diner, and there I was, lighting up the corner of 46th and Broadway. I was so taken aback, I just stood there and took it all in.

Elle nudged my arm. "You're on top of me," she said, finally pulling me out of my daydream to reward her with a smirk.

"This is outta sight," I said, unable to pull my eyes away.

"Can you believe it? You're on a billboard," Elle said. "The first of many. And you were worried you weren't ever going to make it after *Flight*."

No, I couldn't believe it, yet, here I was on a billboard above Howard Johnson's in Times Square. "Peter's nonna's carb pillows really did wonders."

"Also, I have to admit," Elle said, lowering her voice and leaning in to whisper. "You're a stone-cold fox up there."

I looked over. "Oh really?"

She bit her lip and nodded. I always loved when she bit her lip. That meant salacious thoughts ran through her mind. I always benefited from the bitten lip.

"And even though you're in black and white, your eyes are still incredibly striking. I bet they make a lot of people stop and take a second look."

"You think?"

"I'd bet my whole book collection."

I leaned in. "Have you ever gone to bed with someone from a Times Square billboard?"

"No, but we can change that right now."

I didn't care about the billboard as much anymore. I tugged Elle's wrist and walked quickly back to our apartment. It didn't matter if we had been together for almost two years at that point.

Kissing her, holding her, making love to each other was still just as thrilling as the beginning of our relationship.

I buried my face in her neck and slid my hand underneath the lapel of her robe to feel her bare stomach. I squeezed her tightly. I loved how she smelled, a little bit like our apartment, her natural scent, and a soft spritz of perfume I gave her for her twenty-first birthday, Diorella by Dior. She was my favorite smell in the entire world, and no matter how busy and long the day was, she was the perfect remedy to help me unwind. I peeled the robe off, and we got lost in the sheets and the other's naked body.

One of my favorite quirks about her was that no matter how long the day was or if we had just spent the last two hours making love, she was dedicated to her daily journal entry. With the top sheet wrapped around her chest while I continued to breathe in the comforting smell of her, she leaned over to the nightstand, grabbed her journal and pen, and opened to a blank page on her lap.

"I love when you cuddle me like this," she said and then planted a kiss on my forehead. "But I need to journal."

"You know, I've known you for six years, and I haven't ever read what you've written in your journal."

"You haven't…because it's my journal," she said teasingly. "My diary. The whole point of it is to keep all my secrets locked up."

I lifted my head. "You have secrets?"

"So many. Basically, I live a double life." She laughed at her own joke.

I sat up and rested my back against the pillows. "Come on. Give me one little thing you've written in there. You said you would let me read one entry if we moved out of Brooklyn."

"I did say that, didn't I?" She looked over at her journal, as if debating whether to follow through. I gave her my best puppy dog eyes. "Oh, that's not fair."

"What?" I feigned shocked.

"You know that your eyes are my weakness. Actually, you in general are my weakness."

"This is very good news for me."

"Okay, fine." Elle turned back a page and handed me the journal. It felt like holding a vault of her secrets and gossip.

"I see that grin, and I just want you to know that most of my journal isn't eventful. Just boring musings about my day."

"I want to know the boring things."

I looked at the page and noticed her small, neat, cursive handwriting. I found it adorable how small she wrote, as if she was trying to fit as many words on a page as possible.

June 27, 1975,

Today in my English class, I overheard two girls talking about how they saw Chicago *over the weekend and how groovy it was. One of the girls said it was her third time seeing the show and how talented the cast was, specifically the two leads. All I could think was "That's my girlfriend."*

It's not even my dream to be on Broadway but watching Marlie have these dreams and snatch on to them so easily as if they're fallen leaves that she needs to bring back to life makes me feel like I'm achieving my own. Every day I get to watch her come home with this smile on her face that I know runs deep. I haven't seen her this truly happy, and because she has this new special glow to her, I feel like it's swaddled me too. Watching Marlie conquer her dreams is inspiring. I'm so lucky to have her and that she sees a light in me that I don't really see, but she makes me believe I have it. I'm not sure how we've gotten so lucky to get out of Brooklyn with nothing to our name, and now we live in an apartment blocks from Time Square.

It feels like a dream, and I hope I don't ever wake up.

"See, just boring little things," Elle said. "Nothing that interesting."

While the pages weren't littered with gossip, it was still enough to fill me with happiness because even Elle's musing about the little things that happened during her day made me so incredibly glad that she was mine, and I was hers.

"You think I'm inspiring?" I said, turning to her.

Her cheeks flushed. "I do." She snatched up the journal from my lap and set it on her nightstand. I was about to playfully wrestle her for it if she hadn't crawled on top of me, pinned me to the spot, and hushed my curiosity by planting soft kisses along the nape of my neck. Being together for so long, we had memorized the map of each other's bodies and all the spots that caused the other to melt.

"You know, you're making it so much harder for me to allow you to write," I said through ragged breaths as she crawled up from my inner thigh and softly kissed me on the lips.

"But just admit, you're a little less interested in what's in my diary." She plopped on her side, and I scooted into her, burying my face between her breasts.

Her natural scent and Dior clung to the fabric of her robe like I clung to her. "This is true," I muttered into her breasts. "You're too comfortable, and you smell intoxicating."

"That's probably because we've been rolling around in these sheets for the last two hours. Your scent is all over me."

I pulled my face away and looked up. "No, it's all you. I always thought you smelled good. Even at Kindred Hearts. Something about that generic soap."

"You're joking."

"I'm not." I sat up. "I remember when Mrs. Hansen took us to Morsey Records, and we went into the listening booth together, and I think that's when it really hit me."

She raised an eyebrow. "What really hit you?"

I shrugged. "My feelings for you. It's a bit odd. We were still getting to know each other, but I was drawn to you."

Her smile grew. "You were drawn to me?"

I caressed her cheek with my thumb. She leaned into my touch, causing my stomach to flip. "Of course I was. I always thought you were so beautiful. I couldn't keep my eyes off you."

She looked so much softer and warmer from moments before. "Really?"

"I still can't, Elle."

It had been drilled into me since I was nine to not get attached. I grew up thinking that was the golden rule to life. Don't get attached because everything ends. I grew up when the gay community was being beaten and arrested for being gay, and even living in New York City didn't mean instant protection from homophobia. The only solace was our home and those bars.

While part of me hadn't really lived until I'd moved into Manhattan and started getting on with Elle, there was another part not buried that far deep that was also terrified of my growing feelings for her. God, I loved her. I was so in love with her, and it made me so disappointed in myself that almost two years into our relationship, I hadn't ever pulled the curtains back to reveal how much I did love her. It was a whole production behind those curtains, just waiting for me to be brave enough to show her.

The amount of love I had at such a young age shouldn't have been something to be ashamed of. Loving her brought color to my world. It dulled the pain and rejection in my chest. It made me feel worthy to share a life with her. Loving her made me a better person. It made me a happier person. Why should I have felt ashamed about that?

"Marlie," Elle said, low and soft, her face falling farther into my palm.

My heart raced as the confession slipped off my tongue. "I'm in love with you, Elle. I think I've been in love with you this whole time. I know it's taken me so long to say it, and I'm sorry for that, but—"

She clasped my face and pulled me in for a tender yet sizzling kiss. When she pulled away, she rested her forehead against mine. "I love you too, Marlie. And it's okay. I already knew."

"You did? How?"

"I see it in those beautiful eyes of yours, and I can feel it any time I'm with you. We might have grown up wondering if anyone ever loved us, but being with you? I never had to question that for a second."

My heart tore open. I worried that I was too much of a coward for being afraid to say a phrase I'd always wanted to say, a phrase that I'd always wanted to hear back. It was just another moment that assured me that Elle saw all of me, she understood me, and I felt like I saw all of her.

"I feel lucky to have you too, Elle. I love you."

"You do, don't you," she said with a growing grin.

"I really do. More than I can say."

"It's okay. You don't have to tell me. I prefer you show me though."

I kissed her, and we got tangled in those sheets once again.

I liked how telling her that I loved her tasted on my tongue, how it rolled off my lips, and how when the words finally made their way to Elle, how she looked at me like I was her sun.

If I was her sun, she was my universe.

CHAPTER EIGHT

Chicago was up for ten Tonys in 1976 and landed me my first nomination, Best Performance by a Leading Actress in a Musical. I might have lost to Donna McKechnie from *A Chorus Line*, but *Chicago* and the Tony nomination put my name on the list of in-demand stars, at least according to Glenn. It brought in a hefty paycheck that helped Elle and I move out of our tiny Whitby apartment into a two-bedroom townhouse in our favorite neighborhood, Greenwich Village, a few blocks from Peter. I might not have been filthy rich, but I was finally financially comfortable renting a Greenwich Village rowhouse.

Brooklyn was even farther in the rearview mirror.

To celebrate our new home, my new lead role in the musical *Sincerely, Yours*, and Elle not only getting her bachelor's degree in education but also getting a job as an English teacher at one of the best public schools in Manhattan, I decided we really needed to celebrate in style. I rented out the Statue of Liberty Lounge at the hottest new restaurant in the entire city, Windows on the World, on the top two floors of the North Tower of the World Trade Center. Elle and I laughed on the elevator ride to the one-hundred-and-seventh floor as our ears popped the entire ride.

"Hello, Ms. Rose," the hostess said. "Welcome to Windows on the World. You two can follow me."

It was the first time I'd been called Ms. Rose. It sounded formal. Elle and I exchanged a glance, and she waggled her eyebrows at the new title.

The restaurant was nothing like we'd ever seen. It offered a panoramic view of all of New York City, all the bridges that connected the boroughs, and I was amazed that being one hundred and seven floors up made even New Jersey look good.

I scanned the view and spotted the Statue of Liberty. The little figure in the New York Harbor caught my gaze and held it. Whatever the reason, it made me think of how far I had come. I started from the gritty part of Brooklyn with only a suitcase to my name, and now I was being called Ms. Rose at the age of twenty-two and was dining on the hundred and seventh floor of the World Trade Center with my love, sipping wine over white tablecloths in our own privately rented section of the bar.

We were so far removed that the urban decay that had been crawling through the streets over the last several years seemed like a speck of dirt. I felt untouchable.

"I can't believe we're up here," Elle said, leaning into the table, the flicker from the candle contouring her face. "I can't believe we're here. I can't believe I just graduated college and have a teaching job in September. I can't believe you were nominated for a Tony. I can't believe we have a townhouse in Greenwich Village, three blocks away from Peter. Marlie," she said and clasped my hands. "What's happening?"

I squeezed her hands. "We made a life for ourselves, that's what happened. I'm proud of you, you know," I said and reached to caress her hand, not nearly as long as I wanted to because I worried about the bartenders and our waiter watching our intimate moment but long enough for her to know that my comment ran deep. "You worked so hard for that degree."

Both of us let go at the same time. "I did. I can't believe I have a degree."

"You're going to be Ms. Olson come September."

"I just…I don't understand. We went from foster care rejects to being able to afford this menu. Wow."

"I told you not to worry about that," I said with a laugh. "That's one of the many great things about playing Roxie Hart. It afforded us our beautiful Greenwich Village home *and* this meal. Let's enjoy it.

We might have started with nothing, but that's not our life anymore. Just look outside. This is how far we've climbed. We should savor it. For our younger selves who never thought we'd be here."

The way she smiled at me made my stomach flip. She looked incredibly grateful, and God, I wished so much that I could lunge across the tablecloth and kiss her all over her adorable face. "So you want to see what all this hype around caviar is about?"

"Absolutely."

We ordered the caviar as an appetizer, and it didn't matter if I was nominated for a Tony, if we'd moved up into a Greenwich Village rowhouse, or if I could afford a meal at Windows on the World, after one bite, it was my first and last time I tried being fancy enough for caviar.

For the entree, I had the veal and pistachio terrine, and Elle had the braised striped bass, and for dessert, we shared the mocha praline mousse. We ordered another bottle of wine and sank into our seats while flitting our gazes between each other and the sunset coloring the New York sky. I'd seen countless sunsets before, but nothing compared to seeing it from Windows on the World and how it bled magentas and violets into the entire restaurant.

"Everything seems so little from up here," Elle said, running her finger along the stem of her wineglass. "We can see all of Queens, Staten Island, and Brooklyn. I'm drinking delicious wine at the fanciest restaurant in the entire city. I've never been up this high. I've never seen the city from this point of view, and when I look at Brooklyn, I can't help but wonder if my mom is staring up at the towers from across the river."

I bit back my bitterness. There was some reason I wanted to defend Elle from her mother. But after my initial reaction, my heart broke for her. I could see all the hurt and questions behind her irises.

I reached for another thumb caress.

"Sometimes, I think about trying to find her," she said, finally looking me in the eye. "I've been having these dreams recently that I'm walking around in Brooklyn, and I see her on the street. Sometimes, she doesn't recognize me, and in some dreams, she tells me off or runs away."

"Do you want to find her?"

She shrugged. "I do, and I don't. I have to prepare myself to get rejected all over again if she doesn't want to hear from me. But she's had her own life for the last seven years without me. I struggle between wanting to know her, getting answers, but also trying to gain some love and respect for myself."

"You can take your time. Really think about it and be prepared to hear the answers you don't want to hear. But whatever decision you make, I hope you know that I support you."

She squeezed my hand. "Thank you. You've been my family this whole time. Luckily, I'm at a point I don't *need* my mother in order to make my life feel complete. Turns out, all I need is you, and right now, my life feels as complete as it has ever been."

I glanced around to make sure the coast was clear, and we were alone in our own little bubble on top of the world. I pulled Elle's hand to my lips and kissed her knuckles. "My life feels as complete as it's ever been too."

And I meant it.

That was the start to the summer of 1976.

New York City was on the brink of bankruptcy. Unemployment rates were at an all-time high. More than eight hundred thousand people moved into the suburbs to find jobs in what was called the white flight. Others had no choice but to stay and felt neglected by the government after it cut services like sanitation and after-school programs, and they turned to vandalism, drugs, and violence. Crime was rapidly rising.

Times Square, once the beating heart of Manhattan, was now the epicenter of urban decay. More people were deciding to stay home than come to the shows. Instead of drawing in tourists and Broadway spectators, Times Square brought in only brave theater enthusiasts as well as strip club and adult theater goers. The tourist population started thinning after 1975 when pamphlets warned them how to survive "Fear City" and which areas to avoid.

The line of dichotomy was just as blaring as the Times Square marquees. You had to walk past some of the messiest parts of the city to see some of the most wonderful productions just a short distance away from the decay. Elle grew more worried each day about my getting home from the musical. It had gotten to a point where Peter gave us a baseball bat as a housewarming present.

But somewhere in the midst of New York City's chaos, my chosen family had never been stronger. Elle and I were twenty-two and very much in love. After spending nine months in Los Angeles to film his first movie, Peter was itching to be near the water. He purchased a beach house in Southampton in the spring and started seeing his boyfriend, Will Gaines, a production assistant he had met while they both were part of *A Chorus Line*. We relied on each other for comfort while our city eroded, and the three kids who'd grown up as misfits finally had the privilege of escaping.

God, did we enjoy that beach house. It was right on the ocean with its own private beach. We spent the summer bathing in the sun until we became too sweaty, and then the four of us scampered down the beach and into the waves. We utilized the grill almost every night, and it was a great fuck-you to Glenn and his grapefruits. Being from North Carolina, Will really knew how to barbecue, and our stomachs were never empty, especially on the sunny days when we feasted on chicken breasts, burgers, or ribs slathered in Will's delicious homemade barbecue sauce. On rainy days, we blasted records and drank PBRs while Peter led us in making homemade pasta, and Elle always made a wonderful batch of cookies for dessert.

Then there was me, who barely knew how to cook, but the only thing the three chefs requested was piano music as background. Peter bought a gorgeous Steinway grand that sat in the corner of the living room. I played for them while catching glimpses of the beautiful ocean, the woman I loved, and my best friend in the kitchen.

At night, we sat out on the patio chairs in the glow of the colorful tiki lights. We drank, laughed, listened to the soft lapping of the water and the night bugs enveloping us in their chirps while singing along with Elton John, Billy Joel, and Bennett and Sons on the stereo. When the alcohol kicked in, the patio turned into our stage, Elle and Will were our audience, and Peter and I used our PBR cans as microphones while we harmonized to every song that played.

"This is what happens when we date Broadway stars," Elle said one night to Will with an elbow nudge. "As Shakespeare said, 'All the world's a stage.'"

Even when it rained, it didn't stop us from having a good time. I helped turn the living room into our own personal piano bar, playing any song they requested. There was one early August night when a thunderstorm rolled through, and we only had Nonna's gnocchi that we'd spent all day making while drinking a batch of sangria. Three batches in, we were all feeling it. Peter held his microphone—a rolling pin still covered in blotches of flour—and started singing "Don't Let the Sun Go Down on Me." I accompanied him on the piano with the lid closed. The sangria controlled him like a wobbly marionette. He lay his torso on the piano while singing the first verse. I tried biting back my laugh so my playing didn't stop his hilariously dramatic performance. When the chorus came around, Will and Elle joined in, allowing the sangria to magnify their voices.

I thought how wonderful it was that two girls who'd grown up without their parents and two guys rejected by their families had eventually found each other and formed a chosen family. My heart was so incredibly full, I didn't want the summer to end. Even though we had things to look forward to in the fall—like me starring in my new musical, *Sincerely, Yours*, and Elle starting her first year of teaching—we didn't want to leave our peaceful bubble where we could be ourselves and openly love our partners.

Our last night that summer was somber. It felt like the last day of vacation, and the next day, we were back in reality in the hustle and bustle and grit that made up New York City.

"You guys think you'll stay in New York forever?" Peter asked on the patio, twirling his red wine with his legs resting on Will's lap.

Elle and I exchanged a glance. Glenn had mentioned in the spring that I should consider expanding my talents into Hollywood or even record my own album, but I hadn't taken the suggestion too seriously. "Your piano and singing lessons are paying off," he had told me. "You could easily star in a movie, sing the movie song, and boom, your acting and singing careers take off as fast as your stage one."

The thought had been a seed buried deep underneath my other, more relevant thoughts: preparing for my new role as Betty Malone in *Sincerely, Yours* and the fun I was having on my summer off with my best friend and the woman I was very much in love with. I hadn't considered giving that seed a good watering until Peter brought it up. I had a feeling he had his eyes set on Hollywood. He'd talked about his time out there throughout the whole summer, and by the way he talked about LA, I could tell he was eager to go back. I had a feeling if his romance film, *Darlin'*, turned out to be successful, it wouldn't take any convincing to get him back to LA.

"I've never really given it serious thought," I said. "Have you?"

"Are you kidding me?" Will said through a laugh. "This guy has talked nonstop about LA this whole summer."

"What?" Peter said incredulously. "It was a groovy place. It's as bustling as New York, West Hollywood is as gay as Greenwich Village, and the beach vibes are like this but on steroids. The only difference is that it's more laid-back, and you have palm trees as skyscrapers. I know you'd feel the same if you visited."

"I have a feeling you're going to move out there," I said with a bit of disappointment.

I did worry that he would chase the high out there in California. There was something magical hidden in the hills, palms trees, and ocean waves. The more I heard him talk, the more curious I got. I considered flying Elle and I out for a trip just to sightsee, see a brand-new place, escape New York for a bit, but I knew her teaching job wouldn't afford her the time off until the next summer.

Peter shrugged. "I don't know. I've been doing Broadway for seven years. Filming *Darlin'* was a lot of fun. Plus, the city has become a real drag."

I'd grown up thinking Manhattan was untouchable until I moved there, and my career made me untouchable. The land of dreams was dimming right in front of us. After the end of shows, I often worried about the attendees. There was a rule in the city to never cross 42nd Street. Times Square had started filling up with adult shows instead of plays. Urban decay rotted the buildings, dirt filled the sidewalks and streets, and people trying to survive the hard times searched out drugs to ease their pain. The sex workers were always kind to me, and I always said hello and treated them with respect. Others didn't see them in the same light. With Elle starting her new job, I was already worrying about her taking the graffiti-covered and crime-ridden subway home.

But the more I lived in the city and the more the financial crisis turned Manhattan inside out, the more I started wondering if the land of dreams had picked up and moved out, just like the city's former residents.

Maybe the land of dreams was really in LA.

Peter's question must have stuck with Elle because weeks later, as we settled into bed, she rested her head on my shoulder and let out a deep sigh, one I'd learned meant that she was wrestling with some thoughts.

"Mar?" she said softly.

I lowered my script and kissed her temple. "Elle?"

She hesitated.

I tossed the script onto the nightstand and shifted my body to lie parallel with her. I tucked a strand of hair behind her ear. "You have thoughts. I can see them going wild behind your eyes. What are you thinking about in there?"

Another beat of silence before she looked up. "Have you really thought about leaving New York?"

Apparently, I wasn't the only one who'd reflected on Peter's question. I knew that I couldn't do Broadway forever. Not when directors had been calling and begging Glenn to schedule auditions with me ever since *Chicago*. Some of those directors were based in London's West End. If the right opportunity fell into my lap, I would take a gig in London or whatever opportunity that supplied a paycheck that brought Elle and me security. We had grown up knowing what it was like to have nothing. I never wanted to be in a situation where money was a problem again.

To never consider leaving New York in show business was awfully limiting. There would be a job eventually that would require me to get out of the city, and I had wondered what it would look like for Elle and me when I had to fly somewhere for a few months when her job very much rooted her in Manhattan.

"Well," I said, letting out a heavy exhale, knowing this was going to be quite the conversation. "I know that there will be a role eventually that's not in New York. I can't just limit myself to Broadway, you know? Not when there's West End, Hollywood, American tours."

"You'd be gone for a really long time," she said, her voice dropping low. "We haven't been apart since we met."

I grazed her soft cheek, and she melted into it. "I know. It wouldn't be easy, but depending on the job, I could fly back home for a bit. Or if it's in the summer, I could fly you over."

"But what about something permanent in California? Have you thought about that?"

I shrugged. "I don't know. I think, given the state of the city, I'm not fully opposed to moving, depending on the circumstances, and why hold back if there are opportunities?"

She untangled herself from my arm and pulled back to look at me. I knew by the confused expression furrowing her eyebrows that I'd said the wrong thing. "Really?" she said, and I heard the disappointment in her tone.

"Uh...I mean..." I scrambled to find something to say. "The city isn't getting any better. Glenn says the Broadway attendance is dropping rapidly. It might be wise for me to go out to London for a few years or try out a film role or maybe even put out an album. What? Why are you looking at me like that?"

"This is the first time I've ever heard you say this. It sounds like you have a plan."

"It's not a finalized plan, Elle. I haven't given it serious thought, but it wouldn't be smart to limit all my jobs to New York. That doesn't set me up for a successful career—"

"I know that, Marlie. I just...I don't know. It's a big conversation, don't you think?"

"I absolutely agree. But, babe, it's not an issue right now. *Sincerely, Yours* opens in two weeks. I'm not even thinking about what's in store for next season. What about you? I mean, have you thought about leaving?"

"No. I just started my first year of teaching two weeks ago. I'll be there for a while. It might be nice to move to the suburbs. I can commute in—"

It was my turn to pull back. I sat up and squared my body to hers. "The suburbs? Why on Earth would we live in the suburbs?"

She shrugged and looked at her lap. "I don't know. To start a family?"

"A family?"

She gave me an offended look. "What's wrong with a family? You don't want kids?"

"You *want* kids?"

"Of course I want kids. You don't?"

"Of course I don't," I said.

I was light-years away from entertaining a family. I was twenty-two, my career was launching, and my sole focus was that and being with Elle. Opportunities were just starting to fall into my lap. Having a child would stop me from climbing up. Also, my knowledge of families involved either spoiled bratty kids who'd bullied me, traumatized war veterans who'd taken it out on the bottle and their foster kids, or apathetic couples who'd just been desperate for a check. Of course, if I ever decided I wanted to be a mother, I'd strive to be as loving as the McCoys or the Schwartzs, but they were two good couples in a sea of shit. Being a parent was an idea stained from an early age.

"I really want kids," Elle mumbled, sounding ashamed of it.

It was apparent that I'd upset her. She couldn't look me in the eyes for a few minutes after. Instead, she pierced half-moon nail marks on her thumb. I grabbed her picking hand and intertwined my fingers with hers, wanting to take back any hurt I caused.

"It's just that…I don't know. We're only twenty-two," I said and rubbed my thumb over all her indented moons. "I'm not ready. Not at this point in my career where people are actually wanting me. I've never been wanted in my whole life. Not outside of you." I paused, hoping she would chime in with her thoughts. When all she did was stare at our intertwined hands, I continued, "How badly do you want kids?"

"I want a family," she said softly. "I think I have a lot of love to give, love that I had to bottle up when my mother didn't want me, love that was ready to burst open if she ever came back for me. And she didn't, and that kind of rejection made me want to be more of a mother. I want to be the mother that mine wasn't."

A pang rippled through my chest hearing how set she was on wanting a family, something I'd never be able to give her. "If you want kids, then…who do you want them with?"

"With you, Marlie."

"Elle, we're not even allowed to be together. If people knew about us, it would jeopardize our jobs. Hell, we could get kicked out of this beautiful house. You will lose your job. I'd be blacklisted everywhere."

"I know that," she said, her tone rising with defense.

"The world doesn't want us to be a family. We're not supposed to be together. On top of that, can you even adopt as a single parent?"

"I…I don't know, okay?" She swiped her eyes. It sent a pain through my gut. "All I know is that I want to have a family someday… down the road…be a mom, and I know society hates single mothers and gay people. I know they hate us. But maybe things will change. I mean, when we were younger, did you ever imagine going to gay bars every weekend, holding hands and making out in the corner? Absolutely not, especially after Stonewall. And now look around, we're surrounded by a whole community in the Village."

"What happens if things don't change? I have a better chance of changing my mind about kids than society allowing two lesbians to raise a child."

"I'm not a lesbian. I like men too."

I'd almost forgotten about that Robert guy from Howard Johnson's. He was so long ago, and Elle and I were so in love, that the knowledge of her attraction to men had faded in my mind as much as Robert had. But the reminder formed a new worry in me: I'd never be able to give her a child. If anything, I'd hinder her dream of being a mother and starting a family.

I cleared my eyes from the dangling tears. I felt defeated. If society wouldn't let us be our own versions of June and Ward Cleaver, then I had no idea how I'd help Elle fulfill being a mother.

"I can't give you a baby, Elle," I said, feeling like the conversation threw us both into a brick wall. "Unless society changes on multiple levels in the next ten years, then I'm nothing but a hurdle for you."

"What? That's not true—"

"It is. They won't let you adopt, not without a husband and definitely not with me."

"You're right." She reached for my hands, and it was then I realized they were as shaky as her voice. "We don't have to worry about it yet, okay?"

My heart fell into my stomach at how much we both clung to that bit of hope.

But honestly, after that conversation, I was terrified. It ran through me like an undertow. The months continued, and while we never broached the subject of kids again, for the first time in our three-and-a-half-year relationship, I felt the divide. It started as a little paper cut with the conversation, and it slowly started splitting open in the fall and winter.

I often think back on our Southampton summer. I think about how free and how in love all four of us were. It was the happiest I'd ever seen Peter, and it was the happiest he'd ever seen me. If our young and free years in New York were a book, it would have ended with that Southampton summer and a happily ever after.

Life's not a book I can just pull off a bookshelf though. It's a library containing all the eras of my life, and the thing is, when I'm living through them, I have no idea when an era ends and when another starts. The in-betweens just sort of blur together.

My era of being young and in love in the land of dreams ended with that Southampton summer.

❖

The summer of 1977 was the opposite of that happy summer.

I played Grace Farrell in *Annie*, and Hollywood was begging for me to reprise my role as Betty Malone in the movie adaptation of *Sincerely, Yours*. I felt so torn between saying yes to an opportunity that would expose me to a whole other world and choosing to stay stagnant in my Broadway world but keeping my love life intact.

While I was afraid of how my choice would impact my relationship with Elle, I had to be a rock for Peter. He and Will had broken up, and it crushed me almost as much as it crushed him. He sobbed on my shoulder, and I wondered how all the love Peter and Will had for each other had found a way to fizzle and end. I watched him skate through the days without Will, numbing his heartbreak by drinking and dancing the pain away at gay bars.

As my best friend wilted away, so did our city. The subway was a hub for crime, lurid graffiti colored the buildings like the skyline sparkled against the night, and the city feared that the serial killer, the Son of Sam, would strike again. It became impossible not to think about moving just so Elle and I didn't have to worry about stepping outside.

The longer I waited for my city to revert back to the place it once was, the more I grew to dislike it. I was tired of the violence, the dirt, the grit that offered not a unique ambience but one that warned of the decay of buildings and humanity. I was tired of constantly worrying about Elle, Peter, and the people who attended the shows every night.

And when the '77 blackout happened, twenty-five hours was all it took for me to make a final decision about my time in New York.

I was on the Alvin Theatre stage when thick darkness draped the theater like curtains. The audience gasped and chattered while we waited for the backup generators to kick on. Ultimately, the *Annie* show that night was forced to stop, something I had never seen.

Once we were told to go home, I stepped outside in that thick, hot July humidity that had clung to the air the past couple of days. A heat wave had swept through the city, causing temperatures to reach near a hundred degrees. Silhouettes ran around the streets and in and out of buildings. I heard yelling, commotion, and glass breaking. That was when I felt something unsettling in my gut, and after learning to trust my gut at the Chapmans all those years ago,

I quickly hailed a cab and clung to the coat hanger inside the car as the driver weaved around pedestrians freely roaming the streets.

Some good Samaritans tried directing traffic in the midst of the accumulating chaos. I feared that my bad gut feeling had to do with the Son of Sam using the blackout to strike again or that the sudden darkness would erupt in even more crime. My breath was shallow until I walked inside my home to find Peter and Elle on the couch listening to the battery powered radio on the coffee table. Candles flickered around in the living room, more candles than I thought we owned. Both Peter and Elle fanned themselves with magazines.

I sat on the couch and palmed Elle's face. "Are you okay?" And planted a kiss on her lips.

"I'm fine. Even better when this guy showed up." She hooked a thumb at Peter.

"How did you get down here so fast?" I asked.

"Magic," he said, wiggling his fingers.

"He saw a woman get mugged," Elle said.

"You did?"

"Three men cornered her and snatched her purse. It's crazy out there, Mar. I wasn't about to have you two by yourselves. I also didn't want to be by myself, either. So I came over with candles."

That explained all the light. "Where are the generators?" I asked.

"I don't know. They said it could be several hours," Elle said and gestured to the radio.

We curled into each other and listened to the radio all night. The only lights outside were flashing red and blue ones, sirens wailing so often that I could only fill in the blanks and picture what my gut had told me when I'd left the Alvin Theatre. I locked the doors, put a kitchen chair underneath the handle for added measure, and kept the baseball bat within reach.

Peter rested his head on my shoulder while the radio played "Lost Without Your Love" by Bread in between broadcasting updates about the outage. During the song, we sat in silence, huddled on the couch, alternating glances between the flickering candles and the darkness outside with the occasional swirling red and blue lights rushing down the street.

We weren't aware of the looting, arson, and crime that had happened in Brooklyn until the next morning when *The New York Times* and the radio told the tales.

That was the night I fell out of love with New York City. It had been my home for twenty-three years, the only city I'd ever known. But over the years, for many people, the land of dreams had turned into a place littered with broken promises. Even though the dream hadn't failed me, I willed for New York to flicker with hope and life again for all those people who had lost so much. I'd been waiting for years only to watch it shrivel away. It was time to spread my wings.

"I want to accept the role," I said the night after the blackout. I couldn't even look Elle in the eye. Instead, I focused on my plate, pushing the peas around with my fork.

"What?" I heard her deflate. It was so loud that it pulled my gaze up to see the disappointment contorting her beautiful features.

"I can't refuse this role. The pay is enough for us to buy a home, not just rent one. We can have a permanent house, something neither of us have had. We'll be able to move out to the suburbs. Hell, we can move anywhere in the world after this movie."

"Marlie, I just finished my first year. I worked hard to get that job, and I love it."

"I know, but you can get a teaching job anywhere."

"Not when school starts in three months. What? Am I not supposed to work for a whole school year?"

"No. I go film this movie, and then maybe after this upcoming year ends, you can look for jobs out in LA," I said and grabbed her hands, trying to persuade her with a tight squeeze. "Elle, love, please come to California with me. Think of how wonderful it would be. Palm trees, warm weather, an ocean. You can read and journal on the beach whenever you want or outside on the beautiful patio I promise we'll have. I'll make sure you'll have the most perfect reading spot."

"I'm lucky I even have a job given this recession, and California isn't doing that great, either. I don't feel comfortable giving up a secure position. My opportunities aren't as abundant as yours right now." She let go of my hands, and it felt like a puncture to the heart. "You got your start when we moved to Manhattan. I'm just getting mine, and I have a right to see it through. I've worked hard too, you know."

"I know you have."

She set her knife and fork on the counter, and the rattling startled me. She buried her face in her hands, let out a heavy exhale, and ran her hands through her hair. Before she could even speak, seeing how distraught she looked warned me of what was happening. She must have seen the sliver in our relationship rapidly expanding the longer the silence overtook the kitchen.

"Maybe this is just what we need," she said so softly that I wondered at first if she was even sure of what she was saying. "We have no idea who we are on our own. Since we were fifteen, we haven't left each other's side. Hollywood is pulling you over there, and my job is rooting me here. I feel like you've been slowly pulled to the West Coast since the end of last summer."

That was when I knew it was the end of us. My chest tore in two, and I had no control of the amount of moisture on my face. The amount of pain I felt was probably what I should have felt while going through the foster system. It was one thing being rejected by people I had zero connection to, zero love for, but when Elle, my whole world, figured out it was best for us to stop orbiting each other, a crater formed in the middle of my heart. Elle was right. We'd clung so tightly to each other over the last eight years that we didn't have any identity outside of each other. I couldn't see our lack of identity until it finally hit me that New York called for Elle to stay as much as LA was calling me.

And we both knew that staying together wouldn't give her the life she wanted: being a mother.

"This is it, isn't it." I sobbed, barely able to hear when one word ended and the other started. "You're ending things?" The moment I'd met Elle, my life had started. I hadn't known life without her.

"Instead of fighting it, I think we just need to let it happen," she said with a crack in her voice. "If it isn't this role, it's going to be another, and I'm not going to be the reason you don't go after your dream."

I swatted at my eyes. "Just like I don't want to be the reason you don't go after yours." I'd struggled with the decision to move to Hollywood for years. I always wondered, if I stayed in New York, what would have happened to us?

It didn't matter which decision I made. Each one came with their own collection of what-ifs.

I was young, naive, and desperate to cling to my growing success. I grew up watching others live with success and was so jealous of all the things I didn't have. I couldn't turn down the paycheck I'd spent my entire childhood dreaming about.

So Peter and I packed up our belongings and moved to LA. As we unpacked in our rented bungalow in Laurel Canyon, I couldn't believe that it had taken just one dark night to break apart my four-year relationship with Elle.

There Peter and I were in the new land of dreams, completely heartbroken.

I don't even need to think about what to keep or erase. I tell Dr. Pierson to erase being with Elle, being in love, our Southampton summer, and the blackout. While keeping *Chicago*, the *Sincerely, Yours* movie and other productions, and the memories of Peter. The best memories are the biggest ghosts, and I'm tired of being haunted. I'm ready to let go of the years my brain defaults to. It hurts too much.

CHAPTER NINE

The morning after, I wake with a piercing headache, as if I tossed back a bottle of cheap wine all by myself. I fumble through the medicine drawer in my nightstand to relieve it. I know the more I erase, the more substantial the headache. I have no idea what I told Dr. Pierson to erase yesterday, but the headache clues me in that it must have been something significant for it to hurt this much.

God, I must have erased whole years from my memory. I run through my life again, question the milestones for each age, and then I come across a surprise cliff that plunges into a giant hole.

What the hell happened in my early twenties? I can see an outline of it, like a new coloring book, but those pictures don't come alive without color and detail, and that's what I'm missing.

Stop thinking about it. You're not supposed to dwell on it.

I try to sleep off my headache and confusion until my fourth session on Thursday. However, even with the nagging headache that never quite left—even after Excedrin—I upheld my promise to Kristina and looked over the *Hello, Dolly!* script. I'm glad she forced me because after reading it once, I'm almost ready to rip the Band-Aid off and tell her that I'm sold on auditioning. It's a perfect role for my comeback.

I look at my phone to check Kristina's ETA to see if I have a chance to write my manager, Helen, an email about my interest. But right after I see Kristina's text that she's fifteen minutes away, my stomach drops when I see that I have one missed call and one voice mail from Nathan.

Why the hell is he calling?

My mind goes to the worst-case scenario: something happened to him or Elle. Panic snakes around my sternum, and I worry that if I wait too long, the incessant wondering will choke me. I play the voice mail.

"Hey, it's…um…it's Nathan. Just calling to check in to see how you're doing. I know it's been a while but, well, I have some exciting news to share. Call me back when you get the chance. I…I miss you, Marlie. I hope everything is well over there. I've been thinking about you a lot. It would be nice to catch up so, um, yeah, please call me back when you have time. I'll talk to you later."

The message ends, and my phone feels like a brick in my grip. Just hearing his voice again sends my heart to beat in erratic patterns of sadness and nervousness. I replay the message, and after the sixth time, I'm finally able to mute my anxiety, and I hear what seems to be hope in his voice. He doesn't sound as upset as he has in the past. He sounds a little nervous, a little eager, and a little defeated. Hearing him again without the sharpness of anger fills me with hope that maybe he's ready to forgive me.

It's been a year and a half since his wedding, which unexpectedly caused the final break in my relationship with Elle and the first tear in my relationship with Nathan. I've only spoken to him a couple of times since then, but most of the time, the calls or texts ended in an argument about what happened at his wedding. I haven't seen him at all since, and every day that progresses without our once sturdy relationship is another day with a weight added on my chest.

They say time heals all wounds. It was a motto I used to live by when I had bumps thrown my way, but at sixty-two, I'm still waiting for many of those wounds to heal. Even though it's been a year and a half, it's still as fresh as it was back then.

If time healed all wounds, Dr. Pierson and the Farrow Neurological Institute of Malibu wouldn't be in business.

I don't have time to call him back before my fourth session. "Well, Nathan just left me a voice mail," I say as I strap into Kristina's passenger seat.

She hands me my to-go coffee. She seems as surprised as I am. "What did he say?"

I sip cautiously. "He wants to catch up. Says he has some news."

"What kind of news?"

"I don't know, but he didn't sound angry, so that's a good sign that I'll be clinging to."

She backs out of the driveway and starts toward the gated entrance. "You should call him back after your appointment."

"I will. I'm just, well, I'm nervous. We haven't had a good conversation since before the wedding."

"I know, but if he doesn't sound upset, maybe he's ready to put it behind him. A year and a half is a long time."

"I know." I take another long sip. "If I call him, I'll have to tell him about the procedure. I know I need to tell him but…I want to hear his news. I want to have a conversation that doesn't end with him bringing up his wedding."

"The longer you wait—"

"I know. I just…I really need to think about the right time."

"You can tell him about the procedure when it's the right time, but you need to call him back. You don't want to do something you'll regret again."

I run through all the possible reasons why he may have called. Maybe he and his wife, Melissa, are moving to California. Maybe Elle said something to him about wanting to make amends. Maybe he's finally forgiven me, and we can move forward together.

I miss him terribly. But I have no other choice but to put him on hold the second Dr. Wilson puts the helmet on me.

"Okay, Ms. Rose. Should we pick up when you moved out to LA?" Dr. Pierson says.

"Which time?" I ask. "I moved to LA twice."

"The first time. With Peter. How long were you out there?"

"I only spent seven months there. Then, I moved to London for a couple of years." I close my eyes and let the memories fill my mind.

❖

I didn't return to New York City until 1982.

In those five years, so much happened, and at the same time, it felt like nothing really had.

I lived with Peter in Laurel Canyon for seven months, from September of 1978 to February 1979 while filming the *Sincerely, Yours* movie. Peter spent the time trying to mend his broken heart. I was just as sad as he was, though I don't remember why now. All I know is that we both numbed our sadness with some strong weed and people to distract us. For me, that was singer-songwriter, Diane Tyler, and I'm almost certain her song, "Canyon Nights" was about me.

In April of 1979, I reprised my role as Roxie Hart in the London's West End production of *Chicago*. I became friendly with British actress, Elaine Prescott. We dated for a few months while I was in London, used each other to fill the void, but ultimately, it resulted in nothing substantial.

While my love life hit a rut, numbed with secret casual affairs, my career soared in the exact way I had hoped. *Sincerely, Yours* landed me my first Oscar and Grammy nominations, and I was astonished when I won both.

Peter was my date to both the Grammys and the Oscars in 1980, which the media loved. The movie introduced me to the world, not just a niche audience of Broadway enthusiasts. Suddenly, I was a target for flashing paparazzi cameras, people yelled my name, and the world wondered if Peter Arlo and I were dating. He was the young attractive star of *Darlin'* and current Tony in Broadway's revival of *West Side Story*, and I was the star of one of the biggest movies of 1980.

Peter and I exchanged a look after a paparazzo asked. We didn't respond, but Peter did tighten his grip around my waist as we smiled for the cameras.

While walking down the Grammy red carpet, I had a feeling that maybe there was a chance we could win. I'd met singer-songwriter, Joseph Bennett, during my short stay in Laurel Canyon. He was the lead singer of Bennett and Sons, and together, we'd written a song one night around a firepit, Joe on his Hummingbird acoustic guitar, me sitting across from him, improvising lyrics based on an entire conversation I'd had with him about the movie.

The song "Forever Yours" became the movie's original song, and since Bennett and Sons were still at the peak of their career, I had a feeling their talents would help us win the Grammy.

And it did.

Two months later, in April of 1980, was the 52nd Academy Awards. It was daunting to be on the red carpet in the midst of all the A-List Hollywood stars. Dustin Hoffman. Al Pacino. Meryl Streep. Bette Midler. Jane Fonda. I didn't feel like I belonged. I was only a twenty-six-year-old with one film under her belt, but as the night progressed, and those stars, who I had always admired, approached me to tell me how much they loved me in *Sincerely, Yours*, I swatted those thoughts away and allowed myself to fully take in how magical the night felt. The last three years had been hard, trying to find my footing with Peter in LA, to moving to London all by myself without my best friend by my side. For the first time in my career, I was incredibly lonely. No matter how many times Peter came to visit, anytime he left, he took a little part of me back with him.

But that night, it was like those broken fragments of my life started shifting closer into place.

"I can feel it in my bones, Mar," Peter whispered to me right before the Best Actress category.

I didn't believe his optimism until they announced my name, and somehow, I made it onstage with an Oscar that was so much heavier than I had imagined. I had a speech prepared just in case, but when I looked out at the audience and spotted all the TV cameras, I thought of all the people who'd come and gone in my life. The McCoys. The Schwartzs. Mrs. Hansen. Mr. Morsey. My old friend Elle. I'm not quite sure why she took up so much space in my head while giving my speech. I don't think I'd seen her in about eight years, though now, I'm having a really hard time figuring out how. I hate that I don't remember what happened and why we stopped talking.

All I know is that for whatever reason, while celebrating my Oscar and Grammy wins with Peter was one of the many highlights, part of me latched on to my childhood best friend, Eleanor Olson, and how I would have felt complete if she was celebrating with us.

After the Grammys and Oscars, directors were calling Glenn left and right, begging me to be in their musicals. But when one of those begging directors wanted me to play Maria in the West End revival of *The Sound of Music* in 1981, I ignored all the other scripts. The musical that planted the seed of my Broadway dreams had finally landed in my lap.

"I always told you that you were a Maria," Glenn said on the other end of the phone after telling me I got the part.

Peter surprised me by flying into London for the opening show, and knowing my best friend was in the audience supporting me helped erase the loneliness from being in a city by myself, playing a role I couldn't ever fathom playing. Knowing he was in the audience helped my diaphragm belt out the confidence during the title song, filling the entire Apollo Victoria Theatre. Opening night, we performed with a hundred and one percent seating capacity, setting the highest attendance figure for a single week of any British musical production in history.

But what brought me back to Broadway was a script the director was desperate for me to accept: Broadway's production of *Cats*. The musical had been a huge success in London in 1981. I'd seen the original production on one of my night's off, and I'd absolutely loved it. The music was captivating. I knew instantly that I wanted to play the role of Grizabella.

After five years of avoiding my old home, I flew back to the concrete jungle.

❖

Five years is enough time to completely change a person, and it's enough to change a city and the entire world.

When I returned to New York in July 1982, the city was recovering from its most violent year, and the "gay cancer" affecting gay men all over the world for the last year finally had a name.

AIDS.

"Aren't you worried at all?" I asked Peter after he spent the day unpacking my belongings in my new brownstone apartment in Greenwich Village. I handed him a glass of well-deserved wine for doing most—if not all—of the heavy lifting.

"No, not really," he said, taking a casual sip.

"You're not worried at all?"

"Smoking causes cancer. There are thousands of cases of that a year, and there are, what? Almost five hundred cases total? Two hundred something in the city?"

"Yeah, I know but—"

"More people have syphilis than whatever this is."

There wasn't any quiver in his tone that was remotely fearful. It made me stop and think. Maybe he was right. Maybe this was another article that was more of an attention-grabbing headline than anything else.

"Yeah, maybe you're right," I said, shook my head, and drank my wine.

"On a lighter note, have you contacted Elle?"

I'm not really sure why he asked. I hadn't seen Elle in almost ten years. "No."

He pulled his face back as if surprised. "No? Why?"

"Have you contacted Will?"

"What? No?"

"See, there you go."

Now that I'm remembering, Peter responded with, "You and Elle had something, though."

I don't remember what that something was. God, I wish that I did because I'd crushed on Elle all throughout my later adolescent years. While I was in LA and London, I occasionally wrote her a few letters, though I'm confused as to why when we hadn't spoken since 1973. I must have erased something, but I have no idea why I would ever want to erase something of my early years with Elle.

But as time went on, those sparse letters disappeared into empty mailboxes. I hadn't heard from her since I'd won my Oscar two years before.

"So did you and Will," I added.

"But we haven't spoken in five years since we broke up. That ship has sailed." I could see the residual pain still flickering in his eyes. Almost as if he felt what I saw, he tapped my knee. "Hey, you want to know what we need to do? Go out. It's been a minute. Celebrate the fact we're back in New York."

We'd gone out in LA those seven months we'd lived together, and we'd done the same whenever he'd visited in London. It fed into the dating rumors swirling around us that we laughed about. But neither of us cared, especially as the AIDS epidemic swept through the world, and the hate toward the gay community was so strong and powerful, it broke through our little bubble in Greenwich Village and all of New York City. Leaning into the rumors about us being involved diverted any suspicion of us being gay.

Being reunited back in the city where it all started, we enjoyed stumbling drunk on margaritas down Christopher Street with our arms locked. We met up with Peter's friend, Craig Carpenter, and sang karaoke. Craig ushered random people on the street to come inside to "see Tony winner, Peter Arlo, and Oscar and Grammy winner, Marlie Rose, up close and personal."

The bar filled with a decent crowd, all packed into the basement, shoulder to shoulder. As natural performers, Peter and I fully enjoyed the scene unfolding in front of us. We knew exactly what to do with a crowd popping in to get a free show. So we turned that basement into our stage, getting everyone to sing along, and when the two of us sang a duet of "New York, New York," even the bartenders joined in.

We signed autographs for anyone who had a pen. We signed napkins, arms, chests, and I was a little envious of Peter when a woman handed him a permanent marker and asked him to sign her breasts. Poor thing had no idea that she was several worlds away from being his type. Peter Arlo was an attractive man, appealing to the masses.

At the end of the night, Peter, Craig, and I trotted down Christopher Street at three a.m. when Peter stopped walking, clasped my face, and gave me a peck on the lips. "I love you, Marlie Rose, you know that?"

I laughed and wiped his tequila-soaked kiss off my lips. "Peter Arlo, I didn't know you were into me like that. You're going to keep fueling those dating rumors."

"I swear, Marlene Rose Hatcher, if I had a single straight bone in my body, I'd be your guy."

"And I'm sure, Peter James Marotto, if I had a straight bone in my body, I'd gladly be your wife."

"Really?" he said, either very drunkenly or humbly. I feel like it was both.

I kissed his cheek. "Really."

"And I'm just glad to call both of you my friends," Craig said and put an arm around both our shoulders.

I can't tell you if it was one of the best nights of my life because I had my best friend beside me, drinking, singing, and spontaneously performing for all the patrons of those packed karaoke bars; or if it was the fact that it was one of the last nights where some sort of innocence trailed behind us like a gentle wind. Because six months later, Craig Carpenter became the first person we knew who died of AIDS.

And two weeks later, days after the beginning of 1983, Broadway lost Rick Higgins, my Broadway *Chicago* director.

It wasn't just something we read about in the papers anymore. When we lost Craig and Rick Higgins, AIDS popped our little bubble that we'd found comfort in during the seventies. Peter's once cavalier thoughts about the virus turned into an everyday worry that haunted him, our city, the world, and our gay community. It took six months for us to lose Craig, and those gay bars we once found solace in started getting quieter, and the crowds started to thin.

I couldn't help but wonder how many more people were going to get sick and die.

"You better promise me that you'll be safe," I said as we left the church where Craig's funeral was held.

Peter looked over at me. The usual warmth in his eyes had been drained, and fear took over and saturated his stare. "I promise, Marlie."

❖

I didn't muster the courage to call Elle until a month after I moved back. I stared outside at the brownstones lining the street, sipping a glass of pinot noir and feeling her absence swell in my chest. As much as I wanted to hear her voice on the other end of the phone, I was afraid that the significant amount of time would cause tension. The worry gave me time to stall, pour myself another glass, and after the first encouraging sip, I snatched the phone book, plopped back on my couch, and searched the O's. Once I found her name, my heart felt like a bleeding marker staining my chest once again.

I stared at the number for what felt like twenty minutes. My sips of wine turned into gulps until it loosened the knots of anxiety enough for me to pick up the phone. The clicks from the rotary were their own time marker, counting down until I heard a, "Hello" on the other end.

My heart plummeted at the sound of her voice.

I covered the phone to clear my throat. I should have been more prepared. I should have rehearsed what I was going to say, as if this was my audition back into Elle's life. It had been so long, I had wondered if my memory of her voice matched what it actually sounded like, and with just one word, I had my answer. I was amazed that what I remembered of her beautiful voice fit perfectly.

"Hi? Elle?"

There was a loud silence on the other end that might have only lasted for a second or two, but it felt like a minute. "Marlie? Is that you?"

Her soft voice filled my ears, and the way she delicately said my name overtook the nerves that had once fluttered behind my ribcage. I sank into my spot, rested my head against the top of the couch, and closed my eyes. As each second passed of me desperately searching for my words, tears threatened my eyes. We had once been joined at the hip. She used to be my rock. There once was a time I'd shared every part of my day with her, even the boring things, and there I was on the other end of the phone, and the boring parts of my speech weren't good enough to be shared.

And now as I'm recalling it, I have no idea why the hell we were separated for all that time to begin with. But she recognized my voice after only one word, and I clung to the hope that it meant something. "Hi, yeah, it's me. It's Marlie. I, um, how are you?" My heart pounded so hard and loud, I thought it would flop onto my lap next to the phone.

"I'm good. I'm...I can't believe it's you." Her tone wasn't agitated or angry. It wasn't heartbroken or deflated. She sounded confused, grateful, and nervous, all emotions that could either swing toward assuring me I'd made the right decision by calling her or that it was a terrible idea.

But I continued, just wanting to keep her voice filtering through my ears. "I know. It's been a while." Another heavy silence. "I'm back in New York."

"You are?"

"I am. Well, for a bit. Obviously, I don't know how long, but I have a role in *Cats*. It opens in October, so I'm here for the next couple of months."

The hesitation on her end caused my pulse to quicken. "I see you've been doing well," she said. "You have an Oscar, a Grammy, and apparently, a boyfriend named Peter Arlo?"

I laughed, and once I did, I heard the faintest giggle from her. I wanted to tell her that while I was proud of myself for winning those awards, their impact didn't shape me like I'd thought they would. I didn't feel any different. I still felt the same, and sitting on that couch in New York, I felt incredibly lonely.

Awards are just statues if you don't have anyone to share them with, and God, they would have been so much more powerful if Elle had been in my life to celebrate with me.

I couldn't say that, though. I couldn't dump all my emotions on my childhood best friend who I hadn't spoken to in years. "I do, though my love affair with Peter took us both by surprise," I said jokingly.

"I bet it did. Sounds like you made the right choice going to LA."

Somehow, she knew about my moving to LA, and for whatever reason, she wasn't able to truly disguise her disapproval. Underneath her teasing, I could feel the jagged edges of her comment that pricked along my skin.

"Apparently," I said flatly and then cleared my throat, desperate for a shift to put us back to lighthearted joking and not the bitterness that apparently still lingered in both of us. "I, um, well…since I'm back in town for a bit, I was kind of wondering if maybe you'd be interested in grabbing dinner sometime? It would be nice to catch up."

I heard commotion on the other end of the phone. I couldn't quite make out what it was. It sounded like there was someone else with her.

"Dinner? Yeah, um, that might be complicated, but I can try to arrange something."

"Is there anything I can do to make it easier? I see in the book that you're in the East Village now." I didn't necessarily like the thought of Elle living in the East Village. I'd heard it had really succumbed to the city's economic crisis.

"I am, yes."

"I don't have a problem coming to you. Dinner doesn't have to be anything fancy. I…well…it would just be nice to see you."

"Do you mind coming here? I'm a bit tied up at the moment. There's actually something I'd really like to talk to you about."

My heart sputtered at all the different possibilities. Anger still hadn't cracked through her tone, which meant that whatever she wanted to talk about didn't include firing off all the things she had wanted to say to me since…whatever the hell had happened between us.

"I'll do whatever is easiest for you, Elle."

A week later, I took a cab to the East Village. The farther from the Upper West Side we drove, the more guilt sank in my stomach. While I'd gained an Oscar, a Grammy, and accumulated more wealth, Elle must have had no other choice but to move out of our Whitby apartment and into a neighborhood that had been hit hard by the financial crisis. It was a gritty, graffiti-strewn place with what seemed to be as many broken windows as people outside.

After I stepped out of the cab, I found a crack vial on the short walk to Elle's building. Hers was one of the few untouched by graffiti, but it was still worn, and the tumultuous decade had stained the bricks much like it had the rest of the neighborhood.

I exhaled a deep breath, and once she buzzed me inside, I ascended creaking steps, feeling my heart grow heavier with each one. I collected my breath once I made it to a second floor that smelled like a mixture of sautéed onions and tobacco smoke.

I knocked and held my breath until she opened the door slightly, and the beautiful woman I'd spent years admiring in secret stood before me. Her hair was up in a side ponytail with a scrunchie, her once long feathered hair now in tight spirals.

Right as her unrelenting beauty tugged at my chest, she grinned, fully opened the door, and that was when I noticed the toddler in her arms. Any trace of a smile that might have curved my lips faded as I took in the child who looked to be about two years old and with the same sandy blond hair, hazel eyes, and sweet face as Elle.

"Marlie, hi," Elle said.

Apparently, whatever had happened between us, she still found a way to give me a hint of a smile, as if she was happy to see me. Her voice was laced with what sounded like nerves and apprehension, mirroring all the emotions coiling inside my stomach.

However, I couldn't respond. I was too focused on her look-alike toddler as she bounced him in her arms.

She looked at him, planted a kiss on his cheeks, and then said to me, "I want you to meet Nathan."

CHAPTER TEN

"Um." I didn't mean for my utter shock to slip out as an audible noise, but apparently, it did because Elle shot me her furrowed brows, as if questioning if I'd meant to be rude. Just what other noise did she expect with a surprise baby in her arms?

Like the performer I was, I got into character and pretended like I was enthralled with meeting Elle's secret baby. "Hi, Nathan," I said, using the high-pitched voice that all women used when talking to a human under the age of two.

"Hi," Nathan cooed.

I'd never been around babies or toddlers and hadn't expected a full word to come out of his mouth.

"Marlie," Elle said flatly, and when I looked, she gave me a stern eye, as if she didn't believe the act. "Come in. We should talk."

We absolutely needed to talk.

Her apartment was small and cluttered with wooden building blocks scattered like autumn leaves, Fisher-Price trucks and trains, and a Cookie Monster stuffed animal on top of the coffee table. As if seeing a toddler in her arms wasn't enough, seeing her apartment fully engulfed in toys sped up the realization that Eleanor Olson was a mother.

The Whitby apartment we'd once shared together had been downgraded to an even smaller place. She had a front row view of a graffiti-covered building across the alley outside the living room window. I took stock of how everything had changed for her since I'd left, and I couldn't help but feel all the responsibility stacking on my shoulders about how little she'd had to work with while I'd gained even more.

"Do you want anything to drink? I have water, cranberry juice, Fresca—" She held up a can, and my taste buds revolted against the grapefruit flavor. Grapefruit is the devil in fruit form.

I raised my hand. "Anything but grapefruit. I've sworn it off for the rest of my existence, but thank you. I'm okay for now."

She opened the Fresca with one hand and came back to the couch. She took a seat on the sofa, swapped her Fresca can with Cookie Monster, and handed him to Nathan, who put the top of his head in his mouth.

Elle raked her gaze down my body before flitting back up. It lit my body up, as if she had run her fingertips all over me. "You look really great."

"Tell that to Glenn. He monitored my fish and chips intake while I was in London."

"So you're off your grapefruit diet?"

I sat in the lounge chair across from the couch. "Yes, I told Glenn if he forces me to eat another grapefruit, I will regurgitate it on his nicely polished shoes."

Elle let out a little laugh. "Charming, Marlie."

I shrugged. "It's the truth. But now Glenn is all about SlimFast and this Beverly Hills Diet."

"Well, Glenn can shove it somewhere."

"I told him the same thing before inhaling a glorious basket of fish and chips."

She smiled and bounced Nathan. He must have already developed the sense of stranger danger by how his eye contact on me was unwavering.

"So," Elle said and nodded at Nathan "I have a pretty big life update."

"You had a baby."

She met my eyes and gave me a soft smile, one that looked grateful at the same time it told me how she was nervous to talk about it. I wondered if the apprehension was the reason the smile didn't quite reach her eyes. "I did."

"How?"

Elle's face pulled back. I didn't blame her. I had so many questions spiraling in my head that I snatched one flying around like dollar bills in a money booth. By her reaction, it was apparent I didn't hide my confusion well. I really wish I had because I think back to that night often, and every time I recount it, pain ripples through my stomach. I was young: a twenty-eight-year-old who came of age with Eleanor Olson inflating her chest with each passing minute we had spent together. I had longed to kiss her and to have my body wrapped up in her arms. Now, she was a mother, and I was nowhere near wanting to have children. I didn't want to be a mother. I didn't want to sacrifice my time and my dreams to take care of a human being greater than myself.

"How?" Elle said, seeming just as surprised as me that it was the first question I asked. "Do I need to tell you the story about the birds and the bees?"

"No, I know how babies are made. I just…I wasn't expecting this. Who's the father? Don't tell me it's Robert from Howard Johnson's."

She let out a quick hollow laugh. "No, Nathan's father isn't in the picture, as you can see. But it's okay because we don't need him, right, baby?" She planted a kiss on his cheek.

"How old is he?"

"He's two and a half."

I did the math in my head. Nathan was born in January of 1980, meaning she'd had a thing with a mysterious asshole in the spring of 1979 while I was playing Roxie Hart in London.

I imagined myself clocking some faceless guy in the groin.

"Do you want to hold him?"

I said yes only because I didn't have it in me to tell her no.

Babies were as foreign to me as aliens. I didn't know how to hold one or what to do with them. I held him awkwardly with my hands under his armpits. I had never held a baby before, and it was like he knew because he gave me the same skeptical look I'm sure I gave him. He faced Elle and let out a loud cry. I extended him to her, and she scooped him up, bounced him, and he simmered down.

"He hates me," I said.

"That's because it's his bedtime. I'm going to put him down, and I'll be back out shortly. Does that sound okay?"

"Sure. Take your time."

I needed all the time I could get to process the fact that Elle had a baby. I needed the time to take in how much of my leaving New York had affected her. I had no idea what had happened, but she shouldn't have been living in an outdated apartment barely big enough for herself, let alone herself and a toddler. I wanted to help her. Clearly, I was the reason she was living in the East Village where rent was significantly cheaper.

She came back out twenty minutes later, and I still had so much to sift through in my head. She took a seat back on the couch and forced a smile.

"So how's everything with you?"

She let out a long exhale, and I could feel how tired she was from across the living room. "Good. I'm still working at the high school."

"Who watches Nathan when you're at work?"

"I have a teacher friend who is kind enough to help me out. She had her daughter around the same time I had Nathan, and she's a housewife now and offered to watch him while I work. I don't know what I'd do without Lauren. Obviously, I can't afford to work part time, and childcare—"

"Is expensive," I said.

"Yes. Also, really judgmental too. The looks I got when I toured a few places and they found out I was a single parent…" She shook her head and looked at Cookie Monster lying next to her. "I think I almost understand it now. How hard it was for my mom. Being a single mother. Having people look at me differently. I think I finally understand how all that judgment got to her."

A handful of solutions swept through my mind. "Can I help?"

She looked at me with furrowed brows. "What? No, Marlie—"

"Please?"

"It's not your responsibility to take care of me."

"I know, but I want to be there for you. I can make sure you two don't struggle. Don't you want that? Not having to worry about money? I can get you a proper nanny. I can help you move to a better spot in the city. I can help you with rent, or you're more than welcome to stay with me. I have two extra rooms. You and Nathan can have your own—"

Elle frowned. "You're really offering to pay my rent?"

"Yes, of course. I have plenty of space for the two of you."

"I don't need space to make me happy, and I don't think having a toddler in your house is going to make you happy. You made it very clear that you didn't want children."

While I don't remember having a conversation with her about having kids, she wasn't necessarily wrong. Back then, I was too selfish in pursuing my dreams to think about anything outside my career. At twenty-eight, I had no intention of being a mother.

However, I loved Elle, and it made my heart break to see her struggling through life again...with a toddler. Why sit back and do nothing when I was afforded with resources to help her and Nathan?

I could see the worry sparkling in her eyes as she started to empathize with her mother, and given the last conversation I remember having with her about her mother right before we'd moved to Manhattan, it must have taken a lot of worry, anxiety, and sleepless nights to get her to that point of empathy. I didn't want her to struggle like her mother had, I didn't want Nathan to struggle like Elle or me, and the only way for me to change that was to help, and I was more than happy to do it.

"I can help alleviate the financial burden of being a single mother. Please consider it. You're not going to be as much of a burden as you're probably thinking you are."

"Marlie, I'm sorry, but it's been years. We went from sending each other an occasional letter to hardly any communication at all, and suddenly, you turn up in New York again asking me and my son to move in with you?"

When she painted it like that, yes, it sounded like a wild plan, but my heart thought differently. "I know it sounds a bit wild," I said.

"Why do you care so much?"

Her question hit me right in the chest. I thought it should have been obvious why I cared. Whatever had happened between us, it hadn't changed how I felt about her. I loved her, and even then, I knew that a part of me would always love her, and because of that, I felt an eternal responsibility to take care of her.

"I'll always care about you, Elle," I said, though telling her that I loved her thrummed erratically against my chest. "I don't want you to ever have to worry. Haven't we spent too many years worrying?"

Three weeks later, Elle decided to move into my second floor. I was surprised that she chose my place instead of having her own, but I couldn't help but wonder if she had also been incredibly lonely. Of course, I didn't mind the company, either. I hired the best nanny in the city to watch Nathan while Elle and I both worked.

In the beginning, we danced awkwardly around each other, trying to stay out of one another's way. I didn't want to ruin her routine with Nathan just as much as I'm sure she didn't want to ruin mine. I was gone for most of the day, and at night, I stayed in my bedroom. We always checked in on each other's days, sharing snippets of information, and somehow, with each passing day, those little moments slowly stitched the gap in our timeline back together.

The first time I actually held Nathan was after a dress rehearsal for *Cats*. I'd come home to hear him screaming upstairs. I crept up the stairs and poked my head into his room to find Elle bouncing a blubbering Nathan in his bedroom. He was such a well-behaved kid that I hadn't truly understood the terrible twos until I came home that night. There was a soft glow coming from the lamp on the nightstand, but I was still able to catch the gloss in Elle's eyes. She looked absolutely defeated and exhausted, as if she had been trying to get him to stop crying for hours.

"Is everything okay?" I asked.

She shook her head. "Yes and no. It's all because I told him he couldn't eat a cookie. He's tired, but he just won't settle down. Been doing this for about forty minutes."

"Let me take him. You look tired too."

She frowned, probably shocked that I'd offered since I'd made it pretty obvious that babies scared me. "What? No, it's okay. You just got home."

"It's fine. Let me at least try. Help give you a little break."

She cautiously handed me Nathan, who cried even harder in my arms. I regretted the offer as his temper tantrum intensified, and he tried wiggling out of my grip. She stood close to me, almost as if checking to make sure I was holding him right and wouldn't drop him.

"We'll be fine," I said.

"Are you sure?"

He screamed, "No," into my ear. His bright red face contorted into a horrified frown. Toddlers weren't cute at all when they screamed and scrunched their faces like that.

"Yes, I'm sure. Go take a bath. Go relax."

She faltered. "Okay. I'll be out in twenty."

"Just take as long as you need."

Once I heard the bath running, I shut his bedroom door and placed him on the floor. He toppled to the ground in a fit and cried into the carpet.

"Nathan, hon, what's wrong?"

He continued to cry. Two minutes in and I didn't know how Elle could deal with forty-plus minutes of this. I took a deep breath and exhaled out my stress and exhaustion from the day. I had no idea what I was doing with him. I tried handing him his Cookie Monster, but he chucked him across the room. I tried rubbing his back. I tried talking to him in that high-pitched baby voice. Nothing.

So I started singing "Somewhere Over the Rainbow" softly. It was the song that had comforted me the most throughout my life. I can't remember why, but all I knew was that when I heard it, it filtered peace through my body like a soft, briny breeze. By the second verse, his screaming hushed to sloppy blubbers. I scooted over to him and rubbed his back while I sang the rest of the song.

"You like that song?" I asked once he quieted down. I kissed his temple. He smelled like baby soap. "I do too. It's a good song, isn't it? Do you want to hear it again? How about we lie in your bed, okay?"

He nodded before standing and blubbering to his bed. I helped tuck him in, and once he settled into his spot, I ran a hand through his wispy blond hair and sang the song again, watching as his eyes slowly closed.

He was out by the time Elle emerged from the bath a half hour later. She looked extra soft and gentle wrapped in her silk robe, her damp, curly hair falling to her shoulders, the smell of lavender wafting from her. When she noticed Nathan passed out, her eyes widened as if she had witnessed a miracle right in front of her.

"He's out?"

I gave a single nod, afraid too much movement would cause him to wake up and scream all over again. "He's out."

"How?"

"I just sang to him."

She gave me a soft smile as she walked over to plant a kiss on his temple. "Of course you did."

Nathan didn't have many uncontrolled screaming fits, but the very few times that he did, I swooped in, held him in my arms, and sang. A couple of nights later, the night before *Cats* premiered, I heard him crying upstairs. I had already been up from nerves, tossing and turning for at least forty-five minutes before I heard his cries. In a desperate attempt to salvage the rest of my sleep, I slipped out of bed and crept into his room. Once I sat on the bed with him, I heard Elle softly call my name.

"I beat you to him," I whispered.

"Marlie, go back to sleep. I've got this."

"It's okay. I was up anyway."

"You were?"

I shrugged. "First show nerves. The first day still gets me."

Thank God for the dim hallway light filtering through, or I would have missed her soft smile. "You have a Grammy and an Oscar, and you still get nervous?"

"I just want everyone to enjoy it."

"It's really okay, Mar. Please go rest. You have a big day later."

My chest clenched when she said, "Mar," the same clenching that I'd been feeling ever since Elle had moved in. It was like teetering on the edge of the giant hole we'd left between us, and I couldn't help but wonder when I'd lose my balance and fall right into it. She hadn't called me Mar since reuniting. Half of me wondered if it was a familiar slip or if it actually meant something.

I hoped it was both.

"Give me ten minutes," I said. "I want to see if the singing works."

"If you insist."

She curled up in the space next to Nathan on the bed. He rested his head on her shoulder and then looked at me, almost as if giving me permission to start. So I sang him "Somewhere Over the Rainbow" again, repeating the song as many times as needed until his face was dry, and his eyes started drooping, all while Elle snuggled him and rubbed his back.

"He looks like you, you know," I said quietly, keeping a close watch on his drooping eyes.

"You think?"

"He's like a spitting image of you. Same eyes, smile, probably the same hair if he got a perm."

Elle let out a small laugh, but once the moment passed, silence quickly squeezed into the room. It was a mixture of familiar comfort as well as a reminder of the distance wedged between us. But it was the comfort I clung to. So much had changed since the last time we'd seen each other. We tried navigating around the other's separate lives, knowing the only shared piece was our past and living together. But the fact that there were pockets of a familiar silence meant something. To me, at least.

"He really loves your singing," she said. "Even a two-year-old knows how magical it is."

"Magical, huh?"

"You know how much I love your voice. Others love it too. You have this amazing ability to sing a screaming toddler to sleep as easily as you fill up an entire Broadway theater. Your voice soothes just as much as it makes people feel something buried deep within them. You're truly one of a kind. That hasn't changed, and I don't think it ever will."

I pulled my gaze away. Looking at her while the weight of her words lay over me like a warm blanket felt way too intimate for where we were in our relationship. Instead, I glanced at Nathan, who was sound asleep in her arms.

"I'm glad it hasn't changed for you," I said.

"It won't. No matter where we are in our lives, it'll always bring me comfort."

After we headed back to our separate rooms, I slid into my bed alone, holding on to Elle's words and hoping so much that she wouldn't ever let go.

❖

Cats landed me my second Tony nomination for Best Performance by a Featured Actress in a Musical in June 1983. I even performed a song from it during the ceremony and told Elle to tune in. The weight of knowing that the very eyes I wanted on me were actually watching lay heavy on my shoulders. It made me feel like I had even more to prove. I had to prove to the audience that I was my character and not myself. I had to prove my character's story and emotions while performing "Memory," and I had everything to prove to Elle.

I wasn't a writer. I wasn't a reader of novels, only scripts that turned into performances. I didn't know how to collect all my thoughts and feelings into something poetic on paper. If I tried, I'm sure it would have repelled Elle more than whatever had come between us.

She had told me back in October that my singing always made her feel something, and after dancing around her for the last eight months in the brownstone, I wanted to seize the moment with her eyes on me. I was a singer, an actress, and a performer. My voice and my love for music was my power. At least, it was back at Kindred Hearts when I'd played her the piano almost every night. It had drawn her into a friendship. We'd bonded over those records snug in the listening booth at Morsey Records. In our Whitby apartment, we'd danced to countless songs after our long days. I'd sung her favorite love songs by Elvis and Billy Joel on the Steinway. And now that I was on one of the biggest stages, on national TV, knowing that she was at home watching, I was going to try to tell her in the best way that I knew how that I missed her and everything we'd once had.

I poured everything into that performance as if it was opening night with everything to prove. The crowd stood and roared with applause, and I walked off that stage knowing that every emotion still clung to the air in Gershwin Theatre.

It was a wonderful thing that everyone assumed Peter and I were dating because they seated him next to me during the ceremony. During a commercial break, he leaned into me and said, "You've got this, Mar, and you might have gotten the girl too."

I let out a hollow laugh because nothing was official yet on either account. "We'll see."

I knew when I'd first heard "Memory" that the song was anything but ordinary. I knew the very first time I sang the song that it would change my life, and it did.

Finally, in 1983, I won my first Tony Award.

After they announced my name, everything was a daze. Peter kissed me on the cheek, and other cast members congratulated me before I drifted onto the stage, willing for the dream not to end before I held the award in my hand. It was a recurring dream I had since seeing *The Sound of Music* with the McCoys. I'd get up on stage, and right before the Tony was handed to me, I'd wake up. But this time, I could feel the award in my hands and the pinpricks snaking down my spine. I could make out a few of the faces in front of me. They weren't faceless like in my dreams.

What made my stomach coil into hundreds of little knots was the possibility that Elle was watching. I thought if she only watched my "Memory" performance, that meant the feelings I'd had since I was a teen were unrequited. But if she was still watching long enough for my category—even while fighting off tiredness from a long day of mothering—then maybe, just maybe, she felt the same way about me.

As I accepted my award and glanced out at the Gershwin Theatre, I told myself that Elle was watching, and something about believing her eyes were on me gave me the confidence to power through the cameras, lights, and crowd.

"I grew up in a Brooklyn orphanage. I didn't have parents, I hopped from house to house, and the nicest thing I owned was a suitcase that held all my belongings. It was easy to not believe in much when that's the only life you know, but I believed in music. Music kept me going. It helped all of us in that orphanage keep going. It reminded us that there was still a flicker of hope out there for us. And for me, that flicker of hope came from Glenn Kerr, who found me singing outside of the Schubert Theatre twelve years ago, and at the same time, Peter Arlo was inside on that stage playing Jesus Christ.

"Peter, your love and support through the last twelve years have been my guiding light. Thank you so much to all the people who have lifted me up: the wonderful cast, to Elle and Nathan, the American Theater Wing, and the Broadway League for helping this Brooklyn orphan finally find a loving home. Thank you."

As a newly crowned Tony winner, everyone wanted to treat me to a drink at the after-party at Sardi's, Peter especially.

He wrapped his arm around me and presented a champagne flute in the other hand. "This is for you, my Tony winner of a girlfriend." He quickly snuck in a wink as I accepted the glass and took a drink. He frowned. "You know, you don't look like someone who is one award away from an EGOT at the age of twenty-nine."

I glanced at the bubbles rising in the flute. Peter set his glass on the bar, placed his hands on my shoulders, and squeezed them. "Marlie Rose, what's wrong?"

I sat on my words for a moment. I wanted to keep the admission to myself. Once I said it, that meant what I felt was real, and I could no longer deny it. But if I had to say it out loud to anyone, it was going to be to Peter. I trusted him more than I trusted myself. "It feels weird celebrating without Elle," I said.

"I've been telling you to try again with her since she and Nathan moved in with you."

It was true. He had been encouraging me to confess my feelings to Elle for months. But even though we fell back into a familiar rhythm, finding comfort in one another was different than finding romantic passion. I knew it still lived inside me anytime she was near me, but I had to suppress it, and if the feelings were mutual, Elle had done a good job of tamping down her emotions as well.

I had no idea where we stood, and I knew I wouldn't know until I came home and found out if she'd watched the entire ceremony or not.

"It's not that simple, Peter."

"You're clearly still in love with her. Sounds pretty simple."

I'd been denying my feelings for so long, my chest latched on to his words as they settled in me. I was still in love with her, but what the hell was I supposed to do about that? I was offered the role of Audrey in the West End production of *Little Shop of Horrors* opening in October.

"What's simple about telling her I'm still in love with her when I'm moving back to London next month?"

He shrugged. "Didn't you say Elle and Nathan were going to stay in the brownstone?"

"I did. I want to keep helping them, and it's not good for either of them to be constantly moving."

"You fly back once in a while to be with them."

I let out a hollow laugh. "You know our jobs can take us anywhere in the world. That's not simple in the slightest."

"I think you're looking too far into the future, Mar. Sometimes, you should take stock of what's in front of you and enjoy the moment."

He always lived in the moment. He told me that it was the only thing you can control. The past had already happened, the future hadn't, and there was nothing we could do to control those two things. "All we can do is dwell, and that takes away from the now," he'd once told me when we were talking about his family. I couldn't understand how something so sad and unfortunate as his family disowning him could still make him one of the most loving, kind, and optimistic people I ever knew.

"So what, I proclaim my love for her and then bug off to London for God only knows how long?"

He rested a hand on my shoulder. "Maybe you need to stop using all your energy denying your feelings and try embracing them and seeing where it takes you. What's the worst that's going to happen? She doesn't feel the same way? You two remain friends, like you have been since October. Stop hiding from something that shouldn't be this scary."

Even though I had just won my first Tony, that after-party was the one I'd left the earliest, well before one a.m. All I could think about was Elle and if she'd stayed up to watch the entire show. She hadn't left my mind once the entire night, and despite all the complicated twists and turns we had encountered, I still wandered through the night looking for her.

With my Tony in hand, I unlocked the front door and kicked off my high heels the moment I locked it behind me. I rested my head against the back of the door, enjoying how my sore feet felt without the shoes. When I opened my eyes, I noticed a TV glow pouring into the foyer. It had to have been Elle, either still up or asleep on the couch.

Just in case she was asleep, I tiptoed to the living room to find her on the couch jotting something in her journal. She looked up. Her hair was done in a Madonna wrap, and a few spirally tendrils hung over the red scarf.

"Oh hi," I said. "I...I wasn't expecting you to still be awake."

"Marlie," she said so softly, but how she smiled around my name made my chest burst open. She closed the journal as if I could read every word from where I stood, and it was the last thing she wanted me to see. Then, she looked at the Tony in my hands. That's when she smiled, causing my chest to burst open.

"What?" I said, though it sounded more like a croak.

"I'm just so incredibly proud of you, Mar. You won a Tony. It's in your hands right now."

Something as simple as her saying my nickname felt like a lasso tugging on my heart, and God, I could feel it. The only problem was that I had no idea if I was tugging my own heart or hers. "You are?"

She frowned. "Of course I am. Why wouldn't I be? This is what you worked your whole life for. Ever since I've known you, you've been imagining this moment."

I studied the Tony. I was still in a daze, wondering when I'd wake up and find myself in my bed, dreaming the entire night.

She stood and walked over. Her soft fingers guided my hand up, and they skimmed a burning path along my wrist, down my thumb, and onto the black, acrylic glass base of the award before wandering up to the top of the nickel-plated medallion. She smiled softly, and our stares held for a heavy moment. My insides shifted and turned upside down. The way she looked at me had me melting.

I handed her the award, and she inspected it. "It's a little bit different than how I imagined it," I said softly.

"How so?"

"It's silly now."

"Hey," Elle said, placing the Tony on the coffee table before caressing my cheek.

I leaned into her soft, gentle touch. I closed my eyes for just a moment, reveling in the way she held me. It tore my heart open, and I could feel the suppressed feelings bubbling. I opened my eyes to find hers on me. She was so close that I could smell the fresh toothpaste rolling off her words.

"I'm sure it's not silly," she said, so soft yet sexy.

"It is a little bit."

"Why don't I be the judge of that? Now, tell me how you always imagined it." Her stare was so powerful, I could feel it lighting up my lips as she scanned them.

I wasn't afraid anymore. I didn't care about the future and what it meant for us when I went back to London. I didn't care about the past that I can't quite pinpoint now, but I know I reflected back on Peter's words before grasping the moment.

I exhaled a heavy breath, releasing the last knots of anxiety. "I always imagined you being there…in the audience, and every time, I imagined thanking you."

"You did thank me."

"Not the way I wanted to."

She cleared her throat, and I knew that the moment suffusing the room was swaddling her just as much as it was swaddling me. "How did you want to?"

I was so focused on the present that I swatted away the doubts that circled our future. I palmed her face and kissed her. She wrapped her arms around me like she had desperately wanted to do it ever since I'd returned to New York almost a year before. I made sure that I kissed her thoroughly and deeply to match all the unsaid words of my speech. I didn't want her to have a single doubt about how much I'd missed her and how much I still loved her because, God, none of that had wavered.

Elle was always a beacon I gravitated toward.

I wanted her. I wanted all of her, and I wanted her to have all of me. With our tongues still dancing, I walked her back to the couch until she fell. I straddled her, not having a care in the world that I was still in my dress. It pooled over her half-bare legs, her warm skin touching mine.

When those murmurs hummed against my lips, I pulled away and sucked on her neck and felt her breathy moans tickling my earlobe. She sounded as delicious as her minty breath tasted. When a moan broke through her lips, it sent my whole body aflame. I untied her scarf and loved the way her curls fell over my hands. I ran my fingers through them, trying to familiarize myself with this new version of Elle. Her hair draped in front of us, but I was so desperate for her, I continued kissing her with her hair in my face. I didn't care.

I rocked against her hips, and she slid a hand between my legs and grazed along the wet patch on my underwear. I'm sure she felt it because she desperately pulled aside the hem and slipped inside me. I gasped and buried my face into her neck, filling my lungs with the smell of her soft natural scent and the faint Diorella still clinging to her skin.

I rode her fingers until the tension exploded within me. I muted my cries in the nape of her neck and followed it with a soft bite to her shoulder as I came. After I collected my breath, I gladly returned the favor. I wanted her sounds to envelope me. I needed to hear what she sounded like with pure bliss and desire cloaked over her body. So I got on my knees, scooped my hands under her thighs, and pulled until her legs draped over my shoulders so my mouth had the best access. I relished how amazing she tasted and felt, how her hips circled against my mouth, how her cries were soft enough not to travel up the stairs but loud enough to fill the living room while keeping the fire blazing inside my core.

We moved effortlessly, like water. It's odd to think how the first time we slept together was so comforting and familiar, as if I had dreamt about it a thousand times before. The only thing I can think of is that there must have been something there between us the entire time we had known each other, and we hadn't ignited that spark until that night.

Afterward, we stayed on the couch for a while. I laid my head on her lap as she raked her fingers through my hot-rollered curls. We didn't say much. The two of us never really had to. Sometimes, not saying anything was saying everything. The room was as quiet as it could be, but the unspoken feelings I knew Elle felt—based on how she'd made love to me—were extremely loud, like Times Square during the day.

"What now?" she said softly.

The way she asked while still caressing me, I could tell she didn't have any expectations for the future. It was more general curiosity, one I completely felt too. "I guess I go off to London."

"You sure you're okay with us holding down the fort?"

"I'm positive. This is your home…if you want it to be."

"It's not going to be much of a home without you here, but it's a house that I like very much."

"Then please, hold down the fort. Let me help you not have to worry."

Everything left unsaid clued me in that we were on the same page. I think both of us knew in that moment that what had occurred was more of a promise that we still loved each other than a promise of getting together. Our paths were still frayed in the grand scheme of life. It just so happened that for a few hours that night, our paths reached a juncture before we continued. But it still brought us that promise that even with everything we had been through, there was still love deeply rooted in us. We came to an understanding, and the days that followed, that gargantuan hole we had been waltzing around shrunk. It flattened the bumps in our friendship.

A month later, I said my good-byes, kissed Elle and Nathan on the cheeks, and went back to London. Once I settled in my apartment, I scanned the space and realized just how much Elle and Nathan had imprinted on me after a year of living with them. She had started to feel like home again, like how it used to feel when we'd first lived together. There was a tug in my chest when I didn't see her writing in her journal on the couch or see Nathan's toys scattered around the living room. I missed the sound of his uneven footsteps and the smell of lavender soap wafting off her body after a bath.

I missed them so much more than I would have thought.

In some ways, it brought us closer. Unlike the last time I lived here, I made sure to call as often as I could. I stayed up late just so I could hear her voice after she put Nathan to bed. We both poured a glass of wine and chatted about our days, and she always filled me in on how Nathan was doing. On the best days, I heard him on the other end babbling about things that didn't necessarily make sense to me, but he always found a way to make my chest inflate with so much happiness.

While our friendship clicked back in place, the love I had for her continued to accumulate. I didn't know how not to love Elle because if I knew that, all the days without her wouldn't have been as painful as they were.

❖

"What about this memory, Ms. Rose?" Dr. Pierson asks, snapping me back to the present.

"I want to delete my night with Elle after the Tonys."

Once I say it, my eyes water. I try to erase the emotion that naturally spills out of me, but I can't. I swipe at a falling tear. I don't want to forget the first time we made love, I really don't. But I know if I want to unhook myself from the heartbreak, I have to erase this one. My mind says I have to, but my heart screams for it to stay because every part of that memory is wonderful.

And that's the problem. A thirty-three-year-old memory constantly serves up the illusion that I'll get the love of my life back. That's why I need it gone.

"Okay, Ms. Rose. I'll go ahead and target that memory."

I close my leaking eyes and wait for the relief to lighten my mind.

I sing "Memory" in my head while the helmet warms, and the clicking taps against my scalp. I sift through all of my remaining memories, and for the first time during this process, I'm discovering how many holes there are in my life story. Things aren't making sense. My memory of Elle is like scattered puzzle pieces, and I can barely make out her face or how we came to be. Everything is fading and wilting.

I can feel my heart hammering against my ribs the more the clicks tap and zap at the memory until I forget what the hell I just erased. When I try to recover it, I come across another missing piece in my timeline. What felt like a puzzle with lost pieces is now so scrambled that I can't even see a clear picture of my life. Where the hell did I come from? Who the hell am I? What the hell have I done?

❖

In the evening, after I have time to sleep off a mild headache, I pour a glass of wine and sit on my patio. My own personal oasis. Palm trees line the perimeter, an infinity pool sparkles in the dying sun with a view of the Pacific off in the distance. It's such a gorgeous view, one of the things that always offers some comfort on my bad days.

I just wished I had someone to share it with.

I decide then it's a good time to call Nathan. It's almost ten p.m. on the East Coast, but knowing him, he's still up.

So I suck in a deep breath of warm air, take an encouraging sip, and call. My heart speeds up with each ring until I hear his deep voice on the other end. "Hi, Marlie."

My chest bottoms out hearing his voice again. He doesn't sound angry. He actually sounds happy. I push all my anxieties aside so I can finally enjoy the sound of him warmly greeting me. "Hi, hon. How are you?"

"I'm doing good. Just watching some TV with Mel."

"Hi, Marlie!" I hear his wife, Melissa, say.

I smile. "Hi, Melissa. How are you?"

There's a quick beat before Nathan says, "Well, actually, that's why I called you earlier."

"We have some big news we've been dying to share with you," Melissa says.

Once I hear the excitement in their voices, I know exactly what they're going to tell me. Right as I set the wineglass down and place a hand over my stomach, Melissa says, "I'm pregnant!"

My stomach falls like I'm on a Coney Island roller coaster but in the best way because I can hear how happy they both sound, and I can't help but take on their emotions. It fills me with something I've been longing for. My son is ecstatic, and God, that alone cures so much, a powerful antidepressant.

"Oh my God," I say as overwhelming happiness blurs my eyes. "Congratulations, you two. That's so wonderful. How far along are you?"

"Four months," Melissa says.

"We didn't want to say anything until we knew that everything was looking good," Nathan says, "but the doctor told us yesterday that she's very happy. Are you ready for a grandson?"

That's when it hits me that I'm about to be a grandmother, something I would have panicked about in my twenties and thirties. But God, how far I've come. The newfound knowledge settles over me like I'm being tucked into bed with a warm flannel blanket.

"I'm absolutely ready," I say and clean my face. "You have me all weepy over here."

He laughs, and it fills me up even more. "I miss you. I hope you know that." He says it softly and cautiously as the last year and a half finally squeeze into our conversation, reminding me of what happened. I almost feel the need to lower my phone so I can cry out everything I've been trying to hold in for the last several minutes, but I refrain.

"I miss you too," I say, feeling my throat tighten. "More than you know."

A silence falls, and even though it lasts several seconds, it speaks volumes. Nathan and I never had silent moments on our calls. I think back to the Sunday night calls we had together while he was away at college and how we seemed to lose ourselves in an hour or two of great conversation. I always thought how wonderful it was that he could have been going to parties, drinking, and meeting a bunch of women. I'm sure he still did, but the fact that he still blocked off time for me showed me how special our relationship was. He felt more comfortable telling me things than Elle, who was more of the disciplinarian, but I was so grateful that my college-aged son called every Sunday. I'll never forget the one time we spoke for four hours that seemed like four minutes.

Now, a heavy, silent moment squeezes between us. I have to make it right again. I've missed those Sunday calls.

"You know, I've been thinking about it, and it would be so nice to see you again."

It's the last thing I expect him to say. Maybe I misheard. "What? Really?"

"Really. We would love to show you the house. I know it's not a mansion in Malibu, but Mel has fixed it up really nice. I think you'll like it. It's surrounded by woods. It's really peaceful. If not now, maybe when the baby arrives."

I want nothing more than to see Nathan and Melissa. Right as I say I'll fly out, I remember Dr. Pierson and all the gaps punched out of my memory. Visiting him means I have to tell him what I've been up to.

A wave of heavy guilt washes over me. All it takes is hearing him ask me to visit and the news of my grandson. It's scary and confusing because I still have so much I want to forget; at the same time, I'm starting to regret the procedure. All I know is that I don't feel whole and neither does my story.

"If that's something you want," he says.

"Of course that's what I want. I just…I have to nail some things down before I commit. I could fly out next week if that works."

"Seriously?"

With how shocked and excited he sounds, I want nothing more than to purchase my tickets after we hang up. "If that works for you, then it works for me."

"Okay, wow, that would be amazing. I'll let Mel know, and we'll get everything ready. I'm…I'm really looking forward to it."

"I am too, hon. It's going to be so nice to see you again."

I know I'm in the middle of my procedure, and Dr. Pierson advised me to limit my travel, especially to places that hold a lot of meaning—like Scarsdale and New York City—because until the procedure is complete, the chances for a memory to resurface spike greatly. But following the rules seems so insignificant when I hear that my son is excited for me to visit. I want more than anything to clasp this and make up for the rough year and a half without him.

"Great," I say. "I'll send you my flight details once they're booked."

"Sounds good. Well…I should let you go. I'll talk to you soon?"

"Talk to you soon. Love you, Nathan."

"I love you too, Mom."

The last time he called me Mom was at his wedding.

It's the final tug that convinces me to go me back to New York for the first time since Nathan's wedding. I book my flights immediately after the call.

CHAPTER ELEVEN

My fifth session is the only thing in the way of flying back to New York. In twenty-four hours, I will be somewhere over middle America, and the closer I get to New York, the more guilt I'll feel about all the lost time with Nathan. At the same time, I'm anxious and excited to get on that plane.

But there is absolutely no way I'm going to mention to Dr. Pierson that I'm flying to New York. He'll lecture me about things I'm already aware of, and I don't care about the risks. I want to see my son. Nothing is going to prevent that.

Once the helmet is on and the overhead lights flicker off, Dr. Pierson sits behind the table and says, "Good morning, Ms. Rose. How about we start when you moved back to London. What's the first memory that comes to mind?"

My breath hitches, and the nerves and excitement coiling in my stomach about seeing Nathan and Melissa come to an abrupt halt when I realize what I'll be covering in today's session.

Getting through this day suddenly got a lot harder.

"I haven't talked about this in more than twenty-seven years," I say, not able to look any of his team in the eye. I can only focus on my hands in my lap.

"Take all the time you need, Ms. Rose. Whenever you're ready and comfortable."

If twenty-seven years hasn't been enough time to dull the pain, then another minute of avoiding it won't finally relieve it. I've been dreading what happens next. All this time later, it still hasn't gotten easier to think about. Even though my brain already feels like it's been turned into Swiss cheese, I've been thinking long and hard about what I want to do with the series of painful memories that still haunt me. I see the pros and cons of keeping them, and honestly, I'm not sure what I'll do until I relive them again right now, twenty-seven years later.

In the fall of 1985, Peter and I were in London preparing for the premiere of *Les Misérables*. He was Jean Valjean, and I was Fantine. I was so excited to be doing another musical with him and living in our Chelsea apartment. He was the older brother I'd never had, and I was the younger, accepting sister. As long as we were living together, the media continued to paint the narrative that we were dating, though we never confirmed or denied it. And the narrative about us shielded us from the homophobia surrounding the AIDS epidemic.

In October 1985, Rock Hudson died, the first high-profile person to die from AIDS. A month later, I got a call from Elle after she found Will's obituary in the paper.

I don't remember Will too well, but I do remember telling Peter about the news after one of our *Les Mis* shows. By that time, we had lost handfuls of wonderful people in the theater community. Peter had lost his good friend, Craig Carpenter, we'd lost Rick Higgins, the person who'd helped launch my career by making me Roxie Hart in *Chicago*, and then it was Will, the guy who'd always had a spot in Peter's heart.

We were in our thirties and had already gone to too many funerals in such a small amount of time that it felt like we were in the later years of our life. I think that's when it finally hit Peter that this wasn't going away anytime soon. We came of age during the sexual revolution while taking full advantage of the little bubble we lived in in Greenwich Village, a little pocket of acceptance and love.

But it wasn't the seventies anymore. By the time Peter and I moved back to New York in early 1987 to reprise our roles as Valjean and Fantine, the city had become the epicenter of the AIDS epidemic. Many of the bathhouses were forced to close their doors. Unlike when I had moved back four years before, Peter and I didn't have the urge to go out to Christopher Street and celebrate in one of our sanctuary bars. Gay bar patrons were thinning and disappearing, and long gone were the days of us crowded in a dingy and sweaty basement bar, belting Elton John at the top of our lungs.

Instead, he helped me unpack in the brownstone. With Nathan turning seven, Elle saved up enough money while holding down the fort to move both of them into an apartment just a few blocks away. I insisted they didn't have to leave, and Elle insisted that I had offered more than enough help, and Nathan was getting too big and rambunctious—though I knew it was just Elle's pride getting in the way.

But the two of them came over often for dinner and quality time. We drank wine and smiled at how big Nathan had gotten. We spent one entire evening talking to him about school, his friends, and playing with the *Star Wars* figurines I had mailed to him as a Christmas present.

While our chosen family was finally back together, all three of us were terrified about what was happening to our community right outside our door. When we moved back, and *Les Mis* took over the Broadway Theatre, we had no idea how close it was to reaching our front door.

Until that April, when Peter had taken off a couple of shows because he had the flu.

I stopped over with soup and medicine to help with his fever and body aches. He shivered under the covers. His face was warm. I didn't think too much about it because it wasn't the first time I'd given him medicine when he was sick. He got a horrible cold every year, always in the spring when his allergies acted up.

"Take aspirin and drink lots of water," I said, setting two glasses of ice water on his nightstand and brushing the hair out of his face. "I need my Valjean back."

A couple of days later, I invited Elle and Nathan over for dinner. I hopped between the kitchen, where Elle took over making the lasagna, and the living room, where I played with Nathan and his toys. We had a nice, long, delicious dinner, and Nathan was extra chatty, asking me all about Broadway, singing, and being on TV.

When they left, I curled up underneath a blanket on my couch, reading *Second Nature* by Nora Roberts, finally embracing my free time in a way that didn't consist of reading scripts or traveling. I remember thinking how lovely the rain sounded against the window. I struggled to get into the chapter because I was too preoccupied feeling grateful for where Elle and I were in our friendship. I had found a way to tamp down my feelings for her while being able to provide her and Nathan with some stability. We'd found this perfect rhythm of remaining in each other's lives, and I loved when we took time out of our busy schedules to catch up on life, and I loved every moment I got to spend with her and Nathan.

It was going on nine o'clock when a knock on the door startled me. It was the last thing I expected given the weather. I looked through the peephole and saw Peter standing on the stoop completely drenched. His textured, layer curtain hair hung in front of his forehead and eyebrows and started to curl. I whipped open the door so I could pull him inside.

"Peter! What the hell," I said once I closed the door. "What are you doing out in the rain? You're going to get pneumonia or something."

"Marlie—"

"Your teeth are chattering. God, Peter." I ran into the living room to grab my blanket and draped it over his shivering body. I rubbed heat into his arms.

"I have it, Marlie. I have it."

"You have pneumonia?" I pushed his wavy hair back to feel his forehead. He didn't feel warm. Cold, if anything. "Then, what the hell are you doing out in the rain? Let me make you some tea and get you some dry clothes—" I started for the stairs, but he snatched my hand and halted me in my tracks.

"No, Mar, I don't have pneumonia."

I glanced over my shoulder and found a horrified expression in his dark, blurry eyes. The color from his face paled and drained his vivaciousness. That wide, affectionate Peter Arlo smile I'd fallen in love with fifteen years before shrunk into a terrified expression that made everything stop right then and there. Me, my heart, time. All of it halted, yet the world continued turning.

I grabbed the railing as my knees gave out. Peter dropped the blanket, his soaked hands guiding me gently onto the bottom of the stairs.

Everything morphed into a vivid nightmare. I closed my eyes tightly, thinking if I sealed them enough, I'd wake up in my bed with the warm sun shining on my face. But no matter how much I willed myself to wake up, I kept finding myself on the stairs, in the dark, the feeling of my best friend's soaked skin and clothes wrapped around me.

"Peter," I said through the pulling in my throat as I palmed his damp face.

I wanted to slap him hard as the cries filled my throat. He'd promised me he would be safe. He'd promised me for years. I was dumb for believing that doing the bare minimum was enough to skate through it. I was dumb for believing that we were invincible to the fucking virus. We carried on with our lives, singing, dancing, performing, kissing, and fucking like there weren't thousands of our gay brothers and sisters falling all around us.

"You said you were going to be safe—"

"I was safe, Mar!" He cried just as hard as I did. "I promise. It must have been, I don't know. I must have gotten it years ago, but I've been safe ever since Will—" He stopped and buried his face in his palms. "I'm sorry, Marlie," he muttered in his hands. "I'm so fucking sorry."

I pulled him in for a hug and held him so tightly, the rain soaked into my clothes, and honestly, I couldn't tell what was rain and what were tears on my shoulders. But I didn't care because Peter was in my arms. I could feel him. I could feel the rain sticking us together, I could feel and hear his breath against my ear, and I knew a day would come when I'd long for the sound of his breath. In that moment, he was full of them despite the fact that he was running out.

I somehow floated upstairs to get him some pajamas while I dried his clothes. I made us tea in silence, zoning out and waking myself out of the trance because Peter called my name from the living room, the first word in almost an hour.

"You've been stirring the tea for about ten minutes," he said.

Where did I even begin processing that kind of news? The very thing that had been haunting us for the last six years had found a crack and squeezed through, distorting our lives. I can barely remember my life before Peter, and after singing with him as my counterpart for the last three years, he'd become more intertwined with my life than before. He was my best friend and my older brother.

I didn't want to imagine a world without him in it.

"I wasn't going to get tested, you know," he muttered.

This wasn't abnormal. Even if people suspected that they had HIV or AIDS, many didn't get tested because no good came from it. They would get fired, their landlord would kick them out, their family would disown them—if they hadn't already—and eventually, they were going to die. So what the hell was the point?

"Why did you?"

He shook his head and glanced at the turned-off TV. "I don't know. I just…I needed to know."

The shame was loud in his voice. I noticed how defeated he appeared. He was unrecognizable without his wide, goofy smile, and I worried that the virus had already snatched that away.

"Does anyone else know?"

"Just you." He pulled his stare to the mug in his hands. "I'm worried about everyone turning on me. I've heard stories. I heard about Craig Carpenter's time in the hospital. His sister told me how the nurses were too afraid to go into his room and how they threw out everything he touched. She told me they take the beds of the people who die, throw them out back, and burn them. So what? Everything I touch is going in a blaze?"

"Peter," I said softly and placed a hand on his shoulder.

"If people find out, they'll not want to be near me. God, what do I even tell my family? Hey, look at me. I'm diseased just like you've always thought I was?" He slammed his mug on the coffee table and sobbed in his hands.

"Listen to me," I said, gently lowering his hands. When he didn't look over, I guided his chin toward me. His face was pale, wet, and long, and my throat tugged on my words. "You are my best friend. You are my family. You are *not* what your ignorant family thinks of you, you're *not* what all those assholes out there think of you, okay? Do you even see the way Nathan looks at you? He looks at you and talks about you like you're Superman, and that's how you are to the people who matter, to the people who actually know you. Don't you ever call yourself diseased again, you hear me?"

He nodded and threw himself onto my chest, sobbing.

"You're not going to go through this alone," I said, rubbing his back after a long bout of silence. "Do you hear me? We're going to be with you, always, and we are going to make sure you have the best treatment out there. I promise to take care of you because no one can take better care of you than me. If you need to move in, you'll move in."

"What? I can't, no, I can't intrude—"

"You're my family, Peter. You always have been."

He nodded, wiped his eyes, and said, "Can you just promise me one thing?"

"I'll promise you anything," I said and wrapped my hands around his shaking ones.

"Promise me that we're going to fully live until the time comes. I want to see and do everything I can before I can't anymore."

I kissed his hand. "We'll see and do anything you want."

❖

Peter was back at the Broadway Theatre that Thursday, dressed as Valjean and more eager than ever to get back onstage. I watched him perform the prologue from the wings. His voice filled the theater, his presence commanded the stage, and his confidence held the audience captive with each move he made and each word he sang.

But underneath his Valjean costume and makeup, I had almost forgotten that there was a virus that was slowly but surely taking him away from me.

The realization hit me right before I stepped onstage to perform my first singing part, "At the End of the Day." I had to find a way to mask my heartbreak and grief while filling the theater with my voice. This was the moment where I needed to put my fifteen years of experience to the test. I needed to forget everything unfolding outside and imagine myself as Fantine.

But later in the show, when the orchestra below in the chamber played the beautiful melancholy opening to "I Dreamed a Dream," my eyes stung. Music could be powerful like that. Melodies dig up even the most buried emotions. With each lyric, a string of buried emotion spilled out of me. For a moment, I was transported back fifteen years earlier when I'd first met Peter, had the entire city within my reach, and Peter, Elle, and I had found a family within each other.

During the climax of the song, I felt Fantine's emotions so deeply that they drowned me and washed my character away. The words matched so perfectly to the reality outside of the theater that it was impossible for even a professional like myself to swat it away. Something hot and suffocating threaded around my chest as if it was trying to squeeze out the last bit of hope. I came to the realization that, while disguised as a character, in front of a crowd of over fifteen hundred people, my life was supposed to be so different from the current hell that our gay community and others across the world were living in. It was an epiphany that hit me as if one of the lights had fallen on top of me. My best friend was going to die. All his dreams would be cut short. I'd have to continue without him standing next to me. I didn't know my adult life without him, and I didn't want to.

The dream I'd once had was fading too.

Why couldn't this one have come true? Why couldn't Peter and I grow old together as the siblings we'd never had? Why couldn't our Saturday nights be filled with singing Billy Joel and Elton John at three a.m. until we were both ninety?

Why the hell did it have to be Peter?

Singing "I Dreamed a Dream" that night and every night after took on a new meaning. That first night, I tried so damn hard to be Fantine. I tried with every fiber of my being to stay in character, remain professional, and tried shoving all the real-world issues out of the Broadway Theatre so the audience got exactly what they signed up for.

But I couldn't do it.

Peter Arlo had three Tonys and a Grammy. He'd charmed his way on late night shows; hell, he'd made Johnny Carson laugh. He was a highly sought Broadway star, a movie star, and had graced the covers of magazines with his good looks and charisma. He was Jesus Christ, he was the Phantom, he was Jean Valjean. His legacy, even after his death, was that he *made* Valjean, and while others did great, they were no Peter Arlo.

Peter Arlo was HIV positive.

❖

Peter and I took the summer of 1987 to travel the world while he was still able. He invited Elle and Nathan too, and I was so glad she agreed to come. She still hadn't traveled, hadn't gotten the chance between work and Nathan to even get out of New York City, and the four of us together provided just a sliver of something to look forward to.

Enjoy the now, Peter's voice reminded me on our flight to our first stop, Disney World. Don't worry about what's to come. Just enjoy what's in front of you now.

Nathan took Disney World in like it truly was the most magical place on Earth. After Disney, we flew to Paris, and it was Elle's turn to take in the city as the most magical place she'd ever seen. We went to Italy, rode the Venice gondolas, ate the most delicious pasta and pizza in Sicily, and drank the most amazing wine in Tuscany. Elle and Nathan had to go home after that, and we missed them terribly while traveling to Tokyo, Bangkok, and Sydney. We scratched off all the cities he'd been wanting to visit his whole life, and we ended those six weeks from July to mid-August back at his beach house in Southampton.

"That was a hell of a summer," Peter said, taking a sip of PBR.

"Don't Dream It's Over" by Crowded House played through the speaker as we listened to the crickets and the waves while combing through every memory we'd collected throughout our trip.

"Wasn't it?" I said. "What was your favorite part?"

He leaned back in his chair, looked at the clear, starry night sky, and smiled. "I loved seeing the Sensoji Temple in Tokyo, the Grand Palace in Bangkok, I loved drinking Italian wine, staring at the attractive men in Sydney, and eating pastries in Paris. I loved watching Nathan smile at everything at Disney World and riding Space Mountain with him five times. Oh, and how much he was obsessed with the pizza in Sicily."

"He really loved it," I said, feeling the smile claim my face. "I have a feeling this is going to be a memorable summer for him."

"It's one of my most memorable ones. I also loved watching you and Elle have a cute little moment in front of the Eiffel Tower."

I rolled my eyes. He must have caught me because he let out a laugh. "Elle and I didn't have a moment."

Thank God the sun had already set two hours before because I knew the heat claiming my face would have made Peter cackle.

"Oh, don't play dumb, Marlie. I know you know exactly what I'm talking about."

"There weren't any cute, little moments. She's dating some math teacher named Michael who she works with. She seems happy with him."

That was mostly the truth. She had been dating Michael for the last several months, and at that point in my life, I just wanted her to be happy, and it seemed like she was. Even if there were moments throughout our trip of stealing glances, flitting our eyes away if we were caught, or soft touches on the back and wrists while perusing through the cities, my mind told me that spoke volumes about our history and deep connection more than anything romantic.

"Are you happy about that?"

"I'm happy that she's happy, and that after everything we've been through, she's still in my life."

He pulled another sip of beer as he stared out at the Atlantic. He hesitated for a minute before turning to me again. "You know you deserve love, right?"

"What are you talking about?"

"When was the last time you had a serious relationship?"

I thought about it. "The media thinks you're my serious relationship," I said with a laugh, desperate to erase the tension from the conversation.

He gave me a stern look. "It's a serious question. When was the last serious relationship you had besides Elle?"

Looking back on it now, the memories I have about Elle and those little moments on our vacation seem to clue me in that we might have had something romantic, and if I can remember Peter relentlessly asking me questions about Elle that Southampton night, I can't help but wonder if I might have erased something really good.

Why the hell would I erase something good with Elle?

I exhaled and took another sip of beer. "Fine. Do we count Elaine Prescott?"

"Do *you* count Elaine Prescott?"

I shrugged. "Sure. We went on quite a few dates. Picked our fling up again when you and I moved back to London for *Les Mis* and *Phantom*. But the media thinks I'm dating you, the love of my life." I shook his knee, and while it tweaked out a smile, it didn't fully capture his face like I hoped it would. "What? Peter," I said through a nervous laugh. "Work consumes my whole life. Plus, we live in different times now. We aren't as free to love as we were in the seventies. The world hates us even more than before."

"Doesn't mean you should sacrifice love."

I let out a hollow laugh. For some reason, the heaviness of the conversation poked and prodded at me like a mosquito that wouldn't quit. "I'm not sacrificing love. I'm just focusing on the things I know I can succeed at, like singing. It's gotten me this far."

"Don't do that," he said, shaking his head. "Please don't. I've thought a lot about my life these last few months, and my biggest regret is not falling in love. Or rather, not giving that love a better chance. The sad thing is, I don't know if I have time to know what love feels like once more."

"Peter, don't say that—"

"It's true, Mar. We can't keep pretending that it's not going to happen. I'm sure as hell not going to forget. I'm going to fully live my life until I physically can't anymore. And you should too. Stop running away from the things you're scared of."

"I'm not running away—"

"You've been pretending that you haven't been in love with Elle since eighty-two."

If I was going to receive this lecture, I needed more alcohol. I took a large swig of beer. "Part of being an adult is knowing that not everything you want is right for you. Or both of you."

"How are you and Elle not perfect for each other? You grew up together, you've been through the same things. You have this mutual understanding. I wish so much that I had what you two experienced."

I can hear him saying this in my memory, but I can't remember what he's talking about. I could search through every memory of me and Elle as if I'm searching for one phone number in an entire phonebook, but I'm coming back with nothing. I wish I could remember because by the way his eyes sparkled, and a trace of a smile touched his lips, it sounded like what Elle and I had was something for the movies.

So why the hell did I erase it?

"I love that I'm finally at a place in my career where I can pick any role I want," I said. "Broadway. West End. Hollywood, you name it. I can get it. I'm only thirty-three, and I'm one award away from being the third woman with an EGOT."

"Listen, I hear you. We're successful. You and I have proven that in the last seven years. We don't have to worry about struggling ever again. We can afford to visit anyplace in the world. We can afford these nice waterfront homes and row houses in the Upper West Side. We can be picky with our roles. We've been dominating Broadway and the West End, and crowds are flocking to see us. But my clock is ticking. I'm not going to make it to forty."

"Peter." It had become a reflex now. Anytime the tears threatened, I had to try to get him to stop. My once optimistic friend who saw the good in everything and everyone was now becoming a realist. I guess that's what a terminal virus does to even the most optimistic person.

"No, you're going to listen to me, Marlene."

I pulled my face back and lowered my beer. "You've never called me that ever, Peter Marotto."

"Now, do I have your attention?" I hated how he smiled when he said that, and I hated how contagious his smile was that I even felt one.

"You said my real name that I haven't heard in fifteen years. Yes, you have my attention."

He faltered and looked at his PBR can. We were able to dodge the heaviness of the moment for a split second, but when Peter struggled to make eye contact, I knew his next words would plow me over. I tightened my grip around my can to brace for the impact.

"I have three Tonys and a Grammy. When I first started, I thought getting those defined success. I thought I'd feel a million times more fulfilled. I thought having those awards would replace the fact that my entire family had disowned me for being gay and haven't spoken to me since I was eighteen. But it hasn't. I have a lot of money, awards, a chosen family that has healed what my biological family broke. But I'd trade the money and the awards in a heartbeat if it meant I had the love of my life next to me. That's success. That's the stuff you think about when you're dying."

I had no control of my eyes. I set my can down and cried into my hands. Peter dragged his chair over and placed a hand on my back. I told myself to take in how warm and gentle he was, how good it felt to be consoled by him because the moments were fleeting.

I pulled my face up to look him in the eyes. "I love you, Peter. You know that, right?"

"Of course I do. I love you too."

"Can you feel my love, though? It runs deep enough, right?"

"Marlie," he said, grabbing my hands. "I've felt it every day for the last fifteen years. It's what kept me going through my darkest days, and it's what's getting me through my final days. I don't want you to feel sad. I just don't want you to take life for granted. Promise me you won't."

His eyes were just as watery as mine. I wiped mine to get a better view of his face. "I promise."

"And Marlie?"

"Yes?"

He gave me a half-smile as he placed a hand on my cheek and wiped my face with his thumb. "Thank you."

"For what?"

He shrugged. "For everything. For giving me this summer. For being the best friend I could ever have asked for. For always being there. For being you."

He kissed my cheek. I threw myself onto him and cried into his chest.

❖

Only three people knew about Peter's diagnosis: John, the guy he briefly dated when he found out he was positive, Elle, and me. John was gone by Thanksgiving, but Peter was doing okay. He got sick more frequently, but it didn't stop him from reprising his role as the Phantom when *Phantom of the Opera* came to Broadway in January 1988.

Elle and Nathan came to the opening show to celebrate his eighth birthday. He said he wanted to see Peter and me perform, so we got them orchestra seats in the front row. After having the summer and fall off, Peter was eager to get onstage. Part of me can't help but wonder all these years later if he had a gut feeling that *Phantom* would be his last musical. It was the happiest I had seen him in months. That sparkle found a way back to his warm, dark brown eyes again.

When I think back on the hundreds of wonderful memories with Peter, the Broadway opener of *Phantom* always resurfaces. He gave everything to his performance, and for a few moments on stage each night, I forgot that he was sick. It was like we had transplanted ourselves back a few years before when we had performed it for the first time in London. He sang his heart out, like he did with every show, but I'd performed with him so many times, I noticed when he gave a little extra.

"Let's be sure we give both Elle and Nathan a show they'll always remember," he said, nudging me in the arm as he pulled his Phantom mask down, winking through the eye hole.

After the show, Elle and Nathan came backstage. I got to witness the aftermath of Nathan's first Broadway show light up his face. He looked at us in pure astonishment. "That was amazing," he said, barging into my dressing room. "You guys have really nice voices."

Peter ruffled his blond hair. "You really think so?"

Nathan nodded. "Yeah. Mom was even crying."

"I wasn't," Elle said.

I caught her eyes on me, and as if I wasn't supposed to catch her, she quickly stared at Nathan. The sudden contact made my stomach flip.

"You looked really cool in your mask," Nathan said to Peter.

"You mean you weren't scared?" I said.

Nathan laughed. "No! He's Peter. He's not a bad guy."

Peter snatched the mask from his table and handed it to Nathan. "Here, buddy, keep it as a souvenir."

"What? Really?" Nathan said, looking at the mask as if he was holding a brand-new Nintendo.

"Really. I'm not supposed to give you it, but…" He leaned into Nathan and whispered, "Sometimes, I like to break the rules. Keep it a secret, will you?"

Nathan nodded enthusiastically, put on the mask, and sang the melody to "Phantom of the Opera." His arms extended as if he were performing, and he hit every correct note. All three of us laughed, especially Peter.

"You're a better Phantom than me," Peter said.

We had one of our cast members take a picture of the four of us. Nathan wore the mask on the entire way home, even after we hugged Peter good night.

"Are you going to come over, Marlie?" Nathan asked and repositioned the mask.

"Do you want me to?" He nodded. I glanced at Elle, who had this look in her eyes that told me I should. "If it's okay with your mom, then I'll stop by for a bit."

"She says it's okay," Elle said, the smallest smile touching her lips.

It felt like a spontaneous intimate moment, one my reflexes were ready to bolt away from. Then I heard Peter's voice tell me not to run away. So I listened and followed them home.

Nathan jumped into his bed with the phantom mask still on. It kept sliding down his face, but he was quick to adjust it.

"You'll grow into it in no time," I said when I sat at the foot of his bed.

"You and Peter were so cool up there," he said. I couldn't help but laugh as he tried talking with the mask on. "Are you famous? I saw you and Peter on a sign."

I laughed. "People know who I am."

"My mom says you've been on TV before and that you were in a movie."

"I did. I even won an award."

His eyes grew. "Really?" Elle stepped into the bedroom. "Mom, I want to see Marlie on the TV."

"Oh, you do?"

He nodded again. "Yeah. I want to see her being famous."

Elle laughed and pulled the covers over him as he rested his head on his pillow. "You saw her being famous tonight."

"Everyone was clapping for her and Peter."

"It's pretty cool, right?"

"It was awesome!"

Elle kissed him on the top of his head. "I'm glad you enjoyed it. Maybe we can do it again sometime. Would you like that?"

"Yeah!"

After I said good night to Nathan, I followed Elle into the kitchen. Content silence followed us. We exchanged a glance and smile, and then we both looked away.

"You should have seen his face when the music started playing," Elle said through a laugh. "It was like he saw magic for the first time. He didn't peel his eyes off the stage once. He kept whispering, 'Peter and Marlie are so cool. They sound so good.' I think he's going to remember this night for a while."

"I'm glad. I'll remember it too."

Elle looked at the ground for a moment. Her smile faded just a bit. "It was really nice seeing you perform again. Reminds me of the first time I saw you onstage in *Little Night Music*."

When she finally met my eyes, the memory filled my heart, and the fact that tonight mirrored a moment that had happened fifteen years ago made my heart speed up. "Can I tell you something?"

"You can tell me anything." She stared as if she desperately wanted to hear what I was going to say.

I wondered if she was searching for our past, remnants of our young, carefree days. The words slipped easier from my tongue. "The shows are a million times more special with you in the audience. I'm really glad you and Nathan came."

"I am too. I'm thinking I should make it more of a habit. Maybe one of these days, we can take him to a show together."

"I'd love that. I mean, anytime you want to go, just let me know, and I'll see what I can do. If you wanted to go just you and Nathan or one of your girlfriends or if you and Michael wanted to go together—"

"Michael and I are no longer dating," Elle said.

"Since when?"

"Last week."

"What happened?"

She shrugged and let out a heavy exhale. "We just weren't working out. It wasn't exciting anymore. Isn't that what dating someone you love is supposed to feel like? Excitement? Like you're on this continuous thrill ride?"

I laughed. "You're asking the wrong person. I'm in a committed relationship with my job."

She raised an eyebrow. "You don't want to date?"

"It's exhausting. I've dated. Diane Tyler, Elaine Prescott—"

"Peter," Elle added with a smile.

I laughed. "The love of my life, Peter Arlo. Yes, I'd love to date, but how do I do that when my job has me working anywhere in the world? How do I do that when people are terrified of us? I guess it's a 'don't fix what isn't broken' situation, and I don't feel broken."

"Don't you feel lonely?"

"I did when I lived in London by myself. It got better the second time when Peter and I lived together, and now we're all here in the same city, and that feels like enough." I cleared my throat, feeling the emotions rising like bile. I would have loved a partner, a woman I could come home to and cuddle with, a woman to love, but at that moment, it just wasn't in the cards. "Anyway, maybe one of these days, I can take you and Nathan out. I'd love to treat you to Sardi's. We need to have the full Broadway experience."

"I'd love that."

I wanted my schedule to clear up then and there so I could treat them. I wanted to watch Nathan react to an amazing show. I wanted to sit close to Elle and notice every movement she made. I thought, maybe if all went well with the three of us, I could muster up the courage to ask Elle on a date with the expectations low... even though they didn't feel low back then. Just a night carved out for the two of us to catch up and allow those content silences to blanket us, to allow our eyes to lock, to fully envelop ourselves in the other's presence. I could take them to Sardi's or Windows of the World. Windows was a really spectacular place, or so I had heard. We could have time just with the two of us.

All I needed was a little bit of courage.

As the months progressed, so did Peter's illness. In June of '88, when Peter won his fourth Tony for his role as the Phantom, I could see just how much he had thinned. How his cheekbones and jaw were more defined and how his clothes dangled on his body. He started complaining about night sweats and stomach issues and said that was the reason why he wasn't going to make it to the Sardi's after-party.

After the Tony's, he started getting sick more frequently. He developed a cough, continued to drop weight, and was tired all the time, even if he'd had a full night's sleep. I told him he needed to go to the doctor, and he kept refusing. I think he knew what was happening. We both did.

"Marlie," he said one July night when we finally reached my front door.

He was kind enough to walk me home after one of our *Phantom* shows. I wanted to walk him home, since he wasn't feeling one hundred percent, but he insisted. He said he wanted the fresh air, but on our walk, he didn't say much. When Peter Arlo was silent, he was drowning in his thoughts; I had learned that over the course of our friendship.

"Peter?"

He thinned his lips. That look of shame settled into his features, and my heart plummeted. I knew what he was going to tell me before he said anything. I could hear the drop in his timbre before he even said the word, and I could see how much sadness saturated his eyes.

"I think it's time," he finally said, barely audible. My stomach dropped. He stared at the steps as I grasped the railing. "I don't think I can keep performing. I'm tired all the time, and I just feel…I don't feel as strong as I used to. I don't want to be too weak for my last show. I need to go out when I can still perform and sing exactly how I'm supposed to."

We all knew this moment was inevitable. I could have braced myself, but nothing could have prepared me for how hard it finally hit, like a wall of bricks piling on me in a disintegrated heap. No matter how much I wished I could keep him, my partner in crime, for a little longer, I wanted my best friend to go out with dignity.

His final show was a week later. Elle and Nathan came back, though Nathan had no idea that Peter was even sick. I was amazed by how stoic Peter was backstage. He walked into my dressing room, his disfigured makeup on under his mask, his hair slicked back with gel, wearing his black tux. Even though he needed a new tux to fit his thin figure, he stood tall and filled with pride. While most of the cast didn't officially know Peter was sick, it was pretty obvious in our *Phantom* family what he had. The air in the Broadway Theatre was heavy that night, but Peter did everything he could to make light of things. His smile was wide, his laugh was full, and he cracked jokes with the rest of the cast, trying everything he could to cheer them up.

As we stood in the wings waiting for the orchestra to wake the audience up in the powerful opening song, I could feel my chest tighten, and my eyes were ready at any moment to start leaking. Then, there was a warm hand that gripped my fingers. I looked up and saw Peter smiling at me, and that was enough for my eyes to overflow.

"For what it's worth, the last four years, working with you every day, have been my favorite," he said, leaning into me. "This might not have been the way I thought I'd go out, but I'm glad I'm going out with you by my side." He kissed the back of my hand.

"Peter," I said and dabbed my eyes. "You can't make me cry before we start the show."

"I just want you to know that I'm going to savor every second I'm onstage tonight. My last show is going to be with the best friend I've ever had. I might not be fortunate in some ways, but you've made me fortunate in all the other ways. I love you, Marlie."

"I love you too, Peter."

He smiled. "Let's give these people the best show to date."

His last performance and the way his voice filled the theater proved how much passion he had for singing. I didn't have to act like I was captivated by the Phantom during "Music of the Night" because in that moment, I was wholeheartedly. Peter poured everything into that performance. He found strength I doubted he had. The vibrato in his voice caused a wave of goose bumps down my arms; every bit of energy he had came out through his voice, filling the theater with enough of him that it lingered for weeks after, as if his memory clung to the curtains. He sang with his entire heart. The climax of the song was like his voice capturing the theater in his grip, and I was one of them. The emotion in his eyes as he took me in, the audience, the theater, I knew he was trying to memorize how it felt to sing and perform, the rush that filled our veins and stacked in our chest.

Peter Arlo was in his most authentic form that July night. He knew it was the last time he would ever share his voice with the world. We were the only two people onstage, the song and scene belonging just to us and the audience. I watched as he sang good-bye to Broadway and the world.

I wasn't sure how I'd be able to sing for the rest of the show because the entire time he sang "Music of the Night," my throat tugged, burned, and strained. The tears pooled in my eyes as he had to scoop me up in his frail, weakened arms and place me gently on the bed. I told myself to remember what it was like to feel him around me, the way his gentle hands, arms, and voice had cradled me throughout the years.

I never believed in any higher power. I didn't understand the appeal. I don't know how anyone could expect an orphan to believe in God because who the hell would make a child go through all of that? I didn't believe in Heaven or Hell or angels. I've gone through my whole life believing that once a person dies, that's it. There is no afterlife, there is no one looking down on us, there's nothing but the vacancy we leave.

But I hadn't lost anyone close to me, at least, close enough that I'd lose part of myself when they left. Knowing I was going to lose Peter and that I would have to train myself to breathe without him, I was so desperate to keep a part of him that I started questioning the afterlife all over again because I wanted him to stay with me. Always.

His last performance was so perfect and so powerful that it gave me hope that if there was such a thing as guardian angels, Peter Arlo was strong enough to find his way back to me.

❖

The bad days started becoming more frequent. Peter lost so much weight. He started to sleep more and eat less. I hated leaving him, afraid that he would go without anyone by his bed. So he moved in with me in October 1988. I told Glenn I was taking time off. He was pissed about it, but I didn't care. I wasn't going to push my best friend aside when he needed me. I had the rest of my life to work. I only had a matter of months to be with Peter.

That Christmas, we made Elle's grandma's raspberry thumb-print cookies on Christmas Eve. Peter and Nathan kept eating the dough, and Elle had to playfully smack their wrists with the wooden spoon. We all curled up on my living room couch as Peter read Nathan *'Twas the Night Before Christmas*. I couldn't help but watch as his hands shook while holding the book up for Nathan to look at the pictures. There was one point, I had to pull my gaze off the two of them and look outside the window at the Christmas lights outside to stave off the tears.

Elle must have noticed because she slipped her fingers into mine with a knowing look. Her eyes rounded in sympathy, and she squeezed my hand. We sat there for a moment, and I breathed through the accumulating pressure stacking in my chest with the comfort of Elle wrapped around my hand. It served as a perfect reminder that I'd still have her and Nathan.

Six weeks later, Peter was admitted to St. Vincent's Hospital, the first and largest AIDS ward on the East Coast. It offered the smallest sliver of a silver lining that he would at least get the best treatment. They treated him like a human, and we knew being in New York City afforded the patients with better stories than the ones about doctors and nurses refusing to treat anyone with HIV or AIDS in other parts of the country.

I visited as often as I could. Even when he was asleep, I stayed in the chair and waited for him to wake, helped him eat and drink water or juice, told him stories about my day, reminisced on our favorite memories. As he became sicker and thinner, his smile and laughter faded until it was a good day if he let out one contagious laugh.

On that early March day, I stepped outside and breathed in the warmer-than-usual air. It smelled a bit like spring, and usually, that first smell of warmer weather made me smile. It was a sign that the cold dark winter was long behind us. I loved taking a walk through Central Park on those early spring days. I loved watching the city come back to life, families filling the sidewalks, and the greenery starting to bud. But on that spring day in 1989, I barely noticed the beautiful day cloaking the city. Any spring air that filtered through my lungs on my journey to St. Vincent's was sterilized by the smell of disinfectant the second I stepped through the doors.

Peter didn't wake up until about two hours after I had arrived, after I caught up on some reading and finished *The New York Times* crossword puzzle. "Marlie?" he said weakly, extending his hand.

I tossed the paper aside and scooted closer, clasping on to his frail hand. "Hey, I'm right here."

"Can you…can you do me a favor?" he croaked. He clasped my hands, and although his grip was so weak, I could tell he used everything in his power to squeeze them enough to plead with me.

"I'll do anything you want," I said, holding on just as tightly.

"Sing me something?"

I swatted away a tear. "My voice isn't the best right now. I'll sound like a frog."

"You'll sound like the most angelic frog I've ever had the pleasure of hearing."

"I don't want one of your last moments to be tarnished with my horrible cry singing."

He let out a laugh, quickly followed by a coughing fit. I handed him a glass of water and positioned the straw in between his pale lips. Once he calmed, he closed his eyes, lay back on his pillow, and the smallest degree of a smile tugged at his lips. I was glad I was able to make him laugh. He loved laughing. The majority of my memories are of him laughing or trying to make others laugh, and sometimes, he did so at inappropriate times, but that's why everyone loved Peter Arlo. He just wanted to make everyone laugh, and I was so glad I could return the favor one last time.

"You just said you'd do anything," he said.

"I did say that, didn't I? What would you like me to sing?"

"Anything. I don't want to hear silence or that goddamn heart monitor."

I thought about all of the songs that had shaped our friendship over the years, and the songs that instantly reminded me of Peter. I sang him "Don't Let the Sun Go Down on Me," his favorite song by Elton John.

"Can you promise me something, Marlie?"

I tightened my grip around his hand. "I'd promise you the world, Peter."

"Please don't remember me like this. We have almost seventeen years' worth of memories, amazing ones. Think back on those. Please don't hold on to these."

"Every moment with you has been amazing. Even in the darkest moments, there's still a sliver of light. We're with each other. You've been my best friend and my older brother since, *A Little Night Music*."

"You're the best family I've ever had. Thank you for loving me in all the ways you did."

I swatted at the continuous flow of tears. "It was the easiest thing I ever had to do."

I sang him another song. "You've Got a Friend." I couldn't make it through without crying. He held out his hand, and I brought it up to my chest and held on tightly. I hoped he took in every lyric because it was the perfect song for our friendship and how much I loved him. It was another song that always reminded me of him, and how we would sing it to each other, harmonizing because we were singers and couldn't be stopped. I held his hand the entire time I sang feeling his grip weaken as he drifted off to sleep.

The way he looked, the way he spoke, how he was only awake for about thirty minutes out of the entire day, I knew I couldn't leave him that night. My gut warned me to stay by his side, so I did, combing my fingers through his hair, making sure he wasn't cold, making sure he wasn't alone.

Peter died in his sleep right before dawn on March 2, 1989, three weeks before his thirty-ninth birthday. I stayed with him as the sun rose. I looked outside and noticed pinks, purples, and yellows streaking across the Manhattan sky. It was a gorgeous sunrise, and I couldn't help but wonder if Peter had painted the sky to let me know he was finally at peace.

As he requested, I sang "You've Got a Friend" at his funeral that drew in crowds of people from the theater community. I took in all the faces packed into the church and saw how many lives Peter James Marotto had touched and how many people loved him.

Still to this day, that was singlehandedly the hardest performance of my life.

CHAPTER TWELVE

I think this place is a perfect spot for us to enjoy the summer," I said to Elle and Nathan as we stepped inside Peter's Southampton home the summer after he died. "We kind of all need it, don't you think?"

"This is so cool," Nathan said, running into the house and taking it all in. He ran over to the wall of windows overlooking the back patio and the private beach on the Atlantic Ocean.

Since Peter wasn't married, he had distributed his assets to his chosen family and donated the majority of his money to AIDS research. I was shocked to learn that he'd left the house to me. I knew that he would have wanted me to use the house to grieve and recalibrate in peace.

Three months into living without him, I still hadn't allowed myself to fully grieve. I threw myself back into work to distract from being sad, and it took a while to figure out that I wasn't doing myself any favors. Being Christine without Peter as my Phantom drained me more than I ever expected. By the time June came around, I needed a break, a change of scenery, and to be around those who were also missing Peter.

So I invited Elle and Nathan to spend the summer with me in Southampton.

I surprised them both with a few presents to help us enjoy the summer. For Elle: a bathing suit cover-up, a beach hat I knew she would love, and some books that had been getting great reviews.

And for Nathan: a Nintendo and Rollerblades, with a helmet and kneepads, of course. I didn't know what I was buying when it came to the toys. I happened to spot a woman with a kid who looked to be Nathan's age and asked her what a nine-year-old boy would love. She must have recognized me because she stared with wide eyes and seemed very confused, but she and her son helped me pick out presents, and her son told me what Nintendo games were the coolest. When she asked for an autograph, I bought her the *Cats* soundtrack CD and signed it in return.

"Oh my God, Mom, look, a Nintendo," Nathan yelled when I showed him his room. He opened up the box and stared at the toy like it was a wad of cash. He then plowed into me and gave me a hug, stronger than I was expecting. He was getting bigger, stronger, and older every day.

"Don't spend too much time on that," Elle told him. "You have a beautiful beach out back and really cool Rollerblades."

"I won't, I won't," he said.

What a summer we had. Watching Nathan enjoy everything the summer had to offer was like viewing life through a lens of a nine-year-old. Elle and I read while soaking up the sun on the private beach as Nathan swam in the ocean. He convinced me to buy kayaks so we could get out on the water, and both agreed it was one of the best purchases of the season. That and his surfing lessons.

While all those moments meant so much to me, my favorites were the nights all three of us shared. Sometimes, he wanted to go out to eat and feast on his new favorite meal, lobster rolls. Other times, we sat outside on the patio and took in the pristine views of the ocean and all the peace that came with Southampton. One evening, Elle and I had a glass of wine, and he had a wineglass of grape juice.

"Did my mom ever tell you that I used to think Peter was my dad?" Nathan said.

The mention of Peter's name sent a pang through me, but it was Nathan's laugh and smile that quickly pushed the pain out and filled me with joy. I looked at Elle, and when I saw that smile just for me, my stomach flipped. I quickly glanced back at Nathan, attempting to tame the flutter inside me. "She didn't. Tell me more."

He shrugged. "It was only for a little bit, but I thought he was my dad because he'd come visit and play with me."

"He was a lot of fun, wasn't he?"

"He was awesome. He taught me how to solve a Rubik's Cube. I'll have to show you sometime."

"I'd love that."

He paused again, and his thinking face furrowed his eyebrows and scrunched his nose. "I miss him. I miss Peter."

His confession stung my eyes. I swallowed the lump in my throat. I couldn't cry when Nathan was being vulnerable. I had to remain strong. I downed a large gulp of wine to stop the cries from tugging at my throat.

"Oh honey," Elle said and ran her fingers through his hair. "We miss him too. Very much."

"He was, like, the funniest person I ever knew."

I leaned into him. "He was the funniest person I knew too. He was my best friend."

"My mom said that you were best friends. Is that true?"

"Of course it's true," I said. "You know that we've been friends since we were fifteen, right?"

"I did. Are you two still best friends?"

Elle and I exchanged a glance. I noticed the worry reflecting in her eyes softened by the dusk cloaking us. I offered her a smile, hoping to neutralize her worries. "Of course we're still friends."

I held her stare the entire time, watching as the worry faded, and her gaze became heavier. There was something in that weighted exchange that made it feel more important than all the other moments we had shared during the summer.

"You hear that, Mom? She still loves you."

Elle choked on her wine, inspected her shirt, and then said, "Nathan!"

"What? You said—"

"I think you should go play your Nintendo."

"But I want to sit out here with you."

I bit back a grin behind my wineglass. Watching Nathan embarrass Elle, unbeknownst to him, was the perfect way to lighten the mood. I also couldn't help but wonder if Elle's embarrassment meant something more. Apparently, Nathan knew something that I didn't.

"It's going on eleven," Elle said. "It's getting late."

"It's too late to stay out here but not too late to play Nintendo?"

"Good point," I said.

Elle shot me a playful, stern look.

"Oh, you want *adult* talk. Got it," Nathan said. "When am I old enough for adult talk?"

"When you're an adult," Elle said in an authoritative way that wasn't helping to tame the undertow of intense attraction in my gut. "When you're eighteen."

"Ugh, so nine years? Fine, but when I'm an adult, I'm going to *adult talk*, and you'll have to walk away," he said teasingly.

"That's a deal," Elle said and ruffled his hair. She gave him a kiss on the cheek, but he wiped it off and said good night.

"I remember the days when he didn't wipe my kisses," she said, drinking her wine.

"Just wait until he's a teenager."

"I've been mentally preparing for nine years. I know I have four more left, but I don't think I'm ready."

The stereo harmonized with the crickets and frogs. "Fast Car" by Tracy Chapman started playing. I inhaled a deep breath of warm, briny air as the memory attached to this song played in my mind. I closed my eyes and felt my chest bottom out. It's amazing how memories locked on to songs. If everything around me was calm and quiet, sometimes the memory was so strong, it was like I was reliving it all over again.

"The first time I heard this song was last summer," I said, almost feeling my hair blowing back in Peter's Alfa Romeo Spider. "We were driving down Southampton Highway, and this song started playing. I remember about halfway in, we turned to each other, and I think we both sensed that it was probably the last time we would be driving back from Southampton together. Now, anytime I hear this song, I think of that car ride, that last visit."

Elle slid her fingers down to mine and held them. It pulled my gaze off the patio and to her eyes. The intensity there almost had me undone. Stop running away from the things you're scared of, Peter said in my head against the sounds of Tracy Chapman.

He was right. I needed to stop running. I'd been so terrified of heartbreak again that I'd chosen the path of least resistance and stuck with it. I thought back to the conversation we had last summer. I'd found great success in my career, had enough money to live lavishly for the rest of my life, and was one award away from completing an EGOT. It was safe to say I was very accomplished in the entertainment business as a thirty-five-year-old, but that came with sacrificing time to allow myself to fall in love.

As "Fast Car" ended, the radio started playing "Can't Help Falling in Love." I almost laughed at how serendipitous it was. I set my wineglass on the table and stood.

"This song reminds me of you," I said, holding out my hand.

Elle allowed her smile to grow as she grabbed my hand and stood. I secured the other on the small of her back. She was so close that I could feel her soft breath tickling my lips. Our locked stare rushed over me like a warm July breeze. The air between us held a charge as strong as how we held each other. I thought about the first time I played Elle that song on the piano at Kindred Hearts. It was several lifetimes ago, and here she was, finally in my grip, soft, warm eyes flitting all over my face and skating across my lips. Instead of swatting away the low curl of pleasure in my stomach, I embraced it. I let it spread throughout my body. I wanted myself to feel what it was truly like to have Elle's undivided attention.

I realized then just how deep Kindred Hearts ran through me. I had been told from a young age not to get attached. It was drilled into us so well that at thirty-five, I was still exceling at it. I needed to stop running away. I needed to let go of that motto because damn, it made for a lonely life.

I wasn't going to run from the thing I was scared of anymore.

My face fell into her gravitational pull and rested against hers. I paid attention to every part of my hand that clasped hers as our bodies swayed to the song. Her soft breath grazed my earlobe; the warmth of her cloaked over me. I lost myself in that dance. The way her body pressed against mine made it seem like she longed for my touch as much as I had longed for hers.

"I miss dancing with you," I said into her ear.

She pulled back. "You do?" The look in her eyes seemed confused, yet I noticed some hope sparkling in them, almost as if she wanted to make sure that she'd heard me correctly.

As if I needed more of a nudge, I flashed back to Peter and a conversation we'd had after our trip around the world: *You've been pretending that you haven't been in love with Elle since you've come back to the States. Promise me that you'll stop trying so hard to avoid love. Just let it happen naturally.*

"Of course I do, Elle. I miss everything about us."

She pulled me in so our cheeks naturally fell together. I breathed in a deep smell of her, filling my lungs with her comforting scent. "I'm in love with you, Elle," I said softly. The pressure in my chest released. Her grip in my hand loosened as she pulled back to have another look. "I've been in love with you since we were kids, Elle You make everything…well…lighter. Life feels lighter with you and Nathan. I don't know what I would have done these last couple of months without you."

"Marlie," Elle said softly and placed a hand on my cheek.

I caved into her palm, pleasantly heating my skin as her thumb rubbed my cheek. I could almost see a hundred thoughts swirling in her gaze, and the thought of what they could be made my heart race.

"I know it might sound bizarre, but for the last two years, I've been falling more in love with you from the outside, watching you being a wonderful mother to Nathan, a wonderful friend to Peter. Hell, watching you date and get all smitten about Michael—"

"Marlie—"

"And I've tried to find just a modicum of how you make me feel with other women, and no one has even come close to you, Elle."

"Marlie," she said sternly.

"What?"

"Shut up and kiss me."

I didn't hesitate. I cupped her face with both hands and kissed her like I'd been starved for years. It was far from gentle. She caressed my tongue with hers, and my whole body shot off like a firework. Arousal plunged through my stomach and traveled lower. We kissed deeply until it drowned out the sounds of bugs, frogs, and soft waves, and I collected the sound of Elle's faint moans and little gasps. My center throbbed, and I wanted nothing more than to kiss every inch of her body and make love to her, letting all my feelings for her claim us entirely.

"Should we go inside?" I asked against her lips.

When she nodded, I grabbed her hand, and we tiptoed into my room, quietly locked the door, and I got to show Elle with my mouth, my fingers, and my body how much I loved her. It didn't feel like our first time together. It felt like picking up a dance I thought I had long forgotten. I guess all of those years loving her on the outside helped me memorize every inch of her.

The rest of the summer was ours: Elle, Nathan, and me. Countless stares stolen, and I only know because the handful of times I caught her, her cheeks flushed as she quickly turned away. Moments in the kitchen when we listened to the radio while cooking with Nathan lost in his Nintendo. We got lost in our own little world, touching each other's backs and shoulders or sneaking in a quick peck.

While in bed one August night, the end of the summer weighed heavily on me. I wondered what was going to happen once we returned to the city. Were we going to hold on to all those moments that we'd shared, or was our summer fling going to expire once we heard the honks and sirens of the city?

I wanted to hold on to those moments. The summer didn't have to cool into autumn. All I had to do was follow Peter's advice: stay put and grab what I wanted, and that was a life with Elle and Nathan.

With Elle resting her head on my shoulder and one arm draped over my stomach, I said, "I don't want this to end, Elle."

She looked up and grazed my arm, sending goose bumps all over. "Neither do I."

"How do you feel about you and Nathan moving in with me again? Maybe more permanently than last time."

She pulled her face back. "Are you serious?"

"Of course. I want this, Elle. You, Nathan, all of it."

"I thought you didn't want kids."

I don't remember ever telling her that, but at one point in my life, no, I didn't want children. I didn't think I had it in me to be a good mother. But after being back in New York for the last two years and watching Nathan grow and falling more in love with him every time I saw him, there was nothing I wanted more than to form a family with the two of them.

"Maybe when I was young. That was before Nathan."

She sat up. "This is a serious proposition, Marlie. I don't want you to commit to something you can't follow through on. He's already struggling with not having a father. He's having a hard time without Peter. I can't get his hopes up with you just for you to take it back."

I grasped her hands and looked her straight in the eye. "There's nothing I want more than to be with you, Elle. I want nothing more than for all three of us to be a family. That's something I'm certain I'm not going to take back."

"How about this?" Elle said, kissing the back of my hand. "You sit on it until Christmas when we both have a two week break from school. If by December, you still want us to move in—and everything is going well with us—then we'll do it."

For the first time in two years, something warm sprang through all the dead parts of me. It was like smelling spring air after the longest winter.

❖

"I think we've reached a good spot, Ms. Rose," Dr. Pierson says. "Which memories do you want to erase, if any?"

A sharp pain hammers against my chest like something is already nailing regret on my ribcage. Ever since I agreed to do the procedure, I've thought long and hard about this very moment, and now that it has come, I start to panic because both options come with many cons.

Please don't remember me like this, Peter repeats in my head.

After twenty-seven years without him, I can still hear the desperation in his voice.

I watched one of the greatest epidemics unfold in front of me. I think back to all the funerals I had to attend, and each one stacks like a brick on my sternum. I remember all the fear and the shame that followed the gay community around like a stalking shadow. I remember how it slowly sucked the life out of my best friend. I've had to carry that for almost thirty years, almost twice as long as Peter and I had been friends.

I close my eyes. It physically hurts. Still, after all this time, losing Peter physically hurts.

Can I really live with this chest pain any longer?

Even though my memory is filled with so many holes that it's making me question why I'm going through this entire procedure, I know the answer is still no. I feel so much guilt about not being able to spare him all that suffering. Out of the two of us, why Peter?

"I'd like to erase all of it," I say.

"All of it? Can you please be more specific, Ms. Rose?"

I swallow the grapefruit-sized lump in my throat. "I'd like to forget all of it. Peter. Traveling the world, him getting sick, him dying, and that Southampton summer after Elle and I get together. I know that might seem like a lifetime ago, but it haunts me. Every day. Losing him, our community. I've carried that with me for the last twenty-seven years, Dr. Pierson. Peter didn't want me to remember when he was sick, and no matter how hard I've tried focusing on all our good memories, my mind still flashes to losing him and everything I lost when he died. I love him so much, but he told me not to remember him that way, and I want more than anything to forget about him being sick. But I can't just erase him being sick because I know I'll be so painfully confused about what happened with him and our friendship."

Dr. Pierson gives me a knowing nod. "I know, Ms. Rose. That must be very hard."

"It's impossible. I…I feel like I have no other choice but to erase him entirely."

The rest of the team lifts their heads. Everyone, including Dr. Pierson, fixes their stares on me, some with furrowed eyebrows, others with sympathy looks.

Dr. Pierson's furrowed salt-and-pepper eyebrows and glance tells me he understands the extreme difficulty behind my decision. He thins his lips and nods. "Okay, Ms. Rose. If you're absolutely sure about that, then I will target those memories."

"I'm sure. Thank you."

The lights dim, and I close my eyes.

I love you, Peter. Thank you for everything. I hope you understand.

CHAPTER THIRTEEN

D r. Pierson warned me that I shouldn't venture out during the procedure. But there isn't any chance I'm going to put off visiting Nathan and Melissa. Rekindling my relationship with my son takes priority. Anything I rediscover that I don't want, I can always erase again.

So the following day, I power through the headache that throbs throughout my entire skull, and I fly to New York. It's the worst headache yet, and during the five-and-a-half-hour flight, I wonder what the hell I erased that makes this one so grueling.

I set foot in New York for the first time in a year and a half. Just like the last time, there's a tugging in my chest. I can't tell if it's a good tug at all the sweet nostalgia that weaves around the skyscrapers or if it's the ghosts of everything that went wrong haunting me.

Though when I think about it, I'm not sure what exactly went wrong besides my breakup with Elle that prompted me to move out of our home and then Nathan's wedding. I can feel the ghosts of my past mistakes following me in the cab that I hired from JFK to Scarsdale, but I can't see any figures; I don't know where they spawned from. The heaviness saturates the cab as the driver tells me how his mother was a huge fan. While my heart inflates from hearing the sweet things he says, I can't shake the ghosts.

The emotion rising in me as we drive through Scarsdale, the suburb that Elle and I called home for fourteen years. In December of 1989, while I was playing the lead role of Oolie-Donna in *City of Angels*, Elle and Nathan moved into my brownstone. In June 1990, I skipped the Tony after-party after winning my second Tony for Best Featured Actress and celebrated in our brand-new house in the suburbs. It was that house where I finally got to know Nathan, and our relationship quickly inflated and soared, where my love for Elle deepened to my bones, and where the three of us became a family.

Scarsdale provided us everything we needed. It was peaceful, quiet, family-oriented, and had so much more space. While Manhattan was perfect for my twenties, I wanted nothing more than to have a peaceful home to come back to at the end of the night by my mid-thirties. Driving through the quiet roads reminds me of watching Nathan riding his bike and Rollerblading around the idyllic sidewalks. I hope I can see my grandson grow up on these sidewalks like I watched my son.

The cab drops me off at Nathan and Melissa's home, the one I bought them for their wedding. I haven't had the chance to see it in person. I take a deep breath before I knock on the door. When it opens, I find Nathan standing there, and while I was lost reminiscing about him growing up in this town, I'm amazed by how grown-up he looks. He inherited his mother's all-American looks, the kind of face that radiates subtle beauty and warmth. He gives me a vibrant smile, one I wasn't really expecting.

"Hi, Nathan," I say, trying my best not to cry.

"Hi, Marlie." He holds out his hands and barrels into me. He gives the best hugs. Always has.

I close my eyes and take in the feel of him wrapped up in my arms. I missed him terribly.

Finally, he breaks away. "I'm so glad you're here," he says. "Come on in. Let me take your suitcase."

I find Melissa in the kitchen. She turns and gives me a heartwarming smile and hug. I tear up at the sight of her little bump, the first sight of my grandson.

They're quick to offer me a glass of wine before giving me the tour. It's beautiful, and I love so much how it's turned into a home for them. They show me the nursery; there's not much in it besides a dresser, a rocking chair, and a few paint samples of different colors of blue and green. I make a mental note to find their registry and help them with a few things. I'm already thinking about the perfect crib.

After the tour, I offer to help in the kitchen. While Melissa graciously declines, Nathan lets out a laugh. "Marlie, we know your skills are lacking in that department."

Honestly, I'm just glad he's teasing me. I try to enjoy the moment, knowing that once I tell him about the procedure, the laughs, smiles, and teasing may be gone.

I feign shock. "Hey, you act like I've set the kitchen on fire. I have not, for the record."

He turns to Melissa. "There was this one Christmas Day, Mom and Peter were in the living room, and Marlie was yelling in the kitchen because she burned the mashed potatoes, and the entire house smelled. I was upset because mashed potatoes were everything to an eight-year-old." He laughs and playfully taps my arm. "Don't you remember that, Marlie?"

I stare at him blankly. I don't know what he's talking about, and I have no idea who Peter is. I assume he was someone Elle used to date. It makes a little sense as to why I don't remember him if that was the case, but I can't help but pause to wonder why I would erase someone she dated. I remember Robert from Howard Johnson's, Michael from her high school. So why don't I remember someone named Peter?

I stop my wandering mind right there. Instead, I tack on a smile. It's too early for me to tell Nathan anything. "Of course I do," I say and wash away the foul-tasting lie with pinot noir.

"Because that memory is burned into my brain as much as the mashed potatoes were burned into the pot. You should sit. Relax. Enjoy the wine. You're our guest, and you had a long flight. Let us treat you."

"Well, if that's the case, I could always use a massage and one of those cute drink umbrellas."

"Well, lucky for you, we actually do have cocktail umbrellas." He walks over to the bar cart and plucks out a pink one and sticks it in my wine. "There. Now, never say I didn't get you anything special."

I place a hand over my heart. "I'd never. This outdoes all the pictures you drew for me in preschool."

It isn't until dinner when the guilt starts to stack on top of me. Melissa cooked a delicious dinner: her mom's lasagna, balsamic-glazed brussels sprouts, and homemade focaccia bread. It's clear she's gone above and beyond to make us a delicious meal, and I know that whenever I decide to tell them the news, all her kindness and hard work is going to hide in the shadows.

I try to shake my guilt by asking them questions about the baby and doctor's appointments and their jobs. Nathan is still working at the same PR agency in Manhattan, and the three of us cheer his newest promotion. Melissa still runs her own practice as a child psychologist. After the job updates, I ask about their recent travels and hear all about their vacation around Italy.

"The pizza we had in Sicily was amazing, but it wasn't quite as delicious as when the four of us went when I was a kid." Nathan turns to me. "Am I just being nostalgic, or was that actually the best pizza ever?"

"Better than Joe's?" Melissa asks, feigning shock.

"According to my memory." Nathan nudges me. "Marlie, what was the truth? Was that place in Sicily really better than Joe's?"

I don't remember being in Sicily. I take a moment to search my mind, but I come up with nothing. A warm flash of guilt washes over me. The confusion fogs my brain. I down the last gulp of my wine to try to release the pressure.

"The Sicily pizza was delicious," I say, assuming that pizza in Italy has a slight advantage over New York.

The conversation is fun and light until Melissa says good night and heads to bed early to give us alone time. When she leaves, she takes the protective conversation shield with her. The first floor becomes quieter, and everything Nathan and I have been dancing around for the last several hours has all the space in the world now to saturate the living room. He pours us another glass of wine, and as the silence settles, I can almost see the divide between us.

"I feel like I've been talking this whole time," he says as he takes a seat by me on the couch. "I'm done. Tell me about you."

I force a smile and pat his knee. "You know I love hearing about you and Mel. It seems like you two are doing very well."

"We really are, and it's about to get even better when we finally have the little guy."

"I can't wait to meet him."

"I can't wait to meet him either." He pulls a sip of wine. "It's time for me to grill you with questions now. What's new with you?"

"Well…I have an audition while I'm in town."

His eyes widen. "Are you serious?"

I nod. "Yup. This director is begging Helen, my manager, to get me to audition for the *Hello, Dolly!* revival on Broadway."

"So when you get the part, you'll be back in the city…"

"Early next year. *If* I get the part, it would be perfect timing for the baby."

"Wow, that is perfect. I'm sure so many of your fans would also love for you to come back."

"Yeah, maybe." I glance at my wine. It's starting to become much easier to look at than Nathan because all I can think about is how I feel like I'm ready to burst.

"Hey, is everything okay?" He rests a hand on my shoulder.

His question plows through me. I'm not sure how much longer I can sit next to him and swallow the truth. I run through the pros and cons. What would soften the impact? Telling him now may taint the rest of my visit. He may not even want to see me after this. Do I carry the guilt with me and tell him at the end? That seems like the coward's way out.

I take a long drink. "Nathan, I need to talk to you about something," I say, too low and too soft. The guilt and shame swell inside me like a balloon stretching thin from too much air.

He lowers his wineglass. "What is it? What's wrong?"

I falter. How do I compose my next words? How do I tell him that I'm erasing all the painful memories of my life, that, based on how many seem to be missing, some of them have to include him and his mother. In spite of the number of times I rehearsed my speech on the flight over, the words feel like a hair clump stuck to my tongue.

"I'm sorry. This is really difficult to say—"

"Is everything okay? Are *you* okay?" Panic rises in his voice.

"Yes, I'm fine. There's no sickness or death or anything like that."

He deflates. "Thank God." He pauses. "What's wrong then? You seem...I don't know. Off. "

I look up and see the worry in his hazel eyes. God, he looks so much like Elle, the reminder is like a punch to the stomach. I clear the words lodged in my throat. "I've been going through a hard time, a really hard time. I know all three of us have been going through it the last year and a half."

He sets his glass on the end table. "Mom..."

Him calling me Mom breaks the seal. He mostly calls me Marlie, and every time he calls me Mom, my heart tightens around the word.

"I know it hasn't been easy since the wedding. We should maybe talk about that while you're here."

"We should, but I have to get this out first." I exhale and look at his comforting hand on my wrist, knowing he'll pull it back once I get the words out. "There's really no easy way to approach this, so I'm just going to come out and say it. I'm going through this procedure—"

"What kind of procedure?"

I shake my head as the tears break free and fall down my face. I quickly swat them away. "One that helps relieve pain, trauma, heartbreak."

He raises an eyebrow. "Okay...how?"

I can feel my stomach twist into individual knots. "It's called neurological reimaging."

"What does that mean?"

"It means," I say and attempt to dislodge the growth in my throat. "It means erasing memories."

"What?" He sounds like the wind has been knocked out of him. He takes his hand back, and I glance up, and his eyes reflect confusion and fear.

I clear the feelings bubbling in my throat. "I'm having painful memories erased."

He falters as a frown details his face. "What kind of memories?"

"I don't know. I...I don't remember."

"Why would you want to erase your memories?"

"Because they hurt and haunt, Nathan." No matter how many times I wipe my eyes, I can't keep my face dry. "That's what the procedure is all about. Erasing trauma and grief, the things that prevent people from living their lives, and honestly, I've been struggling for a while."

"What...what have you erased?"

"I don't know. They're erased. That's the point."

I see the worry setting in, shaping his stare to a shocked expression. "Did you erase me?"

"Of course not."

"Have you erased Mom?"

I drop my stare to my lap again, feeling my chest absorb all the shame, guilt, and confusion I've been trying to swat away for the last couple of days.

"You erased Mom?" he says with a raised voice. His confused and terrified expression contorts to anger, the very expression I've been fearing.

"I...I don't know. I don't think so—"

"Oh my God. You don't even know?" He stands. "What do you remember about her?"

I dig through my earliest memory, hopping over each hole in my timeline that doesn't really add up. "Meeting her at the children's home, moving to Manhattan, and our first apartment at the Whitby, blocks from Times Square. I know she lived down the block from me when you were little. I know that we were friends for a long time before you two moved in with me for a bit before moving out here."

"I'm sorry, what?" His voice sharpens. "Friends for a long time until we moved to Scarsdale? Jesus, Marlie. Do you have any recollection of you two being together? A couple? When you were young?"

Another cry spills from me. Apparently, what I think in my head isn't the truth. All I can recall is that Elle and Nathan moved into my brownstone with me for a couple of months before we bought our Scarsdale house. Though, when I think about it, I'm not sure how we got to that point. From being friends to Elle and Nathan moving in. My stomach drops when I assume that this other part of my life that doesn't quite add up might very much be because I erased something.

I look at my lap and shamefully shake my head. "No, I don't."

"Are you serious? What the hell, Marlie? So instead of calling her and—I don't know—making up, you decide to erase her instead? Your whole history?"

I glance up at him, feeling my eyes water. "You have every right to be angry with me, Nathan, but I had very good reasons to go through with this."

"Like what?"

I pause. That's when it dawns on me that I don't remember at all what propelled me to do this. "I...I don't remember—"

"You don't remember? Jesus!" He snatches his wineglass and darts for the kitchen.

I get up and follow him, "But I know myself, and I know I wouldn't go through with something like this if I didn't have a good reason for it."

"How do you know yourself when you've erased parts of your life? You can't even remember what prompted you to do this."

I hush for a few moments, but the sharp edges around each passing second of silence feel like a cut against my skin. "I need you to understand—"

He slams his glass on the counter and glares at me. It's like the distance between us doubles and causes me to halt. It's the same look he gave me the morning after the wedding, after I left early because of the argument I'd had with Elle. I can feel the balloon in me burst. It sends a warm, sharp pain through my chest.

"How am I supposed to understand if you don't even know why you're doing this? What was the plan? To erase Mom completely?"

"Not completely."

The way his stare contorts makes me feel like a villain. "And have you found any relief in that?"

"There's been relief, yes, but mostly, confusion has taken the place of the pain. I'm really confused."

"No shit."

I directed a firm point at him. "Don't use that language with me." I'm almost as surprised to hear the motherly tone in my voice as he seems to be. There were only a few times I needed a stern voice with him, even during his teenage years.

He pours another large glass, takes a long drink, and then says, "When are you going to tell her?"

"I don't know."

"You don't know?" He let out a small, hollow laugh. "Have you even thought this procedure through at all, or did you just decide on a whim you were going to erase everything and see how it went?"

I raise my hands in defeat. I don't blame him for being upset. He's handling the news as I would have handled it, I'm sure. But I know that nothing I say is going to help. It's best if I stay somewhere else until he fully processed the news. "You're angry. I understand—"

"Yeah, I'm angry. You're erasing your life. You're erasing my mom, which means you're erasing parts of your family, my family. I know you two have had your differences in the past, but did you really have to erase them because they're uncomfortable for you? I've gone through shit too, and I'm not out here wiping my memory clean."

I want to explain myself and the reasons behind why I chose what I did, but that's the downfall of erasing the memories. I don't remember what prompted me to go through with it. I can't recall the memories of Elle that I wanted to get rid of. I don't have enough of my own explanation to let Nathan in as to why I did it. I just know that I'm doing it, and that I'm hurting…and I'm so confused that it's turning into frustration and anger within myself.

"How about this," I say. "I'm going to stay the night elsewhere. You need time to process, and I don't want to be the thing that makes you uncomfortable in your own home. And when you're ready to see me, hopefully by Sunday, you'll let me know, and I'll come back. I'm very sorry, Nathan."

I wait for him to respond, but he doesn't. He can't even look me in the eye. He rests both hands on the kitchen counter and looks down. My news has bulldozed all the happiness highlighting his face and voice from earlier, and it guts me to know how defeated he looks.

I know the right choice is to give him space. So I find a hotel in White Plains, call a cab, and try to hold in my rising emotion so the driver and hotel employees don't witness me crying. It's incredibly hard. My eyes leak uncontrollably, and I'm barely able to tell the driver thank you as I hand him his tip in cash.

When I walk inside the hotel, the front desk employee stares at me wide-eyed and starstruck, and her hands shake as she types on her computer. Several other people walking around the lobby stop, stare, and whisper. I give them a polite smile, and their grins expand. That always feels good. Something as simple as a wave or smile can make someone's day, and even though I've been recognized for decades, that part never gets old to me. It's something I'm used to and something I'm okay with as long as someone doesn't overstep in my personal space.

Once I'm in my room, I drop my suitcase, text Nathan so he knows where I'm staying, and plop on the bed. I snatch a pillow and hug it, letting out everything I've been bottling up for the last hour.

It's not a surprise that Nathan doesn't text me back.

I do a lot of thinking, so much that my night consists of frayed bouts of sleeping, tossing and turning, and never finding a comfortable spot. I think about Nathan's reaction and how it was just as I expected. I think about Elle and the last time I saw her at Nathan's wedding, how my heart and stomach flipped upside down when I saw her looking beautiful in a violet dress. My body never stopped reacting to the sight of her, even though we had been broken up for years. She offered me a friendly smile. We made small talk about how beautiful the decorations were and how we couldn't believe that Nathan was about to get married. We talked about how perfect a match Melissa was for our sweet, selfless son, and how even though we had our ups and downs, we still managed to raise him into being quite the gentleman.

There was a sharp pang that rippled through me when a woman came up behind Elle before the ceremony started, gliding her hands up her back and to her shoulder. Elle gave her a look like she used to give me, a smile that came on so effortlessly, with a magical sparkle in her eye. The pang sharpened and deepened when I watched the two dance to "Can't Help Falling in Love" during the reception, and how it made me so uncomfortable, I had to excuse myself. She found me twenty minutes later, and that was the mistake we both made. My broken heart spoke before my brain had the chance to mute it. I couldn't get over how she danced to our song right in front of me, and she couldn't believe that I would bring that up at our son's wedding.

I was so heartbroken. It felt like Elle stabbed me in the back and heart by dancing to our song, the one I played her at Kindred Hearts, and the one we danced to countless times in that Scarsdale home together. If our roles had been reversed and I had brought my partner to Nathan's wedding, there would have been absolutely no chance I would have danced to a song that had my ex written all over it. Out of all the sweet, slow songs the DJ played that night, it would have been the one song that I would have been more than happy to skip out on.

After our heated exchange, I couldn't last much longer. I said my good-byes to Nathan and Melissa two hours before the reception ended. I tried to power through the choking and burning in my chest, but with the guests' eyes alternating between me and Nathan and Melissa, I couldn't tack on a smile when I felt like my heart was being broken all over again, this time with an audience at my son's wedding. I wasn't able to act through that kind of pain, and the last thing I wanted was to ruin a beautiful wedding.

So I excused myself early and apologized to Nathan and Melissa the next morning.

But by that time, the damage had already been done.

❖

The next morning, I wake up with swollen eyes, a warm face, and a text message from Elle. I haven't seen her name on my phone in a year and a half. I sit straight up, feeling my heart pound as if I just tossed back ten espressos.

Nathan tells me you're in town and that we should talk. If you let me know where you are, I can come to you.

I text her my hotel and room number, and an hour later, she knocks on the door. I barely have the strength to get through what will be an even harder conversation than Nathan.

When I open the door, Elle stands on the other side, shooting a stern look my way. Her thirty-five year-long teaching career has sharpened her look. Even though she retired five years ago in 2011, the perfection of that expression hasn't wavered. Her jaw is just as structured, her eyes warning that she has no time for the bullshit I'm about to serve her.

But even under the scowl, she's just as beautiful as the last time I saw her. Her hair rests right above her shoulders in long layers, and even with the teacher look directed at me, her beauty still manages to steal just a bit of air from me.

I clear my throat and gesture her in. "Hi, Elle."

She forces a friendly smile. "Hi, Marlie. It's been a while."

"It has. You look…you look really great."

"Thank you."

By how short and flat her responses are, I can tell she's clinging on to our last encounter. I don't blame her. With all the history I'm sure we have, it's probably hard for her to lower her guard.

"It's nice that you're in town again," Elle says. "I know it means a lot to Nathan and Mel."

"I'm glad I'm here too." I sit on the sofa as Elle takes the chair opposite. "How have you been?"

"I've been okay. Excited about our grandson." The smallest smile tweaks on her lips, and naturally, I can feel my own tugging upward.

"Me too. How's Lisa?"

Her smile fades. "We broke up six months ago."

"I'm sorry to hear that," I say and genuinely mean it.

"Me too, but it's okay. I'm okay. The older I get, the more I realize that being alone can be as good as being with someone."

I wonder if that's how I feel or if it's just that I have no other choice than to accept being alone.

"Anyway," she says, exhaling and tacking on the faintest cordial smile. "Nathan called me this morning. He sounded very stressed. Said you were in town and that I should reach out to you to talk. What's this all about? Why is he so upset?"

I glance at my lap. I hate that I can't look Elle or Nathan in the eye. It causes a prickly warmth to snake around my spine. "He's upset because I'm undergoing a procedure that relieves pain, heartbreak, and depression."

"Okay..."

Though I still can't look up, by the tone of her voice, I can picture her furrowed eyebrows and the sharpness of her look intensifying.

"The procedure is called neurological reimaging. It's, um, it's a fancy way of saying erasing memories."

There's a quick beat of silence that yanks my gaze to Elle. Her eyes widen. "What?" Disbelief and confusion saturate her voice.

"I'm erasing painful memories."

Her mouth falls. "*Okay*, what painful memories?"

I shrug and push through the stinging in my eyes. "That's the thing. I don't remember what I erased."

"You don't remember what you erased?"

I flit my eyes to my lap. "I, well, I know that I don't remember some of our beginning—"

"What?" she says with a raised voice. "You...you erased us?"

"Not everything, but—"

"Do you know how we met? Our first kiss? Do you remember living with me and Nathan for fourteen years—"

"I met you at Kindred Hearts. I know we lived together in the Whitby and Scarsdale. I'm…I'm not finished with the procedure. I still have a few more sessions—"

"So you don't remember our first kiss?"

"It was in my brownstone in September of '89. Nathan was at a friend's house, you came over, and we…well…had a nice moment on the couch."

"Are you serious, Marlie? You think our first kiss was in 1989?"

I take it from her red face and the harshness and vulnerability in her voice that what I said wasn't our first kiss or anywhere close to it. I don't realize how much I've lost until Elle asks me about all the things I should have in my memory bank. As I try to remember and come up with nothing but a desert, I break down.

What have I done? I run my hands down my damp face.

"How about this," Elle continues with a firm tone before quickly running a finger below her eyes. "You tell me what you actually remember of us?"

"I remember everything at Kindred Hearts, moving to Manhattan with you, living together at the Whitby, and…that's when things become patchy for a while."

"When does it become clear again?"

I think. "When I was in *City of Angels*. I know we dated throughout the fall, right before Christmas when you told me you wanted to move in with me, and everything after that."

Elle pauses as if searching through her thoughts. "Do you remember Southampton?"

"Of course I remember Southampton," I say a bit flatly. "It was a huge argument when we broke up. We sold it in '04."

Elle rolls her eyes. "Marlie, I'm not talking about the breakup. I'm talking about the summer of '89. That's when we got back together. In Southampton. We spent a whole summer there with Nathan." I blink a couple times when nothing resurfaces. Before I even have time to speak, Elle stands, "Oh my God, Marlie. What have you done?" She throws her hands over her chest and sucks in gulps of breaths. I'm terrified that the stress is mounting in her and that she's going to have a panic attack.

"Elle, are you okay?"

She stares at the opposite wall, and after a couple of moments, she turns and gives me this look as if I have done something completely atrocious. And I have, I really have, and God, I've never been so ashamed of myself.

"So half our lives, it's just gone?" she says.

"It's not all gone. I told you I'm not done with it—"

"So you're in the process of fully erasing our entire story? Is that your goal?" She shakes her head and wipes her face, seeming careful of her makeup. "Who am I to you? Honestly. If everything... if every part of us is gone, what's left of me?" She sits back in the chair, buries her face in her hands, and cries.

Hearing her soft, muted cries and watching her back shake sends a sharp ache through my chest and a burning current through my veins. I think back to all the side effects that Dr. Pierson and his team warned about: the throbbing headaches and confusion so intense, it feels like vertigo. But nowhere in those thick packets do they talk about how difficult it is to tell your family.

Nathan was right. I should have considered that before going through with it. I was so stifled by years of depression that my only focus was healing myself from the memories that had been haunting me for decades.

What the hell was I thinking? "Elle, I'm...I'm so sorry—"

"Don't," she says, snapping her head out of her hands to give me a look of absolute disgust. "Don't you dare say that now."

"I really am," I say with a quivering voice. There's a strain yanking on my throat as I swallow back the cries.

"Forty-seven years just ripped up? Just like that? I don't understand. Why the hell do you want to erase us?"

"Because it absolutely breaks my heart that we're not together. I can't live like this anymore."

"It breaks your heart? I wanted to marry you, Marlie," she says, the loudest her voice has been during the conversation. "I wanted to marry the love of my life when it was finally legal in Massachusetts.

You didn't want that. You were too afraid to do that. So what? You get to free your mind of that because saying no was too hard for you?"

"I wanted to be with you, Elle—"

"And you could have. People had been speculating about your sexuality for years. You really think marrying me would have made a difference?"

"I don't think you understood how homophobic the entertainment industry was back then. Careers were ruined when people came out."

"I was tired of hiding. I wanted to be with the woman I had been in love with since I was nineteen, and it took thirty-one years for me to realize she didn't love me enough to be with me."

"If I didn't love you, Elle, then why do you think I'm going through this? I loved you so much, and the thought of losing you is something I've struggled with for years."

"Having someone erase me from their life doesn't feel like an act of love, Marlie. It's cowardly."

"Cowardly?"

"Yes, cowardly. I know we weren't perfect. Far from it. I know I've hurt you as much as you've hurt me. I know we've been up and down for years, but God, Marlie, I'd never erase you, not for a second." She wipes both of her eyes and sucks in another gulp of air. "You want to know why?"

"Why?"

"Because even the bad times were worth it to me. I loved you, Marlie. I loved you more than I had ever loved anyone, and that means something to me. I was in love with you, and I know you were in love with me, and that alone means, at one point in our lives, we did something right, and that's worth keeping. At least, it is for me. I'm sorry it wasn't worth keeping for you."

My throat tightens in a knot. "I don't like this, Elle. I don't know why I did this."

"You must have had what you thought was a very good reason," she says with a bite.

"I must have, but being here, with you and Nathan, I'm realizing how much I want to remember. I'm so confused right now. I was warned about the confusion. I know it's a side effect until the procedure is complete but...I didn't think it would be this hard to deal with. I feel like I don't know myself or my life or my family anymore."

"That's something you should have thought about before going through with this." She swipes her eyes again and lets out a shaky exhale. "You know, you coming back to New York, I thought it could be the start to us mending our family. I thought we could finally patch things up in time for our grandson to come into this world. I never thought you'd tell me that you put us through the shredder. Luckily for you, you can go back to Malibu and finish your fancy procedure. But the rest of us—me, your son, your daughter-in-law, and your grandson—we're going to be left picking up those shreds, so thank you for that, Marlie."

She gets up and heads to the door.

I stand. "Elle, please, wait—"

But she storms out without looking back.

CHAPTER FOURTEEN

I lie in bed for the rest of the afternoon, replaying the whole conversation with Elle and Nathan, replaying my whole life and all the holes scattered throughout my story. I can feel my eyes swollen and burning. I debate if I should call Kristina or not. She's the only one who might know what prompted me to do this procedure in the first place. Whatever that reason was, it must have been awful enough to make me pull the trigger.

Is that something I want to remember?

It scares me that the answer is yes.

I stare at my phone. Do I really want to go through with asking Kristina? Once I start collecting more information, the more I might start to remember, and what if I don't like remembering everything I erased? What if my memory comes back, and I wish it hadn't?

My phone chirps with an incoming text. It's Elle. I sit straight up, my heart thudding in my ears. I trace the letters of her name. I can already feel her words plow through me, and I haven't even read them yet. I take a deep breath, brace for impact, and open the text.

I found something you might find useful. If you're serious about trying to remember. You should come over if you're interested. Nathan is here, by the way. Let me know what you decide.

My breath sputters out. It's the last thing I expected. I thought my telling her would prevent her from ever contacting me again. My pulse races. I worry if I remember everything, I'll put myself in the same position of wanting to erase my memories all over again.

Pain threads through my body and tightens around me as I weigh my decision.

There's nothing I want more than my family. I want to jump across the gargantuan hole that separates me from Elle and Nathan and embrace them, but that won't happen until I find the strength to make the leap.

I understand why Dr. Pierson strongly advises not to travel during the procedure. Living in a constant state of confusion, and mental vertigo is more difficult than I could have ever imagined. I know it will go away once the procedure is over, and Dr. Pierson warned me I needed to trust the process, but my entire identity is a puzzle dotted with so many missing pieces that I hardly recognize myself. I don't know how I even got here.

I want my family back. I want my story back.

I'll be there in 45 min.

After reapplying my makeup to hide the puffiness, I take a cab back to Scarsdale.

Elle still lives in our house. After we broke up in 2004, I moved back to Manhattan for a few years before starting my break in 2009 to pursue movie roles in LA. Since I was the one who rejected her marriage proposal, I thought it was only fair to allow her to keep the house. It didn't matter to me. We might not have been married, but Elle and I had a life together. The house, the furniture, the summer home in Southampton paled in comparison to losing the love of my life.

The cab pulls up to the end of the driveway, where we're met with wrought iron gates. I plug in the code Elle texted me, and the gates open. As we pull down the driveway, I take in the house that Elle and I turned into a home. The summer nights we taught Nathan how to ride a bike on the driveway. In the front yard, we took prom pictures with him, his high school girlfriend, and their group of friends. The living room is where I taught him how to play the grand piano in the corner, where I listened to him practice for his recitals. The kitchen is where we made raspberry thumbprint cookies every Christmas Eve, and while they baked, Nathan played Christmas songs on the piano while I sang to Elle. The backyard is where we hosted parties, like my favorite one that celebrated me officially adopting Nathan in 1996 when it finally became legal for me to do so in New York.

A house is just a structure that protects you from the weather. A home is a feeling of warmth and peace, a lockbox of love. Our Scarsdale house was my home for fourteen years, and when I step out of the cab, I can almost feel the warmth and peace filter through my chest like a soft summer breeze.

When she lets me in, the smell of the house fills me with comfort. I haven't been inside this house in twelve years. The furniture is different, the living room has dark hardwood floors instead of beige carpet, and the kitchen has been completely renovated. I notice the empty corner in the living room where my piano used to be and all the memories that weaved through the hammers and strings. Nathan is sitting on the living room couch, the same one Elle and I bought all those years ago, in the same spot as when I moved out. There is a small moving box between him and the coffee table.

"Hi, hon," I say.

He thins his lips, a forced fraction of a smile, but I'll take it. "Hi, Marlie."

Elle walks into the living room, and I follow. I notice her swollen eyes and the bags that sag underneath. She looks exactly how I did before hiding it with makeup, and while it sends another pang through me knowing I caused her so much hurt that evidence of it still details her beautiful face, I'm a bit relieved that I'm not the only miserable one.

"What's in the box?" I say, knowing that whatever is inside is the reason she has softened just the smallest bit.

"A Hail Mary," Elle says. Anger lingers in her tone. I ignore it because there has to be a good reason she and Nathan invited me over. I frown at the box. "We read up on your procedure."

"You did?"

"It said on the Farrow Institute's website that after the procedure is complete, there's a twelve percent chance your memories will return with a meaningful enough trigger," Nathan says. "It also said that the risk of uncovering memories is greater during the procedure, and Mom says you haven't completed it yet."

"I have a few more sessions left," I say. "I wasn't supposed to travel during the process because I could easily come across something that would bring them back. The doctor says memories hide in one another all throughout the brain, so parts of memories I've erased could very much be tied to the ones I haven't touched yet."

"So if you really wanted to recover them, we can trigger them," Nathan says.

"Just depends on how badly you want to remember," Elle says. Her stare still shoots daggers at me. It's not as sharp as last night, though. It's dull enough that the choking feeling in my chest loosens.

I stare at the box next to Nathan, wondering what the hell is inside. Elle is watching me carefully. "Did the good outweigh the bad? With you and me? Or are we just destined to be a tragedy?"

"Of course the good outweighed the bad. Almost all my best memories are with you," she says, her tone matching the softness in her eyes.

"Really?" Her words pack a surprising punch. I'm not sure if the punch is more fear of already erasing them or absolute confusion as to why I'd erase something powerful enough to have her deflate. "Then why would I want to erase us?"

"I don't know, Marlie. I honestly don't know."

Silence falls as I search for an answer in the desert of my mind only to come up with tumbleweeds. Skeletons of memories but nothing substantial enough to give life. And just like that, the memory tumbles by.

She stares at the ceiling for a moment. I wonder if she's fighting back her emotions as much as I am. "You and I weren't perfect, Marlie. Far from it. But just because it wasn't perfect doesn't mean…" Her voice cracks around her last word. Once she inhales, she looks me in the eyes. The anger dissipates in her stare, and the hurt comes rushing to the forefront and brims her eyelids. "Just because it wasn't perfect doesn't mean that you weren't the great love of my life. I finally accepted that after Lisa and I broke up."

My heart bursts open, begging for Elle to keep going. I take a seat in the recliner, a new piece of furniture where the piano once was. I might not remember the entirety of our relationship, but those fourteen years of being with Elle in this house still cling to my memory. I'm almost certain that she's the greatest love of my life too. Because if she wasn't, then the pain of losing her would never have driven me to erase her.

"If you want to remember, try the box," Elle says, setting it on my lap. "You always wanted to read my journals. Now you have all of them. All the ones since we were fifteen." I peer inside and see mounds of books packed away. "Not every page has you in it, but there's enough of our story that it might bring your memories back. It's worth a shot."

I glance at them. Their glares have softened, and the anxiety loosens around my chest when I see them looking at me with curiosity and worry more than anger.

"If you want, you can stay here and read them," she says.

"Really?"

She shrugs. "Why not?"

"Because I hurt both of you. I wasn't trying to. I was just…" I let out a heavy exhale and shake my head. It seems foolish to say I wasn't trying to hurt them. "I'm really sorry, but I'm going to do everything in my power to fix it, us, our family."

"How about this?" Elle says. "How about you stay here—if you want—decide what you want to do, and Nathan and I can pick up some pizza. You want the usual from Alessandro's? Burrata salad and sausage and peppers?"

I love how she still remembers my order. Alessandro's was our Friday night meal when we wanted to have a fun night in. Even if I needed to eat healthy, I still snuck in a slice or two in addition to the burrata salad I always ordered.

"You know what? I want to emotionally eat. Forget the burrata salad. Let's get the garlic knots."

"Okay. You ready, Nathan?"

"I don't quite understand why you're being so nice, Elle," I say.

Nathan stands and pauses, flitting his stare to Elle, who looks down for a moment. "I'm doing whatever it takes to not have my greatest love story erased. I have no other choice."

They go, and I'm left with my ghosts. I pull the journals out one by one, opening to the first page and seeing that the first page has the year in Elle's handwriting. I line up the books on the coffee table and arrange them in ascending order. I start with the 1969 journal, the same green and pink flowered journal from her lap the first day I met her when she was in the library. I turn to the first page and her scribbly childish handwriting.

This is the Elle I remember the most, the quiet girl who was the only one to occupy the library instead of the TV room. She comes to life on these pages.

At first, it feels invasive. My memory might be blotchy, but I remember enough about Kindred Hearts to know that Elle's journals were sacred. While I held on to my stuffed teddy bear, she did the same with her journals. Her entire life is woven into the pages of scribbly words.

Nathan fixes me a plate of pizza and garlic knots when the two of them come back. They leave me alone in the living room with the journals while they sit out back. Luckily, reading plenty of scripts over the years has shaped me to be a fast reader. It takes me two hours to get to the 1973 Tonys when I finally hit something that isn't familiar. Apparently, after my first ceremony, I kissed her in our Whitby apartment. I grip the journal on the edge of my seat, feeling my face flush, and my mouth tingles as if her cursive words are coming to life on my lips:

March 25, 1973
She kissed me like she had planned on doing it for years. This can't be something that has taken her aback. This has to be something she's thought about before. I haven't kissed a lot of people, but when Robert kissed me, most of it was on the right side of my mouth, and we fumbled for the first minute or so. Teeth clashing, awkward open-mouthed kissing, and it was only at the end he slipped me his tongue.

But with Marlie, it was different. She kissed me square on the mouth as if she already had my lips mapped out. She held my face, and my God, I felt like putty in her grip. I was entirely hers. When her tongue caressed mine, it was like my mouth was the destination she'd been wandering toward for years.

I don't believe Robert was my first kiss. Absolutely not. Marlie was my first kiss. She kissed me inside and out.

I close my eyes and imagine it. I can see the apartment in my head. I can walk through it, visualizing where every piece of furniture was, but I can't feel her kiss. I can't see us in bed or feel her hands on me. The memory of that apartment dims to a fantasy when I try to imagine Elle and me.

"I'm going to get going, Marlie," Nathan says, startling me from my daydream.

I flinched and see both Nathan and Elle in the entryway. Heat flashes on my face, and I can feel it move down my neck and into my chest and stomach. I stand to give Nathan a hug, but he walks past me to grab his jacket. I accept the rejection and stay rooted in my spot.

"How are the journals coming along?" he asks.

"I reached the first thing I don't remember."

"And?"

"It feels a bit like déjà vu, or I maybe once dreamed it, but I can't really nail down the details or remember anything of it."

"Maybe reading more will help."

"Maybe. I'm going to keep trying."

"Keep me posted."

"I will."

He hugs Elle, forces the thinnest smile for me, and heads out.

It feels like the first time he left the house without giving me a hug since he was a teen. There were about two years when Nathan was seventeen and eighteen, and he stopped giving both of us hugs. The first time it happened, Elle and I sulked in the TV room with large glasses of wine and were pretty confident that he hated us.

While it was only for a short time during his hormonal years, his rejection now hits so much harder than back then.

Elle turns to me, and I know she can't miss the look of defeat I'm sure is written all over my face. I can feel it weighing down my mouth and furrowing my eyebrows.

"I can get going too," I say. "It's getting late and—"

"You can stay and read my journals as long as you'd like," she says. "You are not leaving with my most precious possessions. So just out of curiosity, where in 1973 are you?"

"I, um…" I nervously scratch the back of my head and clear my throat. "I just read our first kiss."

"Oh." The blotches on her neck appear in the same spots they always had when she was nervous or embarrassed. "I'm going to open a bottle of wine. You want some?"

"Please."

I follow her to the kitchen with the box and plop it on the table. It's the same table from when we were together. She hands me a glass and takes a seat in the padded chairs. Our stares meet for a moment before the description of our kiss runs through my head. I can see my Whitby bedroom, and I imagine what Elle must have looked like in a formal dress, both of us fresh from the red carpet. I can't quite see how beautiful she looks, like my imagination is trying to fill in all the fine details of a hairdo and dress I've never seen. But even though I can't see her beauty, I can feel it wrap around the daydream. I can feel it brush against my arms like a ghost grazing them. I can feel it skate across my bottom lip. I can feel the warmth traveling lower in a pulsating throb.

I snap back to the Scarsdale kitchen and stare at Elle's lips, remembering the patterns she used to trace across my lips.

"What are you thinking about?" she says before taking a sip of wine.

Maybe words aren't strong enough to trigger the memory. I think I need to feel it. The realization infuses a warmth on my face and neck. I flit my gaze between Elle's eyes and lips, and at the sudden tingle on my bottom lip, I look at my wineglass and take a large, encouraging sip.

"Marlie?" she says sternly. "I can see a million thoughts behind your eyes."

I take another sip, hoping it helps the suggestion I'm about to propose taste much better. As it flows off my tongue, it tastes bitter. "I think I might have an idea."

"About what?"

"Well, my doctor told me that something tied to a very strong memory increases the chance of the memory resurfacing. He said memories are like trees. During neurological reimagining, we're bulldozing the memories, but because details of one memory are stored throughout different parts of the brain, we can find details of one memory in another. So I could very much have 'old roots' of memories."

"So what's your idea?"

"You might want to drink that wine faster. It's, well, it's a bit risky."

"*Okay*. How risky?"

"Significantly. We might need to do shots of rum."

"Rum?" She lets out a laugh that's not hollow, one that's actually filled with a trace of joy and nostalgia. "Have you actually had any rum since Anguilla?"

"Once or twice."

As if our entire trip to Anguilla resurfaces in her mind, her smile fades, and the blotchy blush claims the same spots of her neck. We both drink our wine as a silence settles, encompassing us in the memory of our tenth anniversary. In the summer of 1999, it was still illegal for us to get married, and we wanted to celebrate a decade of sharing a life and a family together. So we traveled to Anguilla. We had the honeymoon suite for a week and enjoyed our private white beach, turquoise waters, and our bungalow with retractable walls to let the salt air blow inside. The beauty of the island, the intimacy of the bungalow, and the excitement about celebrating ten years together had us acting like a teenage couple being home alone for the first time. We spent the majority of the day in bed, passionately fucking to sweetly making love. One of the nights, we enjoyed a bottle of rum a little too much that we took turns throwing it up. It was enough for me to swear off rum until a couple of years ago.

Our gazes lock. She blinks a few times as if my rum reference finally hits her. "Marlie, what's your idea." It's more of a statement than a question. I think she knows what I'm thinking by the concern in her voice.

"Just hear me out."

Her mouth drops, looking blindsided, but there's a little sparkle of humor lingering in her eyes. "Marlie. Please tell me it's not what I'm thinking."

I falter and bite my lip. I already lost some of the most important memories of my life. There's not much else I have to lose at this point. Why not take the risk? "It's probably what you're thinking. It involves kissing you but—"

"Absolutely not."

"I know, I know. Just let me explain, please."

She lets out a hollow laugh. "Yeah, I'm very interested in hearing your explanation for this."

"When I read our first kiss, something happened. It was like a memory of tomorrow. Like waking up and knowing you had a dream, but you can't quite picture it, but you're close. It's like I can remember the outline. I wonder if kissing you will fill in the blanks."

She looks away and shakes her head, almost seeming to be in disbelief. Even saying it out loud, I have to resist the urge to join in by shaking my head. It's ridiculous. We haven't kissed in twelve years. I don't blame her for being hesitant. I'd feel the same if roles were reversed. My trust in her is fractured too, but she might be the only key I have to digging up any roots to my memories.

"That's…quite the proposition," she says, taking another drink.

"I know, but do you trust me?"

"I do, and I don't."

"That's understandable, but just know that I wouldn't have proposed this if I didn't think it might actually be the missing piece."

She falters. "If this is the missing piece, are you sure you want to do it? It's going to undo everything. All the time and money and—"

"I want to remember more than anything."

Elle glances down at her glass. "I have to ask, what made you change your mind? Deciding to do this procedure is a big deal. It probably takes even more to want to stop it."

It's a big question. Do I really trust myself in this moment, desperate to take back the memories of Elle and I young and in love, when my confusion is the highest it's ever been? When Dr. Pierson warned me that the confusion could be powerful enough to make me regretful? Do I trust myself in this confused state more than I trusted myself when I decided to go through with this? What happens when the memories come back? Will I regret it?

If I didn't see my family reacting to it, maybe I would have continued living life with blinders on. But seeing the look of disgust on Elle and Nathan's faces, that's the strongest force propelling me into remembering.

"You said I was your greatest love, right?" I say.

Elle blinks a few times, seeming hesitant to admit such a confession again. "You were. You are."

"Then that means you were my greatest love."

Elle shrugs. "I don't know, Marlie. The tabloids sure loved you and Elaine Prescott a few years ago."

Elaine Prescott and I reunited at an Oscars after-party in 2010. The world had known she was a lesbian since 2008 when she had come out in *Variety*. The on-again, off-again relationship during my time in the West End blossomed into a two-year long romance.

"They were into it because it was my first relationship after I came out in 2010 and fit their whole 'recently out old lady' narrative. But I never loved her the way I loved you, Elle," I say, pulling my gaze away. The confession felt too intimate for eye contact. "I remember *being* in love, but I don't remember *falling* in love, and without knowing how we got here, I don't feel whole. I'd rather feel something than nothing at all."

She inhales deeply, thinks for a moment, and then exhales as she stands. "Okay, then." She smooths her blouse and then looks up, waiting for me to make the move.

But I can't make any move because I'm so taken aback by how quick she is to agree. After seeing the way she looked at me the night before, I thought I really shattered the last whole pieces of our relationship. "Wait, really?"

She gestures for me to stand. "Let's try this. There's nothing left to lose, right?"

I frown. "I hope that's not what you said when we first kissed."

She pulls back. "Of course that's not what I said." There's a smile in her tone that hardly translates on her face.

I wonder if she's too worried about the kiss for the smile to break free. But the lightness in her voice means something. "I think it needs to be like our first kiss," I say. "We need to commit to this."

"Wait. How do I know this is not some twisted come-on?"

I give her a look. "Elle, if I wanted to kiss you, I would have just brought over a bottle of Pyrat Rum."

She rolls her eyes. "I'm not that easy, Marlie."

"You're right, you're not. But Pyrat Rum made you, well, let's say, very eager."

Her blotchy neck spots darken. I bit back a grin. "Okay, don't make this more awkward than it already is. I'm following your lead."

I close the space between us. She stares at my mouth, and it feels like a spotlight, as if I'm onstage again. I slowly—with shaking hands—reach for her face, and at the connection, there's a zap that lights up my chest. I watch her eyes fidget all over mine, and then my gaze slips like a bar of soap to her lips. I read back our first kiss in my head and immerse myself in those words. They wrap around me like fingers on a pen and direct me until my lips brush hers.

At first, my heart pounds so loudly, I can't think past it. Then, she kisses me back, committing to us using this moment by pouring her remaining hope into me. Our mouths open, and even though I don't recall our first kiss, my tongue instinctively knows where to find hers and how to graciously dance with it. It's a soft and hesitant kiss, but still, it ignites something in me, a warmth traveling down to my stomach and coiling around my spine.

I pull away and notice her eyes are still closed, as if I ended the kiss right as she was going in for more.

Suddenly, my memory is filled with life.

I see her standing in front of me in a beautiful metallic-olive dress. A flash of me slowly pulling the zipper down her spine, and I can feel the curl of arousal when it reveals the soft skin of her back, as if I'm revealing the invisible ink that scribbles in the fine details of the memory. Another flash, and I see the dress hanging around her waist. I can feel my face warming when her naked torso materializes, and I take in the sight of her bare breasts for the first time.

Another wave that hits me square in the chest. I need to take a seat as my mind floods with memories of us kissing in our Whitby apartment, in our Southampton home, but we're young, in our twenties, kissing out on the beach, the patio, and in front of the baby grand that used to be in the living room. Kissing her in the brownstone I lived in when I came back from London and me straddling her lap as her fingertips grazed up the gold dress I wore to the 1983 Tony Awards. I can almost feel her fingers lighting up my core and her soft breaths tickling my earlobe as I ride her fingers.

My chest tightens, my heart quickens. I'm sure my face is blotchier than hers now.

There is a difference between being wanted and being desired. Wanting is a wish. Desire is a need. The details expanding across the memory and infusing my chest with a rush of feelings and pressure fills me up with the electricity that sparked whenever Elle and I were physical. Nancy Osbourne showed me how she wanted me. Elle showed me what it meant to be desired, and she didn't have to use any words.

"Marlie? Are you okay?" Elle asks.

Her question pulls me back to the present in her kitchen. My insides coil, and I try to breathe through the heaviness swelling in my ribcage. I have no idea what's happening. Am I on the verge of a panic attack? A heart attack? I have no idea what's happening, but while my mind suffuses through snippets of forgotten memories, the feelings tied to those memories flood me.

Elle gets up, and I hear the sink turn on and off, and then ice tumbling from the fridge. She hands me a glass of ice water. I take a very cold sip.

"You wore an olive-green metallic dress," I say. "We kissed in our bedroom at the Whitby, and…you looked so beautiful when I peeled that dress off you, and it hung around your waist."

Her eyes widen, and that's when it hits me too, as if I just emerged from the waves and finally caught a breath. There's life in my mind again. "Marlie," she says, her voice dropping. "You're not making this up, are you?"

"Absolutely not."

"It really came back? Just now?"

I nod as another wave of details and forgotten senses flood. "You also used to smell like citrus and flowers. Diorella by Dior."

She gives the faintest knowing smile. "You bought that perfume for my twenty-first birthday. I loved it. Wore it throughout my twenties." She runs a finger over her lips, causing my stomach to flutter. I wonder if she still feels our kiss the way I do. It's a continuous flow of electricity pulsating through my lips. "How do you feel right now? Do you want to read more?"

I want to read more, and I want to kiss her again. She looks at me delicately, a drastic difference from last night. I hate how my stare drops to her lips again. It's like I can't stop looking at how perfect and femininely shaped they are. How delicious they tasted, then and now.

I catch the fall and flit them back up to her eyes. "I want to keep reading, but I don't want to bother you."

"You're not bothering me. If you want to keep reading, please do. You can stay in Nathan's old room if you'd like."

"Are you sure?"

"I'm positive.

"That's incredibly kind of you. Thank you."

I'm even more confused. Twenty-four hours before, I was telling Elle I was in the process of erasing her, and she reacted exactly how I imagined anyone would react. I thought she'd be absolutely done with me then and there. I'm absolutely shocked how she's not only entertained my wild idea of kissing to dig up the lingering roots of memories, but she's even going as far as letting me stay in her house while I read her journals.

"Can I ask two questions?" I say.

"Sure."

"Why are you doing all this?"

"What do you mean?"

"I didn't expect you to want anything to do with me after yesterday. Rightfully so."

"I think you know why."

I down a large sip of wine. *Does she still love me?*

She clears her throat. "What's your second question?"

I think back to her 1973 journal and how she writes about the two of us going to gay bars in Greenwich Village with "Marlie's good friend Peter." I remember all my friends from over the years except for one person who is mentioned in that 1973 journal almost as much as me.

"Who the hell is Peter?"

CHAPTER FIFTEEN

"You erased Peter?" Elle says in a frantic voice.

I don't know how to answer that. Apparently, I did something bad that I don't remembering doing. "I...I don't know—"

"Oh my God, Marlie." Elle puts a hand over her chest, sits, and a faraway glance cloaks her eyes. After a few moments, she blinks herself back to reality. "I can't believe this." She shakes her head and rubs her temples. "I can't believe this."

"I...I'm sorry. I don't know why I did it—"

Elle reaches for the bottle of wine and tops off her glass. "Well, at least I'm not the only one who gets special treatment," she says and takes a liberal drink.

Her comment stings and inflames discomfort in my stomach. "Elle—"

"Peter was your best friend. He was practically your older brother, hell, he felt like my older brother too. Nathan thought Peter was his dad when you two came back from London and were always spending time with us."

I'm not sure what Elle means by London. It could have been a vacation or it could have been something about the West End. But I don't want Elle knowing all the details I don't have and getting more upset with me. I'm sure they're somewhere in her journals.

"I can't believe you really erased him," she says. I try to think of a reply, but when I fall short, Elle grabs her wineglass and gets up. "I'm going to leave you to the journals. There's, well, a lot has happened in the last twenty-four hours that I need to process...with this wine. You have a lot of reading to do. Hopefully by the morning, you'll have a better idea of how much you erased. The guest room is all made up when you're ready for bed."

"Elle—"

She takes her wine and goes upstairs without saying another word.

❖

I wake up to the smell of coffee permeating throughout the first floor. I'm on the couch, cuddling one of Elle's journals, with a blanket over me. I might not remember a large portion of the first half of my life, but I know for a fact that I didn't fall asleep with that blanket.

I hear clanking in the kitchen, and there's a pleasant tug in my chest. Over the fourteen years Elle and I were together, I feel asleep countless times on the same couch reading over scripts. Sometimes I woke up in the morning with a blanket over me or in the middle of the night to Elle draping it, and sometimes, she guided me up the steps into bed or kissed my forehead.

Even after all that we had been through in the last twelve years and my shredding up our beginnings and Peter, she still crept downstairs to put the blanket over me.

And somehow, I was the fool who didn't marry her.

I hear Elle's voice coming from the kitchen and then Nathan's. I glance at my phone and see the time is a quarter past nine. As I start questioning why he's over so early, I notice a large box by my feet.

"Coffee," Elle says, stepping into the living room and handing me the mug.

Nathan trails behind her. By the way he glares at me, almost perfecting his mother's teacher glare, I can tell he already knows about Peter.

I stayed up until two thirty reading through Elle's journals until I came across the memories that I already have. I know from Elle's words that Peter was part of our family when we didn't even know that the four of us were a family.

I could sympathize with the heartbreak that poured out onto the journal as Elle described the last few months of Peter's life. However, I couldn't feel it in my bones. I depleted my memory of him. I couldn't see, feel, or hear him like what should have still been in my head. There was a giant disconnect, like I was reading a novel instead of Elle's journal. My heart knew that he was so much more than a character. My mind just didn't.

"You've kept a whole box of mementos?" I say and nod to the box.

"Just a few things," Nathan says flatly and sits on the other end of the couch. "Apparently, you erased Peter too? Just your entire life? I'm surprised you didn't erase me, honestly."

"Nathan," Elle says as she sits in the chair across from us. "Unfortunately, it's over and done with. Being mad at Marlie is just going to make her more confused and upset."

He frowns. "You're defending this?"

Honestly, I feel like I'm giving Elle the same look. I'm shocked she's stepping in.

She glances at me sympathetically for a moment before turning to Nathan. "No, I'm not defending it, hon, but what's the point of going after Marlie when she doesn't have the answers anymore. It sounds counterproductive. How about you just show her what you were thinking might help."

He shakes his head and sets the box in between us on the couch. Inside it, I find an aged *New York Times* article with a head shot of Peter right below bold text that read, "Peter Arlo, Broadway Idol, Dead at 38." The first thing I notice is his smile. It's so big and warm. He looks like the best friend in someone's story.

"This is Peter?" I say and show Elle and Nathan the front page.

They share a glance before looking back at me. "It is," Elle says.

"How far did you get?" Nathan asks, the annoyance still saturating his voice.

I set the newspaper aside and go through the box. I find pictures, newspaper clips, Playbills, and a white half mask. "Everything. I've read all the journals."

"Seriously?"

"Well, your mom suggested I skip from 1977 to 1982 because apparently, I wasn't in the picture, but yes, seriously. That's what happens when you spend four decades reading scripts."

I pull out a photo album and flip through the pages. Many of them are at the Southampton house. Pictures of me and Elle by the lake in our bathing suits, Elle sitting on my lap with a PBR can in hand, me playing the piano with Peter standing next to me, me sitting on Peter's lap with my arm slung around him.

"Okay, and Mom said you remembered something?"

I glance at Elle. She looks away and scratches the back of her head. "A few things."

"So it worked? Reading the journals worked?"

"Not quite," I say. "I, um, well, I only remember because we… um." Elle shoots me her teacher's look. I stop. "What?" I ask.

"Don't," she says quietly.

"Don't what?" Nathan asks, alternating his glance. "Oh, come on. I'm thirty-six and will be a father in five months. You two aren't doing that adult talk thing right now. Tell me."

"Okay, but it doesn't mean anything," Elle says.

I roll my eyes. "Your mother and I kissed."

"You kissed?" he yells.

"Thank you, Marlie," Elle says sarcastically.

"What? It didn't mean anything, like you said." I turn to Nathan's shocked expression. "I thought if reading wasn't strong enough to remember our first kiss, maybe I needed to utilize another sense, like feeling. It was for science."

"I gathered that," he says flatly. "So what happened?"

"Everything unlocked. It was like all these snippets of memories rushed into my mind, and I could see every kiss we'd ever had." I look at the photo album, flip to the next page, and find a picture of Elle and me. We're in the Southampton home living room, dancing in front of the grand piano. Our hands are interlocked, my other wrapped around Elle's waist, and Elle's hand around my neck. We're in our twenties with our seventies feathered hairdos. The faded and discolored picture proves how much time has passed since that moment, but I remember kissing her in that living room so well, I feel the riptides in my stomach.

"This picture," I say, and pull it out of its plastic protector. "I remember kissing you many times in this living room when we were young."

"Do you know who took the picture?" Elle asks.

I stare at the picture, hoping that a clue or more details materialized. "I don't. Who took it?"

"Peter did."

"So reading journals isn't enough to bring Peter back?" Nathan says.

"I don't think so. It's like reading a script of my memories. It wasn't until the kiss…" I sneak a glance at Elle, and when our eyes lock, I feel the warmth take hold of my face again. I look back at the pictures and flip a page. I stop when I see a picture of me, Elle, a young Nathan, and a man who looks like a thinner version of the headshot from the *Times* article. Nathan looks like he's about eight. He's wearing a white mask that's too large for his face. I know that's the *Phantom of the Opera* mask.

I pull out the mask from the box and inspect it.

"He gave me his mask," Nathan says. "It was my first Broadway show."

I pick it up and examine it. "I know that I was Christine in *Phantom*, but whenever I think of who plays the Phantom, it's a blurry face."

"Okay, so sight isn't strong enough to get them back," Nathan says. "But touch is…and maybe sound. They say music evokes memories, right? When Melissa's grandpa had Alzheimer's, she said that her mom played him music. Even though he had no idea who they were or much of anything, he still was able to sing all the lyrics. It was pretty miraculous."

"Yes, I heard about that too."

He waves a CD. "Maybe we can try this."

I squint my eyes to try to read Nathan's messy handwriting that says, "Peter songs for Marlie," in permanent marker. "What is it?"

"I burned this CD for you like ten years ago. Once I told you that you can make CDs with whatever songs you wanted on them, you had asked me to make you one with songs that reminded you of Peter. I completely forgot about it until I found the mask and the picture in my closet."

"We should try it," I say and take a cautious sip of my second mug of coffee.

Staying up until two a.m., reading Elle's journals like they were a riveting novel pulls on my eyelids. Sleep isn't a priority for me, not when I'm trying to piece my life back together. I desperately want my story and my best friend back, even if that means I will have to remember losing him all over again. While I don't know what that horrible pain feels like anymore, from how Elle described our friendship, I hope that the sixteen years' worth of memories overshadow the dark days of watching him suffer. For any kind of relationship to last that long, there had to be a solid foundation built of wonderful moments.

"You sure?" Elle says.

"I'm positive."

"I think the CD player is in the basement. I'll go get it."

It only takes Elle a few minutes to come back. She plugs it in, and Nathan puts in the CD. "I don't remember what's on this, but I guess we'll find out," he says. Elle takes a seat next to me on the other end of the couch. "Here goes nothing."

The first song is "Vincent" by Don McLean, a song that always made me smile. At first, I don't feel anything. I sing along in my head, waiting for something to take hold of my brain and infuse it with scenes of my past. It's not until Don McLean sings about how the world was made for someone as beautiful as Vincent.

My mind sends me to the studio where we practiced for *A Little Night Music*. I remember someone whistling the melody of the song. In the fuzzy memory, I look up and see a blurry face with shaggy hair in loose waves.

The next song is "Crocodile Rock" by Elton John, and the studio memory fades into the Whitby apartment. There's a blurry man wearing a tuxedo standing in front of me in my gold dress. I turn and see Elle standing behind me in her metallic dress looking breathtaking.

I snap myself out of the daydream as "The Only Living Boy in New York" by Simon and Garfunkel starts playing.

Over the sounds of the strumming acoustic guitar, I turn to Elle, "We listened to 'Crocodile Rock' right before we left for my first Tonys," I say.

She gives me the smallest grin, and while my heart sputters as the new memories keep playing, the way her smile reaches her eyes feels as comforting as a hand resting on my leg. The accumulating anxiety settles for just a moment.

God, I wish so much she would rest her warm, nurturing hand on my leg.

"We did," Elle said. "While you, me, and Peter killed a whole bottle of champagne."

Then I remember gnocchi. Little fluffy carb pillows. "The Only Living Boy in New York" brings to life rolling gnocchi in the kitchen, and I can almost taste how delicious they were.

The next song is, "Lost Without Your Love" by Bread, and I'm sitting in our Greenwich Village brownstone, three of us cloaked in darkness. A discomfort starts rising in me, starting from the pit of my stomach and radiating up my chest. I've had waves of anxiety before, but this is different. It's hot and heavy, like something is filling me up with molten rock.

I turn to Elle. "This reminds me of the blackout," I say. "I can see us sitting on the couch listening to the radio. I can feel…I feel anxious."

"It was a pretty scary night," she says. "And the morning after…"

I remember reading about the breakup in Elle's journal and how heartbroken she was. But it isn't until I listen to "Lost Without Your Love" when I finally feel the heartbreak. My mind became foggy, feeling like the love of my life just broke up with me, and I'm left with the pieces scattered in front of me. My eyes sting. Nathan runs to the kitchen and hands me a glass of ice water. I chug it.

"New York, New York" by Frank Sinatra starts playing, offering me a little relief in my chest from the Bread song. My mind flashes to the dingy dark basement of a Greenwich Village bar and a crowd of people singing and cheering as the blurry-faced man and I belt out the song. Hearing the song makes me smile, it loosens the grip of the "Lost Without Your Love" memory.

"Don't Dream It's Over" by Crowded House is next, and I'm transported to the Southampton patio. The lightness in my chest fades, and the anxiety is back snaking around my lungs.

Stop running away from the things you're scared of.

I turn to Elle looking at me sympathetically.

"Fast Car" by Tracy Chapman. I'm in a red sports car, zipping down the Southampton Highway. No matter how many times I wipe my eyes during the song, it's not enough to keep them dry. My chest constricts, and fighting the sadness only worsens the accumulating pressure.

"Music of the Night" plays next, and it pins me to my spot. I listen to the deep, gorgeous voice singing with so much emotion, perfect vibrato, and so much control.

"This is Peter singing," Nathan says.

It hits me like a tidal wave. His deep, beautiful tenor voice unlocks the dread, grief, and heartbreak, and the tears spill. The further into the song, the more visual details materialize. I'm in the Majestic Theatre watching Peter completely capture the stage and the audience. Hearing his voice colors in the blurriness of his face, and I can finally see him underneath the Phantom makeup and the mask, pouring all his emotions into the song. I can see his brown eyes singing directly to me and how, in that moment, it was just the two of us onstage. No one else.

I snatch a couch pillow, place it in front of my stomach, and hold it tightly, closing my eyes to try to conceal as much heartbreak as possible while I'm finally reacquainted with my best friend's voice. His face fills in all the memories from before, the sixteen years' worth of happiness, fullness, and sense of belonging with him paired with all the pain and heartbreak ripple through me all at once.

Elle scoots over and rubs my back. Nathan sits on the armrest of the couch and squeezes my shoulder.

You could stand silently in the corner of a room, and someone would still find a way to hate you because you chose the wrong corner.

Please don't remember me like this.

And promise me that you'll stop trying so hard to avoid love.

"Don't Let the Sun Go Down on Me" and flashes of us in the Southampton living room. I'm playing it on the piano and holding back my laughter as Peter—drunk on sangrias—lies half on the piano, harmonizing with me. Elle and Will sing along in the corner.

Will. Peter's boyfriend and probably the greatest love of his life. Will, who also died. Another flash, and I see a very thin pale Peter in a hospital bed. St. Vincent's. I clasp both of my hands over his and sing the song.

The last song to play is "You've Got a Friend" by Carole King. I can hear my voice filling the church during his funeral.

More than forty years of emotions flood me, swells of grief and heartbreak pull in every direction. There's an uncomfortable warm tingle that starts at the top of my scalp, twists around my spine and arms, and chokes my lungs as my mind continuously plays each memory, each cycle more vivid and complete than the last time. It feels like a panic attack.

When I've cried out everything and start to calm down, I find myself cuddled into Elle, her arm around me, rubbing her fingertips all over my back and shoulders in invisible patterns. I look up, and she stares at me with sympathy, no trace of anger in her eyes. She looks worried, and by the way she studies me, I wonder if she has the smallest bit of understanding as to why I wanted to forget about these emotions. They're powerful, all-consuming, and paralyzing.

While I feel like I lost Peter all over again, underneath all the feelings I erased, there's an undertow of something exhilarating.

It feels like I'm falling in love with Elle all over again.

❖

I didn't get my first panic attack until I was forty, returning to Broadway after taking a break from 1990 to mid-1994. I was about to take the stage as Norma Desmond in *Sunset Boulevard*. It started as a tingling sensation on top of my head and then flooded all the way down to my toes. It felt like someone was trying to pop my lungs like a balloon. The second panic attack was the following year, in 1995, right before the *Les Misérables* tenth anniversary concert in London. Elle and Nathan were with me in my dressing room, coaxing me through long, deep breaths. Sadness and grief had overcome me. The music reminded me of Peter. The memories we shared onstage together during two productions were threaded around every note. I didn't know how to be Fantine without my Valjean.

Peter Arlo materializes in my memory. His warm smile and his kind eyes replace the blurry face, and I feel a swell of comfort and safety wrap around me like his strong, comforting hugs once did.

The memories and the emotions attached to them flood my mind. Just like the panic attacks I endured before, I feel drained and depleted for the rest of the day. I go back to the hotel to catch up on sleep, relive all the new memories that play on a constant loop, and take a shower. There's so much I have to sort through. Good and bad memories collide together and drench me in riptides of feelings.

But I still want to remember. I still want to piece my life back even though this emotional sludge.

When I get changed, I find that I have a text from Nathan.

Hope you're doing okay. If you're feeling up for it, Mel and I would love to have you and Mom for dinner. We'd also love it if you spent the night.

I respond, *That sounds great. It will be great to do that on our last night.*

I am happy to check out of the hotel and get back on the original visit plan of spending time with Nathan and Melissa. I no longer feel the dread of standing on the precipice when I walk back inside their home. I'm greeted with a big warm hug from Melissa, a glass of red wine from Nathan, and a thin grin from Elle. The kitchen smells like braised short ribs, and I'm amazed Melissa decided to put together another delicious meal.

"I figured I'd do something special," she says to me in the kitchen. "It's been a while since we've had a family dinner."

"Is this all because I can't cook?" I say.

Melissa smiles. "Not at all. You're the guest. Go. Relax and enjoy the wine."

I walk into the living room. Nathan and Elle sit on opposite ends of the couch, and Nathan is pointing the remote at the TV. Somehow, he's gotten YouTube on it.

"Marlie, I found some of your *Les Mis* and *Phantom* shows," he says.

He pats the empty spot between him and Elle. I offer her the smallest smile as I take a seat and look at the TV. I'm shocked that these videos exist, but I settle in with my wine to watch them. Even though the video quality is poor, I smile hearing and seeing Peter and I share the stage and feeling the familiar comfort that his presence and voice always brought me.

Nathan discovers a video of Peter accepting the Tony for his *Phantom* role, and I know now that he accepted the award just a few weeks before his last performance. We watch interviews of him charming Johnny Carson and David Letterman. The more I watch, hearing his voice and seeing his warm dark eyes and that contagious smile, the more of the finer details fill in the memory. I can hear his full laugh before he lets it shine during his Johnny Carson interview. I can feel how big and tight his hugs were, and it's not until we sit at the table to eat that I can feel all his love filling in the holes I had Dr. Pierson carve out.

It's hard to watch these interviews and take in more details of my best friend as the shame stitches into my overall regret for the procedure. I'm so angry with myself that I erased some of the most beautiful moments and people of my life.

Right as the heaviness starts feeling like too much, I scan the dinner table. My family is surrounding me in spite of all I put us through. I have three sets of eyes on me, but instead of daggers, Nathan, Melissa, and Elle's stares hold vulnerability and worry.

"You doing all right, Marlie?" Nathan asks, cutting his asparagus.

I smile. I'm doing more than all right. Although I feel sad and angry, I also feel incredibly loved, that even though I dragged them through my unhappiness, that they still love me enough to share dinner with me. "I'm just really glad to be here with you three. I think this is the first time all of us have sat down for a meal. If we don't count the rehearsal dinner."

"It's nice, isn't it?" Elle says.

Nathan alternates a glance between Elle and me, and if there were any little cracks left in me that the recovering memories didn't patch up, his smile does it. "It is nice," he says.

I know that not everything in our family is fixed. I can still sense the sadness and hurt when they look at me, and I know it's going to take time for all of us, but sitting at the table, sharing a meal, is the closest we have been to being our complete family in over twelve years.

I want nothing more than to bottle this feeling. It's foreign to me, feeling put back together, and while the glue might still be wet, it's the most complete I've felt in years.

After dinner, Melissa tops off our wine, and Nathan opens YouTube back on the TV. He finds my *A Love Letter to New York* TV special from 1999 that won me another Grammy and finally gave me my Emmy, making me the fourth woman to achieve an EGOT alongside Helen Hayes, Rita Moreno, and Audrey Hepburn. I was also the youngest person at the time to have completed the EGOT at forty-five, three months younger than Rita Moreno. It stayed that way for another fifteen years until composer Robert Lopez completed his in 2014 at the age of thirty-nine.

"We have to watch this," he says and presses play.

"Nathan, it's an hour and a half long," I say through a laugh.

"Yeah, and? It's so good. It's why they gave you a Grammy and finally that Emmy, Ms. EGOT." He nudges my arm, and I feel like that nudge clicks us back into place. Light teasing was our love language. We haven't had a moment like this since before the wedding.

He presses play, and the video begins. I remember that night vividly. My love and my son both sat in the front row in the midst of a sold-out crowd of almost six thousand in Radio City Music

Hall. I sang the biggest songs of my Broadway career, plus "New York, New York" and "Forever Yours," the song that won me my first Grammy, and I even brought out the great Joseph Bennett to accompany me on his acoustic guitar.

The audience claps and cheers as I walk onto the stage. Trumpets from the New York Philharmonic blast the opening to "New York, New York," and when I sing the first four words of the song, the crowd cheers louder.

I don't like watching myself or listening to my recordings. It doesn't matter if I have an EGOT and other awards; like most people, I don't like hearing myself speak or sing. "If you're going to play all of this, I'm going to get more wine," I say jokingly.

"Okay, okay, how about just two songs," Nathan says, pointing the remote at the TV to skip ahead. "I want Melissa to hear my favorite."

"I remember my parents watching this," Melissa says. "They were big fans."

"I'm offended you didn't watch, Melissa," I say jokingly.

She smiles. "I was too busy talking to my friends on AOL."

"This is why we need to play the best song," Nathan says, and stops skipping ahead. He pauses the video. "Marlie said her mom used to sing this song to her when she was little, and she did the same with me. Apparently, it was one of the few things that made me stop crying. Anytime I hear this song, I think of you." He looks over and places a warm hand on my shoulder. His smile completely reaches his eyes, and seeing it pushes my heart securely back in place.

The confusion stacks in me again. How come Nathan knows something about my mother when I don't at all? I was raised in an orphanage during my entire childhood.

Fuck, I've forgotten my own mother.

Nathan presses play, and YouTube Me starts playing the baby grand Steinway. Hearing the opening piano notes to "Somewhere Over the Rainbow" forces me to tune out my voice and focus on the melody and lyrics. I can feel it unlocking something in my brain.

"Oh my God," I gasp and cover my hammering heart.

Nathan, Melissa, and Elle turn. "What? Are you okay?" Elle asks with a twinge of panic in her voice.

Nathan pauses the video.

"No, no, no, keep playing," I say, even though I can't look at the TV. I need to hear the song in its entirety.

When Nathan restarts, a small apartment materializes in my mind. It isn't until I hear myself singing that I uncover what must be a root buried deep. A west-facing window, a woman with her back to me humming the same words and melody. Though I can't make out what she looks like, her voice is soft, as if it's not quite confident enough to take hold of the small apartment. But even though the voice holds back a lot, it's beautifully melancholic.

You have the most beautiful voice, my Marlie Rose.

Just like when the tsunami of memories about Peter and Elle came rushing back, my scalp starts to tingle, and it spreads down my spine and my arm. A heavy sadness washes over me and floods my chest.

"I think I might remember why I did this," I say, mentally still in that small apartment watching the blurry woman singing while staring out the window. "My mother is singing this song in a really small apartment. She's looking out the window."

"In your Red Hook apartment?" Elle says delicately.

"I lived in Red Hook?"

Elle tosses a glance at Nathan behind me. "Yes. That's where you lived until you were eight."

"What happened?"

"Did you erase them too?" Nathan asks.

"Them? My parents? I…I must have. Oh God."

I gasp and cover my mouth. Her presence feels motherly and nurturing but also sad. I feel this need to hug her, make her some tea, make sure she rests her feet.

At this point, I can see the fragments of my life piece together, and while there are some holes that linger, I have a clearer picture. Almost. I don't know where I came from. I see Elle as a mother, I already see Nathan and Melissa as parents; I can feel myself being a mother to Nathan. I can see the parent in every family member, but

I have no idea about my parents. I must have had them. Apparently, Elle and Nathan were aware of them in some capacity. Everyone knew where I came from and how I ended up at this exact spot.

Everyone except for me.

"I think I can find out why I did this," I say. "There's only one person who would know."

I pick up my phone, and my hands shake as I try pressing the green button to call Kristina, and I can barely make out the phone screen through my blurry eyes.

"Hey, Marlie? How are you?" she answers warmly.

"Kristina, I remember everything," I say.

"What?" I hear the smile fade. "Is everything okay? Are you crying?"

"I…I just recovered my memories."

"What? How—"

"It's a long story, I'll fill you in later, but I did it intentionally."

"It doesn't sound like it. You can hardly speak."

I blow out a stuttering breath, close my eyes, and try to collect myself. After I wipe my eyes with the back of my hand, I say, "I'm just overwhelmed right now. I just…I don't remember why I did this. Why would I want to erase my parents? Why would I want to erase my whole relationship with Elle? Why would I erase Peter?"

There's a beat of silence on the other end. "You really want me to tell you?" she says.

"I do, I absolutely do," I say as my voice shakes.

She falters again and then lets out a deep sigh. "You've been so depressed. Ever since Nathan's wedding." Everyone must have heard because I could feel their stares drilling into me.

"And that's it? That's why I went through it?"

"That was part of the reason. You'd been depressed for so long, you were desperate to relieve it. You told me that the only reason you became famous was because you were once so desperate to get out of Brooklyn that you had no other choice. You said that the only way for you to be happy was to erase the pain that held you back, that it was your only way out. The thing that finally made you book the first appointment were the results of the investigation."

"What investigation?"

"The…the one about your parents. You hired a private investigator to find out what happened to your mother."

"And? What did they find out?" I look up. Elle's eyes are soft.

"Are you sure you want me to tell you?"

"I'm positive, Kristina."

"It's, um, it's going to be hard to hear. I don't want you to regret finding out the truth and redoing your whole procedure."

"I found out all about Elle and Peter, and I don't regret it at all. Please, tell me. This is the last missing puzzle piece to my life."

She exhales. "After your mother dropped you off at Kindred Hearts, she spent time in a rehab facility. She was an alcoholic, struggled for two years to get sober. Then, she remarried in '65 and had another daughter a year later. She was in Queens until she moved out to Westchester in '69, and then she and her husband retired to Vermont in '92. She died of liver cancer in 2010. I think finding all of that out was the final push to undergo the procedure."

"And my father?" I say through a voice crack. I'm trying so hard to hold back all the cries until I'm off the phone. "What about him?"

"He died when you were six in an accident during work. It was big news at the time. The *USS Constellation* fire. You didn't have many memories of him. You were so young."

As my YouTube self continues singing "Somewhere Over the Rainbow," the top of my head sends the familiar, dreadful tingles down my limbs. I know what's happening, and before I break with Kristina on the other end, I thank her and say good-bye. Once I hang up, the wave of emotions falls on top of me, and I feel like a piece of debris in its wake. I bury my face in my hands, and as much as I hate crying in front of people, I have no way to stop.

Nathan takes me into his strong arms like he did when I first arrived. I sink into his embrace and let out a cry of relief.

"Marlie," Elle says soothingly and puts a gentle hand on my back.

Feeling her console me breaks me even more. My body aches to throw myself into her arms, my safety net since I was fifteen. Elle had this amazing ability to make me feel safe and loved even during the most difficult times. Then, almost instinctively, she glides her hand up to my shoulder and squeezes it.

"I'm so sorry, Mar," she says.

Mar.

With just her calling me by my nickname, I'm reminded that I'm loved. Even though I hurt Elle and Nathan, they're still next to me, holding me, consoling me, and loving me. Once I cry out most of the heaviness, Melissa hands me a refilled wineglass. I can't help but let out the smallest chuckle and take a large drink.

"You want to talk about it?" Nathan says, rubbing my back.

His eyes hold mine in sympathy. The hardness of his stare is long gone, and I see the sweet, caring, and sensitive boy I helped raise. "I don't," I say and force a thin smile to let him know I'm okay. "There's not much to talk about, is there?"

"That's not true," Elle says. "There's a lot to talk about."

I sip my wine and let out a shaky sigh. I watched the woman singing and staring out the window. I wonder what went through her mind when she dropped me off at Kindred Hearts. Was she heartbroken? Was she relieved? Did she think about finding me at all? Did she try and fail? Did I remind her too much of everything she lost? Did she lose so much that not finding me was like wiping her slate clean, like what I tried doing with my memories?

"My whole life, I wanted to belong," I say. "My mother didn't want me. No one in the foster system wanted me, and I spent my childhood wondering if there was ever a place for me. Then, we moved to Manhattan." I look at Elle and give her a small smile. "And met Peter, and the three of us formed our own family, one Elle and I never had and one that Peter lost. I don't care if it's been twenty-seven years since I lost him. People can tell me to get over it or judge me for not 'moving on,' but when you grow up with nothing, you latch on to everything, and I had Peter. I had you," I say, turning to Elle. "I had Nathan—"

"You never lost me," he says, his eyebrows furrowing.

"I did, hon. I lost our joking, our daily texts, Sunday calls. I lost all of that."

"Marlie, that's not—" Elle says.

"Let me finish," I say gently because I want them to hear me more than anything. I can see their broken pieces reflecting in their watery, concerned eyes, and I want more than anything to try to piece them back together like they did with me. "And I think because I still carried the pain and the confusion from my childhood, losing you two and finding out about my mother made me feel like I failed, once again, at having a family. So I thought I had no other choice but to remove the memories that have weighed so heavily on me throughout the years. But it turns out, during this whole process, I was erasing parts of myself, my life, and my family, the very thing I wanted more than anything to have back. I know it's been very hard these last few days for everyone, but I don't regret reading those journals or listening to those songs or calling Kristina." I wipe a falling tear. "God, I'm so incredibly thankful to have my story back."

"You really mean that?" Elle asks.

I smile. "Absolutely. I'm so sorry for hurting both of you. You have no idea how much."

"I think we have an idea," Nathan says. He gives my hand a comforting squeeze. Even through all the anger, pain, and heartbreak from the last couple of days, he still finds a way to understand me. He smiles at me, almost as if he's letting me know it's going to be okay.

"We should listen to that song again," I say.

Nathan goes back to the beginning of "Somewhere Over the Rainbow." I let myself go back to that daydream where I'm watching my mother singing out the window. As I listen to myself sing, more details start to fill in. A memory of me singing with my mother flashes across my mind: I can see a man sitting in a chair reading the paper and telling me how beautiful my voice is. I can feel youth, naivety, and happiness inflating my chest and cooling the anxiety and anger that still flows through my veins.

I can feel Elle regarding me from my peripheral. I turn, and when our gazes lock, she quickly focuses on the TV as if I wasn't supposed to catch her staring.

We are far from where we used to be in our relationship, but it doesn't stop the butterflies from fluttering around after countless seasons of metamorphosis.

The four of us spend the rest of the night drinking wine, watching YouTube videos of me and Peter, and laughing and reminiscing. We stay up until twelve thirty when Elle finally decides to call it a night. She comes to me and extends her arms. I don't hesitate one bit. I'm desperate to feel her comforting arms. "You need a ride to your audition tomorrow?" she says in my ear, her question tickling my earlobe and reaching my core.

It feels so intimate and sensual that it almost feels wrong, given our state of purgatory. I pull away and douse the desire. "Is that an offer?"

"It is. I can take you."

"You sure? I can just take a cab. I'm going to take one right after to the airport—"

"I wouldn't have offered if I didn't want to," she says with a smirk.

"That'd be really nice. Thank you."

She gives me a soft smile, one that doesn't feel forced, says good night to everyone, and goes home.

I find a loose grin while looking at myself in the mirror as I get ready for bed.

"You need anything?" Nathan says when he checks in on me. He plops an extra blanket on the foot of the bed.

"I'm okay, honey. Thank you. For everything."

"For everything?"

"For letting me stay here. I know this hasn't been the most perfect visit but—"

He holds up a hand. "Don't. It might not have been what any of us expected, but in some weird way, I think it was needed. For all of us. It brought us closer together, and I think we all needed a reminder of the things we hold close. We needed to understand each other better, and I think we got that, a silver lining." He pauses for a moment. "So yeah, it might not have been perfect, but I still love you more than anything, Mom. I hope you know that."

Mom. I open my arms and take him in. He hugs me back tightly. "I'm so glad you came to visit," he says.

I break. I hold my son tighter, not wanting to ever let go of him or our family again. "Me too, hon, and I love you too. More than you'll ever know. I'm so sorry for hurting you, Nathan."

He breaks the hug and rests his hands on my shoulders. "I'm sorry that you were hurting so much that you felt like you had no other choice."

I rest a hand on his cheek. I take him in for a moment, and even though he's thirty-six, married, has stubble on his face, and is about to be a father, sometimes I still catch glimpses of the little boy who stole my heart and made me want to be a mother more than anything.

"Have you and Mom talked?"

I let out a hollow laugh and pat his cheek. "Hon, she's still processing the fact I erased some of our memories. One thing at a time."

"You're leaving tomorrow. You're going to just leave without talking about it? I think after telling her about your procedure, this should be a breeze."

I hate how right he is. I know that flying back to California without discussing what happened at his wedding won't sit right with me, and if I want to reconcile with my family and have them back in time for my grandson, back in time for me possibly doing *Hello, Dolly!*, I need to patch up all the holes, no matter how much dread fills me.

"How did you become so wise?" I say with a loose smile.

"I had two amazing moms," he says. "If it's worth anything, I think she might surprise you."

"What do you mean?"

"You think I didn't watch you two this week? Mom has her guard up, she's had her guard up for years, but she was looking at you differently ever since the memories started coming back."

I don't want to get his hopes up, but I noticed it too. Elle softened as the days progressed. Anytime our eyes locked and flitted away, anytime she touched me to console me or took care of me by providing a place to sleep, blankets, water, or just a sympathetic and nurturing look through the pain and heartbreak I'm sure she was wading through, there was a swarm of flutters in me.

Most importantly, Elle willingly gave me the key to unlock my memories. Her journals and her love pieced my life back together, and I see it all so much clearer than I ever did before I started the procedure. I familiarized myself with all the finer details of our relationship, of her. My God, am I still in love with her as much as I was when I first fell for her?

Actually, when I lie awake that night, sifting through the collection of memories and feelings, I realize one thing: I've been falling for Elle ever since I was fifteen.

And it is finally time for me to settle in one place with her.

CHAPTER SIXTEEN

I'm calling to cancel the rest of my appointments," I say the following morning.

The other end of the phone goes silent, but it's obvious the receptionist at the Farrow Institute is taken aback.

I don't need any more time to think about my decision. I want to get the call out of the way before my flight because I know when I get home, I'm going to be too busy desperately missing Nathan, Melissa, and Elle.

"You'd like to cancel the rest of your procedure?" the receptionist asks, clearly confused.

"Correct."

"Ms. Rose, we strongly recommend not doing that as that will drastically increase the chances of memories resurfacing—"

"I understand," I say. "But they have already come back."

"They've come back?"

"Yes."

There's a quick pause. "Do you mind holding for a moment, Ms. Rose?"

I agree, and a minute later, Dr. Pierson greets me. "Hello, Ms. Rose. I understand that your memories have resurfaced?" He sounds just as confused as the receptionist.

"Hi, Dr. Pierson. Yes, they have."

"Ms. Rose, we did strongly advise against you traveling—"

"Dr. Pierson, before you say more, I just want to let you know that I'm not upset at all. I wanted them back. I sought them out."

"You did?"

"I did."

"May I ask how they came back?"

The heat claims my face, not only because I'm thinking about kissing Elle and enjoying the electricity passing through my bottom lip, but because I have to admit to Dr. Pierson that I kissed the woman I was trying to erase.

However, no matter how embarrassing iṭ might be, I tell Dr. Pierson everything. He's probably searching for information about what happens when people put themselves in a similar situation.

When I finish, there's silence on the other end for a few moments. "Music is like the skeleton key to memories," he says. "When an event happens, an emotion and a song connect through implicit memories that are our subconscious and automatic memories. So if a song is paired with a memorable event, it's a cue to bring back the strong emotion tied with it. Also, many of your memories take place in what's called the reminiscence bump period, between ten and thirty years of age. This is when you recall the most. I expect that one unlocked another and created this domino effect."

"I didn't use any music to remember everything with Elle."

He lets out a chuckle, half-genuine, half-hollow. I can hear the disappointment in his tone. I don't blame him. He spent a lot of time listening to my woes only for me to undo all the work. "You know the saying that you don't ever forget your first love?"

"I do."

"Sounds like Elle must be a love that runs deep enough that even our technology can't get to all the roots. We were a little more than halfway through the procedure, and because memories thread through all parts of the brain, there were probably a decent number of roots still connecting to Elle. Explains why something as simple as a kiss brought those back. All those deeply embedded memories worked together to bring the erased ones back. That's why we advise our patients to lock away anything that holds meaning because it can easily bring back everything we've erased at this point in the procedure."

The kiss was anything but simple.

"Can you answer one question, Ms. Rose? How do you feel now that you had everything come back?"

"It was overwhelming. First, they came back visually, and then I felt them, like each snippet drenched me with all the feelings attached to the memory. It felt like a panic attack. It started with a hot, prickly tingling in my head, and it spread down my whole body. It felt like someone was sitting on my chest tying my stomach into knots. It was like losing Peter and my mother all over again. But that was just the immediate feeling. Now, I feel so relieved. I was so confused and frustrated before I left, and I know you warned me about it, and I was supposed to trust the process, but I feel like myself again. Well, actually, a new version of myself. I feel like this journey of forgetting and then recovering is oddly what needed to happen to start repairing my family. To start repairing myself."

"I'm glad it's worked out for you in the end. Not exactly how we expected your journey to relief would go, but I'm grateful that you found clarity, happiness, and the will to move forward."

For years, I was caught in the cycle of everything I had lost. I blamed myself for things out of my control—like Peter's death—and for the things in my control—like my relationship with Elle. The guilt that came with watching those wonderful things end weighed so heavy on me for all those years that color drained from my world. But while there were things beyond my control, there were also things I could have grasped to help bring those vibrant colors back into my life. I let my guilt get in the way.

Now that I have my memories back, I refuse to be paralyzed again. I ran to California in search of color to add back into my life, but this entire time, it had been in New York with Elle and Nathan. I was just too colorblind to see it.

Nathan and Melissa put together a delicious breakfast, and the sadness starts swelling in me. I don't want to leave. The last four days have shown me I still have so much of my life in New York. California was my escape, but New York is my home. I don't want to lose any more days with my son than I already have. I know that once I land in California, I need to call my manager, Helen, and tell her I desperately want the Dolly role. I need to let Kristina know that I'm moving back to New York even if I don't get the role. I want to get back onstage. I want to sing and perform. I want to give the audience a night to remember. I want to be there when my grandson is born. I want to fully be in his life.

Most importantly, I want my family back.

"You'll keep us posted about *Hello, Dolly!*?" Nathan asks when Elle arrives to take me to my audition in the city.

I pull him in for a tight, long hug. Both of us sink into it, unwilling to let go. It's one of the best hugs I've had in a while. "Of course I will. Keep me updated on my daughter-in-law and my grandson."

Nathan breaks the hug and gives me that glowing smile. "Of course, Mom."

"If everything works out, I'll be in New York when he's ready to come into the world."

"That'd be amazing," Melissa says.

I give her a hug and a kiss on the cheek. "Thank you for letting me stay. I'll be back."

"You're welcome here anytime, Marlie."

I give her stomach a rub. "I'll see you in five months, little one," I say.

"Text me when you get home," Nathan says. "I love you."

I'm already home.

"I love you too," I say.

Four days ago, my chest clenched from nervousness and guilt, and now, my chest embraces and holds on to everything that I've been searching for since my twenties: the family that I've always wanted.

Once I buckle myself in, Elle asks, "You doing okay?"

I let out a sigh. "I just don't want to leave."

"You don't?"

I shake my head. "I know this week wasn't exactly how we expected it would go, and I know I hurt you and Nathan, and I'm so sorry for that, but…I really miss us. All of us." Once I dry my face, I let out a quivering exhale. "I miss you, Elle. I know I brought it upon myself twelve years ago, but, damn it, if I could redo it, I'd marry you in an instant." I look at her and see the residual hurt hanging behind her eyes.

She shakes her head and drops her gaze to the steering wheel. "I wanted to marry you so badly, Marlie. It was so devastating to break up with someone I was so in love with, someone I imagined myself being with for the rest of my life."

"Our love was safe if we kept it protected and hidden, and because of my career, I had a spotlight on me at all times. I didn't want society's opinions to distort our love. I watched how we were treated during the eighties, I watched how celebrities came out, and their careers plummeted, and I was terrified. Please believe me when I say that running away from us is my biggest regret. Loving you has been the easiest and most rewarding thing I've ever experienced. I've been replaying all of our memories, and it turns out, you are the greatest love of my life too."

She stares at me with profound loss. Seeing her sad expression tightens the ball in my throat that I keep trying to swallow back. I've cried enough the last couple of days.

"I didn't just get my memories back, Elle," I continue. "I got all the feelings that come with them, and that includes anger, pain, heartbreak, and love. This might sound strange, but getting our memories back has made me feel like I'm falling in love with you all over again. Actually, I never stopped loving you. That's why I felt like I had to forget it because I couldn't imagine a life without you in it. But I'm so glad I remember everything, and now I can see it so clearly. Loving you has been the only constant in my life."

She lets out a cry and covers her mouth. I rest my hand on her wrist and rub my thumb along her hand. I always hated when she cried. The very thing that has tied us together since we were fifteen makes it impossible for me not to cry when I see her crying. I hold her wet face. She closes her eyes and allows her face to fall into my hand. I leave my hand there, feeling the softness and warmth of her skin and allowing it to send a zigzagging current through my body.

"I never meant to hurt you, either," she says, holding her stare firmly on me. "I shouldn't have danced with Lisa to our song at the wedding. That was horrible. I didn't intentionally do it, I just…I wasn't thinking."

"We've both hurt each other and made mistakes, but if this whole thing has taught me anything, it's that after everything you and I have been through, I don't want three minutes to ruin the forty-seven years we've had together. We've made a family, Elle, with Peter, with Nathan and Melissa, and in five months, we're going to have a grandson. We have the family that we spent our whole childhoods hoping we would have."

"I know," she says, a smile touching her lips. "We really do."

"And it makes me sad knowing that the people I love the most are here, and I have to fly back to the other end of the country."

"You don't have to leave," she says softly, putting her hand on mine.

I stop, shocked that she suggested that. "Do you want me to stay?"

God, I want more than anything to hear Elle tell me to move back to New York so we can be together, and we can spend the rest of our days making up for the last twelve years apart. I just hope that I haven't pushed her so far away that it's impossible for me to make up ground.

"I've never wanted you to leave."

"If that's really the case, I have no problem selling my Malibu house and moving back here."

"You'd do that?"

I take her hand. "I'll do whatever it takes to have my family back."

Her grin grows, causing my stomach to flip. Forty-seven years later, and seeing Elle smiling at me causes my body to react. "That'd be really wonderful."

"When I'm all settled, can I take you out on a date?"

She laughs, letting me know that the tears she swipes with her free hand are ones of happiness. The tightness in my chest eases. "A date? Are we twenty again?"

"We're never too old for a date. I'll make sure it's one worth remembering."

"I know this sounds silly, but...I'm going to miss you."

As if the last few days of emotions and memories isn't enough to root my heart back here, Elle's confession cements it. "Why is that silly?" I say.

"Because just three days ago, I was shattered and heartbroken that you erased me and a huge part of our relationship, and now, I'm crying because you're leaving and crying because I'm so relieved you want to move back here. Talk about a roller coaster."

I palm her face and wipe away the moisture. The look she gives me unwinds me completely. God, I want to kiss her. "I'm not leaving, Elle. I'm just going back to sell my house and pack, and once I'm back here, I'd love to take you out on that date and start again. I'm not afraid anymore. There's nothing I want more than to make this right, make us right again."

"I want that to happen more than anything too."

I run my thumb along her cheek and watch her stare fall to my lips, lingering as if she isn't ashamed that I notice. The last reservations about holding back plummet from my chest to my stomach, launching me free to finally kiss her the way we used to. I didn't want us to kiss only to experiment with finding lost memories. I want a kiss that seals a promise to make new ones.

Our lips meet in a gentle reacquaintance at first, slowly waltzing with each other until we fall back into the same rhythm we memorized years before. Once the familiarity sets in, the passion takes over. I slide my hand off her cheek and wrap it around her neck, pulling her closer. Elle lets out a soft murmur, and arousal runs through me like an electric current to my center. I've missed the way kissing her makes me feel. I've missed the way her body claims mine during the kiss and how her warmth blankets me.

As the kiss simmers, I pull away and press my forehead into hers, leaving my eyes closed for just a moment so I can enjoy how it feels to have her again, to feel her soft breaths dance across on my tingling lips, to feel her love and the promise we made swaddle us together like a blanket in the cold.

There's a recognizable squeeze in my chest that only Elle has ever elicited.

"For me, in the last three weeks since I started this procedure, we've had so many first kisses," I say. "But this one, Elle, I have to say this one has been my favorite."

"And why's that?"

"Because I have a feeling this will be our last first kiss."

I wasn't supposed to get attached, but getting attached to Elle was the best thing to ever happen to me. I finally found my way back to her, my love, my home, my constant.

EPILOGUE

2023, seven years later

"It's truly an honor to be here tonight to present a special Tony Award for Lifetime Achievement to a living legend of stage and screen." Blair Bennett says onstage at the United Palace.

I was absolutely blown away when I got the call that I was receiving the Lifetime Achievement Award. Even though I've had a few months to process, it still feels like a hazy dream. I stand backstage waiting for Blair to announce me. It doesn't matter if Blair is reading from the teleprompter, I know she means every word. It means the world to me to have such a close family friend, one I've watched grow up, persevere through her own hardships and become a talented, successful, and admirable woman, present me with the biggest award of my career.

"Marlie Rose's legacy is forever embedded in the world of Broadway. Her voice has resonated through generations and has colored the stage with fifty years' worth of unforgettable performances. From Roxie Hart in *Chicago*, Maria in *The Sound of Music*, Fantine in *Les Misérables*, Christine in *Phantom of the Opera*, and Dolly in *Hello, Dolly!*. Her talents have rightfully helped her become the fourth woman to achieve EGOT status in 1999 by the age of forty-five, at the time, the youngest person to do so.

"She won her first Grammy for the song 'Forever Yours,' that she cowrote with my grandfather, Joseph Bennett. Because of their friendship through the years, I've had the pleasure of not only admiring Marlie as a legendary singer, performer, and actress but as a benevolent person as well. Her passion transcends offstage in her meritorious philanthropic work in the fight against AIDS and who remains a fierce and outspoken activist in LGBTQ+ rights and has helped children's homes all over New York City. While you know her as the great Marlie Rose, I've had the honor of knowing her for my entire life simply as Mar. Please join me in celebrating the incredible life and career of my dear friend, Marlie Rose."

Music and applause fills the theater as I step onstage. All the cameras swivel to me. I kiss Blair on the cheek. I take the award and turn to face everyone in the auditorium and see the standing ovation. Elle, Nathan, Kristina and her wife are sitting in the first row, with Melissa and my grandson, Caleb, watching at home. Having my beautiful wife and son, and my wonderful friend and assistant Kristina there, means the absolute world to me.

I take in the theater and think how truly lucky and remarkable it is that this is my life. It wasn't the easiest, and while there are very dark days in my life story, the good outweigh the darkest and heaviest. I have the family I always wanted, I have a great friendship with Kristina and her wife, and now I really have to come to terms with calling myself moderately successful if I've been awarded with a Lifetime Achievement Award.

And I know Peter would be proud. I can see his glowing smile in my head, and I can feel his love pouring through a hug.

"Oh wow," I say as I continue to absorb the sight in front of me. There are so many people smiling as if I am something truly remarkable. I don't feel remarkable. I feel like a normal sixty-nine-year-old who is somehow lucky enough to still have a really cool, fun job. But the way the audience stares as the ovation lingers makes me *feel* remarkable. "My love for musicals began when I was nine years old, and the foster family I was living with took me to see *The Sound of Music* for my birthday. I was absolutely blown away. It was that March night when my dream was born.

"When I was sixteen, I sang Christmas carols outside of the Mark Hellinger Theatre. Behind me were billboards advertising

Jesus Christ Superstar, and it was there I was discovered. A year later, I was making my debut in *A Little Night Music* alongside Jesus Christ Superstar himself, my best friend Peter Arlo. For the first time in my life, I felt like I belonged somewhere.

"The stage became my home, and all of you became my family. I'm beyond humbled to receive this award. How lucky am I to be part of this magical world for the last fifty years? I still can't believe I'm standing here in front of all of you. This is the highest point of my career. Because I'm old, I have a lot of people to thank."

The audience laughs, and I'm glad I can sprinkle in some humor to distract myself from crying at how overwhelmingly grateful I feel.

"Thank you to the Broadway League and American Theatre Wing for giving me this. Thank you so much to all the wonderful people I've had the pleasure working with throughout the years, from my fellow cast members, to the dedicated crew, and the directors who believed I could bring to life the wonderful characters I've been fortunate enough to play.

"And a very special thank you to the reasons why I'm still on the stage: my amazing friend and assistant, Kristina, and my beautiful family. My son, Nathan, my daughter-in-law, Melissa, and my grandson, Caleb and last, but not least, the love of my life, Elle. If you all thought you couldn't get rid of me, you should ask my wife how she feels about being stuck with me for the last fifty-four years."

The audience rewards me with another round of laughter. I face Elle sitting in the front row next to Nathan. From the stage, I can see the sparkle in her eyes, looking up at me like I hung her the moon.

"Back when we met at fifteen, my number-one rule was to not get attached. She made it impossible for me to follow that rule. Elle, you have been my rock, my family, and my best friend since the moment I sang you 'Somewhere Over the Rainbow.' You have loved me through the toughest battles, and I plan on loving you just as much for the rest of my life." I look out into the theater one last time. "Thank you to each and every one of you."

I don't celebrate my Lifetime Achievement Award at the after-parties scattered around the city, though Blair and a few others try their best to coax me out for an hour to celebrate my award. All I want is to be with my family.

We head back to Nathan's, and when we walk into the house, Melissa and Caleb are still up, a bowl of half-eaten popcorn sits on the coffee table.

"Grandma Marlie!" Caleb says and hops off the couch. He plows into me. He might only be six and a half, but he's already showing signs of having hugs that rival his dad's. I squeeze him back and plant a kiss on his dark blond head. "You were on TV. Mom and I watched you."

"You did? Did I sound okay? Was the speech good?"

"It was! Everyone was clapping for you. Can I see your trophy?"

"You have to be very careful," Nathan says.

I hand Caleb the Tony and direct his little hands where to hold it.

"Not a lot of people get this award," Elle says. "But Grandma Marlie won it."

"And it makes her extra cool," Nathan says.

Caleb glances up at me with the same hazel eyes as Elle and Nathan. "Everyone at school thinks it's cool that my grandma is on TV."

"It's pretty cool, isn't it?" Melissa says, ruffling Caleb's hair. "How about you tell Grandma Marlie congratulations and then let's head upstairs. It's way past your bedtime." Melissa looks at me. "He refused to go to bed until you came home."

Caleb wraps his arms around me. Although I love Elle and Nathan hugs, Caleb's are extra special. "Congratulations, Grandma Marlie."

"Thank you, sweetheart," I say, and plant a kiss on his head.

"Can you come sing to me?"

My heart fills. "Is that what you want?" He nods. "Then I'll be right up."

"How about we let Grandma Marlie rest for a bit while we get ready for bed?" Melissa says.

"After we put him to bed, we're breaking into that bottle of champagne," Nathan says before following Caleb and Melissa upstairs.

Elle smiles at me as she steps forward. She strokes my cheek. "Do you know how proud of you I am?"

I do know because ever since we got back together, she's made sure I never doubted how she feels. As soon as I moved back, our love pieced perfectly back together. She invited me to move back into our Scarsdale home three months after I returned, and our love took off like it had never ended...or been erased. It's why I didn't hesitate asking her to marry me a year later.

We got married at the courthouse, celebrated with a delicious private dinner at Axis by Serena DeLuca, and spent two weeks traveling all over the Mediterranean.

Six years later, I feel like I'm more in love with her than I was when I asked her to marry me.

I scan her, her black dress hugging all the delicious parts of her body, and my God, my wife is gorgeous. The reason why I've been on billboards is because of my job, but Elle deserves to be on billboards because she's so breathtaking.

I caress her cheek too. "I do know how proud you are," I say.

"But tonight's a special kind of proud. Mar, you got a Lifetime Achievement Tony Award. That means that you've left a mark on Broadway big enough to be forever celebrated. You are the most remarkable woman I've ever met."

"You're just saying that because you're my wife."

"I might be a smidge biased, but that doesn't make it any less true. I'm so proud of you, love." She smiles and pulls me in for a simple, yet long, kiss. I feel her love dancing across my lips and filling my chest. "I've known you for fifty-four years, and you never cease to amaze me."

"I feel the same about you, my love." I give her another kiss. "But being with you, creating our family, and finding our way back to each other after so many years apart, all of that is the greatest achievement of my lifetime. Make no mistake about that."

She smiles that beautiful smile that's had me hooked since I was fifteen. "I never would have believed the girl who played 'Somewhere Over the Rainbow' to me while I read the *Wonderful Wizard of Oz* would be the love of my life."

"Me either."

"You had me intrigued right then and there. You were so eager to play the piano. Do you remember?"

I smile and kiss her forehead. "I remember it like it was yesterday."

About the Author

Morgan Lee Miller started writing at the age of five in the suburbs of Cleveland, Ohio, where she entertained herself by composing her first few novels all by hand. She majored in journalism and creative writing at Grand Valley State University.

When she's not introverting and writing, Morgan works for an animal welfare nonprofit and tries to make the world a slightly better place. She previously worked for an LGBT rights organization.

She currently resides in Washington, DC, with her two feline children, whom she's unapologetically obsessed with.

Books Available from Bold Strokes Books

Coasting and Crashing by Ana Hartnett. Life comes easy to Emma Wilson until Lake Palmer shows up at Alder University and derails her every plan. (978-1-63679-511-9)

Every Beat of Her Heart by KC Richardson. Piper and Gillian have their own fears about falling in love, but will they be able to overcome those feelings once they learn each other's secrets? (978-1-63679-515-7)

Grave Consequences by Sandra Barret. A decade after necromancy became licensed and legalized, can Tamar and Maddy overcome the lingering prejudice against their kind and their growing attraction to each other to uncover a plot that threatens both their lives? (978-1-63679-467-9)

Haunted by Myth by Barbara Ann Wright. When ghost-hunter Chloe seeks an answer to the current spectral epidemic, all clues point to one very famous face: Helen of Troy, whose motives are more complicated than history suggests and whose charms few can resist. (978-1-63679-461-7)

Invisible by Anna Larner. When medical school dropout Phoebe Frink falls for the shy costume shop assistant Violet Unwin, everything about their love feels certain, but can the same be said about their future? (978-1-63679-469-3)

Like They Do in the Movies by Nan Campbell. Celebrity gossip writer Fran Underhill becomes Chelsea Cartwright's personal assistant with the aim of taking the popular actress down, but neither of them anticipates the clash of their attraction. (978-1-63679-525-6)

Limelight by Gun Brooke. Liberty Bell and Palmer Elliston loathe each other. They clash every week on the hottest new TV show, until Liberty starts to sing and the impossible happens. (978-1-63679-192-0)

Playing with Matches by Georgia Beers. To help save Cori's store and help Liz survive her ex's wedding they strike a deal: a fake relationship, but just for one week. There's no way this will turn into the real deal. (978-1-63679-507-2)

The Memories of Marlie Rose by Morgan Lee Miller. Broadway legend Marlie Rose undergoes a procedure to erase all of her unwanted memories, but as she starts regretting her decision, she discovers that the only person who could help is the love she's trying to forget. (978-1-63679-347-4)

The Murders at Sugar Mill Farm by Ronica Black. A serial killer is on the loose in southern Louisiana, and it's up to three women to solve the case while carefully dancing around feelings for each other. (978-1-63679-455-6)

Fire in the Sky by Radclyffe and Julie Cannon. Two women from different worlds have nothing in common and every reason to wish they'd never met—except for the attraction neither can deny. (978-1-63679-573-7)

A Talent Ignited by Suzanne Lenoir. When Evelyne is abducted and Annika believes she has been abandoned, they must risk everything to find each other again. (978-1-63679-483-9)

All Things Beautiful by Alaina Erdell. Casey Norford only planned to learn to paint like her mentor, Leighton Vaughn, not sleep with her. (978-1-63679-479-2)

An Atlas to Forever by Krystina Rivers. Can Atlas, a difficult dog Ellie inherits after the death of her best friend, help the busy hopeless romantic find forever love with commitment-phobic animal behaviorist Hayden Brandt? (978-1-63679-451-8)

Bait and Witch by Clifford Mae Henderson. When Zeddi gets an unexpected inheritance from her client Mags, she discovers that Mags served as high priestess to a dwindling coven of old witches—who are positive that Mags was murdered. Zeddi owes it to her to uncover the truth. (978-1-63679-535-5)

Buried Secrets by Sheri Lewis Wohl. Tuesday and Addie, along with Tuesday's dog, Tripper, struggle to solve a twenty-five-year-old mystery while searching for love and redemption along the way. (978-1-63679-396-2)

Come Find Me in the Midnight Sun by Bailey Bridgewater. In Alaska, disappearing is the easy part. When two men go missing, state trooper Louisa Linebach must solve the case, and when she thinks she's coming close, she's wrong. (978-1-63679-566-9)

Death on the Water by CJ Birch. The Ocean Summit's authorities have ruled a death on board its inaugural cruise as a suicide, but Claire suspects murder and with the help of Assistant Cruise Director Moira, Claire conducts her own investigation. (978-1-63679-497-6)

Living For You by Jenny Frame. Can Sera Debrek face real and personal demons to help save the world from darkness and open her heart to love? (978-1-63679-491-4)

Mississippi River Mischief by Greg Herren. When a politician turns up dead and Scotty's client is the most obvious suspect, Scotty and his friends set out to prove his client's innocence. (978-1-63679-353-5)

Ride with Me by Jenna Jarvis. When Lucy's vacation to find herself becomes Emma's chance to remember herself, they realize that everything they're looking for might already be sitting right next to them—if they're willing to reach for it. (978-1-63679-499-0)

Whiskey and Wine by Kelly and Tana Fireside. Winemaker Tessa Williams and sex toy shop owner Lace Reynolds are both used to taking risks, but will they be willing to put their friendship on the line if it gives them a shot at finding forever love? (978-1-63679-531-7)

Hands of the Morri by Heather K O'Malley. Discovering she is a Lost Sister and growing acquainted with her new body, Asche learns how to be a warrior and commune with the Goddess the Hands serve, the Morri. (978-1-63679-465-5)

I Know About You by Erin Kaste. With her stalker inching closer to the truth, Cary Smith is forced to face the past she's tried desperately to forget. (978-1-63679-513-3)

Mate of Her Own by Elena Abbott. When Heather McKenna finally confronts the family who cursed her, her werewolf is shocked to discover her one true mate, and that's only the beginning. (978-1-63679-481-5)

Pumpkin Spice by Tagan Shepard. For Nicki, new love is making this pumpkin spice season sweeter than expected. (978-1-63679-388-7)

Rivals for Love by Ali Vali. Brooks Boseman's brother Curtis is getting married, and Brooks needs to be at the engagement party. Only she can't possibly go, not with Curtis set to marry the secret love of her youth, Fallon Goodwin. (978-1-63679-384-9)

Sweat Equity by Aurora Rey. When cheesemaker Sy Travino takes a job in rural Vermont and hires contractor Maddie Barrow to rehab a house she buys sight unseen, they both wind up with a lot more than they bargained for. (978-1-63679-487-7)

Taking the Plunge by Amanda Radley. When Regina Avery meets model Grace Holland—the most beautiful woman she's ever seen—she doesn't have a clue how to flirt, date, or hold on to a relationship. But Regina must take the plunge with Grace and hope she manages to swim. (978-1-63679-400-6)

We Met in a Bar by Claire Forsythe. Wealthy nightclub owner Erica turns undercover bartender on a mission to catch a thief where she meets no-strings, no-commitments Charlie, who couldn't be further from Erica's type. Right? (978-1-63679-521-8)

Western Blue by Suzie Clarke. Step back in time to this historic western filled with heroism, loyalty, friendship, and love. The odds are against this unlikely group—but never underestimate women who have nothing to lose. (978-1-63679-095-4)

Windswept by Patricia Evans. The windswept shores of the Scottish Highlands weave magic for two people convinced they'd never fall in love again. (978-1-63679-382-5)

An Independent Woman by Kit Meredith. Alex and Rebecca's attraction won't stop smoldering, despite their reluctance to act on it and incompatible poly relationship styles. (978-1-63679-553-9)

Cherish by Kris Bryant. Josie and Olivia cherish the time spent together, but when the summer ends and their temporary romance melts into the real deal, reality gets complicated. (978-1-63679-567-6)

Cold Case Heat by Mary P. Burns. Sydney Hansen receives a threat in a very cold murder case that sends her to the police for help where she finds more than justice with Detective Gale Sterling. (978-1-63679-374-0)

Proximity by Jordan Meadows. Joan really likes Ellie, but being alone with her could turn deadly unless she can keep her dangerous powers under control. (978-1-63679-476-1)

Sweet Spot by Kimberly Cooper Griffin. Pro surfer Shia Turning will have to take a chance if she wants to find the sweet spot. (978-1-63679-418-1)

The Haunting of Oak Springs by Crin Claxton. Ghosts and the past haunt the supernatural detective in a race to save the lesbians of Oak Springs farm. (978-1-63679-432-7)

Transitory by J.M. Redmann. The cops blow it off as a customer surprised by what was under the dress, but PI Micky Knight knows they're wrong—she either makes it her case or lets a murderer go free to kill again. (978-1-63679-251-4)

Unexpectedly Yours by Toni Logan. A private resort on a tropical island, a feisty old chief, and a kleptomaniac pet pig bring Suzanne and Allie together for unexpected love. (978-1-63679-160-9)